These Yellow Sands

Memories of Manteo

Joseph N. Vaughan

ISBN: 979-8-9884255-0-2 (Paperback)

Front cover image by Joseph N. Vaughan.

First printing edition 2023.

Joseph N. Vaughan

Table of Contents

'A Briefe and True History . . .'

Sir Walter Raleigh's 1587 Lost Colony of Roanoke is an enduring mystery in American history. The settlement of eighty-four men, seventeen women, and eleven children, including two English infants born on Roanoke Island in present-day North Carolina, disappeared, leaving only cryptic clues and unanswered questions. The colonists' fate remains unknown to this day through many theories and speculations have arisen over the centuries.

The first of the three Roanoke Voyages, beginning in 1584, focused on exploration, science, and discovery. Led by Captain Philip Amadas and Master Arthur Barlowe, with the maritime expertise of Simon Fernando, the expedition arrived near what would later become Oregon Inlet. The local indigenous people warmly received the English, marking the start of trade and cultural exchange. Two natives, Manteo and Wanchese, even accompanied the crew back to England. Manteo embraced his new surroundings and eventually converted to Christianity, becoming a lifelong friend of the English. Upon returning home, Wanchese saw the English as a threat to his people and became their enemy.

The 1585 voyage, led by Sir Ralph Lane and Sir Richard Grenville, included John White among 108 adventurers. Lane, known for his vanity and fiery temper, remained governor of the colony when Grenville returned to England. Relations between Lane's men and the indigenous people deteriorated, leading to attacks, murder, and disease. Sir Francis Drake visited the colony within a year and offered to return the men to England. Lane abandoned the settlement, leaving fifteen men behind. Ironically, two supply ships arrived shortly after Lane's departure, unaware of the colony's abandonment.

Artist and explorer, John White played a significant role in the Roanoke expeditions. He made several crossings of the Atlantic Ocean, initially serving as an illustrator and mapmaker. On the third voyage, in 1587, Raleigh named White governor of the colony. However, due to deteriorating relations with the native inhabitants and dwindling supplies, he was compelled to return to England for resupplies. The Spanish Armada invasion delayed his return for three years.

When White arrived back on Roanoke Island in 1590, he found the settlement abandoned, with the letters "CRO" carved on a tree and "CROATOAN" on a post. It appeared the colonists had left willingly and joined the nearby Croatoan people on Hatteras Island. However, bad weather prevented White from reaching Hatteras, and he could not confirm their fate or reunite with his daughter, Eleanor, and his granddaughter, the first English child born in the New World, Virginia Dare.

Fearing the loss of his claim on "Virginia," Raleigh left the colony's fate uncertain. In 1595, he mounted a return voyage ostensibly to search for the lost colonists, but it was later revealed that he was searching for the treasures of El Dorado. Despite passing by the Outer Banks, Raleigh claimed bad weather prevented him from landing. Over the years, various legends and theories emerged as the unsolved mystery thrived. No conclusive evidence has been found to support any specific fate of the colonists.

In the years that followed, explorers from the Jamestown Colony continued searching for the Lost Colony. Various stories and legends circulated, including claims that Chief Powhatan, Pocahontas's father, had massacred the colonists. In the 18th century, early North Carolina historian John Lawson visited Roanoke Island and discovered remnants of an English fort and other artifacts. He also collected stories from the Croatoan people, who claimed to have white ancestors who could read.

However, the evidence he gathered, while intriguing, did little more than deepen the mystery.

Today, the Outer Banks is known for its unique culture and natural beauty, as well as serving as a treasure chest of pivotal moments in American history. The Bankers built boats specifically designed to navigate its unpredictable waters and held onto their distinctive brogue into the 20th Century as tourism brought civilization to their sandy doorsteps. Home to lighthouses, fishermen, and "wreckers" who salvaged shipwrecks, the area's winds and tall dunes lured the Wright Brothers to test their flying machine. The brothers' aviation achievements are among many social and scientific experiments that became gateways to this far-flung edge of the country's first English outpost.

Despite 20th Century highways and bridges opening up the Outer Banks to visitors, the mystery of the Lost Colony of Roanoke captivates the imagination of those who seek to discover the fate of the early English settlers, leaving a legacy of folklore and speculation for those who walk its beaches in search of answers.

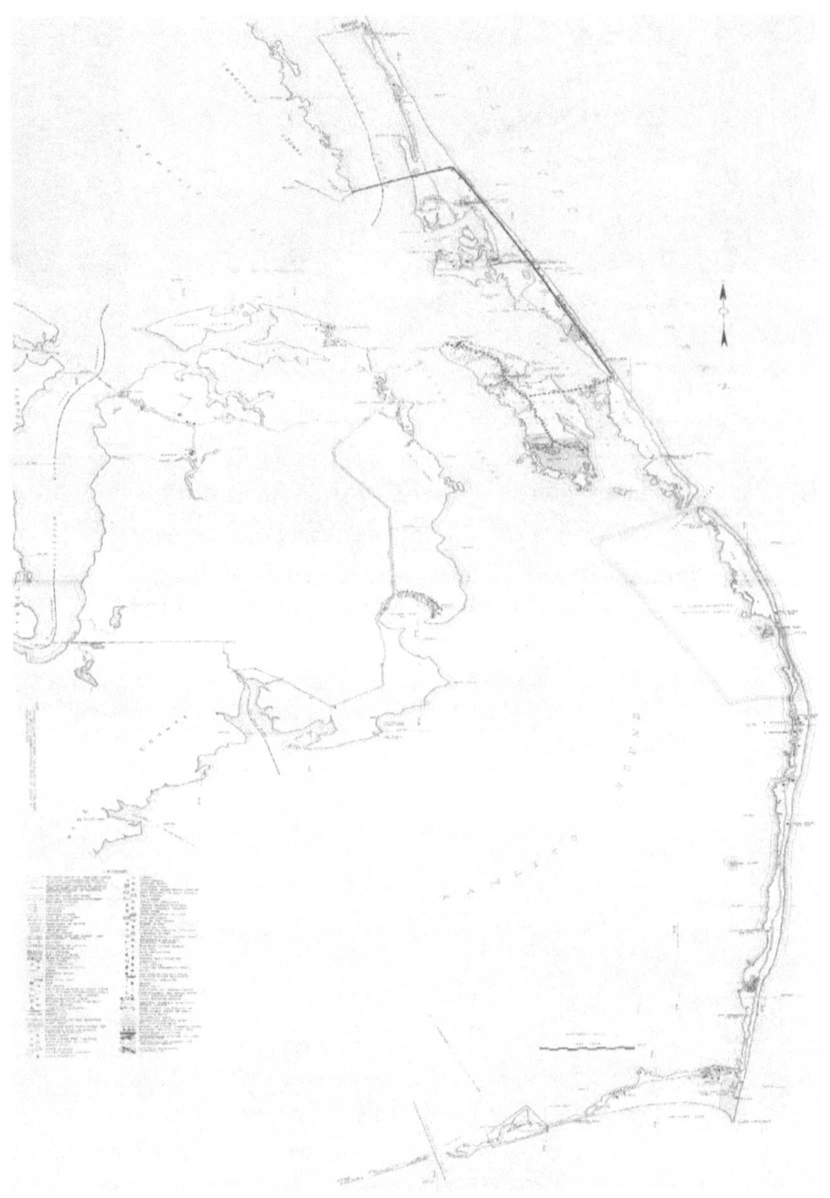

1930 map of Dare County courtesy of N.C. Department of Transportation

Come unto these yellow sands, And then take hands: Court'sied when you have, and kiss'd,-- The wild waves whist-- Foot it featly here and there; And, sweet sprites, the burthen bear.

--from *The Tempest*

1

⌘

Sound of the Surf

Milton Kane slapped his upper thigh to wake his numb leg. His fingers dug into his flesh, coaxing blood toward his left foot. Lost in thought, he paid the price for sitting in one place too long on the ride from Norfolk to Manteo. He was returning to a place he didn't want to be with nowhere else to go.

"Excuse me," the teenage girl sitting on a box across from him said, her voice laced with concern. "Are you okay?"

"It's nothing," Milton replied, embarrassed he was noticed.

In his thoughts, Milton heard the surf pounding on the beach, the ocean's heartbeat pulsing with memories he didn't want to recall. He pictured breezes waltzing across North Carolina's barrier islands. The wind whispered legends born on the narrow strip of land tossed between an impatient sea and temperamental sounds. Carolina's coast was in retreat. Millennial tides pushed the slender crescent of the sandy peninsula and islands toward the mainland. Milton was going there to begin his adult life. In his heart, he felt he was in retreat as well.

He twisted his lanky frame between two boxes opposite the girl. Beyond the truck's flopping canvas, he could once again see the waters of the Albemarle Sound. A few miles across the sound over the rolling sand dunes was where his friend Jack died.

Jack Straw arrived at the Carolina coast on foot. He had walked and thumbed from Westborough, just west of Boston, to begin a fresh chapter in his life. He had taken a job playing piano at the Casino, a white and orange two-story building rising above Nags Head's dunes, where customers danced until dawn on its bouncy second floor. Jack's fingers would never touch that piano. His hopes to build a future were stripped away before they could begin.

Behind the truck, a seagull floated serenely in the calm air, almost as if an invisible force was towing it. The bird tilted its head sideways, spying on the three passengers inside with the hope of getting a meal. The cawing of the gull echoed through the confined space of the cargo hold. The boy, whose cramped position across from Milton had made him grumpy, waved his arm in the bird's direction in irritation.

"Get on, bird. No time for beggars," the boy said.

Milton and Jack met during the Great Depression, working at Civilian Conservation Corps Camp 436 on Roanoke Island. The two teenagers weathered the nation's hard times by planting sea grass and building fences to slow the barrier islands' migration to the mainland. They shoveled the flat plains of sand into dunes, stabilizing the isolated beaches from the ocean's erosion. Long spans of wooden bridges replaced makeshift ferries connecting the automobile to the Banks. Millenniums of separation between the mainland and the barrier islands ended, and tides of people began finding their way to the outer beach. The sounds of ill-tempered surf birds demanding food scraps greeted the newcomers. Honking car horns and the chatter of eager tourists replaced the ancient brogue of fishermen.

The friendship between Milton and Jack began and ended that spring and summer the year before on the deep sands of the Tarheel coast. Jack was unshackled from eighteen years of life at the Westborough Insane Hospital. He was the bastard grandchild of a Boston elite who hid his daughter's pregnancy by committing her to the asylum. His grandfather would not allow his daughter with her half-bred Indian son back into his society. Instead, he secreted them behind Westborough's thick walls.

The asylum erased his daughter's personality and memories with heroic treatments. Jack wore his mother's label of insanity in solitude, passing his days roaming the vast tunnels of the asylum. A ward nurse, whose fondness for Jack exceeded her hatred of her job, taught the boy to play the piano. Even though the room was vast and empty, it came to life whenever Jack played.

"You only get out what you put in." Jack's homespun wisdom came to Milton's thoughts, not unlike the endless dreams about Jack that flooded his mind most nights.

Milton's eighteen years were different. He was the son of Carolina lowland parents until polio forced his mother into an iron lung at a Tidewater hospital sixty miles away. His father, who eked out a livelihood working for a Hertford potato farmer, found employment at a Norfolk shipyard. The shy boy and his father lived in a two-room shotgun rental, seeing his mother twice weekly.

Misfortune wasn't done with this displaced child. A second tragedy struck when his father was crushed between two tugboats on the bustling Elizabeth River waterfront. Ginny, who lived in a neighboring shotgun, added the white boy to her brood of abandoned black orphans. Children were a gift her kind heart needed to protect from a world that had forgotten them. She made sure Milton saw his mother on Sundays. Ginny insisted he stay in school and got him a job delivering newspapers for the morning daily.

"Child, ya ain't goin' to be livin' on the street. Ya got my roof over y'ur head til y'ur mama gets better," Ginny had told the reserved boy, sheltering him from the rough and tumble of a military port city.

Milton's mother continued to survive in the steel cocoon, locked inside a machine that did what her lungs could not do. The doctor back home in Hertford promised a temporary stay inside the cylinder, saying the innovative medical treatment would save her. He had been wrong. She continued to live, fed by her memories, in a trap that robbed her of a tranquil life. She thanked Ginny for the Sunday visits with Milton as grief wore away her spirit, replacing her easy laugh with the mechanical sound of a machine pumping air in and out of her broken body.

Milton was a waif on the waterfront of Norfolk, a wide-eyed child who felt everything and understood little. Weekends of drunken sailors seeking female comfort near Granby Street unsettled him. The fists of his black siblings took revenge on the white privilege of his pale flesh. Each blow deepened an emotional emptiness keeping his thoughts turned inward.

"White boy, you need to run away cuz ya ain't like us," his foster brothers taunted him when Milton strayed from Ginny's watchful eye. He didn't understand why they hated him and learned to keep to himself to avoid the blows of their animosity.

Ginny's affection and gentleness nurtured him and gave Milton a safe harbor. The aging woman reminded him to pick flowers from a vacant lot to give to his mother on Sunday visits. Ginny worked as a housekeeper for a *Virginian-Pilot* assistant editor whose wife was also a polio victim. Unlike Milton's mother, Frances became weakened, not destroyed by the illness. She didn't mind Ginny bringing Milton to work with her. Her husband Frank was a short, round man who took a liking to the inquisitive little white boy of his black maid. The aging, portly editor found the child intelligent and moody. He introduced Milton to the power of words and how people can twist them into falsehoods or straighten them into truth.

"I think it's about time for some bourbon and cookies. Bourbon for me and cookies for you," Frank would say to Milton as the boy waited for Ginny to complete her work. Frank would then reach for the folded copy of his newspaper's crossword puzzle. Whiskey mellowed the gruff newspaperman making him a thoughtful teacher who turned each discovered word into knowledge and vocabulary. Frank unlocked Milton's curiosity, getting him a newspaper delivery route. Frank encouraged the adolescent wordsmith to write funeral parlor obituaries he brought home from work. At first, Milton's clicks on the aging Underwood typewriter were slow. Frank would laugh and rewrite them, finding Milton's mistakes a source of afternoon entertainment. In time, Frank, who was slipping into alcoholism, accepted the boy's copy without comment, as Milton became an uncredited, unpaid journalist.

"Don't add extra facts. Find the words summarizing each life without adjectives or embellishments. Add family names and dates, and you have an obit. What the dead have done, good or bad, is not for us to speculate. We record their deaths, not their lives," Frank said.

Milton's job as an obituary writer took on a new poignancy that spring when Jack died, as he struggled to find the right words to capture his friend's life. He was supposed to join Jack on the Carolina coast by the end of summer, but a death notice greeted the young writer as he opened city desk mail one morning in May. Notes from a stringer read, *"Jack Straw, believed to be in his early 20s, drowned, according to the Dare County Sheriff's Department. Onlookers observed him walking out into a rough surf before disappearing beneath the waves. Police continue to search for his body along the Nags Head beach. Straw, who hailed from Westborough, MA, was a club pianist at the Casino, one of the new entertainment establishments attracting visitors to North Carolina's coast."*

That same numbness swept over Milton when his father died. The same overwhelming destitution he felt when he looked into the empty wells of his mother's eyes washed over him. He sat at the desk tacitly for an hour, seeking words to write, sensing tears in eyes too dry to cry. Milton had dates and Jack's family names, but the words he sought were beyond his reach. The grieving obituary writer wanted to describe Jack as his best and only friend. Jack had lifted him from being a sullen boy into a man who could see the wonder and joy around him. Milton's friend lived without pretense through a dry sense of humor, sometimes mistaken for arrogance.

The two bonded the summer before and were bound for adventures far from their gloomy roots. The slender chain of barrier islands along North Carolina's coast was supposed to be a road trip for the duo. Each of them eager to explore—one through words and the other through music. That adventure never came. There would be no voyage into a future together. Jack's story ended with the few lines Milton was writing. The young journalist looked at fingers that didn't seem to belong to him. The typewriter's black ribbon printed, "He was a musician."

"Ya sure you're alright?" the girl asked Milton again.

"I'm sure," Milton said, aimlessly moving toward the shattered fragments of a future not meant to be, a casualty of lost purpose.

2

⌘

New Beginnings

A dollar would buy passage across the three-mile-long skeleton of reclaimed railroad ties. The beam bridge was an oddity of timbers bolted together by Elizabeth City investors determined to hang real estate signs alongside the freshly poured Highway 34 between Kitty Hawk and Nags Head. Replacing sluggish two-car ferries, the bridge transported people daily between the Banks and the mainland. The trip was a twenty-mile-per-hour, rhythmic rumble over the shallow, lapping waters of Currituck Sound. The swamplands of Eastern Carolina were joined to the gritty, crystal dunes of a wooded marsh peninsula and islands, making way for the human invasion soon to follow.

The Banks guarded its secrets. A sandbar less than a mile wide in some places, the barrier islands held back the Atlantic Ocean. A domain of sea breezes, the coast sheltered the mainland's wealthy landed gentry from the bites of mosquitoes inside the cedar-shingled cottages where they sought refuge in the summer. Small villages, bordered on one side by the ocean and sounds on the other, with names like Nags Head, Colington, Kitty Hawk, and Kill Devil Hills, were in flux. The new Wright Memorial Bridge, beckoning visitors from along the East Coast for getaways, liquor, and jazz, was a siren call of seabirds and crashing waves for tourists.

Hidden behind the 175-mile barricade of narrow sandy strands, Roanoke Island, twelve miles long and three miles wide, endured the centuries as a geographic misfit of American lore. It was where British America began when 115 English settlers disappeared in the late 1580s, abandoned by an England preoccupied with defending itself from the Spanish Armada but remembered by history as the Lost Colony. In the passing centuries, the island witnessed a war ripping America apart, saw an experiment in racial equality fail with its Freedmen's Colony, and watched the Wright Brothers power humanity into the Kitty Hawk sky in their heavier-than-air flying machine. Protected by the sea and sounds, Roanoke Island was an indifferent host to human endeavors. The sounds shielded Wanchese and Manteo, the island's larger communities, from changing times. Yet, guided by a shrouded past, events could yank these tiny villages of fishermen into the extraordinary.

"We just bout there. The bridge don't look like much, but it's safe enough," the driver glanced back to reassure his passengers.

The delivery truck's tires bumped over the Wright Memorial Bridge, open canvas flaps letting in the sparkling chop of the calm, sound waters. The vehicle was Milton's ride into an uncertain future at the Banks, a place of his fondest memories that seemed more like a journey into a nightmare now. He was alone, headed toward an ocean that had claimed his friend's life. Part of him realized the irony of moving to a place of splintered dreams.

Frank knew the publisher of Manteo's *Dare Independent*, Parker Woods, giving Milton a job recommendation. The two older men began their newspaper careers as reporters during the gangland days of Chicago. The Wright Brothers' flights had issued a calling card to Parker, who realized a treasure of advertising revenue might wait for him on the far-flung corner of the East Coast. Parker, a romantic needing to reinvent himself, thought he could trade his knowledge of the newspaper business in a bid for fame and fortune. Milton's background as a Civilian Conservation Corps worker and Frank's support landed him a reporter gig, starting at $20 weekly. Milton accepted the job before Jack's death and kept it since the work meant he would be a half-day journey from his ailing mother.

Not willing to spend what little money he had for a bus ticket between Norfolk and Roanoke Island, Milton found a cheap passage in the back of a delivery truck with two teenagers equally ill at ease with their destination. They appeared to be siblings. With a thin, athletic build, the boy was a foot taller than the girl. He appeared to be her protector, guarding his smaller companion against the world with a reticent temperament. The girl had blue eyes and a Mona Lisa smile dimmed by some past event. A long scar ran the length of her left arm, starting near her wrist and ending above the short-sleeved flour sack dress she wore. The girl's scar was red and swollen, crisscrossed by marks from a hundred removed stitches.

The ninety-minute trip from Norfolk had been quiet, all three passengers reliving moments they wanted to cherish or forget as the driver sang, "Ain't Got No Home." One of the delivery truck's front tires caught a nail as it rolled across the bridge. The driver pulled over to replace the flat tire, stopping beneath the white arch spanning the roadway, announcing their arrival to the jumble of marsh, pines, and oaks that was Kitty Hawk. Adorning the sign were words reading "Dare County" at the top, "1583 Birthplace of a Nation" on the left, and "1903 Birthplace of Aviation" on the right. Beyond the sign, the road was a straight line leading to the Atlantic Ocean. The signage, or perhaps the road itself, awoke a dormant curiosity in the girl.

"Have you ever seen them fly?" the girl asked, looking at Milton with the gullibility of assuming every stranger is an authority.

"No. I don't think the brothers fly here anymore, but there is a memorial to them up the road. It has a light you can see from miles away at night," Milton answered, surprised to start a conversation after a silent trip.

"A memorial? Like a headstone? Did they die?" she asked, genuinely concerned.

"I think one of them is still alive. It's just a big stone tower on top of a grassy hill marking where the brother flew," Milton said, hiding a smile.

"Oh. I see," the girl said, retreating inside herself as her companion climbed out of the truck to give the driver a hand with the tire. The driver was thankful a Texaco station was at the foot of the wooden bridge. Milton studied the girl's face, pretending to look for something in the old suitcase Frank's wife had given him to "make you feel professional on a new job."

"What happened to your arm?" Milton asked, not wanting his thoughts to drift back to Jack, who existed as a memory without a destination. Somewhere in the girl's bright eyes, her quiet demeanor encouraged him to find a better state of mind.

"It was a bear. I got between the mama and its cub. But my brother saved me," she said, touching her arm. "My name is Sparrow. Sparrow Ambrose. That's Finch, my brother, helping that fellow change the tire."

"Pleased to meet you. I am Milton Kane," he said, feeling a flush of embarrassment talking to a child on the cusp of womanhood alone in the back of a truck.

Once she spoke, he could see Sparrow wanted to trust him. People opened up to Milton, laying their life stories before him with uncanny ease. Frank said it was a gift a newspaperman needed, and Milton was lucky to have it come to him naturally. Milton had his doubts. He thought his reserve provided a sense of safety for strangers to share their deepest thoughts and feelings with him, knowing they would never see him again.

The girl seemed to grow older as she talked. She and her brother were from the mainland across from Roanoke Island. The swamps along the Alligator River did not welcome outsiders and had little affection for those who grew up there. It was a place preferring giant cypress trees, black bears, water moccasins, and mosquitos over the disruptions of humans who sawed trees into shingles for beach cottages from the Carolinas to Maine. Once the swamp surrendered its timber, it granted begrudging permission to its adopted inhabitants to brew its dark, tannic water into East Lake moonshine as Prohibition legally turned the clear liquid into a federal sin.

The girl's father moved to Buffalo City, where a million acres of cypress and juniper had grown gigantic, floating undisturbed on the marshlands of North Carolina's Alligator peninsula. He fell the trees during the day while slapping mosquitos and his wife in the evening as he slipped into life without purpose. His wife, a native of nearby Manteo, held the family together with prayer and hard work, taking her children to the Pentecostal church on Sundays, hoping God had a better plan for them than he had for her.

If it were God's intention for Betty Ambrose's fate to improve, the improvement would have to wait for a promised afterlife. Sparrow's mother died of a fever the summer she turned ten. Her brother Finch was a little older. The children were old enough to survive the harsh Buffalo City life but too young to thrive under the eye of an absentee father who ran moonshine once the wood mills consumed the vast forested swamp. Oddly, Henry Ambrose's work ensured his offspring's survival by keeping him away from them. He would split wood for the bootlegger's stills during the day and run moonshine down Milltail Creek after nightfall. The moonshine, sealed in five-gallon jugs, bobbed on a line tied behind his skiff. He crossed the Albemarle Sound to meet trucks waiting near Elizabeth City to haul the illegal brew north. A swift stroke from a fishing knife would send the liquor safely to the bottom of the sound if the law got close. There came a night when the blade wasn't quick enough. Perhaps it was because Sparrow's father consumed too much of the product he used to numb his bleak existence. But there was no escape from the Elizabeth City jail. Henry had reached a crossroads, sending him to state prison without a chance to see his two children even if he wanted.

A 400-hundred pound bear robbed the two of their self-reliance living in a dying town that didn't want to be bothered by human drama. They were balancing on an abandoned timber train rail when Sparrow came between the mother and her cub. The bear's massive black claws dug into the girl's left shoulder, tearing through skin and muscle and exposing the fragile bones of her arm. Finch attacked the bear with equal intensity, bringing a bar of track metal across the enraged creature's head, transferring the mother's fury to himself. Sparrow witnessed both defenders stand their ground as she slipped unconscious and her blood soaked into the mossy understory of the once majestic forest.

Sparrow woke up in heaven two days later; at least, it felt that way to her. She was in the brightest room she had ever seen, laying under the whitest sheets, awash with the antiseptic freshness of a hospital room, unlike the methane-laced, woody aroma of Buffalo City. And then she saw her gauze-wrapped, mangled arm and felt the pain of the massive wound inflicted by the bruin. Having escaped peril himself, Finch found a way to save his sister, begging with the desperate will of a child clinging to his most valued possession. He convinced a rum runner on his way to the Elizabeth City dock to take him and Sparrow with him. From there, seeing the nearly lifeless body of the young girl convinced a riverfront shop owner to take them another hour's journey to the Norfolk hospital.

Sparrow told Milton how Finch would not let the doctors amputate her arm. He told the hospital staff they had an Aunt Deborah, who lived at Manteo, who might take them in. Sparrow's arm healed from tattered flesh, changing from a red flame of skin into a pinkness, leaving a ghostly reminder of her ordeal.

Finch wasn't as lucky at first. Sparrow's heaven was his hell. He was a hungry shadow, standing guard over his sister. The streets of Norfolk were not friendly to Finch, who competed with the homeless for half-eaten meals reclaimed from the hospital dumpsters.

Sparrow retold her story to those who asked, pleading her brother's case to anyone who would listen until she found the ear of another patient. The patient persuaded nurses to let the boy sleep in the hospital's furnace room and saw that he ate a daily meal. Sparrow said the kindhearted woman was very sick herself. The woman died the day the girl was released from the hospital.

"The lady must have been mighty sick. She was inside this big metal shell with only her face showing. Finch said she reminded him of our mother. She had these beautiful dimples when she smiled. I think she was his guardian angel," Sparrow said.

"Oh… I guess. I guess so," Milton said, picturing the kind face and the dimples of his mother's smile.

After repairing the flat tire, the driver and Finch got into the truck, and the gas engine roared as they continued toward Manteo. Milton moved to a box near the open flap of the delivery truck and stared at the diamonds of water sparkling across the sound through the tears glistening in his eyes.

3

⌘

Fishnets and Souvenirs

Roanoke Island was a bank for the Algonquin people five hundred years ago. They polished sea shells into a currency of trade. As he lined a shelf with pork and bean cans, Dick was thinking about sea shells. Dick Nancey, a middle-aged island native with graying hair sculptured with pomade, was a driving force on Roanoke Island. He was an entrepreneur as relentless as the coastal winds sweeping across the amoeba-shaped island tucked behind the Banks' outer peninsula. Dick's father had pressed his son to leave the island where the family had lived for over two centuries. Adam Nancey didn't want his son to follow in his footsteps, sending Dick to the University of North Carolina to learn how not to be a fisherman. Dick took a degree in business and history and then, to his father's chagrin, came home to sell hardware and groceries after declining an offer to join a Chapel Hill accounting firm.

"What the…" Dick said to himself, reaching into the shelf to retrieve a bullfrog trapped in a glass jar, looking back at him. He had discovered another of his daughter's hiding places.

Among Dick's titles and hats, he was a historian who treasured the Banks' history with noted piety. And while Jamestown spawned the East Coast cities called Hampton Roads, Roanoke Island clung on as tiny fishing villages, unable, unwilling, and not eager to leave its isolation. England had attempted to establish a foothold on North American soil in the late 1500s on Roanoke Island. Sheltered from the ocean and the Spanish behind a sandy ribbon of land, the English arrived looking for Old World dreams of exploration, wealth, and new beginnings. The island was a temporary place to stay, never meant to be a final destination. It was an unsafe harbor torn by storms and twisted by the greed of the Old World as the New World carved dark grooves in American history.

"Be gone, fellow. Turn into a prince before you end up in a frying pan," he said, releasing the baffled frog behind his store near Manteo's waterfront.

Dick saw the potential for profits and personal recognition in each Bank's grain of sand. Had he been born where the economy allowed easy success, Dick would not have stood out. He had no desire to rotate through the offices of a Rotary Club or live in a Piedmont town where he might be named businessman of the year every decade or so. On Roanoke Island, Dick was Manteo's king. He ruled over his dominion with a generous, even-tempered, benevolent hand that could slap hard when threatened.

"Wonder what that girl is up to?" Dick said, glancing down the street for signs of his daughter.

The new bridges connecting the Banks and Roanoke Island to the mainland would reshape the area, dotting the sand with hotels, souvenir shops, and strangers willing to trade cash for a day of beach memories. Dick was of two minds regarding his kingdom. He knew the incoming human tide would change the Banks, and he would no longer be the sole lord over it. He would welcome this reinvented coast if he could shape its future without spoiling its past. The coast, long called the Graveyard of the Atlantic, hid its mysteries. Dick considered himself a trustee of those secrets, keeping the Banks polished for public display.

As the Depression hit the country, people lost their savings, homes, and families; a generation became displaced wanderers, losing sight of tomorrow within the blurred hopelessness of the here and now. The isolated coast partially protected Roanoke Island from this despair. People can't lose what they never had. The sea offers its bounty even in the bleakest times. Roosevelt's New Deal brought federal jobs to the Banks. The New Deal gave birth to the granite-covered Wright Brothers Memorial at Kitty Hawk, a short skip across the sound from Roanoke Island. Gangs of once jobless men planted sand fences, grasses, and trees along the oceanfront, and men from the Coast Guard stood watch between the five lighthouses dotting the coast, warning mariners to steer clear of its lethal underwater shoals.

The sea-hardened locals were pillars of salt, easy to break in seasonal storms but quick to reclaim their shape, salvaging the novel treasures washed ashore by angry waves. There were stories of islanders hanging lanterns around horses' necks on stormy nights to lure ships to wreck in the surf. They would loot cargo and salvage the wooden hulls to build homes. The old nags tale might be questionable, but the Banks needed little help to claim victims. The modern islanders were not shoreline pirates. They supplied themselves with seafood, backyard chickens, pigs, and vegetables and bought their hard-to-come-by supplies, such as flour, sugar, and ice, from merchants like Dick.

"What can I do for you this fine day, Mrs. Yarbough?" Dick asked the woman whose sun-kissed skin made her look more like seventy than fifty-four. He had known her since childhood and could recall her family's lineage for three generations. They were related at one of those branches of kinship, though the relationship was too distant to claim. Dick knew her routine as he did most of his Manteo customers. She came to buy flour, lard, and sugar every two weeks for the hotel where she had been the cook since her husband's death ten years before. Deborah was a God-fearing woman thrust more securely into his heavenly arms after her husband's death. Dick was the head deacon at the church they attended together, still angry at a God who had taken his wife and left him with a wild, impulsive child to raise.

Deborah Yarbough and Richard Nancey had known each other since grade school. Dick had been at the top of his class, and Deborah was the reserved church mouse who said her blessings before eating her lunch of cornbread and collard greens on the school's playground. Dick had a dramatic way of presenting himself, showcasing the rusty trinkets he pulled from the sea to the awe of his classmates and the annoyance of his teachers. Deborah was devout in her faith. Her expectations of how people should live for the Lord were high. Yet there was an attraction between the two that lasted throughout their childhood. He had tried to kiss her once. She had pushed him away, threatening to tell the teacher about his amorous behavior.

As the years passed, Deborah married a fisherman from Clark, a small village south of the Chicamacomico Life-Saving Station. Deborah knew her husband Clifton was a kind man, but he lacked the physical endurance to haul fish from the sea. He was an idle fellow plagued by ill health and a shiftless attitude, both cardinal sins for a fisherman. A year into their marriage, tuberculosis stole what remained of his health. He recovered to a degree, but the disease left him with a chronic cough. Respected in Manteo, Clifton was a spiritual man who led prayers on Sunday mornings. Dick liked him, or at least, his fondness for Deborah lingered into adulthood. Dick offered Clifton a job as a handyman once he could no longer endure the punishing work of a fisherman. Dick was an easy boss, forgiving that the ailing man was a poor worker in front of and behind the counter. And though his flaws as an employee were significant, Dick felt Clifton's Sunday morning prayers offset those shortcomings. A few years before Sparrow and Finch arrived on the island, the man's tuberculosis returned with a vengeance, forcing him into a mainland sanatorium. His condition worsened, and by the following spring, all that was left of him to return to his wife was a lamp crafted out of popsicle sticks, blue marbles, and some glue.

Though Dick didn't have noble tendencies, his skill as an honest businessman was unquestioned. As a boy, he wasn't different from his unruly daughter, spending much of his time being lectured by his father. And then he met his wife-to-be, Mary Elizbeth. She changed him, softened his hard edges, and made him more generous in his affairs. And as she nurtured his moral improvement, he rediscovered a love of the Banks that had been dormant since his youth. Following her heart, he learned to shepherd his energies into polishing his hometown into the treasure Sir Walter Raleigh once hoped it might become. Dick aimed to leave his mark on Manteo while keeping his young motherless daughter from burning it down. Some days, he doubted either was possible.

"Fine day, but the sky is unsettled. Gonna rain. I need five more pounds of flour this week," Deborah said. After all their years of knowing each other, she still found herself uncertain about the nature of their connection. She couldn't quite discern if he was a friend. Their interactions in recent years had always been pleasantly guarded and filled with dry banter, but there was an underlying ambiguity that left her questioning.

"Business must be good," Dick said.

"Too good if you ask me. We got these mainland folks comin' in all the time now."

"Visitors treating you well?" Dick asked, wanting conversation more than an answer.

"They're all right, but I don't trust people who throw their money away. Folks spending dollars to wet their toes is peculiar. Well, that is none of my concern," she said, looking in her purse for money to buy peppermint sticks.

"Folks just want to get away. See the ocean, get their minds off things," Dick said, bagging six pieces of peppermint before charging the Fort Raleigh Hotel account.

The Fort Raleigh Hotel was an island calling card for tourism. Its lodgers shot waterfowl and angled fish during the day and made plans to buy and turn the Bank's cheap land into lots of sellable real estate in the evening. Hobby fishermen lodged there for weeks, and the hotel was attracting families with the financial means to escape to the beach on weekends. The islanders heard moonshine money built the hotel, not understanding why people would put money into such an uncertain venue as entertaining people.

Dick knew why. Moonshine money was plentiful, flowing like an inland river muddied after a rain. The Prohibition amendment dammed the flow of legal alcohol while opening the doors to speakeasies that especially welcomed the smoothness of East Lake rum. The days of huge profits from moonshine were numbered, and as sheltered as the Alligator River swamp was, it could not keep unlucky family men out of prison. The sharp, still bashing axes of federal agents known as "The Dry Squad" were plentiful. Greed and jealousy turned friends into enemies and partners into snitches. Dick knew smart bootleg money would become legitimate soon enough. He was counting on a future where the call of the sea and the island's unique history would cement his legacy and fortune without him getting his hands dirty. Yet, Dick had no clear vision of what the legacy might become. He was the "authority," the voice of Manteo without a life's compass after his wife died from a fever. Mary Elizabeth had been Dick's rock. When he sat on the fence between vanity and selfishness, Mary pulled him toward genuine nobility. Dick had lost that guiding smile, the companion who encouraged him to be a better self. The empathy Mary Elizabeth had instilled in him was still there. But he wasn't sure he was the man his late wife wanted him to be.

"I need beans, Mr. Nancey… dry navy beans. Hate cooking 'em because of the effects. But those guests love 'em, so I fix 'em," Deborah said, almost lightheartedly, screwing up her face.

Dick smiled.

4

⌘

Manteo Bound

Rawlee Turnage, his face's red flush made permanent by the sun, didn't like his job, although it gave him substantial pleasure as a people watcher. He had been a ferryman who delivered travelers between Roanoke Sound and Roanoke Island, creating a link with the half-dozen Banks communities like a string of pearls leading down the barrier islands. Bridge tenders were needed when the new Roanoke Sound Bridge opened a highway between Roanoke Island and Nags Head. Rawlee, jack-of-all-trades, fit the bill. He opened the asphalt, steel, and timber section of the bridge, giving the island and the outer banks access to each other. If Rawlee had his way, the swing bridge section would never open, barricading Roanoke Island to visitors.

Rawlee, known for his quick scowls and easy laugh, wasn't a native himself. He was born on Portsmouth Island over seventy years before at the end of the eighty-mile-long strand of Banks. His ancestors were inlet pilots keeping ships off the sandy shoals said to be cursed by the headless body of Blackbeard, eternally swimming the choppy waters off Ocracoke Island. Rawlee's ancestors were grand storytellers, spinning tales, some half true and others lies about Portsmouth and Ocracoke. Ocracoke Island survived the shifting fortunes of time, but Portsmouth did not, becoming a ghost island of empty homes. Rawlee's family home was still there. His father brought his family to Wanchese to work as a shrimper when Rawlee was a youth. Rawlee's nose never adjusted to the decaying smell of seafood, but his heart belonged to the old stories he learned as a boy on the Banks. Awash with salty magic, he saw mainland strangers as the real pirates coming from across the sounds to shatter his way of life. Rawlee was a cantankerous fellow who endeared himself with storytelling and homespun wisdom, increasing his likeability. Faces brightened when they saw him or heard his name, overcoming some people's tendency to see him as a joke. He had become an island tourism attraction, a greeter vocalizing with a preserved brogue more English sounding than American. His sense of melancholy was regularly mistaken for humor.

The Manteo bound delivery truck loaded with dry goods and three strangers motored past the sand-strangled Highway 34, creeping over a road leading to the Roanoke Sound Bridge. The driver, already an hour behind schedule, was impatient to reach his destination and not in the mood for Rawlee's slow-paced permission to enter his island fortress.

"Damn, man, turn the bridge. Ain't got all day," the driver howled, waving his arms.

"Hoi Toide on the sound side. Gonna wait for the bridge to settle. Hope the bird scats on yer glass," Rawlee yelled back, pointing to a seagull hovering overhead as his brogue murdered the words whispered under his breath, "Forkers always in a rush."

Rawlee shook his wrinkled, scaly head topped by a sun-bleached, gray fedora. The sounds bordering Roanoke Island and the Atlantic Ocean were natural enemies, throwing tidal punches at each other. Living on the battered Banks demanded balance and patience. The strips of land between the two surrendered to wash overs and new inlets that sometimes appeared after storms. Rawlee thought mainland dwellers, whom he called dingbatters, were hurrying to go nowhere.

"Look, I gotta get back to Norfolk before dark. I ain't got no time to wait on this pile of gull crap," the driver screamed, thumbing the side of his truck.

"Ya got options. Ya can a-swim over, drive around to the Manns Harbor ferry, or go the hell back to Norfolk," Rawlee grunted. Though he wasn't on friendly terms with the bridge himself, his job as tender kept him and his wife fed. The pain from his disks ruptured from sixty years of shrimping wasn't too severe as long as he sat still, lording over the swing section overlooking his beloved waters.

"Ah, don't get sore. I'm in a big hurry, that's all. Boss sayin' he'll dock me if I ain't back in Norfolk by sunset." The driver grinned at him. Rawlee nodded as he had done sundry times in the past year since the island's first bridge opened Roanoke Island to the automobile.

Milton had half heard the exchange between the two men, still absorbing the second-hand knowledge of his mother's death. A mental wall sealed in his emotions, hardened by flashes of grief and loss. His welcome to Manteo was a notice from a stranger that his mother had died. He didn't want human closeness. Perhaps one day he would feel again, cross paths with others he could care for, but it wouldn't happen soon. He was lost in the moment, staring at a seagull dropping white and black swirls of poop on the bridge railing.

Milton had arrived in a new world. He would have to force himself into his surroundings, keeping his emotional emptiness undetectable. He needed conversation to fit into his new home. The two teenagers didn't count, at least not yet. They were "dingbatters," as was he. Milton sought words to disarm the island's gatekeeper, tone down his roughness, and exchange niceties for information so he could adapt. He used his reporter's instincts to reach out with questions.

"You've been here a long time?" Milton asked Rawlee.

"Don't it look like I've been round for a while? I ain't no spring chicken."

"Not what I meant, sir. I meant living on the island."

"Long time," Rawlee said, hoping the conversation would end.

"Bet you have seen some things opening this bridge."

"Mostly the toide comin' in and a-going out."

"I meant the people you talk to. It must be interesting."

"Yeah, about like this un. A mess of mainland lizards asking questions."

"Sorry. I'm going to work for Mr. Parker Woods at the local paper. Just trying to get to know people around here," Milton said, taking the measure of a man many would've dismissed by now.

"Nothin' happens on the Banks the sea don't cure. Mamas bring babies in a few at a time. They grows up and grows old. The years between are at the Lord's mercy. Life's got no middle; it gives good and bad in big heapings."

"I see," Milton said. He had failed to crack a welcoming door with this bridge tender who was busy stuffing a tobacco chew inside his cheek. This was not a promising sign for a newcomer, especially for a newspaper reporter still wet behind the ears.

Finch fixed his sight on the anxious driver, skipping crushed highway rocks across the shiny surface of a trapped puddle of water. It was a pastime with no bragging right. The hope was each stone would skip three times before disappearing below the surface. Sparrow was squinting and standing on her tiptoes as she tried to make out the towering Wright Brothers Memorial hidden several miles down the road shrouded in sea mist.

Milton's thoughts returned to this girl with a scarred arm and a compelling sense of curiosity. Her calming effect on him evaporated as he saw her misstep on the crushed, imported mainland stone. Her ankle twisted causing her to fall; her arm, still weak, could not stop the fall. Milton didn't take his usual slow, customary route to process her plunge. As Sparrow's body sank below the steel, green-gray waters, Milton hovered midair before descending into the sound. He grabbed the girl by her waist and headed up into a space occupied by Finch. The two lifted Sparrow toward an white life ring tossed into the churning water by Rawlee. Minutes later, all four were sitting inside Rawlee's tender hut.

"Ya okay, miss?" a different version of Rawlee asked, applying first aid to a slight cut above the girl's left eye.

"I'm not hurt. I just slipped," Sparrow replied, uncomfortable being the center of attention.

"Put on my heavy coat. It'll warm ya up some," Rawlee said, wrapping a rubbery jacket three sizes too big for the girl around her shoulders.

"Thanks," she said as Finch dried his sister off with his shirt, checking her, especially her scarred arm, for injury. He eyed Milton for the first time since they left Norfolk. There were no words, just a nod of indebtedness.

Rawlee reached into a beaten-up fish cooler and pulled out three Nu Grape sodas. He knocked off the bottle caps on the chewed-up edge of his station table and handed one to each of the three inlanders.

"Ya know how to hold a fishin' pole?" Rawlee asked Milton as he handed him the soda.

"I do," Milton said, hiding a faded grin behind the bottle.

"I works for Parker and Mrs. Mona part-time myself. See ya about, I reckon," Rawlee added, returning his attention to his job, spitting tobacco juice into tall bean cans on the floor as Sparrow dried off by his kerosene heater.

The driver, down casted by the likelihood his pay would be docked, continued on the paved road after crossing the bridge, approaching a crossroads. One road led to Wanchese while the other veered right towards Manteo. Manteo's main street greeted them with rows of shops and steepled real estate. As the driver navigated through Manteo, the waterfront came into view, overlooking the tranquil Shallowbag Bay before the delivery truck halted in front of a three-story hotel.

Hotel Fort Raleigh sprang up near the Dare County Courthouse in the early 1930s, becoming a Manteo landmark as gossip about its funding source filtered through a population related by blood or marriage, serving to add anecdotes mingled with weather forecasts and fishing reports. The three-story hotel became commonplace as time passed, blending a questioned past with a future softened by the deep pockets of strangers who hooked fish and shot birds for a pastime.

Moonshine money drifted across Croatan Sound from Buffalo City, helping revive mainland interest in Sir Walter Raleigh's long-lost colony once roads and bridges brought automobile passage within easy reach. Manteo, like its Indian namesake, was the more entrepreneurial of the island's two primary towns. Wanchese, a hammock of yaupon and cedar surrounded by a marsh, preferred welcoming fresh seafood over greeting visitors. Manteo had earned a seat at the table of commerce and history Wanchese neither sought nor wanted. The Hotel Fort Raleigh rose above the town's dwarfed oaks and pines, anchoring Manteo to the 20th century. This time, the population of Roanoke Island wouldn't vanish as it did long ago, leaving letters carved on a post to set the stage for a 350-year-old mystery. Manteo used that old mystery as its welcome mat, hanging signs advertising that the village was open for unfinished business.

Three strangers, freshly baptized in the brackish waters of Roanoke Sound, climbed out of the Norfolk delivery truck. Sparrow and Finch were to meet their aunt in front of the hotel, the last leg of their journey to a two-room, sun-faded house two blocks away where Deborah lived alone. The newspaper publisher promised Milton room and board as part of his employment agreement, but until he met with Parker Woods the next day, he would stay at the hotel. Tattered travel bags resting at their wet feet, the trio walked across Lodge Street as a middle-aged woman, wiping flour dough from her hands on a kitchen towel, greeted them with a face stern enough to make Milton flinch.

"Why y'all wet?" Deborah asked, listening without comment as Sparrow greeted his aunt and explained the story.

Deborah Yarbough took her obligations seriously. The foolishness of others never lightened her heart or caused her undue concern. Hard work and disappointment suppressed her sense of humor. A sense of duty more than family got her to agree to take in her young niece and nephew when a Norfolk hospital social worker knocked on her door two months before. Deborah hadn't seen her late sister, Betty, since their childhood in Buffalo City. They had never been close. Deborah's passions were devotion to God and cooking, though the order of that fidelity was sometimes in question. Her world became peaceful when her fingers felt the soft, wet biscuit dough or she heard the sizzling white noise of chicken pieces frying on the stove. This day she made chicken and dumplings from scraps of unused dough and leftovers. Her anxiety didn't show through her blank expression, masked by the aroma of a generous meal to feed her new wards and "lizard" guests at the hotel.

"Smells good in there," Milton said, hoping to break the tension. Like those dunes along the beach, the older lady stood as a sentry, guarding the hotel's front door.

"Are ya from the hospital?" Deborah asked, glancing at the teenagers and then at him. Her brow held a fixed frown as she wiped her hands on a towel.

"No, ma'am, Rode in with them on that delivery truck," Milton said, awkwardly bearing witness to this forced family reunion.

"Well, Hank will check you in at the desk," she replied, suspicious of a stranger who knew more about her family than she cared for him to know. Milton, not wanting to intrude on the unfolding family drama, nodded to the pair, noting the slight smile on Sparrow's face as he banged his oversized suitcase through the hotel's front door.

Deborah continued wiping her hands on the towel after her fingers were clean, eyeing the brother and sister silently, unsure how to proceed. The three were sizing their situation, debating how to begin this new life. Both siblings sensed their aunt's uneasiness. Deborah's routine had been simple since her husband's death. God and her recipe for fried chicken were her fortresses on a small island surrounded by a shallow moat of sounds. The brother and sister saw change as a constant, forcing them to accept whatever came their way.

"I'm awfully hungry. I think Finch is, too," Sparrow said, her blue eyes radiating hope. Finch watched Deborah's face become lineless. A new family was coming together, its permanency sealed over a hot bowl of chicken and dumplings.

5

⌘

Hermit Crabs

The *Independent* newspaper office was barely two years old and looked aged and worn. The internal facade was intentional. Owners Parker Woods and his wife, Ramona, were newcomers themselves. She was from an old South Carolina family, fleeing the charmed mundane life on a northbound train with her parent's blessing when she turned nineteen. Parker was an ambitious beat reporter who had roared through the 20s with Frank working at a Chicago newspaper embellished by glitzy stories about high fashion and high crime. He was an intelligent man of opinions, but he needed Ramona's insight to turn his dreams into reality. Ramona didn't let dreams cloud her vision. Because of her determined, level-headed business sense, the *Dare Independent* established itself as the county's voice. The Woods believed developing tourism on the back of a seafood and timber economy was possible, especially if there was plenty of yellow sand, sun, and seashells to energize the concept. Parker and Mona moved to Roanoke Island to grow a newspaper. They became mesmerized by the coast, falling in love with the fragile environment and plagued by the notion tourism could undermine the Banks in ways storms never would. Though their approaches differed, the husband-and-wife team had lucked onto a coastal jewel. They feared they could become agents of its undoing, promoting its shores into crowded oblivion.

The couple had met in Virginia's Tidewater, working as civilian reporters for a military newspaper in the port city of Norfolk, shielded from the Depression by the massive Naval base there. North Carolina's coast fascinated them. The Banks had the power to lure former soldiers and their families back to the sea for a getaway. The Woods believed emotional addiction to the barrier islands of North Carolina was real, trapping or freeing those who stumbled upon it. Neither one wanted a predictable life without the thrill of the unexpected.

The Depression had cast America on a journey to ruin and aimless wandering. Parker and Mona knew nothing would last forever; the country would recover. Bridges and automobiles would recharge the isolated Banks when the nation's economy awoke. Over the years, Parker had become the front man whose folksy version of himself made him a colorful outsider with measured printed opinions that opened the Banks to new ideas. Mona remained behind the scenes, keeping her opinions mostly to herself and growing the newspaper's revenue by building relationships with small businesses strung along the coast.

Parker, brushed his thinning hair straight back, finishing his third cigarette and fourth cup of coffee when Milton tapped on his glass window door at 7 a.m. Looking over a pair of reading glasses, Parker was reading the mail, a stack of ripped envelopes on his desk.

"Yo. Come on in," Parker said, flicking two fingers to grant Milton entry into his kingdom of cluttered piles of newsprint and the stink of printer's ink that overwhelmed the smell of the sea air.

"Have a seat," Parker added, pointing to the only chair in the office, giving Milton a firm handshake to assert professional dominance.

"How are you, sir?" Milton replied, taking in the man's measure and his office in unassuming glances.

"What you know about hermit crabs?" Parker asked, sounding like a teacher checking a student for knowledge.

"Err. Nothing," Milton replied, wondering if the older man was asking a question or making a statement.

"Let me tell you about 'em. The damn little creatures live in darkness, under shells or whatever dark hole they can crawl inside. You need to feed them and give them water every so often. But they could be dead for six months before you realize you are wasting your time. The water evaporates, and the food dehydrates, making it seem like the crab is eating it. You're just wasting your time on housekeeping such a creature. End up with an empty house and a little sand. Oh sure, you can say you have a crab as a novelty. The truth is you have a crab cemetery."

"I see. Do you keep hermit crabs?"

"Hell, no. I just told you it is a useless thing to do."

"Then you aren't talking about crabs, are you?"

"Smart lad. I like that. No, talking about the future of this quaint little island and the rest of the Banks. You know anything about the Banks?"

Milton recognized Parker's rhetorical strength in asking the question. Milton took his clues from what he saw, and the younger man could see Parker let questions guide his answers. The older man had most answers before he asked the questions. What did Parker want from him? What he gleaned from Frank's history books was the limit of his knowledge of the Banks. Sir Walter Raleigh's 16th Century colony went missing, and the Wright Brothers took to the sky nearby as centuries of storms erased and opened inlets from the sea into the sound. Carolina's Atlantic coast wrote sad histories on the aging bones of ships coming too close to its shallow shoals of sand. England lost its first American colony before it could take root. The Wrights only flew a few feet above the sand. And when hurricanes strike, the landscape is rearranged, outcomes captured in photographs of the bold lifesaving surfmen making headlines as hapless ships met their end on the treacherous shoals.

"Beautiful place. You were kind enough to offer me a job here," Milton replied.

"It's beautiful, but this place could go the way of the hermit crab... be a dead pile of sand. Our job, no, our purpose, is to see it grow. Since the stock market crashed, this country has gone to hell, but businesses still grow here. Not much now, but good times will come if we spread the word. That new bridge brought you over. Roads will bring in the "lizards," as locals like to call outsiders like you and me, to spend their time and money."

"They call outsiders lizards?" Milton smiled slightly. "Well, my family was from Hertford, a few miles inland. Maybe I'm only a half-lizard."

"If your ancestor's toes never touched sound side water to toss a fish into a boat, or there is no Hoi Toider in your words, you are a lizard, my boy... still a lizard."

"Bad thing then?"

"No. Not at all. It's a good thing. But don't tell locals it is a good thing. They won't like you for it and, worst yet, mistrust you. Folks here don't want to see change. The old legends and a fisherman's life is what they know, and all some of them want to know."

"Yeah," Milton smiled again, "Think I met one of them coming in yesterday. The bridge tender, Rawlee was his name."

"I'm surprised he doesn't set fire to the bridge, but he has a family to feed. You see, Rawlee thinks of that bridge as a necessary evil, but the bridge is heaven-sent; it will open up the Banks to tourists. If we do it right, people will make a lot of money. If we do it wrong, it will be like that hermit crab cemetery."

"Yes," Milton said, reluctant to pass judgment on the editor or the land the editor was recolonizing under the banner of tourism and economy.

"You know the Banks' history, Mil. Frank shared a bit of information about you. You know the lore and legends, have a curious mind, and know what it is to live a hard life. You can't spell worth a damn, but you have the heart and mind to open doors. I'll edit your copy. Give me copy that feeds the dreams of lizards." Parker laughed.

Pulling on a thread from his new white shirt, Milton tried to imagine a lizard having dreams, wondering if they dreamed of grasshoppers or frogs.

6

⌘

Hurricane Giggles

One coastal force on par with the Banks' seasonal hurricanes was a twelve-year-old girl with piercing sea-green eyes and a rebellious temperament. Jeanette Nancey was cut from the same cloth as her father, Dick, only she was more rambunctious if not as calculated. Locals made exceptions for her wild, free spirit after her mother died from typhoid ten years before. If Dick was the voice of reason, moderation, and change on the island, Jeanette was the scream of wild abandon confined on an island shaped like an ancient Spanish conquistador holding a shield.

Jeanette acknowledged no master nor thought of anyone as her peer. She was the princess of Manteo, using her father's standing in the community to rule her island. A toothy smile and a "Yes, sir or madam" were enough to disarm the ire of adults. The island's younger residents saw her as an example of what not to be to avoid a father's belt. She wasn't a mean child; her defective sense of right and wrong swayed between sensitivity and impulsiveness. Townspeople were forgiving or dismissive of her escapades as an overindulged child sheltered by a well-to-do widower. She was a demon in a 1932 Ford, barely tall enough to see over the steering wheel to drive the mostly narrow, sandy paths of the island. Dick, unwilling or unable to fill the role of parent, committed to fatherhood by paying for the damages she inflicted on fence poles and porches.

Like an unsure seagull, Sparrow picked up discarded cigarette butts, dropping them into a repurposed bean can in front of the hotel. She heard the urgent repeat of a car horn as she tried to make peace with the unpleasant task her aunt had assigned her. Deborah thought the spent butts were a nasty reminder of the lizard invasion, flicked there by fishermen and bird hunters who migrated to the island seasonally. And too, she needed to give her friendless niece something to do while under her watchful eye.

"Dear Lord, not her," Deborah thought as she heard Jeanette's squeaking brakes slow and then stop along the dirt street where Sparrow sat on the grass, fascinated by a cigarette silk, printed with the image of Col. Lindbergh, lying on the ground. Back home in Buffalo City, men rolled their cigarettes in thin papers, leaving almost no trace of the smoked tobacco behind except their yellow, tobacco-stained fingers. Sparrow had a flash of remembrance; she missed her mother and feared her father.

"Yo, who are ya?" Jeanette asked, thrusting her pony-tailed head out of the driver's side window.

"I'm Sparrow. Aren't you too young to drive?" she asked.

"Heck, no. Been driving for years. Don't need no license, just a good eye and a powerful arm to steer." Jeanette laughed. "I killed Mrs. Migette's cat last year by accident, but the damn thing weren't paying attention."

"Oh," Sparrow said, frowning.

"Hey, ya got any smokes? I need one about now. Had to take a load of beans over to Wanchese this morning. Those folks get on my nerves," Jeanette continued.

"Nope, don't smoke. I pick up these butts for my aunt. She works here. Do ya know her?" Sparrow asked.

"Know her. She is my Sunday School teacher. A little strict," Jeanette said, slapping a mosquito buzzing near her forehead. "You're that Buffalo City kid. Heard about you."

Sparrow touched her scarred arm, wondering what part of her story this irreverent girl knew, disadvantaged in the conversation.

"Folks there make liquor, East Lake rye liquor… the best in the world, says my daddy. Ain't no rules there, and some folks are rich. I'd live there, but I couldn't tolerate those bugs, snakes, bears, and alligators," Jeanette said as she slapped her forehead, leaving a smear of blood and a flattened insect on her palm.

"Ya know, ya got all those things here, too," Sparrow replied, wrinkling her nose.

"Yeah. Ain't the same. This place is too civilized. Too many rules and people telling you what to do. I need some adventure. I got a couple of cold soda pops beside me. Want one?" Jeanette quizzed, tilting her head sideways and adding a sweet smile.

"Sure. Sounds nice," Sparrow said, deciding a girl who liked adventure and offered a Pepsi might be worth getting to know.

Scrubbing gears, VDee's automobile lunged ahead, almost side-swiping a black man dressed in the fading uniform of a Pea Island Life-Saving Station surfman. The man headed toward Nags Head, filling one polished shoe with water draining along a grassy ditch. He shook his head, wondering if the wild girl might one day cause harm to the luckless person who couldn't hear her coming. He should have waited until he got to the station to don his uniform.

Eddie was Number 6 on a crew of six at the Pea Island Life-Saving Station. A man cut from mahogany and sinew, he cleaned the station's floors, checked equipment, and took his shift walking the shell-strewed beach south to Oregon Inlet. Tagging sea foam as his rubber boots sank into the surf wash, Eddie's duty was to watch the horizon between Rodanthe and Clarksville, alert for passing ships caught in the death grip of the shifting shoals. The Graveyard of the Atlantic had claimed over two thousand ships since European barks first touched the Banks in the 1500s. Eddie's station was one of many dotting the coast, scattered between the tall brick lighthouses erected to warn seafarers who ventured too close to shore. Though station crews were often racial checkerboards, Eddie's station was a curiosity. The station's supervisor, called the Keeper, and the surfmen were all black.

Eddie would never climb through the ranks to become Keeper, nor did he want the job. Ernest "Eddie" Etheridge was no kin to Pea Island's legendary Keeper Richard Etheridge, the rescuer of the doomed 393-ton schooner E.S. Newman crew over forty years ago. Carrying the Etheridge name had benefits. Eddie, not saddled with ambition, didn't take advantage of the moniker. He was careless about the future, finding satisfaction in a simple life. He had none of his grandmother's driven passion of more than sixty years before. After the Union Army took control of the island in the first important battle of the Civil War, she swam across the Croatan Sound to Roanoke Island. She believed a better day was near as the Union army created the Freedmen's Colony, only to see freedom slip away a few years later when the government returned the land to its pre-war owners. She found solace in the kitchen and bedroom of Eddie's white grandfather, hidden behind the walls of his four-room house on the edge of California, the island's black district. She never loved him; however, she felt safe, letting the island and this white man's devotion become her fortress. Her legacy to Eddie was leading him on a path where "not so bad" was good enough.

"Hey, Mr. Surfman, ya loot any ships last week?" Nick Pagette called to him as he walked along the Shallowbag Bay dock on Manteo's waterfront.

"No. Did my duty and came home." Eddie grinned. He always walked a little taller, strolling down the main street once his life-saving duty rotation was over.

"That a fact? I heard a steamer came ashore with a load of sugar from down yonder, and the captain washed up on the beach with 50 dollars in his pocket which went a-missin'," Nick shouted, topping off his skiff's gas tank from the Standard Oil pump.

Eddie grinned again, pulling his trouser pockets inside out as he stopped to talk to Nick.

"See. I'm broke. Give my money to Grandma so she can pay the bills. Maybe I got enough left over for crackers and peanuts."

"Well, let me help you there, bud. Me and Sawtooth are goin' night shrimpin' on the big moon tomorrow. We might use some extra eyes and hands," the muscular Nick, who was about Eddie's same age, replied.

"Reckon I can be there," Eddie said, giving Nick a two-fingered salute before heading toward Water Street for the sanctuary of his grandmother's weather-beaten house.

Outsiders thought the respect Eddie received on the island was odd. The island sun bleached most racism out of Bankers, though it was still there, waiting for the tides of human jealousy to resurface it. Eddie didn't fit into either race when he finished his duty rotation and skirted the few miles across the Pamlico Sound to Manteo. He was a surfman, a raceless breed willing to die in a pounding surf to save a stranger caught in the tempest of an angry sea. Eddie was a savior in uniform with a sinewy body and pleasant demeanor. He was willing to pick up extra money by pulling nets for Wanchese fishermen once his uniform was pressed and put away.

Eddie worked for the Pagette brothers, Sawtooth and Nickolaus. The brothers fished the sounds, gill netting seasonal runs of fish and shrimping along the marshland understories. Neither brother was above breaking the law to eke out a living. Few laws were severe enough to call attention to them on the coast, where neighbors minded their business. Nick was generally liked by people on the island, a more agreeable version of his brother. Sawtooth was a drunk, often mean, who earned public acceptance because of his uncanny ability to meet folks' needs without questions asked. When fishing was poor, the brothers made their way up Milltail Creek to Buffalo City, floating five-gallon jugs of the brew on a long string tied behind their boats.

Should revenuers block their rum crossings to Elizabeth City, the pair would cut the line, sending the moonshine to the bottom of the brackish water. Later they would retrieve the prized jugs of East Lake whiskey and continue sending it north to the big city speakeasies of Prohibition America.

Eddie and Nick had grown up together, gigging bullfrogs on Roanoke Island's chilly spring and hot summer nights. They traded plump frog legs for cans of potted meat and crackers at Nancey's store. As kids, they were as close to friends as skin color would allow. Race wasn't as much of an issue away from the cotton fields and row crops of the fertile inland. Still, unspoken codes had to be honored. Bountiful seafood and fishermen's skills held racism at bay, equalized by a profession requiring a dependable back and a cautious nature.

"Is he in?" Sawtooth asked, pulling the starter rope on the shad boat's gasoline engine. The engine sputtered, dropping a spreading, oily film on the water before going silent.

"Yeah, he's in," Nick replied, not looking up as he closed a hole in a gill net draped along the pier.

Sawtooth saw people as prey, especially the colored and the old. Nick and Sawtooth had inherited the same smile. Some serpents are harmless water snakes that unobtrusively swam across the sky-mirrored surface of the sounds. But then, some snakes look like water snakes and tend to go unnoticed despite their deadly venom. Sawtooth was the latter.

7

⌘

Pea Island Highway

A ghostly Jack played "Night and Day" on a grand piano. The white curls of a calm ocean lapped over the piano's legs, washing sand over his bare feet as his fingers danced along the keys. He kept changing the tempo of the music, defying the rhyme of the sea before turning his head and grinning. Milton often dreamt of Jack on the surf. Sometimes Jack was laughing and walking along the beach, which was odd because he seldom laughed out loud when alive. He concealed his playful sense of humor beneath a stoic look inherited from being a ward of an insane asylum, giving him the appearance of a brooding artist.

Milton woke from a chilly night on a late spring day. The quilt felt comforting against his skin as he thought about his conversation with Parker Woods. Newspaper people were bohemians, either direct in what they said or so enigmatic that their words confused the listener. Talking to Parker was like playing a card game without instruction. Milton didn't need rules, just a place to sleep and a job. Pulling the covers close, it seemed he had both. Still, visions of the dream flashed in his head. This apparition of Jack confused him.

A warm biscuit and a hot black coffee cleared Milton's head. He was to meet Parker's wife, Ramona, that morning. As he walked to the newspaper office, the sun hid above the high cloudiness of an orange sky. Out front, a middle-aged woman in blue jeans and a loose-fitting flannel shirt looked at him over her pulled-down glasses. The sand and wind had carved her, reshaped her once elegant form into something more practical for island life. She was checking the tires of her faded black Ford as Milton approached her.

"You must be Milton." She smiled, wiping her hand on her pants as she extended her hand in greeting. An unexpected softness to her touch reminded him of Ginny and his mother.

"I am. Mr. Woods said I should meet you here. Hope I'm not late," Milton said, his eyes meeting the no-nonsense evaluation of the lady's gaze.

"The weather, not the hour, measures days here." She laughed.

"Well, looks like I'm right on time then," Milton said, seeing a red morning horizon creep over the eastern sky.

"Hmmm. That may be a problem. Going to storm this afternoon," Mona said. "We're going down to Hatteras. We'll be back before too late tonight."

"Tires need air?" Milton said, offering to make himself useful.

"No, they need less air going to Pea Island. Likely to get stuck in the sand anyway." She grinned. "But if we do, someone will come along. People here depend on the generosity of others freeing stuck vehicles."

Milton and Ramona crossed the Roanoke bridge and proceeded down the strand of sand and marsh running its 50-mile course to Hatteras, broken in two places by Oregon Inlet and the ever-shifting New Inlet. Rawlee nodded, seeing Ramona brightened his day, and giving Milton a thumbs up as Mona's truck passed over to Nags Head.

"By the way, call me Mona," she said as they approached a line of weathering residences lining the oceanfront. "Those cottages, the Unpainted Aristocracy. Some call it Millionaire's Row because only a millionaire would be foolish enough to build a house near the waves."

"I stayed nearby one summer with a friend. We sat on a porch, talking to girls who were there with their families. They claimed carpenters used shipwreck timbers salvaged from the beach to build their cottages."

"Didn't picture you being one of those folks who spend their summers on the beach to escape mosquito bites." She grinned.

"It was one summer working for the CCC," Milton replied, grinning back.

"Locals see the Nags Head people as outsiders, summer visitors who don't understand the Banks until the wind and water sends them packing for the mainland," she said.

"I get what the locals think. There is a difference between wanting to be somewhere and having to be somewhere," she reflected as she turned right on the paved highway that abruptly changed to sand.

Mona was disarmingly truthful and direct. She took people at face value unless their actions indicated otherwise. She was a chameleon with her surroundings, lacking Parker's bluster. Mona, who grew up as a Charleston socialite, became one of the Bankers tonging oysters, pulling nets, and painting boat bottoms with the best of them. Her face was one of the first people saw after a storm, helping islanders rebuild their lives each time into a patched version of the old one. When she came to their aid, her newspaper put down roots a little deeper, adding pages to its weekly balance of news and advertising.

"Good, you know something about this place. But I have to tell you there is a lot to learn. Just when you think you understand it, something new washes up," she said.

"Are you talking about hermit crabs?" Milton asked, comparing the two Woods.

"Parker is still telling that old cow poop story? You gotta love him," she replied, pointing to the Bodie Lighthouse as she drove to the Oregon Inlet ferry.

Mona's tires cut deep ruts in the sand road the next tide would wash away. The federal government had pushed up artificial dunes along the oceanfront with the CCC labor of young men like Jack and Milton, protecting the Banks from the sea. Scores of sea birds bobbed on broad marsh ponds not far to the right as sand rose on the left. The road was arrow straight since there was no other place for the road to go. The ocean and sounds eyed each other in spots, separated by less than a mile of sand, sea oats, and an understory of dwarfed plants stubborn enough to take root in the marshy wilderness.

Jack and Milton shoved sand and planted grasses along the Nags Head shoreline during the six-month summer of their friendship, thanks to President Roosevelt's New Deal. They bonded as two castaways tossed up by life at Camp Virginia Dare on Roanoke Island's northern shore. The New Deal's Civilian Conservation Corps gave employment to the jobless, turning places like the Banks into national bookmarks, weaving bits of history and isolated natural beauty into a tapestry, a source of pride for an impoverished nation. CCC youth, and its adult counterpart, the Works Progress Administration, planning to recreate Fort Raleigh and carve a waterfront theater out of the north shore of Manteo for an outdoor drama about the 1587 English Colony that had vanished there.

Jack and Milton were among the CCC's barefoot soldiers stationed along the Banks to stop the ocean's advance. The federal plan was to stabilize the surf line, halting an unstoppable ocean from washing over the flat land on its journey to the sounds. Sandblasted and blistered by the sun, the two friends piled sand on dunes and planted sea oats. Overhead, the sky rippled with pastel blue and billowing thunderheads. After a few weeks, the work became numbing and repetitive, though neither Jack nor Milton minded the routine. They found tranquility among the gulls and waves, lowering their emotional guards to talk about childhood memories. The two felt at peace among the shells where pods of porpoises played among the breakers and the boys drew word puzzle boxes in the sand, pantomiming clues.

Milton relived those memories under Mona's charm as she wrestled the steering wheel toward the Oregon Inlet ferry, the *Barcelona*, a wooden deck fitted atop a flatboat carrying a dozen cars across the inlet where the ocean and sound raged in a tidal battle twice daily. Mona's manner put Milton at ease; otherwise, he would have been too private to share his history on the Banks. This ferry dock was his land's end of knowledge about the coast. He knew Rodanthe and a few other small villages peppered the strand to Hatteras, but he had never set foot on Pea Island. Milton wanted to end his grief and nightly dreams by throwing himself into his new job. He knew little about working for an island newspaper, but Mona seemed willing to teach.

"It's no beauty. Still, it gets the job done. Till never lost a car yet," Mona said, pointing to the floating wooden rectangle topped by a small shed. "Bankers can build a decent boat out of a few planks of old drift."

"How many times a day does he cross?"

"Captain reads the sky and water and knows when to stay put. Most families have a boat, so crossing Oregon Inlet wasn't a big deal until sportsmen discovered duck hunting and game fishing."

"Changing times."

"It is hard for things to last beyond a minute. The ocean owns this ribbon of land. It always will."

"So you and Parker won't stay here forever?" Milton asked, wondering aloud what he was thinking.

"We'll stay awhile until someone builds a bridge over this Oregon cut. Yes, our time here will end when there are no more mysteries to add to the history. But who knows?" she laughed, borrowing cryptic lines from her husband's playbook.

Mona's deflated, oversized tires rolled onto the ferry as she braked to a stop beside the Manteo-Hatteras Bus Line, loaded with fishermen staying at Hotel Raleigh. The teenage bus driver slapped his hand on the vehicle's exterior, urging the sportsmen ahead to edge their vehicle forward. Mona said two boys operated the 130-mile round service like the old Pony Express. On a good day, they could make the trip twice. When the weather wasn't agreeable, the journey might be an overnighter with passengers enlisted to free the bus from hungry sand, or the ever-vigilant Life-Saving surfmen would spot them and lend a hand.

"They get stuck often?" Milton asked, trying to figure out how such an improbable vehicle could traverse the sand.

"Often enough to bring out the best and worst in people," she laughed, "Funny to see mainland "adventurers" handle inconvenience. One mighty hunter, who decided he knew more than the boys, drove over his own leg. Took a full day to get him to a doctor to set the bone."

The *Barcelona* chugged across the thousand yards of the inlet on a slack tide, the salt water licking the sides of the wooden hull. Local passengers stayed seated in their conveyances, engrossed in conversations. Visitors lined the ferry's rails, feeding the gulls bits of bread and chicken torn from Deborah's morning fry.

The ferry touched Pea Island's shore and rolled off into the sand. The Midgettes, always on a schedule, cranked their bus's engine to life and bolted down the beach, leaving tracks for the other cars to follow. The next thirteen miles, marked by Midgett's tire tracks, were a landscape of unnamed shipwrecks stripped of anything deemed useful and half buried in the surf.

"How do you feel about black folks?" Mona asked.

"What do you mean?" Milton replied, not understanding what shipwrecks and tire ruts had to do with skin color.

"I mean, do you have problems with negroes?" she continued, this time making eye contact with Milton as she followed the Midgette trail.

"No problems…" Milton said, his thoughts drifting back to the loving spirit of Aunt Ginny and the ass-kicking he got for being a white kid transplanted into a black Norfolk slum.

"Well, that's good." Mona nodded. "Because this strand between here and Rodanthe is a place race forgot. The seven fellows here are black and as close to being saviors as God made men. When the guys are off this narrow stretch of sand, all bets are off. These surfmen become second-class people again. Sure, they have fancy uniforms and get polite respect on the surface, but it isn't enough to overcome the white man's mindset."

"Why are you telling me this?" Milton asked, confused by what appeared to be a test he was not expecting.

"Explaining your assignment. Next week you will live here for three days, staying with the Pea Island surfmen. They are Coast Guard now, the only all-black life-saving crew in the country. Their job is to save people unfortunate enough to shipwreck off Pea Island. Their old Keeper, Richard Etheridge, made this station famous, but skin color keeps them out of the headlines. Your assignment, Mr. Reporter, is to write a feature story about them balanced enough so white folks don't hate them, and the outside world can see the surfmen as another piece of Banks' charm and romance," Mona said.

"Frank told me never to lie when writing a story. Let the facts tell the story. I'm not sure I would be much of a publicist," Milton said, frowning.

Mona laughed and stopped the car, pointing to the Pea Island Life-Saving Station, a tall, sturdy building with a watchtower on its roof.

"Be a wordsmith for a tiny newspaper in the middle of nowhere. Remember how you used to build fences in the sand? Your new job is still about building fences."

"You knew all along that I worked here for the CCC?" Milton said, feeling less smug about his privacy.

"Sometimes it is important to know the answers before you ask the questions," she said with a hint of a smile as she revved up the engine, the wheels spitting up sand toward Rodanthe on the journey back to Manteo. The day had been filled with delays as the Banks playfully toyed with the pair of journalists, blocking them from their destination and giving them time to get to know each other.

"You have to pack your patience here. You can find yourself rushing to get nowhere. About the only friend Bankers have is the chance to try to do it all again tomorrow," Mona said as her Ford left the sands and its tires welcomed the asphalt junction between Manteo and Nags Head.

Milton didn't return to Pea Island for a fortnight. The Banks seldom complied with human agendas. Mona and Milton traveled a little further than the life-saving station. A storm crossed the Banks the night before, carving a short-lived channel between the ocean and the sound. The cut was an old wound, one of many inlets periodically punching holes through the 80-mile-long land bridge. The English and Spanish discovered the swift-moving Atlantic current called the Gulf Stream could sling sailing ships back to Europe from the Americas in weeks. But Spain learned early on the Banks was no place to stop because of its shifting shallow shoals. The English needed more convincing. Over the centuries, the ocean highway continued to tempt captains, adding their crew and vessels to its graveyard.

A sailboat and a steamer came ashore during this latest storm. Both ships were locked in the sand until the surf either buried them or tore them apart as their crews awaited rescue by the Pea Island surfmen. Milton heard about the rescue third hand from Rawlee, who stayed abreast of current events along the Banks by working many jobs without a single occupation. He finished his shift at the bridge, ran his gill nets to harvest mullet, and labored for Parker and Mona, delivering newspapers and doing the odd jobs requiring more time than muscle.

Rawlee kept up with what happened on the Banks. His network of fishermen forwarded the news to Parker's ear in ways that would not have been possible without him. Parker offered his appreciation by handing out dollar bills for each tip. Rawlee kept tabs on the outsiders through the locals employed at the Nags Head Hotel, a central entry point for the visitors. Rawlee regularly docked his small skiff at the hotel's pier to sell fresh seafood to visitors, ironically calling each dingbatter "Cap'n" as he took their cash and traded stories about surfmen rescues with visitors eager to turn tragedy into adventure.

"'Em boys is the real deal," Rawlee said, digging deeper into his storehouse of recalled sea rescues. "My brother was a surfman over at Chicamacomico when the Milo set the sea a-blazin' during the war."

"What happened?" Milton asked as they drove Mona's car onto the flat barge of the Croatan Ferry, going west to drop newspapers off at Stumpy Point before backtracking over soggy roads to Columbia to collect advertising copy from a general store and lumberyard for the next week's edition.

"It was a few years after the surfmen joined up with the Coast Guard. About 1918, I figure. The German subs were like wolves; torpedoes were zipping and zapping everywhere. The Mirlo was a Brit tanker haulin' down the coast. Torpedo got her on a big blow night, waves up maybe 20 foot. The ship set the water on fire, but the boys went out to try and save her. Maybe 50 sailors on board. Keeper Midgett's crew saved 40 or more of them. In all the papers. Big ships come aground, and people take notice of the Banks. Most other times, nobody pays attention, which is fine with me."

"People love a good story."

"I was all lined up to be Number 6 at Ocracoke. I didn't have no pull, so they said I was too slow with the line." Rawlee reflected as the car's wheels bumped off the ferry at Manns Harbor, and Mona's truck headed south to Stumpy Point.

The road to Stumpy Point was as unforgiving as the shifting Pea Island boulevard. Tires mixed swamp mud with the smell of bog gas as Milton and Rawlee continued in silence, each man thinking of paths not taken. Rawlee was a man looking at life through the rearview mirror, and Milton glimpsing forward at a life that would never be. Milton's childhood home was less than forty miles away not unlike the lowland passage whizzing by the open window of Mona's Ford. Life in Norfolk had been a collection of skinned knees and bruised feelings far removed from his sheltered upbringing in the tiny country hamlet of Hertford. That was the price paid for his early innocence, an unbalanced trade between the romance of an idyllic existence and a legacy of hard knocks. Milton had hoped his luck would change on the isolated island where new thruways removed old barriers. Milton looked to his left and noticed a worn dirt road, a sign proclaiming Buffalo City.

"Hmm. That is where Sparrow and Finch are from?" Milton said, stretching his neck to look down a straight road with no apparent end.

"Yeah. Them kids had it hard. Deborah will a-keep 'em straight. Buffalo City ruined Henry Ambrose, made him a drunk and a wife beater."

"You knew their father?"

"Yes, sir. We fished together fore he moved his kin to Buffalo City. He worked for the Duvall Brothers until the lumber business went belly up. Folks had to make ends meet, so they got 'emselves copper coils, bought some jugs and sugar, and turned loggin' equipment into the finest whiskey stills around. They sell that swamp water as far as New York City."

"Yeah?" Milton said, his newshound instincts sniffed, encouraging him to continue probing without labeling the morality of a battle Prohibition had already lost.

"Buffalo City was the place when I was a small fry. Heard trains were rolling over the swamp, steamers coming up Milltail Creek, a couple of hundred Russians, and coloreds moving logs alongside guys like me. A boom town until it weren't. Loggers cut down the trees until nothin' was left but swamp, snakes, and bears."

"Why do people still live there?"

"The moonshine. Lots of folks packed up and left after the timber played out til they figured out how to turn swamp water into money. As bad as times got, some folks there owned two cars. No place to drive them, still they got 'em. Best whiskey in the world. I got five gallons back home I've been working on."

"There must be better places to make moonshine."

"The beauty of it. The swamp protects the stills on three sides. Moonshiners got trip lines strung across the creek and lookouts perched along the edges. They can sneak away from revenuers in a quick minute."

"So why did Sparrow's father end up in prison?" Milton said, embarrassed he didn't include the names of both siblings in the question.

"Ya got lots of questions," Rawlee said, reaching into his pocket for a plug of chewing tobacco. "Lands like this grab a-hold of a person and won't let go. People sink right up to their knees and don't have the heart to lift their feet and go another step."

Milton was quiet as they continued along the road reclaimed by dredging the canal beside it. A white fisher plucked a fish in its beak, taking it to wing as they passed. Milton wondered if he might have qualified as one of Rawlee's "stuck people" if his mother hadn't gotten sick. Perhaps he was stuck differently, mourning the loss of a friendship that had no years to deepen, pondering why he was obsessed over a person he had known for a single summer. Maybe it was the vacuum created by a sudden, unexpected death, selfish regrets of losing a second childhood, a second chance at an innocence he could not get back.

"I pect it weren't all his fault he turned into a mighty sorry bastard," Rawlee said, bringing Milton's thoughts into the present. "Liquor can suck the soul out of a place. If y'ur in that place, well, it'll suck the soul out of ya too. Henry don't get no free pass. He got mean, beat Betty, and gave up on his little uns.

A corner in hell got his name on it, maybe." He pulled the vehicle to a stop and stepped out to relieve himself on the road's sandy middle ridge.

"How well did you know Mr. Ambrose?" Milton asked, realizing there might be history between the two men.

"We're kin, not close kin. Folks on the island knowed the two was comin' to live with Deborah. Now we didn't know y'ur were a-comin'. Mr. Woods is a dingbatter, so he brings lizards to town."

The men took a second ferry across the Alligator River to reach Columbia. The water was "slick cam," as Rawlee called it. The pair shared cans of potted meat and salted crackers for lunch around noon. Rawlee offered Milton a plug of tobacco more out of a playful need to see him turn green than a friendly gesture. Milton took the bait, leaving his portion of potted meat in Columbia beside a carriage post. Rawlee was a fellow who enjoyed minor victories.

Milton's stomach rolled harmoniously with the bouncy dirt road and rocking ferries to Manteo. The return trip to the island seemed longer than he remembered, trying not to show his body's continued rebellion against the tobacco chew. There was nothing left to lose in his stomach; his pride diminished to the somewhat sympathetic delight of Rawlee. Milton felt the tobacco plug was a subtle punishment for asking the old fisherman too many questions. He had paid the price. His nausea appeased Rawlee, and he was in a mood to talk.

"Henry Ambrose was a preacher once upon a time. He sharpened saw blades for the Duvall Brothers, turnin' them white cedar shakes into Buffalo City scrip. Henry was a hard worker at the mill during the day, taking sinners to the Lord on Wednesday nights and Sundays. He a-took himself too serious for my taste. It's what it is," Rawlee said, unwrapping the Ambroses' life story.

"Icy dealin' with folks on account of his short fuse, but he was religious enough for sure. He claimed to be a man of the Good Book, but there weren't much good in him. Betty was the righteous one, a kind woman living under the thumb of a bitter man."

"Anyways, Ambrose lost his job when the milling stopped. He eased into his prayers every night with some East Lake product. Before long, he drank more and prayed less. The man got to haul sugar and glass jugs for the moonshiners, and before long, Ambrose was moving liquor down Milltail Creek to Elizabeth City. I pect he was the last to know he went from preacher to mean drunk. By the time he figured it out, his church already knowed it. They ignored it for a while cuz that's what Christian folks do. Times were hard for everyone. When he started beating his missus, the church gave him the boot. The beatings got worse. Moonshiners don't take to a drunk runner. They set him up to be caught by the sheriff. You know the rest."

"Didn't anyone help his family?"

"When folks see a fellow losing God's good graces, it spills over to stain everybody. People in Buffalo City keep out of other folks' business. Charity kinda dried up with the last junipers they hauled out of 'em woods. Buffalo City, in its day, was a wild west town. Now it grows deader every day," Rawlee said.

"Hum," Milton replied, thinking how his parents had tried to stay the course, hammering hardship into something more durable than the fragile missteps of the Ambrose family. Sparrow's scar was easy to see, but his scars weren't so visible. In Milton's mind, Sparrow was light, and he was darkness. He hoped Roanoke Island might deliver him from the puzzles of his dreams, freeing him of the nightly episodes with Jack.

"I could use a hot cup of Mrs. Yarbough's sassafras tea," Milton said as the ferry docked on the north end of Roanoke Island, the sun filling the sky with a late-day red glow.

8

⌘

A Graveyard Calling

He thought for a moment before lifting his hand to knock on the door. Taking an untried stranger on his trek seemed like an unnecessary hardship for the both of them. He had to follow through. Mrs. Mona had been kind to him and had never viewed him as an oddity in his surfman's uniform. He hoped the favor wouldn't have a bad ending.

"Mr. Milton?" Eddie called off, rapping on Mil's second-floor room in the middle of the night. "Mrs. Mona said to collect you. A ship ran aground at Pea Island."

"Thought we were going to meet at the station next week," Milton answered, half asleep. It was still too early in the night for Jack to enter his dreams.

"No, sir. She said fetch you so you can see how things go firsthand," Eddie replied. "Gotta leave right now, sir. Keeper will want me there on the quick."

A black man in uniform was a rare sight for Milton. And he wasn't used to being called sir by any color. It wasn't a "sir" that raised the barrier between races. Eddie's "sir" was the etiquette of a professional, a man not hiding behind his uniform but responding to a call to action. The surfman's demeanor gave his bearing a crisp polish. Though Eddie was a little older than Milton, he carried himself as if he were far older. The pitch blackness of his skin and the broad flare of his nose gave way to a stone face that hid his emotions as well as Milton hid his own. Eddie's sharp, practiced movements reminded Milton of off-duty Norfolk sailors walking along Bouch Street before the effects of weekend alcohol made them sway.

"I get it. The service motto: "You have to go out, but you don't have to come back," Milton said, trying to break the awkwardness with the sleepy drugs of his dry sense of humor.

Eddie sized up the man standing in the doorway. Milton's lean form suggested a man softened by working behind a desk, his dark brown hair unfurled from a night of restless sleep. The surfman scrutinized this man who would be his companion on a stormy night, deciding if this stranger would be a liability or someone who could carry their weight in a crisis. Milton was uncertain of Eddie's expectations. His dreams of Jack left him in awe and fear of the ocean, filled with images of Jack's lifeless body tossed like a rag doll by waves. A lifetime of uncertainty had given the newspaper reporter a poker face to conceal his anxieties from this guardian of the coast.

"Can you ride a hoss?" Eddie quizzed. Milton remembered his father lifting him on a saddle of a pony tethered in a circle of other ponies at a county fair. The saddle was oversized, and the pony stood motionless, waiting for toddler passengers. It had been a good day, one of a handful he remembered when his father was smiling.

"I'll manage," Milton replied, afraid a truthful answer would mean Eddie leaving him behind.

"Patsy is a good ol' girl. She doesn't spook in a blow," Eddie said.

"The sound is pushed way out, like when Moses crossed the Red Sea. The hosses can walk along the edge. It'll save time. I gotta extra slicker if you don't mind wearing my coat. We are about the same size. It would be a little short on ya."

Milton nodded and grabbed a pencil and paper tightly wrapped in waterproof canvas, donning the storm gear Mona had provided. Wool socks padding a pair of ill-fitting boots would do the job. According to Mona, adding snug boots was as apt to drown a fellow as save him blisters on his feet.

Milton was wet and terrified as they rode on horseback a dozen miles to Oregon Inlet on a stormy night. His heart raced, leaving little time for him to figure out how Eddie could be so calm in the face of adversity.

Patsy was a forgiving nag who rolled the whites of her eyes at first and, after a mile or so of prodding down the waterless beach, made peace with Milton. The scenery was eerie; brackish water had retreated yards from the sound side shore. The ocean threw salty sprays mixed with sand into their faces. As vigilant as the automated lighthouse flashing its Fresnel beacon out to sea in the distance, Eddie was mindful to keep his horse's head angled away from the worst of it. The surfman took the lead, surmising Milton's riding experience was overstated; he kept his mount close to the reporter. The retreating water exposed seagrass and mud hidden from view, along with torn nets, hulks of abandoned boats, and broken rocking chairs that had once graced the vista of Nags Head lodging. Each item marked a lost battle between man and nature. A doll floated in a small pool near a clump of seaweed. Milton said nothing, giving Eddie a questioning look as the reporter got off Patsy and retrieved the figure, stuffing it into his bag.

The riders reached the Pea Island Life-Saving Station before midnight. Once on the island, the stinging wet sand, having inched through their clothes, turned into an icy grit. The scene transformed into a raging leviathan as the nor'easter blew against the sturdy, tall gingerbread-looking building housing the surfmen. The warmth of black coffee pushed aside the storm's veil once they were inside the station. Milton could see duplicates of Eddie, each uniformed black man preparing to brave the weather, risking their lives for strangers who might not acknowledge them on a sunny sidewalk. These surfmen, their personalities suspended by the commands and hand gestures of the keeper, acted in practiced unison, moving a cart and a small banana-shaped boat on wheels toward the tragic symphony playing out on a moonless beach. The dim grayness of another day broke on the horizon.

"She's been out on the bar for a day. Mast straight up into the sky. She was far out, and the storm was too fierce to reach her, stuck on the shoal," Eddie said.

Eddie pointed to the vessel, appearing as a ghostly outline, sitting motionless on churning water, too far out to be reached by a Lyle gun, the small cannon that could hurl a slender rope over the bow of a distressed ship. Once secured by the crew on deck, the surfmen would add a heavier lifeline to haul passengers one by one to shore as the hapless victims sat inside a breech buoy, pants woven into the canvas of a buoyant doughnut.

"Will I go out in the boat?" Milton asked, hoping the answer would spare his pride.

"Nope. It's dangerous work, and you don't need savin'. Best to keep it that way. Stay here and take it in," Eddie replied.

Seven surfmen guided the high-walled boat over the packed sand and through the surf. They tried three times to launch the heavy craft over the pounding breakers, only to have the sea return men and splintering boat to shore. On the third attempt, a wave caught the boat by its stern and flipped it backward, tumbling all seven crewmen under its white churn. The men lifted themselves, righted the craft, and, without hesitation, broke again through the breakers, this time undefeated by the ocean's might.

In the distance, the silhouette of the sailboat was losing its fight to stay whole. Its geometry of near-perfect lines was changing, bending, and breaking into submission to the sea. The surfmen, robbed of their engine when the boat overturned, gripped oars, pulling away from the shore and heading toward the dying vessel being torn apart on the shoal.

As the surfboat pitched in the tempest, the surfmen sat rigid in their seats, their arms pistons for the oars and controlled by the chants of the keeper to keep going, maintaining human harmony in the chaos. The keeper guided their forward motions toward the ship which was crumbling on the horizon. The shore was filling up with the ship's cargo of juniper wood, soon to be salvage for the islanders. Sand-crusted lumber drifted ashore, covering the surf line with boards. A sail, still flapping against a broken mast, had drifted ashore, adding a new sound like freshly washed clothes flapping on a line. A body was tangled in the broadcloth, a shroud half concealing a broken man no older than Milton. The carnage had crushed and disfigured his skull. His left arm was tied to the broken mast as a testament he had tried to save himself. His body was bloodless, vital fluids washed away from his pale corpse. His final shocked expression frozen in death by the watery horror he witnessed.

Milton's stomach heaved, and an image from dreams about Jack poured into his consciousness. Milton seldom saw the death mask on Jack's face in his haunting, but he was seeing this dead man's face, and it was worse than any nightmare. He looked away, out to the surfboat. He had an odd, disjointed thought, wondering if those seven black faces would be as pale if the sea returned them as broken shells to shore. The surfmen showed no willingness to yield to the sea. The surfboat, a tiny dot on the water, circled the doomed ship, determined to finish its mission. Unexpectedly, six smaller dots of humanity moved around the deck of the larger vessel. Hope surfaced as a gloomy day replaced the dark sky.

An hour later, the surfboat loomed large on the beach, sitting low in the water, carrying the seven surfmen and six new passengers, one an infant, crying against its mother's breasts, wrapped in a surfman's jacket.

"You alright, ma'am?" the keeper asked the young woman. She cried, finding comfort in his giant ebony arms. Milton recalled how Ginny held him in her arms after his father died, remembering that human comfort.

"We got 'em all," a tired Eddie said, not forgetting his obligation to the reporter who tagged along. "Most of the ship will be up on the beach in a few days. People be salvaging. Looks like a good load."

"Not everyone," Milton said, nodding toward the sailor still entangled in the broken mast.

"Give him a proper burial once we get them people dry and fed," Eddie said, his left cheek flinching, showing a trace of emotion, a pang of regret hidden by the salty spray on his face.

Standing in the sand among the timber boards floating on a placate surf, the keeper held the shivering mother and a child who would never get to know his father.

The surfmen buried the dead sailor among the dunes of Pea Island. Eddie handed the toy doll he had found in the sound to the grieving widow, knowing token gestures would bring her little comfort. The surfmen continued their services into the next life, giving a frightened widow and fatherless child solace. Two boards reclaimed from the ship marked the grave, the sailor's initials whitewashed on the wood with paint from the station. In a short time, the marker would be gone, that too erased by the sea's winds and sands. The sailor's widow needed closure. The surfmen and Milton were silent mourners. A week later, a Coast Guard boat picked her up from Oregon Inlet, giving mother and child passage to Norfolk. As she said her goodbyes, she shook the Keeper's hand, grateful for his thoughtful care.

Milton's return to Manteo was longer than the one on the night riding horseback through the liquid nightmare of a nor'easter. The Manteo Hatteras Bus broke an axle, leaving Milton and Eddie stranded on the southern shore. Eddie had lowered his guard around Milton; the shared tragedy had created another wordless between people living along the coast. Milton got to know the man behind the uniform. The official apparel and his surfman status was a shield allowing Eddie, a freedom impossible to obtain away from his duty station. When wearing the uniform, he wasn't second-class to any man. Eddie lost that self-assurance once he was home on Roanoke Island. He was a man without ambition, and he knew it. He had reached his pinnacle, and there was nowhere else to go. That was enough for him.

"Gonna let Mrs. Mona read what you write before you put it in the paper?" Eddie asked. "She'll make it so folks don't get upset. Some people got issues with the Pea Island crew."

"What issues?" Milton asked, awed Mona had gained the trust of both races on the island.

"Don't write down words that upset folks. The colored will get the notion I'm uppity, and some whites believe I don't know my place," Eddie said.

"You care?" Milton asked, knowing he cared even though his government job was secure and the Etheridge name carried weight among the locals.

"The island can be touchy. Say the wrong words, and the words fester like a bad cut that don't heal right. Hear nothing for a long time, and then they come to haunt you. Savin' folks from the sea and fishing is enough for me."

"Want to be a Keeper one day?"

"Nope. Keepers got to make decisions. Come here and do that is all the keepin' I need." Eddie nodded. "Eat some flat fish on Friday, listen to the radio on Saturday night, and have the preacher say some righteous words over me when they put me under."

Milton couldn't tell if Eddie was being sincere. He imagined the surfman had spent a lifetime telling white people what he thought they wanted to hear. Ginny was an expert in disguising thoughts. Whites bought into her disguise of being a wrinkled, brown-skinned, simple-minded woman. She had aged into a heavy-set granny smiling her way into the odd job and handouts from the privileged. When a hospital nurse told her Milton couldn't see his mother locked in an iron shell, another Jennifer Cooke emerged. Her words peeled away levels of race and misdirection becoming a heated, honest minute to reunite a son with his mother. From that day, when Milton required the presence of God, the deity took on the appearance of Ginny.

"What do you do when there are no shipwrecks?" Milton asked Eddie, scribing notes on a pad, sitting in the shade of the sand-locked, broken-down bus.

"Truth told, most of what surfmen do is drills. More cars than ships go by the station these days. Time's changing, and maybe the surfmen's days are numbered. Could turn us into a museum like they did Fort Raleigh so folks can remember how things was. Hope I can keep my job." Eddie said matter of fact, ending Milton's attempt to collect his thoughts in a notebook made rebellious by a blustering wind. The surfman brushed sand from his uniform pants and moved toward a horse-drawn cart delivering a new axle for the bus. Milton stuck his notebook in his back pocket and followed Eddie's lead to repair the bus. Bankers wore many hats. Often those hats looked the same.

9

⌘

Jeanette's Island

Dick Nancey had three true loves in his life. He failed to cherish them in a timely order. He realized the depth of his love for his wife the day before her death. He had devoted himself to his mistress but his paramour wasn't a woman. Dick reserved his deepest affection for the island and Manteo, where he was the Banks' visionary and leader. Mary had been his moral compass, keeping him level-headed and compassionate. Without her, he was like a seashell tossed up by the ocean, limited without his kind-hearted, generous partner. Without Mary, he risked destroying the things he valued. Dick understood his shortcomings and prayed to his dead wife for direction, petitioning her heavenly presence to serve as his conscience. Without her guidance, he feared he might slide into the shadows, remembered as a name and date on a headstone. Dick was more of the person he pretended to be than he thought. He saw himself as his father's son, driven by ego and not a man who cared much for the welfare of others. But Dick wasn't a copy of his father. Mary had brought out his better self, leaving his veneer of vanity in place while stripping away his selfish tendencies.

The third love of his life stood to derail him in the form of his tomboyish 12-year-old daughter, Jeanette. She was unfiltered and brash. She did whatever came into her untethered, adventurous mind without fear of reprisals. Older men on the island adored her, and women shook their heads at this unruly girl with no mother to tame her. These mothers fretted their children might fall under her spell of impulsiveness. The island's inhabitants split between envy and loathing for Jeanette. The young girl could inflict as much damage as a nor'easter on her birthplace. Things got broken or went missing when Jeanette sped through the streets of Manteo in her father's 1932 Ford Phaeton Roadster.

There is a legend that the spirit of Eleanor Dare's child, Virginia, roamed Roanoke Island woods as a deer, waiting for her grandfather, John White, to sail across the sea to reclaim his abandoned, lost colony. The older fishermen called Jeanette, VDee, an abbreviation of Virginia Dare. In contrast, others saw her antics akin to Sir Walter Raleigh's Queen Elizabeth, doling out proclamations of eminent domain over the island. The seasonal residents across the sound at Nags Head viewed Jeanette as a hooligan, trespassing on their summer memories and creating chaos where there should be none. Dick had given Rawlee Turnage orders to bar Jeanette's passage over the Roanoke Sound bridge to Nags Head after Jeanette stole a truckload of pumpkins from the row of cottages called the Unpainted Aristocracy the year before. Manteo's matrons told Dick his daughter was bad for business and he should reel her in before there was real trouble. Dick, who was often at a loss for words when it came to Jeanette's behavior, tipped his fedora and said, "Will do."

"Have some peppermint," Jeanette said to Sparrow, waving a large glass jar of the candy in front of her.

"I don't have money for it," Sparrow replied, her eyes feasting on the long red and white swirled sticks.

"This is my daddy's store. I can take what I want and give it to anybody I please," Jeanette said, shaking the jar impatiently.

Sparrow studied this girl with curly blonde hair made more uncivilized by the salty ocean air. She was a head shorter than Sparrow and three years younger. Jeanette was unlike anyone

Sparrow had known. Jeanette embarrassed Finch an hour earlier, telling him how cute he was before ordering him to disappear for the afternoon. Sparrow had looked sympathetically at her brother, her eyes telling him she would be all right.

"I can't pay," Sparrow replied without seeing Dick walking up behind her.

"Who's this young lady, Jeanette?" Dick said, smiling at the two girls.

"She's the girl with the bad arm. She and her brother killed a black bear with their bare hands," Jeanette exclaimed, never afraid to turn a simple truth into a lie.

"I see. You must be Deborah's niece," Dick said, assuring Sparrow it was ok to take a piece of peppermint.

"My daddy. He's lord of Manteo and all nearby parts," Jeanette said, nodding as she crunched into her peppermint stick.

"Stop it, Jeanette." Dick laughed. "What are you girls up to today?"

"Oh, we're going over to the Ice Plant. Look for a few shipwrecks on the beach," Jeanette replied, giving Sparrow a head's up on her plans in the same breath.

"Don't think you will find any there… just people out for a walk, picking up driftwood and shells. Be careful," Dick said, footnoting. "And, oh yeah, stay on this side of the bridge."

Though the car was not old, the sea air had dug into its shiny black finish. The impatient adolescent driver had forced its gears to the point they scraped, making a sound like someone clearing their throat before beginning an arduous task. Jeanette's lips curled into a smile as the car lurched forward, and Sparrow's eyes widened. The trip was brief despite Jeanette's fanfare. She drove several hundred feet from one end of Main Street to the other, parking the car along Dough's Creek as the girls continued barefoot to reach the ice plant now standing in ashen ruins.

"This is where the world began," Jeanette said, outstretching her arms to the forest and low-growing shrubs encircling her.

Sound waters lapped against the tan shore, sparkling through the trees.

"You mean the colony? I thought that's down the road where they built the theater," Sparrow said, allowing her curiosity to fall under the spell of the island's history since arriving at Manteo. Milton fed her imagination as he researched the Banks for his newspaper articles. Easy conversations between the two budded into a friendship deepened by tales of the island's history and the aerial exploits of Amelia Earhart that Sparrow gleaned from magazine articles. The two spent evenings working on crossword puzzles from a nearby daily newspaper. Each solution strengthened their growing bond as they sat under the stars of Manteo and listened to the nightly concert of hungry insects and lonely frogs.

"Which colony? Negro one or the white one?" Jeanette laughed.

"I thought there was only one," Sparrow replied, unaccustomed to the mention of race.

"There's the Lost Colony one, island folks have been celebrating with a pageant forever. And there's that colored one when the Yankees gave the island to black folks during the Civil War. Yep, freed them all and gave the land away, but it didn't last long. The government made 'em give it back after a while," Jeanette said.

"I know about the Raleigh one. John White couldn't come back to save his family until it was too late," Sparrow said, envisioning a fleeting image of her father.

"Croatoan! Croatoan!" Jeanette yelled, the sound echoing through the trees. "I'm still here, grandaddy… waiting for you to save me. You know people call me Virginia Dare, right?"

"You aren't Virginia Dare. You just act wild to get people's attention," Sparrow said, looking down at broken sea shells on the beach.

"Neither of us has a mama, so we can do as we please," Jeanette replied. "You can be in the new pageant, too. My daddy knows people. Probably have to be an Indian girl, though."

"I'd like that," Sparrow replied, pointing across the sound. "Have you been to the Wright Brothers Memorial? Amelia Earhart came there once. I'm going to meet her someday."

"Yep… a big ol' funny-looking lighthouse that is goin' to blow off the dune someday. My daddy helped 'em Wrights with their equipment. He said they were nice guys. One was a little stuffy. That Earhart lady was there when they turned on the lights. My daddy said she reminded him of me. She ain't afraid to wear pants just like me," she said.

"I want to fly like Amelia Earhart. Wish I could meet her. One day I will. I'll soar in the sky and see everything down here from up there." Sparrow cast her eyes skyward.

"Well… you are a sparrow, so go fly, little bird." Jeanette laughed.

10

⌘

Shared Meal

Steam from two plates of baked ham and boiled cabbage rose above the table like a calm fog over the sound. Parker and Dick stared at the lifting vapor. The two men ate dinner together on Wednesdays at the Sir Walter Raleigh Restaurant. It was their meeting night. An interest in history brought them together for this weekly pork feast topped off with banana pudding and black coffee. Their vision of the Banks' future forged a bond between the newspaper dingbatter and the island's lord of commerce.

Neither man trusted Nags Head's seasonal residents. Parker was wary his island newspaper might fall to competition from larger Elizabeth City and Norfolk newspapers; its small-town charm drowned by mainland hunger for current events. Dick knew outsiders' interest in real estate along the narrow band of sand was growing. He couldn't compete with those deeper financial pockets and broader connections that would one day steal control of the Banks from him. Dick didn't want Roanoke Island to go the way of Buffalo City, big business gobbling up local resources, only to see its fruits dry up and leave behind a local economy sinking into denuded marshland. Dick understood history shrouded in mystery was the Banks' valuable resource. The two men wanted to be legendary but needed a larger audience first. They sought to brand the Banks with their labels dipped in the same ink that had sent Sir Walter Raleigh's venture around the ocean in 1584. Parker and Dick wanted to protect the colony Raleigh, that ancient captain of commerce, had forsaken once he realized the Bank's isolation and natural beauty would not yield the wealth he sought. Though the quest for wealth didn't drive either man, they wanted to be remembered.

According to Parker and Dick, Roanoke Island belonged on gas station road maps, a place for mainlanders to spend money and not overstay their welcome. Across the island's causeway, along the new asphalt road linking Nags Head to the three-mile-long bridge on the rural peninsula south of metropolitan Virginia, the flow of vehicles thumping over its wooden span continued to grow from spring until fall each year. Over the years, their Wednesday pork meals changed from sharing pipedreams to brainstorming how to grow fishing villages into tourism attractions.

"May never find the exact site. I think it's under the sound now. Erosion has taken its toll. People find a shard of broken pottery now and then. Jeanette brought this piece home the other day," Dick said, placing a broken fragment of ceramic next to a bowl of fried okra.

Parker toyed with the small chip and lit a cigarette. The smoke was drifting above the table, replacing the pungent smell of cabbage from their meal. He had seen hundreds of such pieces since he had been on the island, convinced most of them were worthless glaze discarded over the centuries and not from Raleigh's colonies.

"People dump their trash away from neighbors' prying eyes, but trash tells a story. The government wanted to search through trash piles they can find to resurrect the vanished City of Raleigh. Roosevelt is pouring money and creating jobs to fund dozens of similar projects across the country. Sphinx is determined to dig the nation out of this Depression."

"I know you don't want to hear this. Does it matter if we are a few feet off? Thank God they covered those two entrance stones with log guard towers. At least it doesn't look like a cemetery gate anymore." Parker chuckled, referring to memorial posts near where Sir Walter Raleigh sent explorers to claim a chunk of North America in the name of the English Queen Elizabeth I.

"Details make the history stand out. We can't say the Lost Colony was sort of on this spot. When the government built the Wright beacon, they marked it with a stone. That is how it should be," Dick said, irritated by the local under-funded effort to preserve the ancient real estate.

"There must be a dozen buildings there, and I don't believe one is anything like what Raleigh's colonists built. You got to love the chapel, though. Folks are growing fond of it," Parker said, recalling how he and Mona fell in love with its rustic charm, hailing it as Manteo's community center.

"It's shifting sand, Dick. A few hundred yards to the right or left doesn't matter. The island is washing away. People will feel they are standing on the hallowed ground no matter where the government plants the next marker," Parker continued, dismissive of Dick's passion for historical correctness and his devotion to America's Cradle Song pageant.

"Well, this year's pageant isn't a mile away… only months. The first English child was born here three-hundred-fifty years ago. People remember Virginia Dare's birthday. It gives locals something to celebrate," Dick said.

"The historical association has been at it for a long time. If the association hadn't bought those sixteen acres from the Dough family, the Lost Colony's location might have jumped over to the Unpainted Aristocracy by now. The Casino could have booked Manteo and Wanchese dancing the night away with the crowd sipping Pabst Blue Ribbon. Ras Wescott may end up buying the joint since it has already failed twice. He has a head for business," Parker said. The men laughed, relishing unguarded moments of banter.

"I want to make the pageant permanent, Parker. The WPA theater is supposed to be a one summer show to give starving artists a job, showcase how Roosevelt is saving art and history, and putting people back to work. We can turn it into something lasting. We can build on it, bring people from all over to spend their money where America began," Dick said, crunching into a cold piece of greasy cornbread from a bowl beside his empty dish of pudding.

"Humm. I like that.... where America begins. Possible, I guess. It's a big step up from entertaining duck hunters, wayward history buffs, and weekend partygoers. It means opening up the island and the Banks to a new way of doing business. Would the Banks still even be the Banks?" Parker questioned, watching crumbles of Dick's cornbread fall onto his plate.

"You know damn well things will change. Instead of catching a boatload of fish, fishermen will haul around a boatload of fishermen. They'll go from picking up salvage and seashells on the beach to stocking shelves with them. The old way of people getting by from storm to storm will be gone. The new way will turn the old way into merchandise to peddle in souvenir shops."

"Understand what you are saying. Locals become innkeepers for tourists looking to get away from hard times. The sea can heal a soul on a weekend getaway, and the rich pockets of Yankees will fill the oceanfront with rows of summer cottages."

"One thing about sand; it never stays put. Still, the wind won't blow the coast away for another thousand years. That's enough time for two old-timers like you and me to make a decent living," Dick said, smiling as he asked the waitress for another cup of coffee.

11

⌘

Pews Have Ears

Ginny figured church people bargained with God or lied to keep up appearances with the neighbors. Since Milton decided that Ginny was right about most things early on in his life, he strayed from his mother's faith in God to seek devotion on the streets of Norfolk. These two women whom he treasured, didn't see the same Heavenly Father. His mother trusted in faith, whereas the eternally smiling Ginny counted on what she could see with her earthly eyes.

Milton kept his distance from God, avoiding disappointment in the outcome of his prayers. Jack and Milton had talked about the Bible and God under the starry vault above the pulsing sea and crackling domes of thunderstorms that summer they worked for the CCC. Jack thought of himself as a biblical expert. While growing up in the insane asylum, he read daily devotions under the righteous fist of an evangelical ward nurse who battled the demons of mental illness with a swift hand and a leather belt. Jack's knowledge of the Bible was extensive, and his shared stories left Milton enthralled. Jack was equally confident God didn't exist. He said if a God in Heaven existed, people wouldn't suffer, and life wouldn't be a dark tunnel like the underground passages between the asylum buildings. Jack's passion for a faith that he saw as a myth puzzled Milton. When his friend died, Jack's journey into an afterlife troubled Milton. As for himself,

Milton accepted churchgoing with a respectful apathy, keeping the door cracked for God just in case he could put in a good word for those he loved.

Milton sat on the third pew of the Manteo church. The curved seat bottoms were hard. He figured they were part of God's punishment for the self-righteous. Church eyes watched him, waiting for gossip to answer why he sat with Sparrow and her aunt every Sunday. Finch avoided Sunday service, finding a part-time job cleaning a Wanchese fish house as acceptable penance. Deborah didn't object strenuously to Finch's employment since she had two extra mouths to feed. Though Deborah was polite to Milton, it displeased her that Sparrow reserved a place for the young reporter during worship. She knew Sparrow and Milton had become friends. She had heard accounts of how Milton helped pull her niece out of the sound, and she trusted Mona's instincts about people. Her own judgment was less accommodating. Deborah viewed Milton as a man interested in her teenage niece and believed men have a way of upending a girl's life. Deborah thought it was bad enough Sparrow was friends with Dick's teenage island terror. Sparrow's friendship with Milton compounded her worries, adding extra words to her evening prayers.

The Most Reverend Thomas Boggs was known for solid sermons and loose living. He was a seemingly congenial man who comforted his parish with well-placed words, a genuine love for the island, and his belief in a heaven where sand didn't blow the streets away. The minister worked to keep the name of John White's long-vanished granddaughter, Virginia Dare, on the tongues of the faithful. After all, the infant was the first English child born in America, a national symbol of the Christian purity he idealized.

Boggs had the ear of key state and federal legislators. He sought to transform Virginia Dare from a partial myth into a lasting legacy. He was flexible in the company he kept. The minister could conform to more secular audiences over glasses of East Lake Rye, making deals in cities far from the sandy shores of his parish. He hoped God might forgive him for his sins in the name of his beloved Virginia Dare. Boggs didn't know his transgressions closer to home in the arms of an Elizabeth City merchant's wife were the ones that echoed on the winds of Manteo. The islanders, tolerant of the burning sun and sinking sand, wouldn't continue to look away from his indiscretions forever.

"There was a day when I put church ahead of the community, placed love of my faith above God, and followed the rules without convictions. Those days are in my past," Boggs said, beginning his sermon.

Boggs could move people with his words, using those words to hide his secret life during his frequent trips off island to preserve Virginia Dare's memory. He was a brilliant orator, and his Sunday sermons lightened the daily load of his congregation. They were reluctant to challenge his hypocrisy; at least, they overlooked it to let God determine Boggs' seat at the heavenly table. His charm and sympathetic ear were a foundation in the community not easily corroded away by gossip on the six days outside of the Sabbath. Island people saw him as a flawed man whose Sunday words offered hope. Had Boggs known his secrets were so poorly hidden, he might have crumpled like a sandcastle built too near the surf.

"The day will come when Jesus sets us free. We must have the courage to wait for his deliverance. As Eleanor Dare, that blessed mother of Virginia, waited on these shores for her earthly father's return, we must wait. God's hand protects us in our darkest hour and will deliver us at the end of our days to be with our Heavenly Father," Boggs continued. He never prepared his sermons; they welled up in him as he spoke, scanning his audience for hints of inspiration.

Rawlee Turnage chewed his bottom lip, craving a plug of tobacco as he sat on the back pew as he had done for thirty years. He had no faith in Boggs, knowing him as a man whose actions and words were a poor mix. Rawlee's religion was the sea, and his house of worship was a small fishing boat tied to a rundown pier behind his home on Doughs Creek. The aging fisherman had mentioned Boggs once to Milton during their regular Sunday afternoon fishing trips, offering few words about the minister among his recollection of tales about the Banks. Rawlee entertained Milton with his opinions as they fished on the sound, but he kept his thoughts about the minister to himself.

Dick and Parker sang in the chorus, screaming at God from a distance. Parker's bass was more off-key and noticeable than Dick's solid baritone. Their spiritual fidelity was secondary to a desire to keep up with island happenings. The eight women who formed the core of the church's chorus were well-connected muses of current events. On Thursday nights, the two men paid the church's bills, practiced songs for the next service, and collected chatty bites of candor useful to the merchant and newspaperman.

Mona played the church's old Steinway piano, struggling to keep the poorly tuned instrument guiding the euphony of the congregation's favorite hymn, "The Old Rugged Cross." She made Milton think of Jack when she played, searching for harmony among the keys that failed to deliver it. She had played since childhood. Unlike Jack's haphazard training on the chipped keys of an asylum piano, Mona had classical training in her youth. She was now hampered by the less nimble fisherman's hands she had earned since coming to Roanoke Island. Milton suppressed a grin at her sour notes, hallmarking her struggle, not her defeat.

"Mrs. Yarbough, would you lead God's people in the reading of Ecclesiastes 3:1-8?" Boggs asked Deborah. He called on her often, which was novel among churchgoers where public requests for God's guidance and mercy came from male voices. Boggs sensed Deborah didn't hold him in high regard. She magnified his hidden guilt, passing an unspoken judgment. Though Boggs didn't show it, she unnerved him. The minister found penance in giving his youth Sunday School teacher a voice in the morning service, aware people didn't care for her overt piety.

Deborah was conscious of Boggs's feelings toward her. She saw Boggs as a man of pretense, barring him from a godly path the same as her imprisoned brother-in-law. She viewed Boggs as a damnation with good intentions. One day he would bear the fruit of his sins.

"I have seen the travail God hath given to the sons of men. He hath made everything beautiful in his time; also he hath set the world in their heart so that no man can find out the work that God maketh from the beginning to the end," she read, emphasizing certain words to Boggs' discomfort.

A flush colored Boggs' face. He asked the chorus to lead the congregation in "Amazing Grace."

12

⌘

Where Legends Roam

Jeanette had a problem with God for making her wear a dress on Sunday mornings. She forgave him by the afternoon as she roamed Roanoke Island in blue jeans and a flannel shirt, sporting the pale freckles highlighting her nose. Mrs. Yarbough got on VDee's nerves, making her learn the books in the Old Testament by heart. If God had wanted her to know that stuff, he would have made it as joyful as finding a cluster of bullfrog eggs, as wondrous as lightning forking across the sky, or as entertaining as having the police chief chase her over the bumpy ruts of the town's unpaved streets. VDee tried to be charitable. Mrs. Yarbough needed rules, but even her father wasn't as hard-edged as that woman. VDee was afraid Mrs. Yarbough would ruin her new friend, changing her into a younger version of her aunt. Sparrow deserved more than the strait-laced complications of an overbearing Deborah Yarbough.

"Hop in. Afraid ya would be stuck at the hotel. My daddy said a lot of fishermen are staying there this week. Some folks at Hatteras are takin' lizards offshore to fish. My daddy says they are payin' big bucks to catch a few fish. Crazy, right?" VDee laughed, pounding her hand on the side of her vehicle.

"I've been reading. Men staying at the hotel bring magazines, and they let me keep them. I put them under my bed. Anyway, sport fishing is what rich people do. They want to catch trophies to mount on their walls, which is good because Finch and I don't have to clean 'em." Sparrow giggled.

"Y'ur brother is a strange bird. And don't get me started on your aunt."

"She wants what is best for people, and Finch is…. quiet."

"He is dreamy when he doesn't smell like a fish. Tried talkin' to him. He won't say much, and he thinks I'm a kid."

Sparrow knew her brother and aunt were not dreamers. Their minds were as elemental as the sea, surviving and accepting the simple majesty of forces too mosaic to comprehend. They dealt with the facts laid out before them and didn't look far into the past or future for answers. Sparrow tried to keep her dreams to herself. She shared them with Mil, who listened and encouraged her, yet sometimes, he seemed more distant than her aunt or brother. VDee was different. She looked like a kid and acted with a feigned maturity. Sparrow thought of Jeanette as being older than she was because she had little filter talking to adults. VDee freed Sparrow's imagination. Sparrow was grateful for this island sprite. She was like the legendary deer changeling of the first Virginia Dare that locals said haunted the island. Jeanette was both pirate and princess, a force of nature and a source of strength for the more outwardly reserved Sparrow.

VDee sought to be more of a pirate than a princess this day. She was determined to break her father's rule of not crossing the bridge to Nags Head. VDee's past encounters with the seasonal residents and visitors didn't turn out well for them or Dick. VDee was as unpredictable as a waterspout, leaving degrees of destruction in her wake that taxed the ability of Dick's finances and social graces. She once reclaimed the nameplate from a shipwreck nailed to the side of a cottage, claiming those lizards had no right to keep it. Eddie found the nameplate floating on the surf and gave it to Dick, who returned it to the cottage owner with an apology. A little pirate himself, Dick told the owner a close relative perished on the wreck, polishing the story with $20 to get his outlaw daughter off the hook. Jeanette's notoriety became fixed later that summer when she sold a bushel of mussels to a summer visitor for $100, showing the eager buyer the promise of mother-of-pearl inside a shucked mollusk. Her last pumpkin heist sealed Jeanette's fate, barring her from crossing the bridge.

"Thought you couldn't cross the bridge anymore?"

"The only one keepin' us from goin' is Mr. Turnage, and I got it from good sources he ain't workin' today."

Sparrow became thoughtfully quiet. There was an opportunity in VDee's plan to escape the island, and the possibility intrigued her. Sparrow first saw the Wright Brothers Memorial when she arrived on the Banks and wanted to stand on the spot where wings first lifted men into the sky on the windy dunes of Kill Devil Hills. Her heroine Amelia Earhart had visited once to pay homage to the brothers. VDee's plan was Sparrow's chance to set foot where Earhart had walked on hallowed ground, that distant vista across the Croatan Sound from the Manteo waterfront.

"We shouldn't go. You'll get in trouble," Sparrow warned.

"Well, little bird. It is my trouble to get in, and I wanna go. I get bored waitin' for the world to come to me, so let's ride," VDee replied, grinding the Ford into first gear as she headed toward the bridge and causeway.

The memorial sat atop a grassy hill, itself a marvel of human ingenuity taming the shifting sands. It was a granite-clad monolith looking more like a lighthouse than a place of remembrance, a gift of the New Deal to celebrate overcoming the impossible, giving hope to a country disenfranchised by a failed economy. The Art Deco beacon was another symbol planted by Roosevelt's idealism. The Ohio brothers, who stood on the dunes and flapped their arms in imitation of birds, captured the imaginations of Bankers. Corralled by water and wind, their ancestors understood the aerial ballet better than most, watching pelicans glide over the waves and seagulls hover above them with open wings.

"Well, we're here. What's so special about this place?" VDee said, uninterested in making another pilgrimage to her father's favorite spot.

"Wish I could fly with them," Sparrow said, staring at the monolith as the girls walked uphill from its base among the swirl of gulls begging for a meal.

"If one of 'em craps on me, we're goin' to leave," VDee retorted as Sparrow smiled, sitting on the grass in the memorial's shadow.

Sparrow could see beyond the grassy dune across the sound to the sliver of land that was Roanoke Island and out into the pale blue ocean to the east. She wondered if Raleigh's colony had the same vantage point when their wooden boats passed through Trinity Inlet because shoaling had closed that opening between the Atlantic Ocean and Croatan Sound long ago. Her thoughts morphed from images of ancient mariners lowering sails on calm waters to two brothers moving a canvas-covered machine to soar into the heavens. Though the visions were disjointed, those pivotal moments defined history without redefining the natural world. Mil and Mr. Turnage said the Banks were changing, and this memorial in the sand was just the beginning. She couldn't make sense of what they meant. The Banks had saved her and her brother from the misery and uncertainty of Buffalo City. Even though times were difficult on the Banks, it was a comforting place to come of age, predictable in its extremes, but a safe harbor for her and her brother.

"Don't pull the plants," a uniformed man demanded, looking at VDee, who was collecting wildflowers where the girls sat.

"I'm not. I'm pickin' flowers. You can't tell me what not to do?" VDee retorted, defending her right to act as she pleased in her self-proclaimed domain.

"I'm in charge here, young lady. Took a bit of Mr. Roosevelt's money to turn this dune into a grassy paradise, so we don't allow picking," the uniformed man replied, trying to soften the edge of his demand.

"Like the sand better than this old grass. It ain't natural," VDee said, eyeing the man as she pulled another flower to test the fellow's resolve.

"This is federal land, and there are rules. You and your friend must follow them, or you must leave," he said.

"Leave? Don't you know who I am? Virginia Dare is my name. I own this place. I have been here before there was a Mr. Roosevelt." VDee replied, deciding to play the role she would have been too self-conscious to attempt on the island. If she used her secret identity, perhaps she could avoid her father's wrath, keeping him from finding out about her escape.

"That would make you a mighty old woman indeed. Now you and your friend move along. Go get some sodas at the Casino, rest your bones, and don't undo Mr. Roosevelt's good work," he replied, again softening to the girl's mischief.

Sparrow remained silent during the exchange. She couldn't understand VDee's boldness with adults. She thought Jeanette's attitude was impolite but admired the girl's spirit. Sparrow, wishing Jeanette would curve her indignation, wasn't ready to leave the open hillside capped with its tower honoring the first flight. She hoped Amelia Earhart would step out to greet her and ease the tension.

"Sir, did you meet Amelia Earhart when she was here?" Sparrow asked the man, who smiled for the first time.

"Why yes, I was here."

"May I ask what she was like?"

"She seemed to be a fine lady, friendly with a big smile, always in a rush. You know she is going to fly around the world soon."

"She was a skinny lady with big teeth. She was standing over there, talking to my daddy." VDee pointed to the left, revealing more about herself than she intended.

"Thought I had seen you before." The man frowned.

Sparrow, taken aback that VDee hadn't told her she had met Amelia face to face, rescued her younger companion from more questioning as she nodded and thanked the man for the information. Her disappointment became more profound as she looked into space and imagined Amelia standing nearby. Sparrow had hoped a bond would form with Earhart by standing where the famous aviator stood. And then she realized the bond was there, hidden inside herself. It dawned on Sparrow she could become the master of her realities.

13

⌘

Dare Stone

Dick studied a mouse as it scurried across the storage room floor. He needed to add another cat to his feline arsenal. The trouble with cats is they eat more frogs than rodents. He hated to upset Jeanette's fondness for the green-skinned creatures. The mouse darted into the storage room where Dick's guest kicked at the frightened creature as it ran by his white and brown Oxfords.

"Parker, we need to talk." Dick's voice crackled over the phone as Parker sat at his desk, finishing his weekly editorial rant on the state of affairs on the Banks. Dick's voice suggested urgency, its calculated statesmanship missing.

"Yeap, what's up?" Parker asked, inhaling before crushing his cigarette in a shell ashtray overpopulated by butts.

"Can't talk about it on the phone. Too many ears on the exchange. If what I'm seeing is real, it will change things. Need you to see this for yourself," Dick requested with an earnest eagerness Parker hadn't heard from him.

"Your place or mine?"

"Mine. Got this guy here I want you to meet. Got him waiting in the stockroom. Come on back when you get here."

Dick's store was a five-minute walk from Parker's office. His thoughts strayed to Mona, wondering which Banks port of call she had landed on that day. The warmth from the late morning sun was pleasant as the sky had lost its red and was turning blue. Parker debated why he didn't leave the office more often. The pale-skinned man with thinning white hair lived sheltered from the sun in self-imposed office exile, thanks in part to a limp inherited from a World War I mortar. That old wound gave Mona dominion over the Banks while he remained tucked behind mounds of paper and cigarette butts, pressing his wireframe, round lens glasses with his index finger to keep the printed words in focus.

The Banks' sun had aged her. Mona looked ten years older than her husband. Inwardly she had the grit Parker never possessed. She had the energy and ease of personality that had welcomed the couple to Manteo. Mona was the newspaper's public face, and Parker was thankful for it. He knew his sense of humor was caustic to many locals. He remained at his desk amidst the smell of printer's ink, exchanging courtesies with middle-aged women who wrote social notes and having an occasional sip of whiskey with local politicians looking for kindness in the printed word.

Parker had never been a people person. He tolerated them, glad Mona was the honest, hard-working woman islanders respected. Without her, Parker was another mainland lizard looking for a place to warm himself in the Manteo sun. He didn't mind being in the shadow of this woman who allowed him his space, found amusement in his enigmatic, bit of a smartass demeanor, and gave him unquestioned loyalty. Mona's boundless, restless energy provided Parker with the audience who read his words, which was enough. Besides Mona, his only trusted friend was Dick, whose straightforward, sometimes awkward common sense he had come to admire.

Dick was sitting on a crate stacked with flour sacks when Parker entered the back room. A shaft of sunlight cast a bright rectangle of light through a side window in an otherwise dark room. A stranger, tipped back in a straight-back wooden chair across from Dick, arms folded, nodded to Parker as he entered.

"Parker, this is L.E. Hammond. He is a grocer from California," Dick said.

"How are you, sir? You're a ways from home," Parker addressed the stranger while looking for a flat surface to sit on.

"Mr. Hammond is traveling across the country, taking in the sights. Apparently, grocers in California make more on a sack of flour than grocers do in Carolina," Dick said, all three men laughing as Dick gave Parker a head's up on his skepticism.

"Yes, sir. I've been all over this country. A couple of weeks ago, I was in South Dakota when the boys chiseled out the face of Thomas Jefferson on Mount Rushmore. It was a sight. They are cutting out the face of the wrong Roosevelt beside him," Hammond said, gauging the reaction of the two men.

"Some people think the wrong Roosevelt is in office now. He has been good to this part of the state, saving the beaches and putting people to work," Parker said, eyeing a melon-sized object resting on the crate hidden by a strip of burlap.

"I don't get too much into politics. I want to see this glorious country while I can. Plan to visit every national park. Passed through here to see the Kitty Hawk monument. Impressive. I stopped by Fort Raleigh, too. Yeap, this is where it all began. Too bad they haven't put this little spot of heaven on the maps yet," Hammond said.

Having a late morning talk with a tourist wasn't what Parker expected. He wondered why Dick was wasting his time with this fellow. Small talk was something Dick could handle on his own, so why had he interrupted his day for this meeting? Dick sensed Parker's pending boredom and pulled back the burlap covering the object on the crate.

"Mr. Hammond was headed down south when he took a break beside the road," Dick said. "Found this stone near the Edenton bridge on 17."

Parker looked at the rock, an unremarkable stone that didn't show signs of a remarkable history. The rock might have been the ballast of an ancient ship, a natural chunk of river stone, or a scoop of road rubble. He was unimpressed.

"Look closer. Turn it in the light. The stone is engraved on both sides," Dick said. "Mr. Hammond and I have spent the better part of the morning writing down what it says."

Dick moved a sheet of paper before Parker, who squinted and held it toward the incoming light.

Ananias Dare &
Virginia Went Hence
Unto Heaven 1591
Anye Englishman Shew
John White Go Via
Father Soon After You
Goe for England Wee Cam
Hither / Online Misarie & Warre
Tow Yeere / Above Halfe Deade ere Tow
Yeere More From Sickenes Beine Foure & Twentie /
Salvage with Message of Shipp Unto Us / Smal
Space of Time they Affrite of Revenge Rann
Al Awaye / Wee Bleeve it Nott You / Soone After
Ye Salvages Faine Spirits Angrie / Suddaine
Murther Al Save Seaven / Mine Childe /
Ananais to Slaine wth Much Misarie /
Burie Al Neere Foure Myles Easte This River
Uppon Small Hil / Names Writ Al Ther
On Rocke / Putt This Ther Alsoe / Salvage
Shew This Unto You & Hither Wee
Promise You to Give Greate
Plentie Presents

EWD

"I see," Parker said, staring at the stone and handwritten paper. The stone held his interest. There was something believable about this rock that could solve a 350-year-old mystery. It would rewrite the opening chapter of American history. The Lost Colony would no longer be lost.

"It took a while to read the carving. I don't know what all the words mean, but Mr. Nancey here says the story is clear. I found your Lost Colony, Mr. Woods. That should be something your readers will eat up," Hammond said.

"Mr. Hammond, let's not be jumping the gun here. It's early to make assumptions," Dick said, holding the stone edgewise into the light flooding through the storeroom window.

"Seems clear to me, gentlemen. You are the man who would know, Mr. Nancey," Hammond retorted.

"Why don't you take a room at the Hotel Fort Raleigh for a few days? It's $2.75 on the American plan. I tell you what, it is on me until we dig into this stone a little further."

"Can't rush history." Parker smiled, offering Hammond a cigarette. "And I tell you what, I will arrange a fishing trip with this local fellow who knows how to catch 'em."

"Can't stay more than three days. I'm on schedule and don't want this stone knocking me off," Hammond said. "Give me $300 for the stone and study it all you want."

"Take Parker up on his fishing trip. If the stone pans out, it could be worth much more than $300," Dick said. "Let's go to Edenton tomorrow and look for the second stone. We can make it worth your while, Mr. Hammond."

Dick organized an excursion to investigate Hammond's discovery that afternoon. At first, only Mona and Rawlee were to make the journey. They planned to drive Hammond to where he found the stone, squeezing the alleged Californian for inconsistencies in his story. Mona wanted Milton to tag along and take notes for what could become a national headline if Hammond's claims were valid. Knowing Sparrow's compulsion to explore, Milton asked Mona to invite her to accompany the party, afraid Mrs. Yarbough would nix his invitation. Deborah gave her permission, Rawlee took the day off from bridge tending, and Hammond showed up wearing a black fedora and a green and red plaid shirt. Milton greeted Sparrow just after sunrise in front of the hotel the next day. Mona was late, reducing her day-to-day tasks to the ones Parker could complete from the office telephone.

Mona looked through the rearview mirror at Rawlee. She was amused. The bridge tender's raised left eyebrow so clearly revealed his discomfort. She turned left on Highway 34 and headed north, passing the towering memorial on the left, accelerating well beyond the speed limit on the smooth, asphalt-paved beach road, no longer slowed by her everyday rutted sandy paths.

Milton recalled his treks to the Wright Memorial, remembering how he and Jack climbed the hill to watch spectacular sunrises and sunsets. He listened to the rhythmic bump of wheels rolling over the almost three-mile-long Currituck Sound bridge to the mainland. Milton was a professional newspaperman, yet inside, he was a half-empty vessel of dreams keeping a dead boy alive. It had dawned on him this day's travel would take him through his birthplace of Hertford. He wondered what he might remember of his first home.

Milton studied Sparrow's profile as she looked out of the vehicle window. He had noticed a change in Sparrow over the past months. A more relaxed person was emerging from the shy, curious girl. Under the guardianship of her aunt, Sparrow lived in a structured world that was broadening, albeit thanks to magazines visitors left behind at the hotel. The emotional scars ingrained in the girl faded, as did the red scar running down her arm. Like the lines of sand fences etched along the artificial surf line dunes, the scar was a conversation piece for hotel guests. Her bear attack opened visitors' eyes, immersing them in the raw forces shaping the Banks. In exchange, the visitors added to Sparrow's knowledge of a world inhabited by the globetrotting Earharts of her dreams. Milton thought of Sparrow as an innocent version of Mona, a person of fantastic willpower, determination, and spiritual kindness. He tried to see her as a younger sister, someone to hold dear at arm's length. His attempt never quite worked.

"So, he found a rock with writing on it. And Mr. Parker and Mr. Dick think Virginia Dare's mother left it here? That means the colony isn't lost anymore. It's a good thing to know what happened." Sparrow whispered to Milton as Mona filled up Dick's car with gasoline before crossing the bridge, and Hammond disappeared inside the Texaco station.

"Not sure. We are going to check out Mr. Hammond's story. Thought you would enjoy being part of history," Mil said.

"VDee says all yesterdays are history. We leave our footsteps in the past and shouldn't look back. Today is a beautiful day to look for a rock," Sparrow replied.

"When did she become such a philosopher? You sure that wild spirit who becomes a white doe roaming the island, eating people's vegetables and tearing through their gill nets and garden fences is a good influence," Milton laughed, finding Jeanette's misadventures entertaining misdemeanors. Sparrow and Milton were good at reading each other's thoughts. Sparrow's intuition overwhelmed Milton's defenses in a way he found non-threatening. She knew Milton was joking and not passing judgment on Jeanette.

"Mil, VDee believes she is Virginia Dare. She makes me laugh, and I enjoy her company," Sparrow said, protective of her younger friend as she told Milton about their escapade at the Wright Memorial.

"Dick told me you two want to audition for the Lost Colony play."

"We're gonna try. VDee wants to be Virginia Dare, but Mr. Green's play needs an infant for that. I told her a hundred times, but she says Mr. Green will add the part when we audition," Sparrow said. "No reasoning with her."

"After today, Mr. Green may have to rewrite his play," Mil quipped as the travelers got back in.

Milton liked Sparrow sitting beside him, their arms touching in an intimacy forced by the limited space. On the other side, Rawlee was uncomfortable, holding an empty bean can in his lap, working up his first spit from a chew of tobacco. He was a hostage, his loyalty to Parker and Mona stretched to its limits. He didn't like being in the vehicle with the man who said he was traveling with a piece of Banks' history in his suitcase.

"Mr. Hammond, what do you think of our state?" Mona asked, breaking the silence as the travelers moved through Elizabeth City. The port city was a watery gateway to the Banks before the bridge connected the dots. Even now, the port lorded over the Banks. The town was the artery through which East Lake moonshine flowed north and the center of commerce where deals carved up the coast's real estate of sand, making Roanoke Island a lesser player in determining the Bank's future.

"You boys know how to make history. The nation started here. Sir Walter Raleigh knew what he was doing," Hammond said.

"Why, Mr. Hammond, Sir Walter didn't put much heart into trying to find his "lost colony." His advisors knew enough about the Banks to know this wouldn't be a place to start a country. They sort of got stranded and had trouble making the most of it." Mona laughed.

"Hmmm. Stranded, you say," Hammond replied.

"Well, yes… until the bridges crossed the sounds, the Banks were isolated. Nor'easters kept folks focused on staying alive until the New Deal saved us with those dunes and sand fences," Mona said, trying to get a reaction from the stranger.

"Mr. Roosevelt… a mighty fine man. He saved this country."

"Don't know if he has saved it yet, but he has some ideas. Do you have family close by, Mr. Hammond?"

"No one close. I left the grocery business and decided to travel and see the country before it was too late."

Mona pressed the conversation, adding anecdotes about herself and Parker to fuel the exchange. Milton had seen her work this magic of trading insights with people before. She was an expert, gaining a clearer picture of situations and people, disarming the uninitiated with direct honesty making it difficult for lies to take root. Milton learned from a master as Mona tightened her wrinkled upper lip, deciding how to maneuver her next question as the vehicle passed through the edge of Hertford.

There was nothing about the town to evoke memories for Milton. He saw his parents' faces; however, those visions were without time and place. If Hertford had once been home to him, those recollections were locked away as tightly as his mother had been sealed inside a metal drum to die alone. Sorrow washed over him as Mona pulled into a gas station for a soda. Sparrow asked for a Nugrape, and Rawlee poured some roasted peanuts into his Pepsi. Milton watched Rawlee's soda fizz as the salted peanuts slid down the glass bottle's neck.

US 17 started in the mountains of Winchester, Va., rolling downhill to the palm trees of Punta Gorda, Fla, 1,206 miles of Coastal Highway. The road didn't pass within twenty miles of the Banks. It was the national highway Hammond claimed carried him south to find a 16-pound stone half buried on the side of the road near an Edenton swamp. His story made sense. It fit with the facts of documented history, though those facts had gaps wide enough for myths and legends to slip past. Yet, it seemed unlikely a man from California accidentally stumbled upon the rock while picking up wild nuts.

"Mr. Hammond, why did you stop here?" Mona asked.

"It was a beautiful day, and I was about to cross that Chowan River bridge. Needed to stretch my legs," he said. "To be honest with you, ma'am. Mother Nature called, and these woods seemed as good a place as any."

Three of Mona's companions grinned. If Mona thought the idea was funny, she didn't show it, pulling the car onto a side road Hammond indicated with his finger.

"You turn there, ma'am. Down there a little way," Hammond said, not giving anyone a clue as to whether he was anxious and eager to pinpoint the location.

"You must be a very modest man, Mr. Hammond," Mona said as she followed the road for several miles before Hammond told her to stop the car.

"I love back roads, Mrs. Mona. Got a genuine passion for 'em," Hammond said, pointing to a narrow creek draped by cypress trees wrapping along the dirt road. "It was here a few yards into the woods."

The band of young and old, local and foreign, realists and dreamers, picked their way through the green briars and bramble of the swamp. Rawlee and Mil held the prickly thorns out of the way for Mona and Sparrow to pass, opening a passage into the swamp. Hammond, etched by crimson scratches of blood on his forearms by the undergrowth, blazed a haphazard trail near the cypress knees of the Chowan River. He stopped to rest on a fallen log coated in green moss.

"Believe we are near the site. I recall these fallen trees," Hammond paused to catch his breath, fishing in his pocket for a pack of Lucky Strikes. "We can't be far now."

"Fellow, we be walkin' for a long while. Seems we's walkin' circles," Rawlee said, spitting out a dark brown chew of tobacco mixing with the muddy goo left by his boots.

"These woods look the same to me. I should have marked the path, but the stone was heavy. I got excited and wanted to get back to my car," Hammond fended.

"Yeah, ya should have done that," Rawlee agreed, reaching into his pants pocket and pulling out what appeared to be a small caliber handgun.

"Rawlee, what the hell…." Mona questioned before the others spied the white mouth of a moccasin a few feet from Hammond's muddy trousers. The gun issued a soft pop echoing through the woods as the thick snake settled peacefully into death.

"Snakes all over. Got to be mindful where ya set y'all's foot," Rawlee said. It wasn't easy to tell if Rawlee was more pleased with his marksmanship or getting a raise out of Hammond.

"Much appreciated," Hammond murmured, monitoring each step with a more cautious eye. "I remember that shaggy tree. It's taller than the rest. It was to the right of it.

Near the bottom of the tree was a sunken depression matching the size of Hammond's rock. The group encircled the cavity, weighing its potential as the spot to reveal a sad testament to the Lost Colony. Time stood still as Milton noted the look on each face. Mona's face pinched, her thoughts suspended between awe and skepticism. Rawlee would have none of it and walked further into the swamp to relieve himself and grumble unheard obscenities before returning. Sparrow found a snail and traced the shell's swirl with her fingers as Milton continued to collect his thoughts in his notebook, writing sketchy details of what could be the end of an age-old mystery.

"There it goes. I knew I could find it," Hammond beamed.

"Mr. Hammond, ya took us on a snipe hunt. We could've bagged more rusty nails and buttons back on Pea Island. That hole ain't nothin' more than a bear's print. Don't see nothin' cept a waste of time," Rawlee said.

"Don't know what to tell you, Mr. Turnage. Found the rock on this spot. This is where it was," Hammond said.

Now, gentlemen, the stone speaks for itself, and the hole matches, so let's not have words. Mr. Hammond is our guest," Mona said, calming Rawlee's discord as she sought a middle ground for the fisherman and the tourist.

Mona knew Dick had avoided the trip, staying behind at his store on purpose. He was not above using Hammond and the stone to his advantage to secure Roanoke Island's place in American history. The island statesman wanted Mona to do his dirty work and hold Hammond accountable with finesse beyond either his or Parker's ability. Dick would support Hammond as long as the stranger didn't turn the discovery into a well-conceived ruse. Dick's influence could elevate the stone's importance, making it more or less than what it was.

Standing near his inland birthplace, fifty miles from the ocean, Milton pictured Jack's body drifting along an empty beach, troubled that every decision people make is a crossroads, the best choice eventually made clear by hindsight.

14

⌘

The Meeting

Dick and Parker viewed Rev. Boggs much the same way they saw God through different lenses. To Dick, God was a distant, unforgiven stranger he held in reverent regard because of his saintly deceased wife's faith. He saw Boggs as a weak link toward questionable salvation. This preacher played politics with a devotion best reserved for the Creator. He respected Boggs' ability to negotiate compromise, making deals to benefit his beloved Manteo. But Dick's disdain for the imperfect shepherd made him wish Boggs would leave the island and not return. Roanoke Island was at a crossroads, and Dick felt guilt for finding the preacher useful. To Parker, Boggs with an amusement. Hw saw the preacher's conflict between duty to heaven and desires of the flesh as comical because he was terrible at hiding his disconnected struggle. Parker, whose belief in God was window dressing to clothe his island role, had sympathy for the preacher who was a living billboard, Bible in hand, advertising the Banks into commercial prosperity. Dick and Parker judged Boggs as a practical hypocrite, not insightful enough to see himself, yet having a grand ability to herd travelers down the newly paved roads and bridges to the Banks.

"Is the stone real?" Boggs asked the men, all three sitting in the minister's office, sipping hot coffee from mugs printed with the word "CROATOAN." Their meetings became more frequent over the past year, with Dick calling the group the Croatoan Club to honor the word carved on a post at the disassembled Elizabethan settlement that vanished from Roanoke Island three and a half centuries before.

"If that's the case, the colony moved in with the Hatteras Indians. Looks like Green's Lost Colony play needs a rewrite before the first curtain goes up," Parker said.

"There are no curtains at the waterfront theater. And let's not jump to conclusions this early." Dick nodded, knowing Parker was trying to get a reaction.

"Gentlemen, we should take this situation seriously. It could change how people look at our history," Boggs said, seeing no humor in this stone that felt like a weight around his neck. He aimed to bring mainland interest to what some elected officials viewed as a useless sand pile. They felt the shoals of North Carolina handicapped the state, making it a poor cousin of South Carolina and Virginia, where harbors were deep. Developed roads and rails bypassed the coastal plain, making it convenient for another version of Raleigh, this time the state's capital, to avoid its marshlands. Boggs wanted to shepherd national attention to the Banks. Movers and shakers, including President Roosevelt himself, were willing to overlook the barren sand and embrace its historical legacy. Boggs convinced himself God wouldn't mind him bending the rules to bring his people employment and a better life. If he sinned a little to make it happen, so be it; his Lord was a loving, forgiving God.

"No one is taking this stone lightly, Reverend. We don't want to rush to judgment, and all three of us realize federal money coming from the New Deal could change the Banks forever," Dick said.

"To be honest, Dick, the Banks is not a forever place. It will change all by itself, burying its treasures and mistakes under the sand," Parker said, lighting a cigarette, knowing that Boggs wouldn't object though he didn't care for the tobacco smell.

"When did you get so profound, Parker?" Dick quizzed.

"Nothing new there. The way I am. Don't you read my editorials?" Parker replied, avoiding the topic as he watched a puff of smoke float toward the office's ceiling, debating if the stone's message was an echo from the past or a warning of the Banks' future.

"We should look at the facts before deciding our next move," Boggs said. "The new Fort Raleigh is in place. The island has spent decades trying to honor the birthplace of our first American princess, Virginia Dare. It is a blessing from God that the nation will finally come to know our Christian angel and how our ancestors suffered to begin a new country here," Boggs said.

"Save the preaching for Sunday morning, Boggs. I don't believe people will come here on religious pilgrimages. They will take in the sights, walk on the beach, and leave some money behind. I want to be sure the little history they soak up is the real deal," Dick said.

"We should probably leave history to Mr. Green's play and that new waterfront theater, thanks to Mr. Roosevelt," Parker said. "Let us polish this little spit of sand so people can see it as a great place to spend vacation dollars. This bend of the coast is where America was born, and tourism may turn this yellow sand to gold."

"Sir, that dirty stone has no message from God to prove your point. That damnable stone says our little angel died as a child; her mother and the others were cast into the wilderness to die. God wrapped Sir Walter Raleigh's Lost Colony in a mystery for a reason. That mystery is better than some lie told by a stranger peddling goods," Boggs said, his voice modulating as if standing in the pulpit.

"Crank it down a notch, Reverend. This stone is still a rock supposedly found in an Edenton swamp. Don't want to jump to conclusions or rewrite what people hold to be true. Many Bankers believe the colony lives on in local blood. You and your cronies created this lost business to shake the dollars out of a government money tree," Dick said. "Don't get me wrong. Who knows? Your story may be true, and the mystery is real. But don't we owe everyone the benefit of considering this stone legitimate?"

"No matter which way this stone turns out, we get a better story, one that is richer, even if the details add tragedy to the account," Parker said. "Haven't you guys heard the expression of leaving no stone unturned?"

Neither Boggs nor Dick found the humor in Parker's pun as the newspaper editor lit his fourth cigarette. Parker was on the fence when it came to the rock. If the stone were real, it might cause a stir good for the island. On the other hand, once a mystery is solved, legends tend to lose their luster.

15

⌘

Fish Trap

Finch Ambrose had no affection for the Pagette brothers. Never one to pass judgment, his sea-green eyes saw them as petty thieves, robbing good people of a source of income. They openly bragged about their luck gained by stealing from their neighbors' nets and traps. Finch was easy to overlook among the lean-muscled fishmongers of Wanchese. He blended into the sturdy stock who harvested food from the sea. But to the Pagettes, the newcomer was a fresh novelty until the young man stood his ground or they broke him. Finch's mother had told him evil men must answer to God, not to man. Finch kept to himself, creating distance from a conflict he had no hope of winning. His father was in jail for his abuses. Maybe one day justice would call on the Pagettes as well.

The brothers baited Finch with names—Goatee, Frog Boy, Birdbrain being popular— because the young man didn't speak often, and when he did, it was to the point. The brothers sold much of their ill-gotten catch to Ice & Seafood Company where Finch had worked since coming to the island. Finch was an asset to the business. He didn't ask questions, glad to see a paycheck to support his aunt and sister.

Nick was the kinder of the two brothers. Sawtooth, a rough and tumble mariner with a mouthful of teeth broken by an oar wielded by his father when he was a child, considered kindness as a weakness. Sawtooth delighted in belittling Finch, insulting him for unloading the day's catch too slowly. Finch could tune people out, but not today. Sawtooth was in a bad mood and needed a victim.

"Unload dat box, Birdbrain. Make quick work of it," Sawtooth demanded as he killed the motor, bumping his boat hard against the Wanchese pier. A trail of oil skim on the slickcam waters followed him up Mill Landing Creek. Sawtooth jumped on the dock without saying another word, leaving a muscular black man behind to help Finch unload. Finch thought the fellow had the bearing of the Navy men he watched outside his sister's hospital as he began tossing fish from the Pagette's boat with his straight back and fluid movements.

"Hello, Name's Eddie Etheridge," the man said. Finch recognized the name from stories Milton had shared with Sparrow. Eddie was the hero, a lifesaving surfman. Finch couldn't fathom why he was fishing with the island's two chief miscreants.

"I'm Finch. I work here," he said, unaccustomed to conversation while working at the fish house.

"Figures." Eddie tested a good-natured smile. "Us being here in the bottom of this boat and all these here fish waitin' for the pan."

"My sister says you are a hero," Finch hesitantly said, his interest spilling over his inverted personality.

"I don't know for sure, but I imagine even heroes have to work," Eddie said, handing Finch a wire basket filled with thrashing fish, unsure if Finch's remark was a compliment or sarcasm.

Finch hauled the basket inside the fish house, leaving Eddie feeling more alone after spending a grueling night with the Pagettes on their boat. The brothers were a bad habit he inherited at an early age. Eddie knew associating with the duo could be dire for him. They made him feel second-class, but their familiar company filled a void of loneliness. They were childhood companions he trailed behind through the Roanoke Island marshlands fishing, frogging, and hunting. The brothers were reminders of who he didn't want to become while he drifted through life.

Eddie, as many mariners did, lived inside himself. It was the safest place he could find. His reflexes were quick, relying on muscle memory to take him through days of repetitive tasks as a surfman. He practiced rescues with his crew, waiting for disasters that were becoming infrequent as technology made the Graveyard of the Atlantic less deadly. His grandmother, living on the black California side of the island, suffered from what she called "that thing," cancer draining her life away. Eddie's family was small; he lived with his grandmother and a sister. He worried about what would happen to his sister when his grandmother passed. The world seemed less charitable to females. He would provide for her.

Eddie was thinking about his family's fate when a box of mullet loosened by the slippery ooze of the day's catch struck his right shoulder. The pain was intense, and Eddie couldn't react to save himself as other boxes shifted, threatening him with more significant harm. He braced for the calamity that didn't come. Strong arms slowed the collapse, and Eddie moved to safety as the skewed containers spilled a ton of silvery fish over the dock. He thought one of the brothers had lessened the blow until the pain eased to reveal another face. Eddie locked to his rescuer's green eyes; they were wells of empathy. The fallen surfman accepted Finch's hand, a friendship glued between palms coated in fish scales and slime on a Wanchese dock.

16

⌘

Silver Screen

Sparrow and Jeanette walked down Lodge Street to the Pioneer Theater. Going to the movies was a rare treat for Sparrow, though Jeanette frequently made her way to the movie theater with the Tutor facade. Her father thought it was wise to keep her imagination confined to the screen rather than inflicting her mischief on the property of Manteo's villagers. Townspeople were thankful Jeanette's actions gave the aging townsmen who could no longer fish something to do. Her aunt's impulses limited Sparrow's free time. Deborah, a dutiful guardian to the brother and sister, mothered Sparrow by filling her hours with hotel kitchen chores and errands. In rare moments, she sensed the weight of her overbearing nature on her young niece and tried to make amends by providing money for an afternoon matinee.

The Pioneer Theater had been a part of Manteo for over a decade. The Creef family moved the theater into a new home on Lodge Street as cinemas reinvented themselves, giving voice to the black and white actors moving across the silver screen. Jeanette had seen the current feature twice and was eager to spoil the scenes for Sparrow with her advanced knowledge. Sparrow didn't mind. She could tune Jeanette out and become lost in the flickering lights in front of her.

Aunt Deborah considered going to movies a waste of time. She would have preferred Sparrow to use her time studying

God's word. However, Deborah wasn't about to force Christian teachings upon her niece as her father had done to her and Sparrow's mother. Her father's tyrannical attitude had driven Sparrow's mother away from home and into the arms of a worthless man. Deborah trusted God would bring Sparrow and maybe Finch into the Lord's fold in good time.

Jeanette hooked Sparrow's interest in the feature by telling her there would be a newsreel of Amelia Earhart planning her around-the-world trip, and the film was about giant flying machines saving the world. Sparrow needed no coaxing. It was enough to cloak herself in the dark theater, eating popcorn and escaping from the sandy sameness of her adopted island home.

"Why they always gotta call her Lady Lindy? She ain't no relation to the man. It ain't like they're husband and wife. I don't get it," VDee mumbled through a mouthful of popcorn.

"Shhh," Sparrow said, watching three kernels of popcorn fall to the floor from Jeanette's overeager hand.

"She likes tomato juice. I sort of like it too. Maybe that is why she is so skinny. She was quiet, kinda like you. Told her the colony cut that word, *Croatoan,* on a tree so Virginia's granddaddy would know where they went. She said somethin' funny. She said maybe the word means a direction, not a location," VDee said, recalling her conversation with Earhart at the memorial dedication. Sparrow wrinkled her nose.

The theater was hushed in silky darkness as one of the Creefs changed reels on the projector. Sparrow frowned as VDee fished under her chair for a place to stick her gum before offering her friend a fresh piece. Sparrow held up an open hand, declining the offer. Sound filled the room, heralding the opening credits of *"Things to Come."*

The world projected on the screen upset Sparrow. People poisoned each other, spread disease, and rebelled en masse. She was thankful for her island and her quiet life, unsettled by thoughts of a future where war ruled people's lives. Sparrow pictured herself piloting the Flying Wing of the movie, which made her heart race, yearning to be free of the land, soaring among the clouds. She liked to think that one day Amelia would return to the island. Amelia would look down on her little island, eyeing its sister barrier reef as the white curl of waves raced toward shore. One day Sparrow would fly in the clouds with her hero.

"All the universe or nothing? Which shall it be, Passworthy? Which shall it be?" VDee shouted, repeating dialogue from the movie. "I could be an actress. We'll get a part in the Lost Colony pageant together. They'll let me be Virginia Dare, and you can be… a colonist's wife."

Sparrow nodded, paying minimal attention to Jeanette. Her mind was in another place, above the island, on white patches of water vapor resting on purple bases drifting over the sea. Mr. Turnage said it was a sure sign of thunderstorms, and she needed to get VDee and herself out of harm's way as her imaginary plane banked back toward Roanoke Island's Skyco airfield.

As Sparrow drifted off to sleep with a vision of mastering the sky, Milton awoke in the middle of a dream. It was the same troubled jumble that plagued him since Jack's death. Jack was an apparition taunting him with images. It was as if his dead friend were sending fractured messages from the grave, a burden of confusing glimpses.

Milton sat up in a sweat. No matter how unsettling the dreams were, sometimes Milton welcomed Jack's ghostly reappearances and questioned his sanity for taking comfort in them.

In this visitation, Jack was sitting at a baby grand piano with the worn keyboard on which he learned to play as a child. The instrument's legs sank into the surf, stretching along miles of dunes trapped by sand fences and grasses. Jack didn't speak; he gave Milton an unfamiliar smile. Strange though, his smiles were peaceful, almost playful, suggesting he kept a secret he was unwilling to share. Milton thought about the dreams and wondered if solving the enigma might end them. But he didn't want the ghost to leave for good, so Milton tried to make peace with the specter.

This dream was more cryptic than most. The scene shifted with Jack playing Mozart's Piano Sonata No. 11 atop a high dune in the shadow of a shipwrecked Irma that dominated the Nags Head surf line for a decade. Even though Jack was pressing the keys, the piano went silent. Milton heard the rhythmic swoon of a pulsing morning tide as an unseen sun painted purples, yellows, and reds from below the horizon. The rays caught the right side of Jack's face, glowing with colors. Oddly, the scene reminded Milton of Jack's Indian heritage.

Milton knitted his brow, disturbed by the transformation. The wind rolled in a fine mist from behind the dune, and Jack's body dissolved into sand, lingered for a moment, and then blew in a curved arch out over the ocean. Milton blinked in the dream, and Jack's body reformed as the sand touched the foam. This time, he was shirtless, his upper body covered in tattoos, one side of his head shaven, and the other sporting a long, braided ponytail. He wore the Elizabethan coat and breeches of Green's play, carrying a shiny white stone. Letters like the ones on Hammond's rock appeared on the chiseled quartz as Milton attempted to read the inscriptions.

Jack dropped the stone, and the sand swallowed it, leaving the sleeping Milton disappointed. Milton didn't know this version of Jack and was sure he didn't want to know him. Milton stepped away as the stone resurfaced and changed into a piece of floating wood inscribed with the word "Croatoan." Jack opened his mouth to speak. The mischievous smile of his dream self was not there, replaced by an expressionless stare. Jack pointed to a pod of pelicans gliding south feet above the ocean. One bird swooped down, mistaking the carved piece of wood for a fish, missing his target. When Milton looked back, Jack was gone.

Milton lay in bed, covers wet from his cold sweat. He didn't want to sleep because he feared Jack would reappear to haunt him. Clueless to find meaning in the images, he tried and failed to erase them from his mind. Milton thought he might go insane from his dead friend's relentless reappearances. He didn't see this dream as an omen; it was confusion built from unresolved fragments of memory. Milton needed resolution and these cryptic messages to end because they were trapping him, holding him in the past.

Milton turned on his table lamp and rolled on his side, reaching into his bedside drawer for one of the unfinished crossword puzzles he and Frank had worked on before he left Norfolk. The newsprint was yellowing.

17

⌘

Marking the Spot

Hammond's stone, staging Green's play, and Parker's determination to turn the Banks into an economic goldmine was playing through Milton's awake mind. Milton rolled on his side. It was 5:30 a.m. He could stay in bed for another hour before meeting Sparrow and Jeanette who were auditioning for the play later that morning. Parker said local auditions would pique islanders' interest, investing them in a drama the country would notice. In a few months, the President of the United States would travel by train and ship to discover the Lost Colony, and then Roanoke Island would be on the map, according to Parker. Mil wondered if this map would be any more precise than ones John White penned centuries ago.

VDee's car chattered, prematurely aged from the harsh, salty air and hands of its adolescent driver. VDee viewed the vehicle as part automobile, part boat, and part tank, unmerciful in her treatment of the conveyance. The islanders were thankful the car bellowed in protest, warning them to escape VDee's sway of minor destruction. Mil had options. He could walk three miles to Fort Raleigh or brave a ride with VDee. Sparrow convinced him Dick's daughter's legend was more myth than fact.

"Morning, Mil-a-ton. Don't care for that name Milton. Like Mil much better. Ya gonna write a story about me when I get to be Virginia Dare in the play?" Jeanette asked as Milton climbed into the back of her Ford.

"Don't think there is going to be a speaking part. Virginia Dare is still a baby in the play," Milton said, recalling how his mother used to call him Mil. He liked the shortened name replacing Milton, which he found too stuffy and formal. The name Milton Kane was good for his newspaper bylines not his life.

"Mr. Green can change that. My daddy has pull," Jeanette said, intentionally sounding more arrogant than she was, sensing the bond between Sparrow and Mil and feeling threatened by his intrusion on this special day.

"You're right, but your father has his limits," Milton replied. There was no purpose in debating with VDee. Her thoughts came with changeable certainty.

The new play was not so new. Roanoke Island had celebrated its Lost Colony through annual pageants for decades, holding the original Virginia Dare in a sacred canon accompanied by reenactments, fish fries, and homemade desserts. Past commemorations of the first English settlers took on the appearance of a church social.

Green's play would be different, morphed into a celebration funded with federal money and the passions of people who knew little more about Roanoke Island than words printed on a page. No matter what fresh energies might steer the story, Virginia Dare would remain an infant, a blank page with infinite possibilities. The mystery worked better that way.

"We'll see about that," VDee said, flooring the long-suffering gas pedal. "Gotta skedaddle. I accidentally ran over Mrs. Manley's cat last week, and she don't have no Christian heart."

Milton's and Sparrow's eyes met through the rearview mirror. Fascinated by VDee's free spirit, they overlooked her impulsive nature. VDee could be who they dared not be. VDee's father had tried to cushion Jeanette's mother's death, allowing his only child's grief an indulgent release. She was a daughter of privileged status, the offspring of the island's most civic-minded patron. Neither Milton nor Sparrow had such a buttress to ease their sorrows, yet they could relate to this uncensored version of themselves, sometimes feeling envy.

The entrance to Fort Raleigh had changed since the Burnside Expedition claimed the island as a Union prize during the Civil War. Granite pillars, placed on the site before the turn of the century, had a graveyard feel. The markers honored the location in an unintentionally mournful fashion by the well-meaning Roanoke Island Memorial Association struggling to mark the historic spot. Federal grants concealed the stones inside twin guard towers leading to the construction of a dozen reimaged buildings from the 1500s. Locals were losing control of how Fort Raleigh returned from the past, willing to make the sacrifice so long as the spirit of the first colony remained intact.

The site reminded Milton of a scene from a Saturday Western matinee, causing him to question if the rush to reclaim Fort Raleigh might erase its accurate history. He had researched the location as best he could with Parker's limited resources. The publisher footed the bill for him to return to his first adopted home and dig into the more abundant archives of the Norfolk Public Library.

He had not been in contact with Ginny since he had moved to Manteo, barred from communication by his foster mother's illiteracy. He had looked forward to seeing those knowing brown eyes and her broad toothy smile. Milton was crestfallen when he learned Ginny had vanished along with her neighborhood, leaving vacant lots with roots of foundations gnawed down to the pavement. Mil had already mourned the loss of his two other Norfolk mentors, Frank, and his wife, who had died the year before driving down Granby Street, victims of a drunken sailor's night behind the wheel of a borrowed car. Milton's connection with his first adopted city was gone.

There was no one to ask what happened to Ginny except a few remaining small store owners whose businesses survived on the fringes of the old neighborhood. From their accounts, Ginny had moved in with one of her street orphans, an unknown daughter informally adopted as he had been by this kind-hearted woman. The girl moved north and lived in Connecticut in some place named after water. Mil settled for the answer; it was soothing among the other possibilities. He knew Ginny would not willingly leave her beloved Tidewater city.

While researching, Mil discovered gaps in the current Fort Raleigh's authenticity; the recreated buildings weren't accurate. Three hundred and fifty years of clawing a living from fishing, roaming livestock, a civil war, and unending storms had expunged most of the fort's detail in favor of generalities and hearsay. The new Fort Raleigh, built on a guess, was as much a mystery as what happened to the colonists. The exact location of the colony was a wishful assumption, more akin to an X on a dubious treasure map than fact.

Native islanders didn't care about the details. They knew the first colony's location was a misstep, a side adventure to creating a new nation, a hidden island behind a barrier of tedious sand, little more than a military base to loot Spanish galleons sailing up the Atlantic's Gulf Stream. The deep waters of the Chesapeake Bay had been the colony's true destination. Roanoke Island was rugged and enchanting, a place for lost people to stay lost, a spot for tourists to stop, and not meant to be a place to plant a new nation. Parker told Mil the Banks were the first tourist stop in North America, and Manteo had waited long enough to become its port of call for tourists to leave their money behind, laughing as he said the words. Mil forced a smile, finding the thought somehow doleful.

"Which building do we go in?" VDee said with her typical blend of antsy, impulsive anticipation.

"I think the auditions may be in the chapel," Mil said before allowing VDee to gain a toehold on answering her own question. Of the buildings comprising the new Fort Raleigh, the chapel was beloved by the islanders, its status elevated to a house of God without the Sunday sermons.

Work on the waterfront theater had enthralled the island's most diehard isolationists. It was a marvel of wood, using the island's natural slope for seating 3,500 people, a feat that left people like Rawlee in awe. Its designer and architect was a force of nature himself. Skipper Bell was an Englishman who moved from Canada to Edenton in the 1920s as a landscaper. The Works Progress Administration provided the money; Bell raised the fort and its waterside theater along Roanoke Island's northeastern shore. Skipper was unstoppable, building on the notoriety of playwright Paul Green to transform Roanoke Island into a national showplace for one summer to celebrate Virginia Dare's 350th birthday, complete with the President of the United States as an honored guest.

Local nets were no longer limited to the daily haul of seafood. There were new fish channeling the sounds, mainland strangers with money to spend on renting rooms, buying souvenirs, and eating fresh catch. The island was becoming crowded, putting money in the pockets of locals without them toiling under a blistering sun or finger-numbing cold. Kitty Hawk and Nags Head, across the causeway, were growing as mainlanders purchased tiny parcels of shifting land, not understanding how a storm could take their sand boxed houses away in a single blow. Mil wondered how this drama would end, picturing an editorial cartoon he had seen of tourists flopping ashore like beached fish littering the shore with money. Even though the image made him smile, he didn't know if he cared for the vision of this wild, free coast tamed by the dollar.

"Do they show?" VDee asked.

"What shows, Jeanette?" Sparrow replied, looking at the line of islanders waiting to audition for a role.

"My boobs. I know they ain't showin' much yet, but I taped them down, so 'em folks won't notice. They don't want no little woman for the part of Virginia Dare," VDee said, patting her flat chest.

"I think you are ok," Sparrow said, shaking her head as Mil's face turned red.

Rehearsals were more of a sign-up than an audition. The casting person, a WPA worker grateful for employment after years of theatrical drought during the Depression, screened islanders at face value, smiled politely, and cast them as one of the one hundred men, twelve women, and nine children who vanished from history in 1587. Jeanette and her determination to be Virginia Dare tested the lady's demeanor. Attempting to please, the casting lady asked the girls to sing. The girls sang "Jesus Loves Me." Sparrow's voice was that of a songbird; however, the sounds coming from VDee's throat had the melodious rawness of the bullfrogs that blanketed the island's small ponds.

"Could she be an Indian, maybe an Indian princess?" Sparrow asked, catching the lady behind the desk off guard.

"Well, we have some parts," the lady replied quizzically.

"Oh, yes. That would be grand. You could dress in buckskin and shells and dance like the Indians in the movie we saw at the Pioneer last year," Sparrow said, genuinely excited.

"You mean Peter Pan, the one with the fairy and pirates?" Jeanette answered, sensing Sparrow was offering a path away from rejection.

"That could work," the lady nodded, pushing paperwork toward the pair. Jeanette initially eyed the compromise as a defeat but soon rationalized the turn of events as a situation more to her liking. She realized the potential of being a savage on stage. After all, didn't the real Virginia Dare become America's first Indian princess?

"Thank you, ma'am," Sparrow said as Jeanette silently debated her new status.

18

⌘

Caught in a Net

Nick Pagette wasn't cruel, though life hadn't steered him on a course to become a decent person. He had the potential that once might have led him toward a more generous affection for his fellow man. However, his brother, Sawtooth, had none of this tendency. His hard edges of darkness dimmed any chance his younger brother might escape a dishonest, selfish existence.

Islanders knew the brothers lived lawless lives and were not men to be trusted. But they were native sons, as much a part of the island as fish left to spoil in the sun. One day the putrid flesh of their misdeeds would meet a cleansing rain of judgment to wash away their smell. The sheriff knew they were trouble; however, their larceny was minor, stealing small percentages of the bounty offered from the sounds and sea. As long as they weren't too greedy, people turned a blind eye to their thievery. It was simpler to ignore them than incur their ire.

Sheriff Ben Owens, a man who walked an uneven line between law and order, understood the spirit of the law protecting Dare County. The letter of the law was a thin, sandy line prone to being washed away by politics. Owens and the brothers had connections to Buffalo City. The moonshiners knew when Owens would look the other way. In return, they were okay with him getting his picture in local newspapers by busting up a few worn-out stills near election time. Those same moonshiners wore many hats on the Banks. They were not ordinarily violent but they could count on the Pagettes to twist an arm, ax the bottom of a sloop, or cut a few fishing nets to reinforce the Bankers' natural tendency of minding their own business.

The brothers were akin to a strong storm coming ashore threatening ruin, keeping people mindful the economic lubrication of moonshine balanced their petty misdeeds. Prohibition had lost its grip on the country and its hold on the state. It was a matter of time before the water brewing East Lake spirits remained untapped in the brackish coastal swamp. It would be replaced by the flow of seashells and souvenirs hauled home by summer tourists. The sheriff, a calculating man, realized there was a degree of larceny in each.

The legacy of Buffalo City had run its course. Legend suggested the swamp hid the first English settlers from the Spanish as the colonists watched for John White's return. While White arrived too late to save anyone, the land waited for the 20th century to reveal its timber treasure. The Alligator River peninsula, vast acreage held together by towering cypress trees, yielded its wealth of roofing shakes for the homes of the wealthy in the early 1900s.

Buffalo City was once Dare County's largest settlement, a community floating on saw chips and railroad lines. The town, populated by thousands of local whites, blacks, and Russian workers moved there by northern timber lords, grew until the forest ran out. Once sawmills harvested the majestic trees, the barren understory exposed the swamp's people to a sun that held no sanctuary for them. People either left or turned the abandoned rail and mill equipment into moonshine stills. Moonshining for the swamp people was a mixed source of pride and shame. They were proud of how their formula, a blend of rye, sugar, and the tannic waters of Milltail Creek, produced world-class product;

yet, it vexed them that the liquid was the Devil's brew, leading even the righteous down the thorny path to damnation.

Sheriff Owens knew each moonshining family by name and, if needed, could uncover the location of most Buffalo City and East Lake stills. He half-heartedly sought to smash them when public sentiment ran high; otherwise, he left them alone, knowing the product kept food on the tables of poor families with few other options.

As long as the brew flowed north and created no visible problems for his county, Owens made peace with his staged attempts to ax the swamp's stills. He accompanied his mainland law enforcement brethren looking to build reputations for themselves as still bashers. It amused him that these government boys thought they could outwit people who walked among the cypress knees and cottonmouth snakes for a lifetime. The revenuers would get lucky occasionally, find and smash a still. Arrests meant a year in jail. The sheriff maintained a widows and orphans fund to dull the pain of the luckless.

"There ain't no shame in running shine. The shame is in getting caught," Owens once told the teenage version of Nick Pagette. Nick had been hauling a load of five-gallon jugs up the north beach. He was playing tag with the waves when he drove too close to the surf, and water stalled his truck. Owens, then fond of the boy, knew his brother Sawtooth would eventually get him killed or jailed. Nick had crossed the county line when he crashed into the sea where a life-saving station surfman found him. Owens got Nick's sentence reduced to six months. The sheriff figured he would find a reason to cull Sawtooth from his populace in six months. But Sawtooth was mean, not stupid. The older brother was a model citizen without someone to take a fall for him.

Sawtooth and Owens were two sides of the same coin; one turned up, shining in the light of public opinion, and the other buried in the foul goo of a swamp's underbrush, shunned for his darkness. They were men who wielded intelligence behind unexpected facades and could see trouble coming from a distance.

They were Hoi Toiders who used the brogue of their speech and the sun-etched features of their faces to disarm people while sizing them up to get the upper hand. Owens's motives were more altruistic, and he weighed what was good for the island on nearly equal footing with what was good for himself. Sawtooth had no filter; the man was a feral dog ready to snap at any hand holding something he wanted.

The president of the United States was coming to Roanoke Island. That thought sat well in the minds of both Owens and Sawtooth. For Owens, it played on a bigger stage. The visit would mean the shiny side of his coin would glow brightly. He was realistic, however. Owens knew his role as sheriff would relegate him to a dim corner with federal agents not wanting his help. His duties would be ceremonial, and that was fine with him. He didn't relish the weight of protecting a president in a wheelchair. There were complications unfolding beyond what federal agents could fathom. Sawtooth understood the potential outcomes, as did Owens.

Roosevelt's upcoming visit to Roanoke Island promised to put island's natural splendor on display, surpassing even the grandeur depicted in Green's Lost Colony drama. For Sawtooth, this meant an opportunity to secure his fortune and bid farewell to the grueling task of dealing with gill nets that had taken a toll on his weathered hands. On the other hand, Owens feared that his reputation would suffer a devastating blow should the moonshine run make national headlines, leaving him stranded like a tattered ship, damaged and without hope of rescue.

On the very night when the country buzzed with excitement over the president's visit, one of the largest bootlegging operations in the nation's history would be set in motion just a few miles away from the waterfront theater, hidden within the depths of Albemarle Sound. Both men were unaware of the operation's intricate details, as they each had their own reasons for wanting to keep it concealed. Owens, unable to prevent it, resolved to ensure that the planned run remained hidden from public view. Sawtooth would organize a covert flotilla of repurposed boats, carefully concealed from the prying eyes of the Coast Guard and revenuers, too preoccupied with presidential security to notice a procession of vessels clandestinely transporting thousands of gallons of illicit alcohol across the sound.

19

⌘

Stone Man

Boggs laced his fingers together, drumming his index fingers with a quiet, nervous tap. In an odd way, his clasped hands looked like the steep of a church opening and closing.

"I've had enough of this stone man. Dump this piece of rock in Shallowbag Bay and move on to support the play," Rev. Boggs said, irritation overwhelming his ordinarily overstated civility. His polite nature and well-spoken charm melted before Dick and Parker, two men who saw the minister's contradictions. Boggs was the pawn for these men. They were willing not to draw attention to his character flaws as long as he remained a faithful servant of the island home.

"Don't know about that. Everything about the stone checks out so far. Hammond seems to be who and what he says he is," Dick replied.

"I have an editor friend in California. He said the fellow checked out, and the people he spoke with recalled Hammond. They remember little about him, in any case. It has been easy to vanish during this Depression of ours," Parker added, encircled by cigarette smoke in the back of Dick's store.

"Experts in Raleigh, Norfolk, and Richmond say the stone and its message could be real. They think it would be hard to fake. Eleanor Dare's husband was a stone carver. She would have had access to the tools, maybe," Dick continued, attempting to read Parker's face.

"Those buildings at Fort Raleigh are supposed to be the real deal too, but they aren't," Parker said, smashing out the butt of his cigarette on the top of an empty cheese hoop box.

"No one ever said those buildings are authentic. They serve a purpose. They are a starting point for things to come, and the federal money was there to make it happen," Dick said, shifting his weight on his straight-back chair.

"Not complaining. A lot of history seems to be smoke and mirrors to me. But it makes for a good story," Parker said.

"Well, the story of this dirty rock could harm us. It could rewrite Banks' history into a version no American wants. Our mystery becomes a matter-of-fact tragedy. Why would anyone come to see where America failed, where savages slaughtered Christians, and sweet little Virginia Dare is a murdered infant?" Boggs said.

"Ahh… a little much, don't you think, Reverend?" Parker said, losing his grin.

"Facts speak for themselves. If the message on the stone is real, we should keep looking for the other stone. Solving a mystery will not keep people away from the Banks. They will come to see for themselves," Dick said.

"It's a matter of timing. We have the nation's attention. The president is coming. Thousands will visit. Let Green tell his story. If this stone is real, we can share those facts when the mood is right," Parker argued.

"We don't need this remotely possible bit of tragedy to undo our hard work. God gave this nation to an English-speaking people. The stone is a lie planted by Satan to dishonor the memory of Virginia Dare," Boggs rallied.

"Humm. Dick, is it ok to cut off a piece of cheese?" Parker asked, not waiting for an answer as he carved off a chunk, dropping it into his cup of coffee as it bobbed and softened in the steaming liquid.

The bell on the store's front door dinged as Sparrow opened it.

"Mr. Nancey, are you here?

"Yes, dear. I was in the back. How is she doing?"

"I put Aunt Deborah's poultice on her face, and she drifted back to sleep. I think she will be alright, but she keeps asking for you."

"I'll be getting ready to close up here. Have a little business to take care of first. Thanks for sitting with her. You are a dear friend to her."

"I'll stay longer if you want."

"No need. You got to go practice for the play this afternoon. The island needs you there. I'm headed home now."

Sparrow was no longer a child. Four summers on the Banks had darkened her skin to the color of honey. Time had metamorphosed the girl into a woman made wiser by evening talks with visiting fishermen and the reading and rereading of the magazines they left behind. Her mind was a sponge, curious to take in a bigger world, especially anything related to Amelia Earhart. Still, her innocence remained, shielded by her aunt's overbearing nature. Sparrow looked for the good in life's uniqueness. The scar on her left arm had faded under the Roanoke Island sun, though it was still visible. Sparrow's scar was a conversation starter with these transit strangers as they took their evening meals at the hotel and talked about the day's catch with exaggerated bravado. Visitors offered crumbs of facts about the outside world for Sparrow to ponder, and she left an impression of quiet strength on the visitors, enthralled by her life's journey. Deborah stood watch, never letting her niece get too close to these outsiders who wasted their time and money on the island, calling fishing and duck hunting a sport.

Sparrow was a safe harbor of calm behind her blue eyes, taking an interest in a world beyond the confines of the Banks. At least, she was to Milton, who had been her friend and advisor since they first met. He had seen her shyness melt away, replacing the girl as a person who had taught him to be more trusting of his own waning innocence. His newspaper reporter instincts protected him with skepticism unless he spent an idle hour with Sparrow. His guard was there, but he lowered it around her, letting her into his thoughts. Mil saw himself as too damaged by his past to trust. Still, if Sparrow could survive her fractured past and emerge into young adulthood as authentic and unpretentious, he would try to be open to the possibility of his own redemption.

Summer nights were long on Roanoke Island. The sun took its own sweet time to sink below the mainland horizon across Croatan Sound, and twilight lingered with a rosy grayness on the island's western shore. Mil and Sparrow sat on a crumbling pier at the foot of the Croatan ferry, waiting for Mona's return from Mann's Harbor. She had crossed the sound without her automobile. Her vehicle refused to begin the daily journey that morning, thanks to the antics of a dirty carburetor. Mil's job was to retrieve his waylaid employer, who was already an hour later than expected. Driving her repaired vehicle, Mil was to pick her up at the ferry dock.

Sparrow's usual ride with VDee was canceled. VDee remained home, her face swollen by the stings of ground wasps who had no patience with her antics. She had refused to venture beyond Dick's doting affection that afternoon, telling Sparrow the Lost Colony would do fine without her at practice that night. Mil had offered Sparrow a ride since the waterfront theater was on his way to pick up Mona. Deborah reluctantly sanctioned the arrangement, thinking Mona would be nearby. A brief thunderstorm changed the plan. The practice rained out, and Mona was nowhere in sight. The turn of events pleased Sparrow. She enjoyed her time with Mil, and Aunt Deborah would get over her worry when Mona brought her home.

"Are those bats?" Sparrow asked Mil, sitting beside her on the craggy pier as minuscule, white curls of sound rippled to a stop and retreated from an uneven shore.

"Nope. I believe they are purple martins," Mil said, his thoughts unsettled. Sparrow was still Sparrow; however somehow, she was not the same.

"What are they?" Sparrow asked.

"They are swallows, I think. People build birdhouses for them on the island, so they can feast on mosquitos," Mil said, slapping a mosquito perched on his left hand.

"I guess they missed some." Sparrow laughed, followed by a sideways grin from Mil. "They look blacker than purple."

"Yes. The birds are visitors like the fisherman and the mainland families who stop by Dick's store for ice cream."

"Where are they from?"

"I think they are Spanish ghosts searching for the Lost Colony reincarnated as little black birds," Mil laughed, instantly regretting his randomness, "No, they come from South America to build nests, raise little ones and then fly home. They return to the same nesting spot every year."

"I like the idea they are Spanish ghosts. Maybe they could tell us stories like Mr. Turnage."

"There are plenty of storytellers on the Banks already, Sparrow. Don't know if there is room for any more."

"The martins are good flyers. I like how they soar and dive, their wings tucked in."

"I could probably get you a ride on a plane. Barnstormers come to the memorial a lot."

"Yeah? Aunt Deborah would probably say no."

"Probably. Just like she would say no to you being with me now." They both laughed.

"You always seem sad, Mil. Even when you laugh, you seem sad."

"You think so? Yeah, I guess I am," Mil said, his uneasiness increasing as their conversation headed in a new direction. Mil wanted to force himself to see Sparrow as the child she once was.

"Why?" she replied, disarming his emotional distance with a word. Mil was a master of the question "why." The word was his bread and butter, his professional tool to extract facts for his news writing as well as his insurance to keep others from asking him that same simple question. He was grateful Sparrow was the one asking. He didn't have her unconditional faith in human nature; however, he had faith in her.

"Do you remember your dreams?"

"Sometimes… Especially the ones where I am flying. It is always with Amelia Earhart. She is there telling me what to do."

"I kind of have nightmares. Well, maybe not nightmares, more like confusing dreams about this dead guy. He was a friend. His name was Jack."

Sparrow stopped looking at the martins, her eyes locking on Mil. Jack's story flowed from his lips with quivering emotion he didn't believe he could show. Sparrow silently listened as she learned about Mil and Jack's friendship. The unexpected intensity of Mil's feelings for Jack overwhelmed her, but she did not react. Mil was no longer her rock, the man Sparrow trusted and adored, who had helped save her life when they first met. He was broken and she wanted to understand. It was the moment she became his equal, and both knew there was no forgetting of Mil's vincibility.

"Did you love him?"

"You mean like romantically?" Mil asked, pausing as Sparrow nodded. "I've thought about it. Why would a guy have that kind of feelings for another guy? I don't know. It wasn't physical; we connected. Maybe we were spiritual brothers."

"I read in a magazine that everyone has a soulmate, maybe more than one," Sparrow added, touching Mil's hand where the mosquito left its red mark.

The amber light of the boat's night crossing glowed, making them aware Mona's long-awaited ferry was approaching. The sky became darker as light from the ferry made the stars disappear. The vessel blindly bumped into the makeshift dock. Mona's arm was waving high over her head in greeting.

20

⌘

The Decision

Sawtooth pulled hard on the gill net, dragging the wet web onto his skiff. Over a hundred mullets snared in the trap brought a grimace to the man's sour face. Gray whiskers sprouted from the sun-dried cracks of his weathered skin. He hated the ache of his fingers as the squares of netting cut into his joints. Still, the pain was not as bad in the summer without winter's fridged water adding to his agony.

"Hey, boy… what bout ya haul this in?" Sawtooth said, turning to Eddie, who was moving the silverfish into a large container shading the catch from the Pamlico Sound sun.

Eddie had joined the brothers as he did on his days off from the monotony of surfman duties. His job on Pea Island was a ritual of cleaning the Lyle gun, repacking the gun's line and breeches buoy again and again, as the surfmen practiced launching the cannon's projectile toward an imaginary mast. This constant preparation for disaster and drills lulled his mind into a profound calm. Eddie's duty at the Pea Island Life-Saving Station reinforced his waffling sense of self-worth. There was the occasional sea rescue, surfmen rowing out to a boat pinned on an underwater shoal, and the sound of the Keeper's confident command to save terrified people from the untamable ocean. The single-minded purpose of rescue created an adrenaline rush for Eddie. However, the Pagette Brothers held the young surfman's test of mettle. He had disliked Sawtooth since childhood. Now as an adult, his childhood friendship with Nick soured into the customary drama between races in the South. The brothers were anchors, holding Eddie in a troubled place.

"Gettin' too old to catch bait y'urself?" Nick called out to his brother, his hand guiding the sputtering gasoline outboard motor.

"Naw, that boy is a strong, young buck. Needs the exercise after loafing over on Pea Island actin' like he is all important," Sawtooth said, in better humor than usual, scanning the ashen sky for signs of afternoon storms.

Sawtooth's slurs were commonplace, and Eddie ignored them. Today, the older brother had something on his mind, and Eddie found himself curious. Sawtooth seldom attempted to acknowledge him as more than muscle unless he wanted an extra favor.

"You know the president is a-coming to the Banks. He is y'ur boss man, right? He loves yall coloreds," Sawtooth said, flicking fish scales from the craggy skin of his forehead.

"I heard," Eddie replied, prying a large mullet from the net.

"Need ya to do sumthin'. Those Coast Guard boys will be hell to deal with when Roostervelt comes a-callin'. Won't hardly be able to put a boat in the water. Want ya to tell me where to find 'em when he comes," Sawtooth said.

"They don't tell me that stuff. I'm up at the Pea Island station. Not much news coming out of there," Eddie replied.

"In case ya' hear anythin', I want a heads up," Nick said, shifting the motor in gear as Eddie pulled the last of the net into the boat. They headed back to Wanchese over the visceral sound of the engine's propeller churning up a jet of white foam.

Sheriff Owens waited for the trio as the Pagette's skiff entered into Broad Creek. He and two deputies were standing on the dock of the new processing and packing plant, standing with their feet apart, a sign of official business.

"Hoy, sheriff. Ya here to cause me some grief," Sawtooth yelled as he tossed the docking rope at Owens, splashing the sheriff's uniform with the oily slime from the boat. Owens bit his bottom lip, not baited by this man he held in low regard, as he looped the rope around a piling.

"I'm here to take ya to jail. Seems ya are grief enough. Stealing a man's fish and destroying his property is a crime, and it's about time ya three learned the truth of that." The sheriff moved aside, allowing his deputies to handcuff the three men and load them into the back of a pickup truck.

Owens watched Sawtooth and Nick leave the jail after making bail. A stranger wearing a three-piece suit, flipping a gold pocket watch in his left hand, paid the money. Owens assumed the man was a Northern boss working with the Jersey bootleggers who supplied the big city bars up the East Coast with East Lake brew. The sheriff took unspoken pride in the quality of local whiskey. It was the best of the best, coming from the amber waters of his childhood roots. Owens knew Banks' moonshining was a dying art, unraveling as alcohol sales became legal. Bootlegging on land protected by swamps and snakes would be exposed from overhead by planes spotting stills from the sky like vultures soaring, waiting to remove the remains of the dead. There was little left of Buffalo City as the stills disappeared; the swamp's sassafras gold was a free novelty, its giant trees gone, and its water soon to be no longer transformed by copper coils. Dare County's once largest village would be another lost colony, hidden from the present by a greedy past.

Eddie remained in jail until the next day when Mona posted his bond, transferring her displeasure to the jailor before unleashing her full anger on a freed Eddie.

"What the hell have you done?"

"I went fishin', Mrs. Mona," Eddie sheepishly replied.

"Well, I know that, mister, but you hooked up with those two thieves again, and you are in a mess this time," Mona said, mistreating the tired engine as she pulled away from the jail, taking Eddie to his grandmother's west side home. Eddie studied Mona's face, realizing she would never understand the different rules that applied to each of them. Eddie, unlike Mona, didn't have the privilege to nonconform.

21

⌘

Crossing Over

Boggs poured three fingers of East Lake whiskey into a tumbler as he stood at the hotel window overlooking the Pasquotank River waterfront. It was 7 a.m., and the Elizabeth City harbor was busy. The reverend looked over his shoulder at his mistress of three years, the wife of a timber mill owner who had made it big in the decade before the Depression. She was curled under the covers, pretending to be asleep. Boggs thought how bold their affair had become. Once so guarded with elaborate plans to meet secretly, Boggs and Frances cared little about who saw them together, at least not in Elizabeth City. Neither Frances nor her husband kept secrets anymore. They had found a balance, separating themselves from their marriage while enjoying the trappings of wealth. Frances' husband was aware of the affair and welcomed Boggs' usefulness in oiling deals between local and state officials.

Boggs simply couldn't keep his indiscretions secret, no matter how convincing his lies were to himself. His congregation needed him to be the shepherd he appeared to be, the charismatic man who led them on Sunday mornings. Boggs realized he lacked the integrity to please God, so the minister sought to appease his creator, hoping the Lord would delay judgment. He was a compass on a broken pedestal, suspecting he had no true north.

Handsome, well-spoken, and hollowed out by greed and hubris, Boggs commanded the room if he was inside it, but when he left it, the illusion dissolved, his spell broken by the humor and gossip at his back. His sheep grazed on his good intentions as long as he didn't bring his sinfulness to the island. They prayed for his soul and hoped rumors about him were exaggerations.

Even Dick and Parker didn't know for sure how far Boggs had slipped from his godly perch. Parker could have figured it out with some newspaper work, but the publisher didn't waste time researching a man he considered vain, useful but harmless. Parker had underestimated Boggs, not understanding it was the minister's weaknesses that gave him worldly strength. Hard times, politics, and a religious zeal to be on the winning side had transformed Boggs into a backroom dealmaker. Though he might frequently fail God, Boggs convinced himself he could turn his human shortcomings into a victory for his native island and the memory of Virginia Dare. Perhaps if he were successful in his quest, the ends would justify the means, and God would forgive him.

"I will be back in a while. Will you be here?" Boggs asked Frances as she greeted the day with a fake morning stretch.

"Don't know," she said, rolling over in the soft covers, looking beyond him at the bright day unfolding through the window.

"I hoped we could drive to Norfolk for dinner and stay over. I have no plans for tomorrow. We've spent little time together lately," Boggs said, wondering if the fire of their affair was becoming embers.

"Have to see. I'm not sure yet," Frances said, annoyed that his silhouette was blocking her view.

"Very well," Boggs said as he closed the hotel room door behind him. He had spotted the man he was to meet from the hotel window. Unlike most men who walked and worked along the dock, the fellow was well-dressed and at ease in a suit. The fellow glanced at his pocket watch, sliding its thick, gold chain through his fingers.

"Good morning, sir," Boggs said as he approached the man witnessing a seagull gift his suit with a dollop of runny black and white scat.

"Damn this place," the man said, fingering his splattered coat.

"We can go over there. It should wash off if you take care of it now," Boggs said, pointing to a small restaurant without shaking hands with the visitor.

Once the man cleaned his coat, he sat opposite Boggs and looked at the menu board.

"What are grits?" the man asked, showing greater disdain for the town following the bird's speckled greeting.

"It's ground corn. We could have met in Norfolk. It would have been more convenient for you."

"Na, Na… I wanted to see the place. Once you get the product here, my boys will take over. I don't want any surprises."

22

⌘

Gone Fishin'

Mil and Rawlee bobbed on the brackish water just beyond Shallowbag Bay. Water at the island's northern point had been too rough, tossing the men about in Rawlee's skiff more suited for breaking bones than fishing. Rawlee motored his small craft to the northeast side, placing the outline of Manteo's waterfront on his left and the Wright Brothers' Memorial in the distance on his right. Rawlee had taken to sports fishing as more mainlanders visited the island on fishermen's holidays. He saw light tackle casting as an impractical way to harvest seafood. However, the money these "muckcrusters" offered helped pay his bills and allowed him to save money that he stored in an old fruit jar. Rawlee enjoyed the serenity of waiting for fish to jiggle a line as his skiff rolled on top of the pulsing sound. He was selective about the charters he accepted — no families, no women, and only those mid-aged men who seemed more intent on fishing than talking.

Rawlee's regular fishing invitations to Mil were not for profit unless there was a reward in people of different generations and ways of thinking spending time together. Rawlee was direct and apothegmatic in what he had to say, while Mil's conversations became more relaxed as he discovered a true fondness for his fishing partner. Rawlee thought of himself as the younger man's advisor, his surrogate father, on matters of common sense. The younger man learned from him and was open to the islander's honest, if not biased, reflections on humankind. Mil accepted Rawlee's reasoning as sincere, his truth forged by island isolation and shaped by an affinity for the unforgiving sea. When Mil disagreed with Rawlee, and those times were frequent, he didn't seek a compromise. The islander's truth was his truth, and the younger man wouldn't risk Rawlee's companionship to prove a point. Good reporters listen and let the facts shine through the maze of opinion. To be honest, Mil liked Rawlee and considered him to be a friend. Rawlee's uncomplicated wit was endearing to the younger man.

"Those damn new floodlights are a-gonna cost the taxpayer a bucket of money. It's a waste. Once Roosevelt is done, there won't be no country left," Rawlee said, looking toward the memorial.

"No way to stop changing times," Mil said, scanning the horizon. To the west, the sun mixed in a touch of pink with the late afternoon sky. In the east, clouds with puffy white tops stretched out over the sea.

"Don't get me wrong. The gov'ment saved the Banks a thousand times over. A mess of new jobs and post offices to call the mail over. The price is high, though. No rangin' livestock anymore, and there's talk south Banks could get bought up by the federal boys. I reckon some young fart, no offense, buck, is going to tell us how to spend that new gov'ment check that us ol' boys will be a-gettin'," Rawlee said.

"The government gave me a job once, throwing up those dunes with a shovel and laying in sand fences. It wasn't a terrible life," Mil said, picturing Jack digging out sand fleas burrowing into the wet sand to avoid becoming fish bait.

"Life's good if ya keep it simple. People be wantin' to claw their way to the other side like crabs a-shredding bait in a pot, nothin' to show for it 'cept a full belly. They still trapped in a cage, bout to be steamed up on a dinner table," Rawlee said, offering his homespun wisdom.

"Will you be tending the bridge when the president comes to see the play?"

"No meehohkey on that day. Every soul gotta be in place. The state hired some extras to see things go smooth. By God, there'll be bushels of dingbatters stayin' at Manteo; the whole damn island may sink. It'll be a people nor'easter, and I want a front-row seat to be a-watchin' that storm."

"Secret Service agents stopped by the newspaper to check things out. They are no-nonsense guys in tailored suits, their collars too tight to let in the sand. When they dress down, they still look like federal agents."

"That dog don't hunt. They're a funny bunch. One saw a blaze in the marsh. Told him it won't be nothin' cept water fire. He looked plumb fuddled until I spelt it as gas light from the swamp."

"I remember seeing that glow one night with Sparrow," Mil said, wishing he had kept quiet.

"Ya won over Deborah to your side?"

"Don't know what you mean?"

"Ain't no need to fret none, buck. Deborah is a-goin' to let ya court her. It was meant since we pulled that little gal out of the sound. Ya had to wait for her to get old enough."

"Old enough?"

"Old enough to court. I know you ain't no Casanova, and I ain't no matchmaker, but a spark is a spark. Saw it that first day. That girl ain't no girl no more. She's a woman."

"Sparrow is a friend," Mil said, recalling the look the bridge tender must have seen. Rawlee had witnessed his grief learning of his mother's death and interpreted it as an attraction for Sparrow. The younger man mused at the irony in Rawlee's observation. Grief was his attraction.

The men fished in silence as the sun dipped closer to the horizon, adding fresh colors to its palette. Their rods flexed as Rawlee and Mil brought flounder into the boat, the flat fish dancing against the boat's gunnels. The fish captivated Mil with their eyes closely spaced on the same side of their bodies. Mil realized the creatures had no choice but to look up, tempted by a finger mullet dangling from a size four hook. That thought disturbed him.

"That's a nice 'un," Rawlee said as Mil pulled a three-pound fish banging its flatness against the boat's deck, making a hollow sound echoing across the flat expanse of water.

"It's a slickcam evening. Quiet on a slack toide. Too bad it ain't like that on the island now. Lizards a-comin' and a-goin.' The island a-gettin' too crowded for decent folk," Rawlee said, spitting a chew of tobacco over the stern.

"Think the Lost Colony play will change things?"

"We've been findin' excuses to celebrate little Virginia Dare long before Mr. Roosevelt got it in his head to send 'em theater folks our way. This play ain't nothin' new. What's new is the people, the damn asphalt roads and bridges letting in the dingbatters. Not a day goes by when I'm not wishin' a storm would haul those bridges all the way to Virginia. Even if God were in agreement, those government folks would throw up a bigger one to let more people cross over."

Mil considered Rawlee's words, aware they entangled his friend in a life he disliked. Rawlee was unwilling to notice his shifting fortune. He adapted like the rest of the Banks. Mil had not seen himself as a government servant planting seagrass with Jack to tame the waves, but it was a fact. One day the Banks might retreat to Roanoke Island, squeezing the sounds smaller and freeing the island to face the sea, ending its hiding spot behind dunes of sand. Mil had an image of his altered adopted home, picturing a future he hoped he would never see as another flounder flexed the end of his rod, bringing him back to 1937.

"Only island folk cared about Virginia Dare for three-hundred-fifty years; even then, most didn't get excited cept at pageant time. Once Roosevelt is back in Washington and those WPA artists go home, things'll get back as they ought to be. The country can go on a-thinkin' the colony was lost," Rawlee said.

"You don't think it was lost?"

"No, buck, it weren't lost. Those Englishmen got ate by the salt and sea. They are still about. I know folks who claim 'em as kin."

"Kind of hard to prove after all this time."

"Don't need provin'. Just is. Their blood is here, be it in the skin or buried in the sand. Ya ain't an islander, buck, so ya don't feel it. I ain't a-holdin' it against ya. You're all right for a lizard and a newsman, not whopperjawed like most. Reckon we better head on back."

Rawlee edged his skiff toward the dock on Shallowbag Bay. Waterfront buildings were outlined as dangling electric lights glowed yellow in the darkening sky. The men tied up the skiff and unloaded their catch in the back of Rawlee's truck, icing up the fish as a gift to Deborah. Rawlee cautioned Mil he needed insurance to stay on her good side. Keeping pace with the older man exhausted Mil. That night he didn't dream of Jack. The day had filled his mind with an imagined Virginia Dare walking along the bottom of the sea encircled by flounders swimming around her, their fish eyes looking up.

23

⌘

Stone Witness

Mona and Deborah had little in common except for the church chorus. Yet they had an unspoken respect for one another. Deborah had a certain distance envy for how Mona took on a man's world, though she didn't approve of the newspaper woman's manly attire. Mona admired anyone with a work ethic, and Deborah had one of the strongest on the island.

Neither woman saw any virtue in their minister, though Mona was less troubled by Boggs's haughtiness. They said their goodnights to Boggs and Dick as they headed home, playing different scenarios in their heads as they left the church. Mona was worried about Parker, who was under the weather. And Deborah needed to check on Sparrow.

"This has got to stop. This stone will help no one understand what happened to Raleigh's colony because it is a fake. It will cripple interests in Roanoke Island, destroy the play, and stop the flow of money that will make the island a better place, the place God intended it to be," Rev. Boggs said, touching the white collar around his neck as the last choir member disappeared into the Manteo night.

"I'm not privy to God's intentions, but I think the Banks is already a great place. We've to be careful so history doesn't repeat itself. The Banks could become a tourist mecca. We can tame these sands without destroying them and still give history a proper nod," Dick said, drinking cold coffee in Boggs' church office after Thursday's choir practice.

"My God has nothing to do with Mecca. If your words are true, Christians will visit and learn how the English brought God to America. We must preserve the Christian memory of Virginia Dare."

"You sound like a damn broken record. Allow facts to speak for themselves. You want to turn the island's story into a sermon, not preserve its history."

"We're on the cusp of something big that will benefit the island and our nation's Christian views. The stone has no place."

"Not all views in the country are Christian, reverend. History leaves its trail behind. Christian and non-Christian people rewrite it to their liking."

"The stone doesn't bear witness to what happened. If it were real, why haven't you discovered the other stone, the grave marker stone?"

"Because, if it exists, it's in a ten square mile swamp. I've hired fellows to poke around those Edenton wetlands. It might take another three-hundred-fifty years to find another carved-up stone there."

"Why didn't you get the state involved if you were so sure? That would have been the thing to do, right?"

Dick sipped reheated coffee. His headache, which had been pounding all day, was easing off as the bitter brew assaulted his taste buds. He had asked himself why he hadn't sought help from the state. He told himself he didn't trust them but knew the honest answer was more complicated. Perhaps he didn't want the stone to be authentic. Revealing the stone would rewrite the colony's final chapter, reducing the colony and island to a minor footnote in America's story. Common knowledge of the stone might show how Hammond tricked him, his standing in the community tarnished by some wild speculation. Perhaps he agreed with Boggs more than he would have liked.

"The message of the stone might overshadow work to promote the Banks. I don't think so. Schoolhouse history books celebrate Jamestown and Plymouth Rock. Until now, the country had no more than a passing interest in the Banks. Still, the stone can't be ignored."

"I didn't say ignore it. Ask God to point the way; he will lead you to the truth. The stone is an attempt to draw attention away from Christian knowledge. The Lord protects true believers in their times of need. Now the door is opening for a better tomorrow for the children of Virginia Dare. Don't need that stone as a doorstop."

"Boggs, I don't know what you are thinking. I suspect much of what you do off the island isn't very Christian. Judging is up to God, not me. If you must ignore the facts to protect a lie, I'm not sure that's God's will. There is a degree of politics in preserving history, and I admit I don't have the mindset to navigate it. I have trusted you in the past to handle the politics. I'm not sure I trust you on this," Dick said, standing up, leaving an empty coffee cup on Boggs' desk.

"You know the story, Dick. The colonists never had a chance here. A stolen cup sealed their fate. Some savage stole a silver cup, and Raleigh's soldiers couldn't retrieve it, so they burned an Indian village in retribution. Nothing that happened after was good for the English. Was a village worth a cup? Is a stone worth a future? You're the man who moves this village forward. What will history say about you?"

Surprised, Dick wasn't accustomed to a Boggs who didn't pull his punches, revealing a candor he thought the minister incapable of showing. He was unsure what brought on the reverend's unexpected openness. Dick needed sleep, wanting his returning headache to go away. It had been a long day of business dealings, compounded as the number of people visiting the island grew. The thought crossed Dick's mind that he needed a vacation away from the Banks, thankful his sense of humor remained intact. He envisioned himself on the road like Hammond, touring the country. The Banks was where he belonged. He had no urge to roam.

24

⌘

The Storm

The clouds were in a hurry as Mil headed back to Manteo from Kitty Hawk. Parker had sent him there to interview the Wright Memorial superintendent as Amelia Earhart prepared to circumnavigate the world. He thought it would be a good angle, another national calling card to the Banks as federal dollars and local labor continued to restore Fort Raleigh and build the waterside theater. Mil disliked writing puff stories. They were more advertising than news. He kept his displeasure to himself. Parker and Mona were good to him, becoming the family sorrow had taken from him. The couple had a plan for the Banks' future with little room for debate, so Mil kept his thoughts to himself. Perhaps spending time with Rawlee had divided his loyalty, making him more aware of the Banks' past and less inclined to embrace a tourist-filled future.

Mil asked Sparrow to accompany him on the interview. Her love of all things Amelia Earhart would have honed his questions and brought the dreamy, faraway look to her blue eyes he adored. He liked it when Sparrow marveled at a bigger world than either of them had experienced. An approaching hurricane made it impossible to sneak Sparrow away from the vigilant eyes of her aunt. A thousand miles wide, the behemoth storm was churning up the Atlantic waters from Barbados, making a beeline for the Banks. It was time to tie Roanoke Island down and store those harmless things resting on the ground waiting to be weaponized by the storm.

Thick, low clouds tinged in ebony swirled across a jumbled blue sky hundreds of miles ahead of the storm announcing its approach. It would be the thirteenth one of the season. Chances were the tempest would be an inconvenience, charging toward land and following the warm off-shore current up the coast and away from the Banks. The sea would rage for a few tides as people untethered their property so island life could return to normal. But Rawlee had warned Mil this storm would be different, too wide to ignore the narrow strand of Carolina sand. He told the young reporter to go home and help Parker board windows before the ocean paid a visit. Mil believed him; however, it was Parker who signed his paychecks. He rushed to finish the interview and head home across the bridge. Mona's vehicle choked as Mil plowed through a small lake of water across the black asphalt of Highway 34 and coughed to a stop.

Mil was unwilling to abandon the vehicle, afraid of getting stuck if he pushed his ride off the highway. He held the steering wheel in one hand as he nudged the rusting motorized box toward the Whalebone Junction Esso station. A pink Packard Six pulled beside Mil as he inched the car through the blustering northeast wind.

"You seem to be in a pickle, fellow. Get back in, and I'll push you to the junction. Maybe Midgett can get you back on the road," a thin man, his long graying hair lashing out from under a flapping straw hat, said.

"Appreciate it," Mil hollered back over the howl of the wind.

Jasper Howe was from the landed gentry of the coastal plain's rich bottomland where his ancestors had turned peat bogs and ancient forests into wealth. The plantation days were over, snuffed out by a nation that no longer built fortunes on the backs of slaves, at least in name. The blacks of Howe's world continued to work as serfs and servants, or they could escape the trappings of the past and go north to a life that promised slight improvement. Jasper was a man who believed everyone had a place in life except for himself. He despised the station where life dropped him. Jasper felt like an outcast, a privileged individual without purpose, gagged by his silver spoon. He hid his disappointment in contradictions, being a good ol' boy in mannerisms and a brooding intellectual in thought. He kept his distance, cloistered behind the amber veil of barreled Buffalo City whiskey and the volumes of books lining his Nags Head cottage. The building was one of the nearly indestructible summer homes built from timbers of ships tossed up by a merciless ocean, known as the Unpainted Aristocracy, a name coined to celebrate the dwellings' unpainted exteriors, shuttered windows, and wraparound porches.

The front bumper of Jasper's car nudged Mona's black Ford into the Esso station, giving it an extra throttled push before braking as the vehicles coasted to a stop. Nearby the 72-foot-long skeleton of a whale, reclaimed from the surf near Hatteras and reassembled by the station's owner, ignored the weather. It was a landmark, proclaiming entry to Roanoke Island once the two new bridges and a single strip of asphalt ended the island's isolation.

"Nobody's home," Jasper yelled, holding onto his drooping straw hat as his reedy voice pierced through the sandy, soaked whistle of a strengthening wind. "Get in. I'll take you to my place until the storm passes."

Mil thought for a moment, considering the invitation. Walking to Manteo in the furor wasn't an option, and he didn't relish riding out a hurricane in Mona's leaky car. The flamboyant, middle-aged man in front of him seems like an image borrowed from one of his dreams. Mil studied Jasper for another minute, scrutinizing his demeanor and face as water ran down the round lens of his glasses, soaking through his brown tweed vest and making his skinny legs visible through his white pants.

"Much appreciated," Mil said as he slipped into the passenger seat, trying to keep the notes from his interview protected from the wind-driven rain.

"I'm Jasper. Sent my folks home to Hertford once I knew the storm was coming. My wife is no fan of an angry ocean," Jasper said, extending his hand to Mil, who was anxious about the storm and bewildered because this man was from the birthplace he had fleetingly known as a child.

"I'm Milton Kane. Good to meet you."

"Seen that name. You write for Parker's newspaper."

"Yes. I've been working there for a few years."

"Yeah, Read your pieces. Spelling isn't your strong suit."

"I'm aware… working on it," Mil said, hoping his flush of embarrassment didn't show.

"Parker should do a damn better job of editing. Can't say I like the guy. My wife says his wife is a fine lady, though."

"I think so too."

"Well, there she is, ready to weather another storm. The windows all shuttered and the chairs inside," Jasper said, nodding toward a dark gray house, sitting on a flat expanse of sand, facing a sea clawing its way toward its front door.

"My father moved it back from the ocean once years ago. Guess I might have to move it again after this blow."

"How long has your cottage been here?"

"Over seventy years. There's no need to paint it. The sand would strip it off. My father claimed its lumber came from the schooner Patriot after she wrecked with Vice President Aaron Burr's daughter, Theodosia, onboard in 1813. Some folks say the place is haunted by her, looking for her traitorous daddy. The locals haven't always been the peaceful fishermen they would have you believe. They were wreckers, luring ships onto the shoals by hobbling a horse, hanging a lantern around its neck on stormy nights, walking it up and down the beach, and making sailors believe they were safely offshore. Once the ship got stuck on the shoals, locals would salvage the ship's cargo and timbers and murder the crew and passengers. Not a pretty picture, is it?" Jasper said, holding his destroyed hat against his head and motioning Mil upstairs.

"Heard those stories. They seem a tad overstated. People find a use for what the sea leaves behind. I don't believe many were land pirates," Mil said.

"Probably right. Still, I love a scary tale told around a campfire on the beach. They make my little girls scream and giggle. No one will be walkin' a nag along the shore this night," Jasper said, stuffing a towel under his front door to muffle the howl of the wind.

"Do you think the ocean will breach over to the sound?" Mil asked.

"Not a case of if, but a matter of when. The sea and sounds play games on nights like this. The sand moves aside and lets them have their frolic. Could be a new inlet cut by morning. Storms are forever rearranging real estate," Jasper said, pointing toward the upstairs staircase again.

"By daybreak, sand will cover the downstairs. I've a sitting room overlooking the surf, which is more like a study. It had an extra thick window pane facing the sea, two leather French Club chairs, and a jug of East Lake's finest. I offer you my hospitality and hope your personality is as agreeable as your writing," Jasper said.

"I'm better at listening than being a conversationalist," Mil replied, slipping into the seat Jasper offered.

"That's fine. I get tired of listening to myself. I welcome your company. After a couple of glasses of whiskey, I'm apt to ramble for a while. Have one with me?"

Mil, never developing a taste for anything more robust than sassafras tea, sensed the command in the invitation. He accepted a half glass, its clarity painted amber by the yellow flicker of a kerosene lantern sitting on a table between the two chairs.

"It is good stuff… smoothest liquor on the East Coast made right here in the swamps of Buffalo City," Jasper said, pouring himself a second glass, "Have you ever been to Hertford?"

"I have been through there; not that close to Buffalo City. I thought the rye turned the moonshine brown into whiskey," Mil said after a pause, mystified by the coincidence of this man asking him about his birthplace. He wanted to steer the conversation away from questions connecting him to Hertford.

"No. That color comes from aging in oak barrels for a time. I have a few kegs back home spruced up for special occasions. Sometimes in the middle of a hurricane, one needs to see the glow of crystal moonshine in plain clear glass. You can study your demons in the clarity until the storm passes or it kills you," Jasper said.

"You have demons, Mr. Howe?" Mil asked while considering his own.

"The other side of the sound over there. The place where I pretend to be someone else. The demon hunts me, so I pretend to be someone else to hide from him."

"Who do you pretend to be?"

"Myself, of course."

"Sounds more like a riddle than an answer."

"Could be. Sometimes I confuse myself, but this me sitting by the ocean in the middle of a hurricane, drinking East Lake, telling a reporter all my secrets has a clear mind."

"I don't believe you tell people more than what you want them to hear."

"Absolutely. That is what movers and shakers do, Mr. Kane. My ancestors have been at it a long time. They were masters of self-deception Maybe we, or at least I, should stop since I am the last of my kind. It is a new day, Mr. Kane—a day of imported conch shells sold along with cold Pepsi. Think of the asphalt road where I picked you up. It will not disappear tonight. The state will dust it off and pour more tar until nothing is left of the Banks except sea and blacktop," Jasper said, raising his glass to the unseen highway covered with sea foam and sand as the sea washed across the strand.

"You could change that, right? The land is yours. You have the power," Mil questioned.

"The land is useless." Jasper laughed. "People come here for the view. The sea doesn't care much for permanent tenants. It's a temporary host until Mother Nature does its annual cleaning. Power is in the hands of people who divide a pile of sand into tiny chunks of real estate. Not for me. My family is bound to the land and growing things. You can't grow much in the sand. Mind you, my folks never did the heavy lifting. We had coloreds for that. Some of my best pals growing up were those colored boys. My family worked them half to death. Didn't seem right at the time. Doesn't seem right now."

"Then why do it?" Mil said, finishing his first glass, frowning as Jasper poured him a second.

"My kin's negroes cut trees, picked cotton, shook dirt out of peanuts, and pulled potatoes out of the ground to make a living. My daddy said coloreds don't mind the sun, so my folks could sit in the shade and supervise." Jasper paused, distracted by an unspoken thought. "There was that time Buck Lazareth, the best peanut vine shaker I ever saw, took too much sun patching the roof right over our heads, and he fell. He didn't live more than a day. The sand broke his fall, but the sun got him. He had no kin, so we buried him on the east side of Jockey Ridge. Not much of a funeral. I went back and said a few words, spelled out his name with shells. We never brought colored help to the beach after that summer."

"Sad not having a family to remember you."

"Buck was a little older than you. He was a good listener. He would sit with me at sunset and listen to me go on about this and that. I still climb the ridge, go on about this or that, and leave a shell where I remember his grave was."

"He was your friend."

"No one gave two shits about him. He worked his ass off for the family. If I could find him buried under all that sand, I would take him to Hertford and give him a proper burial, including a headstone: "Here lies Buck. He ran out of luck.""

"Sounds a little… whimsical," Mil said, relaxing under the influence of Jasper's liquor.

"You're right. Buck had no luck, just the soul-killing my family forced on his kind. Some of my best buddies were those colored boys. My family worked them to death. Didn't seem right at the time. Doesn't seem right now."

"I think it takes more than hard work to break a spirit."

"Those boys aren't slaves anymore. They're employees under contract to the sweetest soil under the cope of heaven, free people chained to a land they can't leave, living out their days slapping skeeters and sweating in the sun to make my family richer."

"You don't seem to be a fan of wealth."

"I'm well off enough to reflect on the sins of the past, just not motivated enough to stop it. Status quo keeps me comfortable and gives me room to be troubled while I take my family to New York City twice a year and steam over the ocean to Europe once in a while. And, of course, let's not forget this hiding place — the Howe family's great escape."

"What are you escaping from?"

"Locals despise my kind. We are the outsiders, throwing up cottages on the oceanfront, partying away in the summer, and then going away in the autumn, leaving these gray houses as calling cards."

"Locals don't hate you. Maybe they aren't too disappointed when your cottages wash away. It isn't painless being servants to the privileged, no matter the skin color," Mil said.

"I like you, boy." Jasper laughed. "You speak your mind."

The wind was picking up, breathing its salty soaked breath on Jasper's cottage, whistling through the building that had once been part of a ship. Even as water entered its first story, the structure was solid. Rising water lapped against walls and floated the few pieces of furniture remaining in harm's way. Unlike Mil, who developed a lump in his throat as the storm banged unseen objects against the house's exterior, Jasper was at peace. He had a history of surviving hurricanes since his boyhood. Mil couldn't tell if Jasper enjoyed the pounding outside or if the older man had a death wish.

"Would you mind pouring me another glass?" Mil said, pointing to the half-empty jug of moonshine.

"Here ya go," Jasper said, topping off Mil's glass. "My kind don't want the Banks to change. The thought of trading joyous isolation for a thousand people picnicking in our front yard isn't ideal. The Nags Head beachfront has been ours for seventy years. Locals stay on the sound side, up in Colington and over in Manteo. There is a truce between us. This balance ends once that play opens in Manteo and the president comes to visit. People will be as thick as sea turtles on the beach, tourists draining away the harmony until nothing is left but a waitress checking to see if you want your eggs fried or scrambled."

"Seems harsh," Mil said, mentally comparing Jasper's thinking with Rawlee's foreboding that tourism would transform the Banks into a parking lot. These two men, who saw the world from different points of view, were in sync, fearful new bridges and paved highways might overrun their sandy realm. They were both helpless to block a future already decided by reconstructing a three-hundred-fifty-year-old story lost in the past.

"It will be over soon," Jasper said, seeming to speak to himself, inspecting the refracted light from the lamp shining through the beveled glass he was holding.

"The storm?"

"No. the rum-running. I smeared my family's name by associating with bootleggers. When the timber business failed at Buffalo City, people turned to bootleg. Making the whiskey is honest work; selling it requires a degree of damnation. Maybe God can forgive those who brew the Devil's drink as long as the product is superior."

"What is your connection with Buffalo City?"

"I'm in the supply and transportation business. Send the old sharpie, Hattie Creef, up Milltail Creek with a hundred pounds of rye, three-hundred pounds of sugar, and five pounds of yeast, and wait for the product to return, sealed in five-gallon jugs in the keel of a shad boat."

"That's the same boat the Wright Brothers leased to bring their equipment to Kitty Hawk?"

"Yeah. That tugboat has been useful for many ventures over the years. There's nothing illegal about hauling sugar and glass jars. Buffalo City folks love their sugar. Ask the revenuers. Every family there orders pounds of sugar. I suppose they bake a lot of sweets." A smirk reflected from his glass.

"I'm sorry, Mr. Howe. You telling me you are a bootlegger?" Mil asked, feeling Jasper's brew's warm, heady glow take effect.

"What if I am? No one cares. People are on the hush, but they know what is happening. After a while, the revenuers tire of trudging through the swamp of ticks, chiggers, and water moccasins to bash in stills. The bootleggers and police have an understanding. The bootleggers sacrifice a few stills so police can smile for a few photographs. Makes it look like everybody is doing their job…." Jasper said.

"People do go to jail. I have covered their court cases," Mil replied.

"Yes… for a year and a day. Because they had an uppity attitude or did something stupid, like make a bad batch. People come together and take care of their families until they get out of prison," Jasper said.

"You make it sound, well, better than what I believe it is," Mil said, remembering Buffalo City had destroyed Sparrow's family and almost ended her life.

"People getting by as best they can is all it is. Prohibition is over; it is a matter of time before legal booze gets taxed. Nobody will hide in the swamp to make a batch if there is no money in it. I'm going out big, though. I've got enough jugs sitting under a house of God to water every classy bar in Boston and halfway up the seaboard. I'm waiting for the Master to give me a sign on how to move it to the promised land," Jasper said as the men drifted into a drunken silence broken by hurricane winds whistling through cracks and thumping the cottage's shutters.

By morning, the storm had swung out to sea, delivering a glancing blow to the Banks and Roanoke Island. The hurricane assigned new addresses to a few buildings as the Banks waited for seawater to drain back into the ocean. Jasper and Mil walked along the altered beach, noting damages and debris awash in the surf. All the cottages of Millionaire's Row were still standing, waiting for their mainland owners to return to repair and close them for the season. Jasper gave Mil a ride to Manteo, lifting his storm-tattered straw hat as he drove away.

It would be the two men's first and only meeting. Jasper's death came shortly after their evening together. He fell on the blades of farm equipment, trying to free one of his employees from a tangle of belts as the dark loamy soil of his Hertford home became black, drinking the blood of generations seeping back into the land. Mil told Mona about the conversation with Jasper, needing to share Jasper's claim of having moonshine hoarded in a church. If Jasper had a secret, Mil and Mona were willing for the man in the pink suit to carry it to his grave.

25

⌘

The Understanding

Sheriff Owens felt his influence over the Pagette brothers had slipped beyond his control. He had hoped the arrest would warn them that eyes were upon them. The only person affected by the arrest was Eddie. His standing as a surfman didn't sit well with some islanders. They saw him as an uppity black man. His arrest would be a reason to bring him down. Owens thought of Eddie as a decent guy who made poor choices in friends. Still, there was not much he could do to save him. The charges against him were public, and the tide of justice had begun. Eddie's day in court was unlikely to have a happy ending.

"Hello, Mrs. Mona," Owens said, tipping his hat to the newspaper woman as he walked up to the *Dare Independent*'s office. Mona, dressed in her casual fishmonger attire, was in her familiar business mode, complete with an air of urgency to finish her list of tasks that renewed itself each day.

"Good morning, Ben. What brings you by?" she asked, not needing an answer.

"Came to see Parker. Is he in?" the sheriff asked.

"Since when is he not in? He is always in unless he eating down at the restaurant. Anything other than seafood, he hates that." She laughed.

"That's drime. No wonder folks don't like him as much as they do you," Owens said with a dry laugh.

"Ben, why did you do it?"

"Do what?"

"You know… arrest Eddie?"

"Doin' my job, what the taxpayers elected me to do."

"Nonsense, Ben. Eddie stole nothing. He is a straight arrow, and you know it."

"He got himself a-mixed up with a bad bunch. Let the court do its job. Things'll work out."

"They will not work out well in Eddie's favor. You know this, and you need to make it right," Mona said, getting into her truck and closing the door.

"Mona, I know. I'm a-gonna do what I can."

"You shouldn't have arrested him in the first place," Mona said, bringing her noisy, sad engine to life, leaving Owens alone on the street, smelling the exhaust from her vehicle, slowly dying from a harsh life of sand and salt water.

Owens found Mona charming for an outsider. She was more native than most locals. She understood living by the sea was an ongoing trial by nature. Her tan lines were wrinkles, her body sanded by traveling a daily circuit, keeping the Banks glued together by her will as much as the weather would allow. She sacrificed herself to such a daily grind for a reason. Owens could see she loved the Banks, and her dedication to his birthplace moved him. He needed to figure out Parker. The man, who spent his days surrounded by his movie set office, was an enigma through his teasing wordplay in the newspaper. Owens got along well enough with Parker. They were not friends, though they had an amenable relationship as police and press. Life was a contest of the mental fittest to Parker. Owens didn't care for games he couldn't control or understand.

"Morning, Sheriff," Parker said, waving to Owens through the office window, pointing to his cup of coffee. The sheriff gave him a thumbs up, acknowledging his interest in the black liquid growing old and bitter in the pot.

"I thought your piece on our senator was a tad mommucked," Owens said.

"I call 'em as I see 'em, Ben. The folks over in Stumpy Point had waited too long for a decent road. This is the 1930s. There is no reason not to have good roads in Dare County," Parker said.

"Believe the coast has its own reasons. Could be cuz you are tired of your wife getting stuck in the mud every time she picks up advertising," Owens said.

"One day, the Point is going to be booming. Pamlico Seafood is a golden goose. That ice plant is going full blast, and business needed better roads," Parker said.

"There weren't but one road in question. That is all the state will push through the swamp." Owens grinned, privately thankful the *Independent* could sometimes get things done he couldn't.

"What's up, sheriff? I know you didn't come here to talk about roads."

"Couple things I want to run by you if you have a minute?"

"It is a slow day," Parker said, sipping his cup and offering the sheriff a cigarette which Owens declined.

"Parker, Mona got on me about arresting Eddie. Don't know what she wants me to do about it."

"The ideal outcome would be to un-arrest him. The island needs its heroes, and Eddie qualifies."

"It ain't qualified him to stay away from those Pagette boys. Our hero seems to be a dumbass on his time off."

"On that point, we agree. There is too much going on this summer for a jury to debate the character of a colored boy. Every racist thought people harbor will see the light of day if Eddie goes to trial. We're trying to get people to view the Banks as a tourist attraction, not some racial sideshow."

"I reckon you are right. The best I can do is to keep the case off the docket until late fall. By then, all the tourists and our president will be back home."

"Hmm," Parker said, sure the trial could be an editorial opportunity at the expense of a pure soul. He could rant and rave about racial inequity; no matter what he wrote, a white jury wouldn't be sympathetic to Eddie. Old memories of white property owners temporarily losing their land to the Freedmen's Colony lingered. Enslaved people had fled the mainland to Roanoke Island as the Union army took control of the island during the Civil War. These freedmen began carving out a fresh start for themselves until the government deemed the black settlement project a failure. Eddie's family was among a handful of former slaves who remained on the island.

"That brings me to why I stopped by."

"I'm listening."

"What if we had a little added excitement during the visit? What if this whole thing goes off-script? Not sayin' it would. Tell me how you a-see it playin' out with the national press comin' to town?"

"National press… going to be big time, a couple of sea levels above my little masthead."

"The Banks mean something to you. I'm not sure your national brethren would be as considerate."

"All right. Tell me what you are alluding to then," Parker said, pouring Owens a second cup of coffee.

"Let's say those boys from Stumpy Point started running moonshine instead of moving fish. In a big way, I mean enough to keep East Coast bars in liquor for a few seasons. Suppose those boys want to move their hooch when everybody and nobody are watching them all at the same time."

"Sounds like a riddle. I'm still all ears."

"Let's say some big shot is passing through, so many eyes looking one way nobody notices nine, ten, or maybe a few more boats sail right past them with jugs in tow."

"Sounds like you are talking about those Buffalo City boys, not Stumpy Point."

"Well, Mr. Newspaperman, I won't being particular. Said that from the start," Owens said, pushing back in his chair on two legs.

"Why are you telling me this, Ben? You are not the kind to dance around with something."

"True. You are much better at dancin' with facts than I am. I need fresh eyes. I know what to expect from Bankers; they are my people. We got folks comin' to call that I don't understand and can't bear to tolerate. I'm an old dog. I could bark all night on the pizer, and these strangers will still be standin' on my beach in the morning."

"My eyes are as old as yours, sheriff. I don't know what I can offer," Parker said, probing why a man as guarded as the sheriff admitted his limitations.

"Parker, ya're an outsider. No matter how long ya stay on the island, that fact stays the same. Ya and Mona are like them turtles come ashore to nest. They find a spot in the sand, lay their eggs, and bother nobody. Ya got the good sense to nest in y'ur office most times, throwing some words out on paper that ain't too whopperjawed. And Mona, God bless her, understands this bar of sand like she was born here."

"What is your point?" Parker asked, not amused by being compared to a sea turtle.

"I ain't makin' a point. I'm statin' facts. Ya and Mona understand what is on the line," Owens said, pointing west to the mainland. "I think a storm a-comin', and I want to tie down what I can before it comes on shore."

Parker, a man of ready answers, said nothing, inspecting the burnt-down butts of cigarettes in the ashtray on his desk. He felt the sheriff was honestly seeking advice without his typical heavy-handed bluster. Parker was uncertain how to react to him.

"This storm has been brewing for a long time. I don't think anyone knows where it will land. The Banks were built from salvage. Homes raised from repurposed timbers of ships and commerce washed ashore in cargo boxes. It's no different as tourists roll in from across bridges. What happens next is up to us," Parker said.

"I don't want the editorial, just the editor's off-the-record opinion. Those bridges could let in a mess I'll have to clean up. My daddy and his daddy did just fine cleaning fish. I can go back to it," Owens said, regretting this conversation with a lizard.

"Those days have passed. You're who you are, and I don't see how you or the Banks can go back in time. Sure, Mona and I came here riding on a wave, seeing the island as undiscovered and waiting for a better day. If that day means more lizards or even turtles spending their money, enjoy the fruits. Sir Walter Raleigh would be glad his New World dream is becoming true gold," Parker said.

"All this Lost Colony stuff gone to people's heads like seawater up the nose, not much to show for it except the burn, red eyes, and a headache. The colony is where it has always been, Injun blood mixed in with the salt and sand," Owens said.

"I've heard that before," Parker said, unwilling to continue on a tangent neither man would win. "So, what about this hypothetical moonshine flotilla you were talking about?"

"Never mind, Mr. Newspaperman.… Just an old lawman spinning a tale. Bankers love to tell a good yarn," Owens said, standing. "Tell Ms. Mona not to go gallivanting up and down the shore when the president comes. I got two special seats for both of you near Mr. Roosevelt."

"Appreciate it," Parker said, nodding toward Owens as the sheriff left. He was suspicious of Owens, and that distrust was taking deeper roots, moving toward dislike. The editor wasn't in the mood to edit Mrs. Mary Beth's social comings and goings across the sound at Otila. He grunted to himself, thinking the post office there would close soon, and another small hamlet would disappear, absorbed into neighboring Kitty Hawk made famous and more permanent by the Wright Brothers' flight more than thirty years before.

26

⌘

Mullet Trap

Finch and Eddie found words to be liabilities. Their friendship thrived without words, surrounded by seabirds squawking, salty breezes puffing around buildings and boats, and the rhythmic splash of water against the dock. Their eyes had learned to listen in harmony with the fluid landscape. Eddie was adrift in a storm he should have seen coming. His friend's inexplicable bond with the Pagettes irritated Finch. The brothers' hold on him made no sense, entangling him like a mullet trapped by its gills in a net.

"Hop in. I'll give ya a lift to home," Finch said, offering Eddie a ride in his patrol car as he walked toward Good Luck Street, leading toward the island's black section, California. It was his third week on the job as a deputy. Sheriff Owens saw potential in his soft-spoken delivery and cool head which was sometimes mistaken for a brooding nature. Finch had earned Sheriff Owens's notice when he stood up to the brothers, dumping their haul of stolen crabs back into the creek after Sawtooth pistol-whipped the rightful owner for challenging him. Finch clenched fists as Sawtooth approached him, screaming obscenities. The dock's supervisor intervened, firing Finch and telling Sawtooth he would double the price next time around. Owens escorted Finch to his patrol car, and a few miles up the road, the sheriff asked the young man if he wanted a job since he no longer had one.

Eddie didn't know if he cared for this new reality. He was supposed to be the one in uniform. Still, the deputy attire suited Finch. It wrapped him with an authority that might have gone ignored otherwise. Eddie understood how clothing could give the wearer prestige and a sense of purpose. It had been his armor, protecting his sense of self. Finch, the protector, detested any force that claimed victims, and Eddie was a victim, granted he had victimized himself by associating with the Pagettes.

"Can't pay you or Miss Mona for helping get me out."

"Didn't get you out. Ms. Mona did that. She raised a fuss until they set bond," Finch said, pulling his car into Eddie's grandmother's yard, its red light spinning, giving a public reason for the two remaining in the car for so long.

"Times changed since we met. Lots of things I can't undo."

"My aunt says God hands out second chances. Says it is in the Book of Jonah. I don't know what verse."

"That's bout right. I let the whale swallow me, and I gotta pay."

"Sheriff said to give this to you. Let fur grow on your face, and keep away from the Coast Guard. Plenty of water jobs are there. He says no one is apt to come lookin' for ya with fur on the face. Mrs. Mona will talk to ya bout it later," Finch said, handing Eddie $50 rolled up in $5 bills.

"Ain't going nowhere. This is home," Eddie said, waving off the money.

"Home is where ya are free. If ya ain't on Pea Island, ya ain't home. And it don't look like ya goin' back," Finch said, sticking the money in Eddie's shirt pocket.

"Could be," Eddie replied, climbing out of the sheriff's car and going inside the paint peeled shack. His grandmother's cancer didn't slow her down as he found Delores sewing buttons on costumes for the pageant still a few weeks away. He took the money, pressed each bill flat, and laid the bills under his grandmother's chest of memories, tiny seashells glued onto an old cigar box.

27

Sassafras Dreams

A squadron of pelicans cruised in a single-line formation over the serene morning sea. The air had brightened from its foggy gray to white mist, bleaching the periwinkle blue sky with its yellow rays. Mil sat on a dune, looking at the flat beach littered with gifts tossed ashore on the night's high tide. Sparrow sat beside him, the sun glowing on her face as her blue eyes scanned the horizon's edge. Mil told himself not to look into those blue wells of warmth, focusing instead on the coquina clam shell he was toying with in his sand-encrusted hands.

Mil thought the morning was the best time of day, filling his lungs and lifting his spirits before burning sand and midday heat claimed the beach. He remembered days like this when he worked for the CCC. Those were the finest days of his life, letting him live in the moment and not dwell in his past. The shifting dunes had buried those fences he and Jack pushed into the grit. They had done their job for the moment. But times were quick to change as life passed slowly on the beach, marked by the seasons and the storms that came to visit.

Sparrow was wearing a white dress crocheted from cotton. The garment covered her almost completely, leaving her face and forearms bare, showing the bear-clawed scar on her arm. Not looking into her face, Mil studied the borders of the scar. It had been dark red and angry when he first met her. Over the years, the scar had fainted, losing its anger.

The awkward girl had grown up. Sparrow was a woman, and Mil saw her without the passive guilt of his earlier attraction. She had become a beautiful woman with simple charm unchanged by the years, an innocence skillfully tempered by her time on the island. His impulse was to touch her hand, lacing his fingers with hers to feel her energy float through him.

"Sparrow, I..." Mil attempted to speak, his thoughts too scattered to make sense.

Mil caught sight of a sandpiper darting across the sand, scouring for a morning meal of sand fleas. His attention shifted to a form on the beach buried in the sand. As he drew closer, he saw the figure was a person lying on their side with an arm outstretched overhead. Mil had the urge to shield Sparrow from the unsettling sight. When he looked back, however, Sparrow was nowhere to be found. In her place stood a ghostly apparition, his once-copper skin now ashen, sipping what smelled like sassafras tea from a gleaming silver cup. He was the shirtless demon Mil had envisioned in his earlier dream, his body as pale as his face and his eyes transfixed on an indeterminate object in the ocean.

"Jack. What are you looking for, or is it me looking for you?" Mil said, startled awake by another cold sweat. He wondered if Mrs. Yarbough might have sassafras tea to relieve his sick feeling. He needed to see Sparrow.

Sparrow spent her mornings and afternoons at the Hotel Fort Raleigh, assisting her aunt in preparing breakfast and dinner for the burgeoning number of strangers arriving daily on the island. The hotel was abuzz with activity as hundreds of unfamiliar faces came and went. Some were connected to the Lost Colony pageant, while others were WPA technicians, the curious, or traveling salesmen. Federal agents were also making their presence known, preparing for the president's visit. The sportsmen made seasonal visits during the spring and fall, when the migrating fish congregated near the shore, and ducks and geese glided over the marshes for a meal and a safe haven. The new rush of visitors sent the fishermen further south to Hatteras, where locals like Ernal Foster, ribbed by his neighbors that he was hanging an albatross around his neck, were determined to start the state's first charter fishing business. Deborah didn't mind the changing demographics. Even though they tipped well, she was tired of the daily tide of the bloody fish and bird guts bringing flies and stray cats to her pizer. Islanders had opened their homes to visitors. Renting a room or two created a cash flow they were learning to welcome.

"Morning, Mrs. Yarbough. Could I get a cup of sassafras tea?" Mil said as he walked into the dining room, scanning the room for Sparrow.

"Milton," Deborah said, greeting Mil with her typical sternness, "people don't ask for sassafras. Rawlee brought me a couple of roots last spring. It'll take a minute. I'll see what I can do."

"Thanks, Mrs. Yarbough."

"By the by, she isn't here. Sparrow is collecting the mail from the call over. She'll be back by the time I brew ya that tea," Deborah said, finding his interest in her niece endearing as well as troublesome. She had her concerns about Mil, unsure where he stood with God. He seemed to be among the faithful; at least, he was trustworthy enough to sit with Sparrow on Sunday mornings. In her mind, the young newspaperman had two strikes against him; first, he was an outsider, and second, he was a man. She didn't believe any man, even one with good intentions, could be friends with a woman without eventually hurting her. Mil's face flushed with a trace of red as Deborah returned to the kitchen. No tables were open, and he considered sitting on a bench outside Lodge Street.

"Join me," said a man approaching late middle age, made more noticeable by his white-haired temples, sitting alone by the front window, wearing a three-piece suit over a rigid white collared shirt, the tie knobbed tightly against his throat. Missing was a fedora. In its place, he sported a working-class flat cap lying beside his half-eaten plate of fried eggs and link sausage.

"I appreciate it, but I'm just here for a minute," Mil said, dismissing the man as another out-of-place dapper gentleman who frequently appeared on the streets of Manteo in recent months.

"Don't you work at the newspaper? Milton Kane, right? I saw you the other day when I was visiting your boss. Read a couple of your pieces. You have interesting ways with words."

"Thanks."

"Please have a seat until whomever you are waiting for comes."

"Didn't say I was waiting for anyone," Mil said, screwing up his face a little.

"My mistake. Please have a seat anyway," the man replied more forcefully than reflected in the politeness of the request.

"Sure," Mil said, nodding as he slipped into the seat across from the man as Mrs. Yarbough brought his cup of tea.

"Smells different. I would say that's more of a local blend, not yaupon, though, something else."

'It's sassafras."

"Ahh, yes. Sir Walter Raleigh's miracle plant was worth more than gold in its day. I'm Jake Winslow. I work with the National Park Service as a consultant."

"So, what I hear is true. The government will turn the Banks into a national seashore," Mil said.

"Well... not all of it. The villages will remain private, and Roanoke Island isn't part of the plan. Uncle Sam wants to preserve the beaches and dunes before developers fill them with rows of beach houses. Think of it as a continuation of what you started when you worked for the Civilian Conservation Corps."

"How do you know about that?" Mil said, irritated by the man's knowledge of his past.

"You don't have to be a reporter to research." Winslow slightly grinned. "I always do my research."

"I see. That is how you know about Raleigh's gold, wherever that may be."

"Of course. You know, Raleigh never set foot on these islands. He was a bureaucrat who wanted wealth and a name for himself. There was certainly more to him than that. Still, at the end of his days when he lost his head to King Charles' ax, he was an arrogant man in search of glory, not a patron attempting to find his Lost Colony."

"Most people adore Raleigh. What you are saying is not the information that will help establish a national seashore."

"I get it. People want fairy tales and happy endings. People don't want to hear Raleigh sent ships here to harvest sassafras, not look for his Lost Colony. Sassafras was worth its weight in gold then. People thought it was a medicine to cure syphilis. As long as his colony remained lost, Raleigh kept control of the land under the queen's charter."

"Interesting story," Mil said, wondering what point this unexpected historian was making.

"No, too depressing. People will like Paul Green's version of the story better. John White's search for his granddaughter, Virginia Dare, is a more romantic, sympathetic tale. It is the version where hope survives, and people spend their vacation trying to piece together a mystery."

"Have you solved that mystery?"

"I don't solve mysteries; I collect facts. Understanding how facts fit together is up to the individual."

"I used to work crossword puzzles. Still do. Once you fill in the blank boxes, you have solved nothing — just a collection of words," Mil said, fascinated by this stranger.

"Good point. Your boss has a stone that may add to the collection."

"Ask Parker about that, which I'm thinking you already have," Mil replied, shocked but not reacting to Winslow's knowledge.

"Of course. I have talked to Mr. Nancey as well. And I tried to speak with the inscrutable Mr. Hammond, but he has disappeared from town…. lost if you will," Winslow said, sipping the last of his cold coffee.

"Don't think I can add much," Mil said, thinking about how Parker would react to this maybe not-so-chance meeting with Winslow.

Mil looked through the rippled panes of glass distorting the view down Lodge Street. He saw Sparrow walking briskly toward the door with an armful of mail cradled against her chest. She reached for the knob and opened the door as the mail tumbled to the floor; her face contorted with the troubled lines Mil knew she reserved for uncertainties. As he helped her reclaim the letters, Mil saw she was holding a magazine. Smiling from the cover was Amelia Earhart standing beside her Lockheed Electra. Mil thought how much Earhart's smile was like Sparrow's.

"She's gone, Mil," Sparrow said, tears welling in her eyes.

"She is circumnavigating the globe, seeing all the places you want to see," Mil said, smiling.

"No," Sparrow said, frowning. "She has disappeared. It was on the radio last night. She didn't make it to Howland Island. She vanished, Mil."

"I didn't know. I'm sorry, Sparrow. People have gotta be looking for her," he said.

Sparrow cried without making a sound, tears running down her face as her hands trembled, her sadness drawn from the apprehension of not knowing. It was a feeling best observed from a distance. He was so consumed by the emotions of this changeling woman that any sense of distance evaporated. He reached out to her and held her, Sparrow's face against his chest. Deborah was horrified by the gossip this hug would generate as she witnessed the embrace as she was leaving the kitchen. She felt a lump in her throat, turned on her heels, and headed back for the kitchen. She wanted to feel angry, but there was no vexation, only calm as she stirred the chicken pot and dumplings simmering on the stove.

"I don't know if they will, Mil. The ocean is a big, empty place," Sparrow said, trading her upbeat outlook for gloom.

"It's going to be all right. Remember the purple martins. They find their way home no matter the odds. Mrs. Earhart will too," Mil said, self-consciously releasing his embrace, noting Winslow had disappeared, leaving his card beside Mil's half-empty cup of sassafras tea.

28

⌘

The Sermon

A dragonfly hovered over a sunflower crown opening in Mrs. Abram's garden, one of many dotting the streets of Manteo. Mil and Sparrow trailed behind Deborah as they walked to church on Sunday morning. They watched the insect suspended in flight, its four wings buzzing on the warm June day. Sparrow stared at the darner, enthralled by its colored patches. She touched Mil's arm, pointing to a praying mantis, its legs folded under its giant eyes, squatting on a snap bean, huddled beneath the plant's broad leaves. Mil welcomed her touch, thinking how beautiful Sparrow was in the new dress Deborah had meticulously stitched together from a new batch of flour sacks.

"I think she's going to be all right. Amelia was in my prayers. Aunt Deborah says prayers give hope because God listens to them," Sparrow said.

"I hope so," Mil said, glad to see Sparrow's mood brighten, though he harbored considerable doubt God answered prayers. He believed the Almighty didn't interfere, letting human drama play out in moments of gladness and lingering sadness. He disliked his pessimism, finding comfort in Sparrow's warm conviction that things always work out.

Deborah walked ahead, not looking back. Even though she was drawn to Mil's quiet, polite manner, she wouldn't allow herself to trust him. Deborah had married young and had found happiness in those first years. Then her life crashed like a rough surf coming ashore. First, she lost a baby, and then she lost her husband, Clifton. He didn't have a constitution to stand up to coastal hardships. She couldn't forgive him for not protecting himself. And she never forgave Sparrow's father, Henry Ambrose, for not removing her sister from a miserable existence in Buffalo City. He had betrayed Betty and his children with East Lake liquor as Clifton had betrayed her by dying young. She knew the comparison was wrong. She still loved her husband as much as she despised her brother-in-law.

After her husband's death, Deborah discovered a haven at the hotel, cooking for strangers and devoting herself to God's House, even though another weak man controlled the church. She prayed for Boggs' soul with reservation and hoped his sinful ways would one day bar him from her beloved island like God forced Adam out of Eden.

"Thank you, Milton," Deborah said as he opened the church door for his two companions. Unlike all the other Sundays when she kept Mil and Sparrow apart by sitting between them, this Sunday, she took the aisle seat on the middle pew, no longer being a physical barrier between the two. If people were going to talk about their public embrace, she would send a message she had things under control by loosening her reins on Sparrow.

"Praise God for this glorious morning on our beloved Roanoke Island. Welcome to the Lord's House as we greet a new age as America discovers its roots. In the coming weeks, our nation will rejoice and join us in celebrating the birth of our sweet Christian child, Virginia Dare," Boggs said, starting the morning service with vocal vigor and dark circles under his eyes.

As the congregation sang 'Blessed Assurance,' Boggs' thoughts were muffled by the throaty, off-key sound of old men and the blended soprano voices of their wives. His affair with Frances was over, and his plans to use bootlegging money to pave the island's way into the future were in play. He couldn't divert the course of either. Boggs had become a pawn in his own game, hoping God would understand his moral sacrifice. He had sinned to bring recognition to his island home. If he had damned his soul, at least his actions might lead the nation to know Virginia Dare as the sainted first child of American Christianity. The weight of his decisions crushed him. He prayed to God to numb his thoughts.

"To know God is to know joy. In a few days, the curtain on Mr. Green's play will rise, and the country will see how God brought his word to the shores of this land, creating hope where there was despair. As scores of people, including the President of the United States, come to witness God's grace, Roanoke Island will emerge from the lost sands of time and take its rightful place in history," Boggs said, looking at several unfamiliar faces among the worshipers.

Even though he realized they had taken advantage of each other, Boggs felt used by Frances's selfishness in their transgressions. Frances wanted her hoary husband's jealousy to rekindle her status as a wealthy timber matron. She needed her husband's interest to return her to the social pedestal of her youth. God's rules were for lesser men. She never understood that Boggs required a free hand to serve his Master. Frances and Boggs were thin shells, best left untouched lest their empty vanities become crushed under the footfalls of gossip.

"Three hundred and fifty years ago, God returned John White to this sheltered paradise. White left his daughter and newborn granddaughter behind as a covenant between the Old World and the New as he sailed back to England for supplies. When the governor returned, the colonists had vanished, leaving behind a spiritual legacy that lives on at this hallowed island today," Boggs rambled.

Boggs' head was pounding; there had been too much liquor the night before in Elizabeth City. He had sealed the deal to float millions of dollars of East Lake whiskey across the Albemarle Sound on the night FDR would watch actors lift an infant Virginia Dare in the air at the island's new theater. As the actors told the Lost Colony's story, fishing boats would haul moonshine, hiding in plain sight a few miles up the sound to waiting trucks.

"God requires sacrifice. As Abraham offered his son to please the Lord, our devotion will change the island from a fishing village into a showcase of America's beginnings. As visitors witness our glorious past, we will trade the hardships of our storm-tossed lives to become caretakers of our countrymen's thirst for this new Christian dawn. Businesses will grow; our community will flow with God's blessings as we keep the memory of Virginia Dare alive," Boggs continued, noticing Winslow seated by a stained glass window, the sun sketching rainbows on his white jacket sleeve.

"I hope the bastard returns to Washington soon," Boggs thought. Winslow had become a thorn in Boggs' side. At first, the preacher assumed Winslow was another federal agent paving the way for FDR's visit. As the dapper stylist's visit lingered and Winslow started asking questions about Hammond's stone, Boggs became suspicious of his true intention. Thankfully, Hammond's rock was no longer an issue. The mysterious tourist from California, who said he kicked up the stone while hiking in the woods along Route 17, had disappeared himself. The reverend was relieved Hammond had packed up his dirty engraved stone and left. According to Boggs' northern connections, Louis Hammond was on the road, well away from Dare County, heading south with his troublesome rock. Parker and Dick took Hammond's disappearance as a sign to let its message evaporate into the ether of their doubts. They were free from its weight, even though Dick and his energetic daughter continued to spend weekends searching for an ancient grave marker that might rest on the eastern shore of the Chowan River.

"God is a beacon of truth. As a lighthouse guides ships to safe passage, God shows the way for the righteous believer. We must not turn our backs on his truth or turn away from the Lord's guiding light. As faith guided White's colony, they were not lost in the wilderness but held tight to the Creator's loving breast. We are the keepers of Virginia Dare's legacy as we open up our island home to visitors," Boggs said.

There was an emptiness in Boggs that his prayers to God could not fill. Soon America would find the island's lost colony shrouded by shells and trinkets, hotels and cottages of breezy summer days, daily specials and night-long parties, and the spines of unlucky ships weathering in the surf. The soggy shores of Roanoke Island might not compete with the flat sandy beaches of Nags Head, but Fort Raleigh would bring wealth to the island and Christian purpose to his people. The island sanctuary would be a lasting attraction, a pilgrimage to honor Virginia Dare, until storms peeled back the sandy strands of Kitty Hawk and Nags Head, leaving Manteo open to the sea. That distant future wasn't his concern. He would be long dead by then, suspended between a heaven and hell of his own making.

"May we carry forward being the faithful servants of our Lord. As a new day breaks on the Banks, may we continue to be Christian stewards, setting an example for our neighbors and our visitors. Through the grace of our little angel, Virginia Dare, God has provided us with this holy station to save the souls of the fallen. It is through his will we honor this heritage," Boggs said.

Boggs was ill-at-ease, shattered by doubts as he witnessed his long-standing mission to turn Virginia Dare into a national symbol was drawing to a close. He had been negligent in safeguarding his secrets, and the effects were now becoming evident. Fueled by adrenaline and blinded by arrogance, he had veered off course, and the perception of his congregation weighed heavily on his mind. He contemplated confessing his sins to them after the president's visit, engaging in a mental tug-of-war with his own pride that would likely prevent him from such an admission. The thought of facing his community with the truth about his actions had become unbearable, to the point where he would rather disappear into the crashing waves of the sea than acknowledge his wrongdoings.

"Let us turn to Psalm 23 as I read, 'The Lord is my shepherd; I shall not want...'" Boggs read as the congregation joined in, the preacher's baritone disappearing within the drone of a collective voice.

29

⌘

On a Turtle's Back

Rawlee was annoyed by the cypress knees that seemed determined to grab his ankles as he returned again to look for the second Dare stone. The green briars tore into his arms and legs, and the low buzzing air assault of deer flies and black mosquitos on the back of his neck and hands made him swear as he forged ahead. On the Banks, breezes lessened the attack of these tormentors. There was no reprieve in the swamps near Edenton as he, Dick, VDee, and Sparrow zigzagged through the green, watery understory looking for a stone marking the single grave of Ralph White's lost colony. Hammond's quartz rock described the resting place of Raleigh's colonists, or at least some of them, including Virginia Dare, as being four miles east of the Chowan River. Dick hoped blind luck might lead him to the mass grave tombstone.

Experts Dick knew agreed the stone seemed genuine, a message from the past left by a grief-stricken daughter letting her father know the fate of her husband and his granddaughter. The Manteo businessman's thoughts were conflicted. He wanted the stone to be authentic while wishing Hammond had never found his way into his store months before. If the engraved stone were genuine, the romance would be peeled back from the Roanoke mystery and replaced by a documented tragedy, a sad footnote in American history. Dick reasoned it was better for Virginia Dare to live on in legend as a ghostly white doe in a maritime wood than as a pile of bones decomposed in an Edenton swamp. He knew the stone's message would haunt him for the rest of his life. Dick's frequent forays looking for a second stone seemed futile. The trips were token gestures to remind himself that he was doing the right thing.

"'em damn flies big as a hoss," Rawlee said, smacking himself hard on the neck.

"That's why they call 'em horseflies, Rawlee," Dick said, holding back a thicket of green briars so VDee and Sparrow could pass.

"Mr. Dick, this is it for me. I'm done with this lizard swamp. If'n some colony is buried here, rest in peace. No need for me to be a-troublin' 'em bones. At least 'em flies ain't biting the dead," Rawlee said.

"This'll be the last trip, Rawlee. And I don't believe after all these years there'll be any bones left to find," Dick said, poking his boot into a clump of moss. The moss folded back, revealing an earthworm wiggling down into the wet earth.

"Good to know, Mr. Dick. This here rock huntin' is a-takin' away too much fishin'. I ain't seen Hammond in Manteo for nearly two weeks. He done disappeared anyways."

"He has indeed, Rawlee. I may know where he is. He mentioned he was going to Georgia to look at some carvings at a place called Stone Mountain."

"Never trust a lizard, specially a California one with a wife nobody ever seen," Rawlee said, smearing chewing tobacco juice on his arms to fend off the insects.

"He appeared to be legitimate, Rawlee. I've reservations too. I offered him $500 to leave the rock behind, and he declined," Dick said.

"Good riddance to that ol' rock. It's a bad omen the Banks don't need," Rawlee said.

"What's an omen?" VDee asked, lining a worn basket with shaggy clumps of gray green moss.

"Sign of somethin' a-comin' like thunderheads poppin' up on a summer's day," Rawlee said, "Time to get a-shore before the wind hits."

"Aunt Deborah says God gives a lot of signs, and people don't pay attention. She says that is what's wrong with the world," Sparrow said, looking at the orange and black shell of a box turtle disappear behind cypress knees poking up from the swampy floor like sinister fingers of a sinister forest creature.

"Well, she ain't here," VDee said.

"Who's not here, Jeanette?" her father asked, absorbed by examining bear scratches on a nearby beech tree.

"Virginia Dare. She ain't in this swamp. She's alive back on the island, running through the north woods and eating squash from Mrs. Ida's vegetable garden," VDee said.

"Ahh, you're talking about the ghost; the child's spirit lives on as a white doe," Dick said.

"Yeah. We chased the deer from all the way down Highway 345 a while ago, didn't we, Sparrow?" VDee said. "It kept driftin' in and out of sight cause it was rainin' hard that day."

"Yes. It was the same day you ran over Mrs. Ida's rooster," Sparrow said, forgetful of the audience.

"I remember that day. And I thought you said you were late for rehearsal, not chasing after some white deer," Dick said, offering his daughter a jaded look of disapproval.

"The rooster did kinda kill itself, Mr. Dick. He walked off the road when Jeanette blew the horn and flew right back on the hood," Sparrow said, trying to make amends.

"Told Mrs. Ida she could use the rooster for chicken salad. I told her I would clean it myself, but she won't havin' it," VDee said.

"It worked out fine. I caught two dozen crabs with that old rooster's carcass. They was good eatin', better than that tough old bird could have ever been. I gave Mrs. Ida four or five of 'em," Rawlee said.

"You've good friends, my wild daughter. And the way you stay in trouble, you need good friends," Dick said, pointing to an elevated clearing ahead.

The two men and girls pushed back undergrowth as they reached higher ground. Rawlee pointed to an object near the top of the clearing as Dick spied the rounded shape. Dick's heart raced as he touched the thing with his boot, lifting a vacant snapping turtle shell above the leaves. Its occupant had found a peaceful place to end its days. Dick paused, looking inside the empty husk before letting it fall back to earth.

"Think it's time to go home," Dick said, leading his companions back to his automobile for the hour's journey back to Manteo.

30

⌘

Blind Justice

Mona leaned in closer to Sheriff Owens as they sat together on the back of her new 1936 Ford flathead V8 pickup. "I think I know what you're after," she said, a sly smile playing at the corners of her lips. As the Banks' economy flourished, the newspaper went bi-weekly, prompting Mona to remove her old vehicle's engine and roll its salt-rusted shell off the Croatan ferry, giving, as Rawlee would say, fish a new home. Parker's editorials had won him notice in the state as a progressive working to reimagine North Carolina's troublesome shoals of nautical sea traps into a tourist destination. Mona had unconsciously picked up a trace of Banks brogue in her quest to gain the ear of locals. She has proven herself Dare County's friend, even earning her a tug-of-war friendship with the county's sheriff.

"Now, Mona. Always got my eyes open to look after the Banks. What do ya think ya have that I want to hear?" Owens asked, looking out over Manteo's waterfront docks.

"Ben. You get your way here. Most folks who live on the Banks and along the Alligator River are kin to you. Law enforcement is your side job," Mona said as Owens smiled, offering the sun-dried newspaper woman a cigarette from a fresh pack of Lucky Strikes. She waved her hand, declining the offer. "No thanks, I get my smokes secondhand from Parker."

"Ayee Miz Mona, y'all be more of a Banker 'n Ah is, 'cept ya don't got dat brogue right," Owens drawled, drawin' out his words as he snagged an apple from a bushel basket in the back of Mona's shiny new truck.

"Don't run for office, sheriff. You already have my vote," Mona said, frowning. "Enjoy the apple. I don't think the folks in Manns Harbor will miss one if they know the thief is the sheriff."

"As ya say. They're my kin, and kin can cause pain in the backside."

"Ben. You were fishing for information the other week when you stopped by to see Parker."

"And what would I be a-fishing for?"

"Everyone's bait… information."

"A lawman, like a good newspaperwoman, needs the facts."

"Ok, let me be plain. Something is rotten on the Banks, and you are worried the national press will feast on it when Roosevelt visits the island. You tried to play Parker's rambling games to get his insights, and you're not as good at it as he is. You went to the wrong Woods to get help."

"Maybe ya are right. Parker and me don't agree on much. He strikes me as a mainland dandy," Owens said, biting into the apple with a loud crunch.

"That's funny." Mona laughed. "Parker feels the same as you. But I don't believe he sees you as a dandy. It is a matter of style, not inclination, that puts you at odds with him."

"Devoted wife. I like that about ya. Never had a taste for marriage myself. Seems the man always ends up wearing the dress," Owens said.

"Don't be silly, Ben. You would look ridiculous in a dress."

"For sure."

"So, tell me what is going on. I'm thinking it has something to do with East Lake."

"Seems like your crystal ball is a-workin' extra," Owens said. "I'm thinkin' Buffalo City is gonna to send a boatload or two of brew across the Albemarle when the president comes a-calling. The country don't need to see us as bootlegging pirates."

"Noble thought, Ben. I didn't realize you value lizard opinions. You have your informants. Stop it from happening."

"As a rule, you'd be right. This is something bigger, different. A couple of local brothers are involved, but big shots up north are pullin' strings. These boys think they are smarter than they are. The last time they got this smart, their hooch blew up and turned a boat into a fireball smack dab in the middle of the sound. Two runners got killed. I don't want shenanigans going on when Roosevelt comes a-callin'."

"You opposed to the moonshining or against the attention?" Mona asked.

"A little of both, mostly the second. Time to turn Dare County's swamp water into somethin' a tad more legal. Moonshinin' has fed a lot of families, but its day is over."

"Hmm. You sound like Parker."

"Not my choice of someone to sound like. The man has his good points, though. I read y'ur paper."

"You're looking at the pictures. A month doesn't pass without a photo or two of you posing beside something, or someone ends up on the front page."

Owens was a man who didn't like having his attention drawn to his vanity. Mona understood the slight. She saw it on Parker's face when a reader didn't care for his opinions or disliked his mainland manners. The brand of vanity was part of both men's nature, an open-mindedness with shallow roots when provoked by a differing opinion. Mona had made peace with the weak sides of their characters. They were bold men who reminded her of her father. They were not opposed to being unique to remain in the public spotlight. She had fallen in love with one man who had led her to the Banks, and once she arrived, Mona needed the other man to open the doors to island life. For all her independence, she was a woman playing by man's rules; she was a skirt in a pair of pants relying on her wits to make her mark.

"Mona, Don't need that from ya. Posin' for newspaper pictures is part of my job. It makes little old ladies feel safe."

"Well, you're damn good at it." Mona laughed, aware of the sheriff's seldom recognized playful side.

"So, why are we a-sittin' on the back of y'ur truck in the middle of Manteo, Mona? Locals got enough to gossip about already. You ain't sittin' here this long without reason."

"There's something. Suppose I could help you address your concerns about FDR's visit?"

"How in the dickens would ya do that? Let me see. It's got somethin' to do with Eddie," Owens said, blowing a curl of cigarette smoke into the Manteo air.

"Kinda. Not exactly, though. You know if Eddie goes to trial, he'll go to prison and never return to the Pea Island station. Being a surfman brought honor to his family."

"Should have considered that before workin' for them Pagettes. No matter what, Eddie is never goin' back to the station."

"Agreed. Those brothers are trouble. I don't understand why he feels obligated to them. He is facing jail time for something he didn't do. You know it. I know it. The island knows it."

"Justice is blind, Mona."

"Justice isn't so blind it can't see the color of his skin. Eddie will never get out of this unless you help him."

"Took him into custody to keep him away from those boys, at least, until the president had come and went. It worked right good until some do-gooder newspaper woman bailed him out."

"I don't believe you shared your master plan with me, Ben. How was I to see that? So if you know he is innocent, make the charges go away."

"You askin' me to do somethin' illegal?"

"Nope. I'm asking you to do the right thing. Level the playing field, and don't make Eddie's race a crime."

"Can't make the paperwork disappear. I might have buried it if ya hadn't made a public scene by bailin' Eddie out. Shine too much light on somethin', and it shows up where ya don't want it to be."

"Hum… the Pagettes involved in your presidential rum running?"

"Never say too much to newspaper folk cuz they latch on to information like a seed tick and don't know when to let go. Yeah. They are involved, and I can't figure out exactly how. Normally I would have known yesterday what was a-goin' to happen tomorrow. Not this time."

"I may have some pieces you are looking for."

"How could you probably… without being part of it yourself?"

No, not me. I just haul apples over to Manns Harbor as a favor to an advertiser." Mona laughed.

"Then what da you have?"

"Did you know Jasper Howe?"

"Yeah. He's been dead for a while ago. People said it was an accident, but he won't stable, so who knows?"

"Could be his spirits live on. My young reporter Milton got caught in a storm, and Howe sheltered him. He told Mil he had thousands of East Lake jugs in storage. I don't think he planned to drink it all himself."

"And y'ur just tellin' me now? No one within fifty miles can store that much booze without me knowin' where."

"Well, Mr. Sheriff, I guess you aren't privy to all of mankind's secrets."

"Ya blackmailin' the sheriff, Mrs. Woods?"

"Do what you think best. I've got these apples to deliver." Mona smirked. "I was going to tell you, no matter what. You will do the right thing by Eddie whether or not I tell you what I know.

Mil had reservations about believing a drunk man dressed in a pink suit during a hurricane, but Jasper told him liquor is hidden inside a church at Buffalo City."

"I'll do what I can, Mona," Owens replied, wondering to himself why the situation kept getting more complicated.

31

⌘

Waterside Showtime

The final nails were being driven in Waterside Theatre as cars filled the parking lot of Old Fort Raleigh on July 4. It was opening night for Green's play, but Roosevelt's visit to the Banks was over a month away. Sparrow had a role as a milkmaid dancer, and VDee made peace with her part as an Indian savage. Her mark on the earthen stage would be closest to where FDR would view the play. VDee found satisfaction in being a nameless character who could scream and dance with the ferocity of her nature.

Mil climbed out of Rawlee's truck, wondering what or who had convinced the older man to attend the play. For years Rawlee had balked at going to pageants staged to commemorate Virginia Dare, even though he enjoyed the carnival-like atmosphere of ball games and food accompanying those events. Performances, in his opinion, were nothing but unnecessary theatrics, reminding him of the days when evangelicals would call out the demons of ordinary people possessed under a tent on hot summer nights.

"Looks like Skipper got dis place done right on time," Rawlee said to Mil as the two walked among the log cabin buildings of the new "Citie of Raleigh." Rawlee was ill at ease around Albert "Skipper" Bell, an Edenton man with an English accent who had used New Deal workers to resurrect a forgotten fort. Rawlee saw Skipper as a larger-than-life personality better suited for building his thatched roof replicas than for the practicalities of coastal life.

"Seems so," Mil replied, not wanting to set Rawlee off by saying the buildings were not authentic, the product of men with a rushed vision of history to thrust Roanoke Island into the modern day. Encouraged by Parker, Mil kept those details out of print, thinking an odd placement of logs shouldn't derail the first English colony's restoration.

The men felt a sense of tension spread over the island as they strolled from the parking lot to the waterside theater. Both locals and thousands of newcomers were eager to see Green's depiction of a 350-year-old Roanoke Island, but islanders were wary, unsure if it would truly be another birthday celebration for the long vanished infant princess. This time, strangers would be staying in their homes and eating their food. The flow of cash would change their lives. Islanders donned their Sunday best, not knowing what to expect from Green's "symphonic drama" under a sky illuminated by floodlights on the north edge of the Croatan Sound, lights of Nags Head blazing across the water.

"It's a-gonna be a whopperjawed drime," Rawlee proclaimed as he and Mil took their seats midway among the two thousand people filling the amphitheater on opening night. Jake Winslow, cloaked in his familiar ether of mystery, slid next to Mil on the hard bench, the smacks of mosquitos between hands and necks audible amidst the audience's chatter, anxious for the play to begin.

Mil wasn't sure why Winslow made him feel uneasy. Maybe it was because Winslow had witnessed his embrace with Sparrow at the restaurant. That embarrassed him; his ability to hide his feelings forsook him, exposing the painfully emotional person he was generally successful at hiding. He knew the hug wasn't a big deal, a brief whisper of community gossip evaporating like a summer morning's dew. It troubled Mil that this articulate man seemed to appear and disappear at will, creating unspoken anxieties everywhere he materialized.

"Rawlee, have you met Mr. Winslow?" Mil said.

"I knowed he's about," Rawlee answered, nodding toward Winslow without making direct eye contact.

"I hope you are doing well tonight, Mr. Turnage. Surprised you aren't working at the bridge with this vast crowd on the island," Winslow said.

"Problem weren't getting' 'em over. The problem is getting 'em off. Half the families in town took in boarders. Where's ya stayin', Mr. Winslow?" Rawlee asked with weak courtesy in his voice.

"I'm on the other side of the sound, Mr. Turnage… near where the Irma ran aground in 1925," Winslow replied.

"She was a grand lady, a three-masted schooner haulin' nothin' but sand and bad luck… a decent spot to build the Croatan Inn," Rawlee countered.

"That is right, Mr. Turnage. Perhaps after tonight's performance, you and Mr. Kane would join me for a cup of coffee, or as Mr. Kane prefers, a cup of sassafras at the Wigwam," Winslow said as the stage lights flashed, signaling the beginning of the pageant.

"Can't do it, Mr. Winslow. My wife is ailin', and I reckon Mil here has a pretty little girl to see after," Rawlee said, grinning at Mil.

The sound of an organ permeated the amphitheater, soaring above the dwarfed maritime trees caressing its perimeter. The starry vault above the stage's angled thatched roof turned a deeper hue of purple as the ocean merged with the night, changing the island's landscape and crowding it with people. Rawlee, seldom driven by conscious reflection unless he was telling one of his well-rehearsed folktales, looked around, feeling a fledgling grief the island would not recover from this evening.

The wide-eyed visitors, who had braved the rickety bridges and the loose surface of shifting roads, invaded its shores, searching for a place to stay and a meal to go along with a slice of America's past. Rawlee wanted to throw them all off his island. They were invaders incapable of understanding the Banks. Grudgingly, Rawlee admired these visitors' determination to cross the sounds. The journey could be perilous and even deadly for the ill-informed. Perhaps it was ignorance that gave them luck and kept them safe. Rawlee thought of Lost Colony pageants as sugar-coated affairs for polite society. He would have preferred to spend his Sunday night in front of a radio sipping Pepsi and nibbling on molasses cookies while listening to Charlie McCarthy on the *Chase & Sanborn Hour*.

Lights came up on the left side of the stage, revealing a chorus of twenty men and women dressed in gray. The organ's wind died down as the choir began singing, "O God that madest earth and sky and hedged the restless seas around...." On the right side of the stage, concealed in shadow, was a tiny figure sitting in a tree, pretending to survey the horizon like an Indian Peter Pan. Mil smiled, curious if Jeanette might upstage the months of hard work that had gone into the drama.

Mil eyed the people near him to see if anyone else had noticed Jeanette draped in the off-stage tree. He studied faces in the audience, many of them were unknown, reverently watching the play's minister encircled in light, addressing the audience with a prayer before gazing out at the silhouetted group, calling them friends honoring the spiritual birthplace of a nation. He delivered lines about free men and liberty before introducing a historian sitting at a little table in an alcove. The historian spoke of how English men and women under Sir Walter Raleigh's guidance dreamed of founding an English-speaking nation in a "fitting place for a first settlement."

"This here pageant minds me of Boggs' preaching, but my pews more comfortable than this here hard-arse seat," Rawlee said, shifting his weight from one hip to the other.

"Poor fellow. These islanders are going to be a challenge. Thank God for deep pockets and no timetable," Jake thought to himself with his customary detached amusement, seeing ahead to a future that would take decades to unfold.

Mil expected the play would pull him back in time, making him feel connected to the Elizabethan past. It didn't happen. He looked on stage and saw locals in costumes. The lights and sounds of the production created a disjointed awe, making him want to return to the Manteo that greeted him when he first stepped on the island. He didn't recognize this Manteo dressed for theater. His adopted island home was covered in a sea of cars scattered over the island. He wanted to flee. No one would miss him except for Sparrow. But Parker had assigned him to write local color for the newspaper's next edition, reserving writing a review of the performance for himself.

Mil held the souvenir program over his head to swat a mosquito, thinking better of it and settling for a slap from his hand. Smacking the insect with the program might seem disrespectful. His focus shifted from the actors before him to the lettering on the program — rustic, tan sticks forming the words, **The Lost Colony**. Beneath the lettering was a group of hand-drawn 16th Century soldiers searching for something in the sand, some pointing to the word CROATOAN carved on a gnarled tree. Grouped around the image were seven smaller hand-drawn scenes from the present — two men fishing, a speed boat cruising, a beach filled with people, the Wright Memorial, the rolling dunes of Jockey Ridge, two deer hunters transporting their kill, and the slender needle of the Cape Hatteras lighthouse pointing into the sky. The visual evolution of three and a half centuries of Banks' history fascinated Mil. He had researched Queen Elizabeth's court for months, giving him a clearer understanding of how Sir Walter Raleigh was a profiteer who left his colony abandoned with little intention of finding them. This performance might have been borrowed from one of his frequent dreams about Jack. He recalled Jack saying the loss of innocence is the price of knowledge. Mil's early life had dulled his innocence, and he was finding it difficult to suspend his disbelief as costumed characters moved across the stage.

"There's our girl," Rawlee said, pointing to Sparrow coming on stage with other girls to dance around a laughing Sir Walter Raleigh as the organist played *Greensleeves*. An unscripted yell greeted the dancing girls from the trees on the stage's far side. Mil looked toward the noise. Jeanette was sitting in her tree as if to remind the audience Indians were the first to dance on Roanoke Island.

32

⌘

Half-Dollar Thoughts

Mil had intended to rendezvous with Sparrow after the play, but Deborah Yarbough had other plans. She harbored suspicions about the male actors who had descended upon Roanoke Island for the summer production, and she had good reason to do so. Some actors who had rehearsed for the play had abruptly departed from the island just weeks after their arrival. Their penchant for carousing and heavy drinking might have been overlooked had they been locals, but they were not, and Deborah was relieved to see them shipped off across the sound when their behavior became too unrestrained.

The theatrical performance brought about a transformation on the island that Deborah struggled to comprehend. An influx of cars and vendors threatened the island's harmony more than a nor'easter. And Deborah knew the best place to be during a storm was at home. She told Dick that Jeannette could spend the night with her after the play. She agreed to hunt down the little Indian prankster, knowing that finding Jeanette in the thickest crowds would not be too difficult. Dick wasn't sure whether he was protecting his daughter from the strangers or protecting the strangers from VDee, but he welcomed Deborah's offer nonetheless.

Mil wanted to see Sparrow after the show but realized such a meeting was unlikely. He was fearful the inland invasion of playgoers would bring more bizarre dreams into his sleep. To make matters worse, he and Rawlee couldn't free Rawlee's truck from the tangled jumble of parked cars on the island. Rawlee decided that walking the two miles home was his best solution.

"Helluva of a pageant. Seen nothin' like it. That Green fellow was worth the money Dick and the gov'ment paid him. Was one fine show," Rawlee said, surprising Mil with his positive review.

Only days before, Rawlee had wished the stack of timber and thatch that was the amphitheater would wash out to sea and take the bridges with them. Mil's own less-than-enthusiastic thoughts about the show shocked the young reporter. He realized the production was too brilliant not to run for more than a single season. The play's future would be set once the president came to call in a few weeks. The island would become a bullseye on roadmaps. The play and Fort Raleigh were gifts from the New Deal to one day challenge the Banks for its real estate, sharing dunes and marshes with rows of buildings fronted with flashy signs. Human footsteps would compete with the tides, thanks to a drama and a fort whose real-life counterparts had disappeared in the mist of time.

"The night is still young on this Manteo's island, Mr. Kane. I'm afraid I don't have any sassafras tea, though I do have a vacuum flash of black coffee. Please join me?" Winslow asked, a degree of friendliness in his voice.

"Sure, Mr. Winslow," Mil replied, distracted by his disappointment at not being able to spend time with Sparrow. He had wanted to listen to her relive her night, which he was sure would be an upbeat reflection that might lift his mood. Life seemed more honest when he saw it through her eyes.

"Shall we return to the theater for a seat? I have an extra cup."

"Let's sit on Rawlee's tailgate if you don't mind. I don't think the good Lord made my bottom for those seats. The back of Rawlee's truck is more to my liking."

"So, what are your thoughts about the evening, Mr. Kane?" Winslow said, pouring two cups of coffee as Mil dropped the tailgate with a bang.

"I'm better at interviewing than answering questions, Mr. Winslow."

"Oh, I don't know. I was a reporter myself once a long time ago. It is sort of a trade-off. One must offer information to receive it," Winslow said.

"Fair enough, Mr. Winslow. Seems you have most facts before you ask the questions," Mil said.

"The hallmark of a talented reporter, or the nonsense of a man who believes he knows more than he truly does. The best fact checker is to have the facts in advance," Winslow said, sipping his coffee as he watched the departing guests walk toward their cars.

"I'm not open when it comes to details about myself," Mil said, realizing the stranger had a self-effacing sense of humor.

"You seemed preoccupied while watching the performance."

"And you watched the audience instead of the show."

"Touché, Mr. Kane," Winslow said, his serious face breaking into a laugh. "Let me change direction. You have questions. Ask them, and I will answer them honestly if you promise to keep my answers out of your newspaper."

"Who do you work for, and why are you here?"

"You cut to the chase, as the silent movie people used to say."

"Do you work for the Federal Theatre Project, Mr. Winslow?"

"I work for myself, Milton. I am a quintessential hired gun. I go where I'm asked and don't always know the intentions of those asking me to go."

"Interesting."

"I believe you are a man who enjoys a mystery. I prefer to think of my work as an exercise in piety."

"Then you work for some.... church?"

"No, not righteousness in the traditional religious sense, but I guess there are similarities. Think of piety as fidelity to fundamental obligations."

"All of us seek some level of truth, Mr. Winslow."

"People tend to invent truth. I'm a collector, a sorter of facts I pass along to others. Those others decide which facts are worth keeping and which are to be placed in storage."

"What has this got to do with the Banks?"

Winslow reached into his left pants pocket and pulled out a silver half-dollar. He rolled the coin between his fingers as if he was about to reveal a magic trick and handed it to Mil.

"I am familiar with the coin, Mr. Winslow. The Roanoke Colony Memorial Association is selling them.

"The thing is… Mil. May I call you Mil?"

"Sure."

"The mint pressed twenty-five thousand in January. The association sells them for $1.65 each, and the group ordered another twenty-five thousand coins this month."

"Sales were slow. Some question the wisdom of ordering more. Mr. Woods says sales don't matter. The coins advertise, inviting tourists to visit and spend their money."

"Promotion is the bread and butter of free speech. Newspapers do well at telling any story they can wrap advertising around."

"You don't care much for newspapers, do you, Mr. Winslow?"

"Not true. Newspapers are my source of general amusement. They raise the red flags that aid me with my work. I understand them. As I said, I was a journalist once."

"What is your work again?"

"I think I have already told you, Mil. Repetition is the broken record of a reporter's quest for information. It's like fishing. Bait the hook enough times, and you catch something."

"Maybe we are just cautious about the truthfulness of the answers."

"Without contradictions, there is no conflict, no story. Things are seldom what they seem to be. Look at this coin. On the front is a left-facing bust of Sir Walter Raleigh, who resembles the actor Errol Flynn by the way. On the back stands a figure of Eleanor Dare holding her child, Virginia, flanked on each side by sailing vessels and a pine branch on the right.

"It seems direct enough. I don't see a contradiction."

"Examine the wording… Obverse inscriptions, United States of America, E. Pluribus Unum, Liberty, 1937, Sir Walter Raleigh, a half dollar, and on the reverse side, The Colonization of Roanoke Island North Carolina, The Birth of Virginia Dare, 1587-1937, In God We Trust."

"Seems that sums it up pretty well."

"Perhaps, if truth exists in a collection of words."

"Are these words not factual, Mr. Winslow?"

"They are authentic details divided between the obvious and the implied. They are like a… pageant, if you will, where the accuracy seldom stands in the way of a good story."

"You have doubts about the truthfulness of Mr. Green's play?"

"No. Paul's symphonic drama is a masterpiece. It is an account people want to hear, a chronicle of courage and inspiration turning the Outer Banks into the promised land Sir Walter Raleigh at first assumed it to be."

"And what promised land is that?"

"A thirst for fame and fortune blended with an outward appearance of humility, a quest for wealth disguised as nobility, and the human need to hide imperfections in recorded history."

"That sounds judgmental, Mr. Winslow. Locals aren't looking for those things. Bankers are people humbled by the sea, living in simple harmony."

"My job is to collect, not judge. I document the unexpected so others can decide which truth is real," Winslow said, holding the half-dollar in a better light. "For example, the government considered four different spellings of Raleigh's name. The designer, whose foremost authority is to design coins, used one of the arcane spellings when he created the coin. His superiors would have none of it. They were adamant the spelling be standardized by adding the letter 'i' to Raleigh. I wonder if Sir Walter would care how the 20th Century spells his name?"

"I expect he might. What do you want to know about me, Mr. Winslow? I have only been on the island a few years, so I'm as much of an outsider as you are, sir. Why are you here, Mr. Winslow?"

"Why, Mr. Kane? I'm an insignificant man of letters who adds missing words to America's English heritage. What can you tell me about Hammond's Dare Stone?"

"I think you are asking the wrong person, Mr. Winslow."

"I'm asking the person who will most likely give me a direct answer, Mil. Mr. Turnage will share his somewhat skewed opinion, while Mr. Woods and Mr. Nancey will further master the art of evasion. Rev. Boggs will assuredly lie, further complicating the issue. I could ask the two girls, but you would prefer I leave them out of this inquiry. And Mr. Hammond may be more myth than fact himself."

"So, you are not with the National Park Service, then?"

"Oh, but I am. The service's mission is a tad more complex than it seems. Heritage and preservation are built on geology and geography. Few places on the globe are bound by nature more than the coastal shoals of North Carolina."

"I'm not your man, Mr. Winslow."

"You are as close as I'm going to get to being the right man. I thought I would have another five years, but it turns out 1937 is my deadline. Paul's drama, this surge of tourists visiting a re-imaged Fort Raleigh, and road building have created a sense of urgency I hadn't envisioned a year ago. The benefits of the president's New Deal..."

"I'm a reporter for a local newspaper. I have no special insights or knowledge."

"Oh, but you are wrong. You have something more valuable. You have the perspective of being an outsider who has made his way inside. You may not be a native son. However, you are an adopted one."

"Mr. Winslow, you don't know me."

I know enough. I know your history, or better yet, your cultural landscape. Your mentor, Frank, was an excellent wordsmith. We worked together during our Chicago days. I know how you lost your parents, how you worked with the CCC building those sea fences… I know about your unfortunate friend Jack and how he met his fate and altered yours. I perhaps grasp more about Jack than you do. But that is a story for another day."

"What's your point?" Mil asked, maintaining an outward composure while his thoughts were reeling. Why would this man dig into his past? How Winslow gained access to his life following a thin trail of sad crumbs puzzled Milton.

"Knowledge is power, Milton. It is not my goal to gain an advantage over you. Your life's story is unremarkable among human tragedies. The question is, are you up to reversing your misfortunes? Do you believe the Dare Stone is authentic?"

"I don't have an opinion yet. And both of us realize opinions aren't facts. I have to think about it."

Winslow rolled the silver commemorative half dollar over his fingers before handing the coin to Mil.

"Keep this… a memoir of the evening. Maybe one day, it will be worth more than $1.64. The price of silver is bound to increase. Good evening, Mr. Kane," Winslow said, sliding off the truck's tailgate and disappearing into the Manteo night. Parked vehicles had thinned enough for Mil to save Rawlee a return walk to collect his truck in the morning. Once back in his room, Mil had a few hours to write before his deadline. There would be no mention of Winslow in his article.

33

⌘

The Cover of Apples

Tranquil ripples of waves greeted the Pea Island shore with tiny whitecaps. The sky overhead was milky blue with no clouds, and the air smelled of sea life tossed up to rot on the beach. Rawlee, in hip boots, was wading knee-deep in the sound, gathering a mound of seaweed with a long rake. He nodded, gesturing a welcome as Mil approached him. An accumulation of seaweed rose on a flat barge, forming a human shape. The mass of vegetation slid away, revealing a native from Green's play, the man's skin stained brown and his body banded by geometric patterns of white paint. The figure held Hammond's stone, its lettering glowing in his right hand as the man approached Mil. The apparition dropped the stone with an audible plonk into the water as if to say, "You do not belong here. Go home."

Mil woke up with his face resting against the article he was writing. It was 8:30 a.m. He was late for work, and his tardiness would displease Parker. He had slept an hour before a late-rising rooster's crow called him from his dream. He splashed cold water on his face, dressed quickly, and stepped out into a warm, breezeless July morning headed for the newspaper office.

"Glad you could make it," Parker said, absorbed in polishing the finer points of his review. The newspaperman ignored Mil's lateness. "What did you think of the play?"

"It was great."

Parker grinned, pulling a sheet of paper from his typewriter and handing it to Mil.

"If this keeps up, we will have to go daily." The young reporter paced his reading to give Parker the appearance of appreciation. Parker liked the dances and the ending scene where faithful colonists headed into the darkness to face their fate.

"I like it," Mil said, wondering if he was convincing as Mona walked into the office carrying a mail sack.

"Morning, Milton," Mona said, hoping he hadn't got cold feet about what they were planning to do. "How do you think Sparrow did last night?"

"She was great," Mil replied, aware of a trend developing in his answers.

"Remember when we took in shows in New York and Chicago? They had nothing on this play. It is a calling card to the nation. It is going to put Jamestown and Plymouth Rock in the backseat," Parker beamed.

"Sometimes history needs to stay put. I have never seen so many people on the island. The play will end in a few months, and things will return to normal," Mona said.

"There's already talk about making Paul's symphonic drama permanent. I think you will have to learn to share the island roads with tourists," Parker said.

"Maybe," Mona said. "Mil, did you spend time with Sparrow last night?"

"Nope."

"Sorry. You two have been the talk of Manteo since the day in the restaurant. You almost made Mrs. Ida's social column if Parker hadn't done a little editing," Mona teased, her smile following the weathered lines of her face.

"It's not like that. Sparrow was upset by Earhart's disappearance. Amelia has been her heroine for years. She needed a shoulder."

"It appears she has one. Parker, I need to make a run to Columbia today. I should be back on the last ferry."

"That town feels wronged after the state whittled down the size of Tyrrell County, but we are winning them over. Going to take Rawlee with you?" Parker asked.

"No. I'm crossing over with the new deputy. Ben wants me to introduce him to the store owners along the way."

"Working for Owens now?" Parker replied, not sure if he was joking or annoyed.

"Staying on good terms with the law. Finch seems like a pleasant fellow. I'm sure you know him, Mil? ...since he is Sparrow's brother."

"We know each other. We don't talk much."

"In that case, why don't you go with them, get to know your girl's brother since he is a deputy now. Do some reporting and get the mainland's reaction to the play. The ferry between here and Manns Harbor has been extra busy. If this keeps up, they will have to build another bridge," Parker said as all three of them laughed at the possibility.

Mona smiled. The first part of her plan was coming together.

Mona's truck rolled off the Manns Harbor ferry with a thud and headed north up the muddy dirt road to Columbia. Finch and Mil were quiet as the ferry crossed the Croatan Sound. It was a tight fit; three people squeezed inside the cab, packed shoulder to shoulder. She assaulted her new gears moving westward, guided by the grooves of the well-traveled path. Mona could sense an uneasiness between the two men. Mona hoped the trip would relieve tension and create some connection. She knew they were both committed to the arduous task ahead.

Her concern wasn't for the men riding beside her but for Eddie, concealed under a tarp and jammed between four bushels of apples on the truck bed. Mona was breaking the rules, abandoning the letter of the law for a cause that might end badly for the passengers in her westbound truck. The risks were apparent. Keeping Eddie out of jail might mean prison for all of them. Mona sensed Ben must have sanctioned sending Finch, who had become one of his most dependable deputies. The sheriff hedged his bets, not risking his job to disentangle Eddie from a justice system that had no sympathy for a black man, even a Pea Island Life-Saving Station surfman. Finch had a track record of loyalty to the people close to him. The deputy had grown to appreciate how laws could calm people, protect the meek and curb the appetites of the greedy. Yet, he knew those manmade rules alone could nullify justice, twisting it to serve the politics of the powerful. Finch didn't think too deeply or often about right and wrong; his friend needed a second chance, and he would oblige.

Mil's sense of right and wrong was conflicted. His reporter cynicism wasn't as deep as he wanted it to be, untested by his youth and willing to seek adventure for a cause. This trip was Mona's sojourn, and Mil didn't question her fidelity to do the right thing even when it was illegal. Mona offered to let Mil return to Manteo on foot as they waited for the Manns Harbor ferry. He would have none of it. Eddie was his friend as well.

Each bounce of Mona's truck shoved the bushel basket wire edges into Eddie's shoulders. That pain was better company than his thoughts. Mona had talked him into ending the life as Ernest Etheridge, Pea Island surfman No. 6. He accepted her guidance. She was offering him a new path, though it was one that might keep him from seeing his grandmother and sister again and would bar him from returning to his beloved Banks. Tears and sweat ran down his face as he lay under the tarp, sweating under a Carolina sun. He had traded his future for an obligation from the past. It tore him apart emotionally, wondering if the price of repaying his debt was worth the cost.

Eddie told his story to Mona one afternoon when she picked him up while he wandered back from Pea Island to Manteo. The suspended surfman sheltered in the brotherhood of his fellow surfmen every week or so. She lectured him on how foolish he had been tying himself to the likes of the Pagette brothers. Mona had been harsh and angry. He hung his head, listening as she blasted him for his unwise conformity to the Pagettes' will. And then he became angry, not at Mona, but at history. Eddie had had enough of listening to the intentions of people born under the hue of a different color skin.

His past crashed out of him like waves breaking from a stormy sea. The Pagettes' father had taken on Eddie's mother as an employee to repair his cotton gill nets. Eddie's mother started working for the older Pagette after he lost his wife to malaria. At first, she fixed the webbing, and within a few months, she became his housekeeper and nanny to his two motherless boys. Soon he wanted more from her. Within a year, Eddie was born, the unclaimed brother of two boys soured on life by their father's cruelty, forced to pull nets too heavy for his young shoulders.

Sawtooth was old enough to see Eddie as the odd piece of the family puzzle he was. Eddie and Nick accepted each other without the lens of race as the toddler Eddie learned to avoid Sawtooth. Sawtooth's abuse of Eddie was indirect, cushioned by the mutual affection between the two younger siblings, until one day, there was no affection. The bitterness at Sawtooth's core matured into a bully, especially towards Eddie.

The Pagette's father cut his hand on a rusted nail while salvaging a sunken skiff pulled from Broad Creek. While the cut was insignificant, the tetanus infection that followed was deadly. The senior Pagette died four weeks later, his last hours spent with muscle spasms coursing through his beaten body, leaving Sawtooth to follow in the footsteps of his practical cruelty. Eddie's mother disappeared a few months later, leaving Eddie in the care of his two half-brothers until his grandmother Delores came for him. A few people on the island suspected Eddie was a Pagette. It wasn't a conversation pursued, even as gossip. Sawtooth maintained his hold on Eddie after he went to live with his grandmother back on the California side of Roanoke Island. Delores protected him as best she could, but she had little time for her grandson or herself, finding solace and income in repairing the nets of more kindly island fishermen, cooking, and hiring herself out for odd jobs. When Eddie became a surfman, Sawtooth's resentment turned to hatred for his half-brother. He insisted Eddie remain connected to the toxic brotherhood. Eddie's misplaced loyalty kept him in the family as a servant indebted to a blood bond he wouldn't forsake.

Mona absorbed Eddie's history, biting her lip as she listened and hatched a plan to rewrite his saga. She didn't share the details of Eddie's battered heritage with anyone, not even Parker until she enlisted the help of Mil and Finch. She gave the young men versions of Eddie's past that, while truthful, were abbreviated. Mil filled in the missing pieces. Details were less critical to Finch. Having faith in Mona's judgment, he only needed to know how to help his friend.

The drive from Manns Harbor to Columbia was a half-day trip, much of the time spent waiting on a motorized barge to ferry vehicles across the Alligator River. Mona made the regular journey to build a rapport with the small town's merchants. Her efforts added to the newspaper's growing subscription list since daily publications in Elizabeth City and Norfolk barred the Manteo newspaper's expansion to the northwest. Without the lure of tourism, Stumpy Point, Manns Harbor, East Lake, and Columbia people lived in an uncomplicated straightforwardness that appealed to Mona. One day, she reasoned, a second bridge might cross the Croatan Sound linking Manns Harbor and the island, making Columbia the state's inland gateway to the coast, removing Elizabeth City's maritime chokehold on Roanoke Island.

For now, the drive across the marshy lowland was arduous. The body odor of her two sardined companions vented out the rolled-down windows. Mona worried about Eddie stuffed in the back. She had wanted to spirit Eddie away at night until Finch convinced her the plan would be too dangerous for her alone. She had agreed with the young man's sagacity that the best way to get Eddie off the island would be during the day. Finch's presence would prevent questions, adding a layer of security to the escape. Mona peeled back the tarp, revealing a sweat-soaked Eddie as the four waited in line to cross the nearly three-mile wide Alligator River.

"Why didn't you pull back the canvas to get some air? A fellow could die under there with all those apples and yellow jackets," Mona said, touching Eddie's arm to get a sense of how his body was dealing with the heat.

"Guess so. I thought it was best to stay put," Eddie said, taking a drink of warm water sweetened by the sun from a Mason Jar.

"Everything is going well so far. Getting across on ferries is the hard part. Folks can be nosey. We're far enough from Manteo for noses not to matter, though."

"Been under this tarp a while now. A little longer won't hurt."

"It's going to be all right, Eddie. Starting over isn't bad. I have done it twice. Both times things got better."

"No disrespect, Ms. Mona. You ain't black."

"And you ain't stupid. Your feet just won't be on these sands. You have a life ahead of you. If you had another choice without going to jail, that would be one thing. As I see it, you don't. They'll throw the book at you. The court will make an example of you."

"May I have an apple, Ms. Mona?" Eddie asked, grabbing one with a rotten spot from the top of the bushel, brushing away a yellow jack, and crunching his teeth into the red fruit.

"Have you looked over the documents in case you are questioned?" Mona asked and Eddie nodded.

Mona possessed an inherent talent as a forger, a skill she did not intend to cultivate but one passed down to her from a misfit uncle. This skilled printer meticulously replicated official documents with accuracy. She used those skills to create Eddie's new identification, thanks to Mil's chance encounter with Jasper Howe in the middle of a hurricane. The Hertford planter, whose generational privilege had led to self-loathing, held the key to Eddie's salvation. From an unmarked grave, Eddie became a resurrected Buck Lazareth. Mona had used old government documents saved by Mil from a sack of Jack's belongings to craft an identity as well as a bit of Mil's past. Eddie was now Buck Lazareth, born in Hertford, carrying a letter of recommendation from Jasper's ghost attesting to his skills as a craftsman.

Eddie would continue alone from Columbia, taking a boat across the broad Albemarle Sound to Hertford and then continue on another 60-mile hop up US-17 to a job at the Norfolk shipyard. The man-hungry shipyard would gobble up the new Buck Lazareth, glued together from the hurried records of Roosevelt's Civilian Conservation Corps.

"I'm going to miss you, Eddie," Mona said, wrapping her arms around the stoic lost man. "Write to your grandmother and mail those letters to me. I will read them to her, and she can write back to you through me."

"Thanks, Ms. Mona," Eddie said, sliding out of the back of her truck parked near a canal on Scuppernong River.

"Wish there was more I could do," Mona said, touching the back of Eddie's ashy hand.

"You done what you could. Won't your fault. It's mine. One day I'll make it right," Eddie said, wondering why these three cared about the fate of a single black man. His grandmother said some whites carry guilt about the old ways. And though she might be right, these three had taken risks to aid him. They were faithful to him without reason and he shared none of their blood. He didn't understand them any more than he understood himself, trying to resolve the years of misplaced loyalty he felt toward his two brothers.

Eddie said goodbye to Finch and Mil with a handshake before climbing aboard the waiting boat. Smoke and oil percolated the amber water as the vessel's engine idled. Buck stepped on board, and Eddie begin a crossing to disappear from the only life he had known.

"I'll see you the day before Thanksgiving. You know where to meet," Mil said, reminding Eddie to rendezvous with him at Ginny's old neighborhood.

The trio was silent for the first ten miles as Mona drove east from Columbia toward Manteo, each dealing with Eddie's exile. The plan was for Mil to meet Buck in a few months once he settled into his new life in Norfolk. Mil wasn't sure Eddie would follow the direction in which Mona was pointing him. The former surfman would find it hard to resist the urge to travel fifty miles to return home. Mil suspected Eddie would keep going. He would need to put distance between himself and his memories of the Pagettes. Still, Mil felt the call of the Banks would bring Eddie back one day to a place that might no longer feel like home.

34

⌘

Swamp Ghost

Mil generally enjoyed the silence, letting the sounds of nature soothe him. But there were too many unbearable thoughts dangling on the rush of air passing through Mona's open truck windows.

"Are there alligators in that river?" Mil asked as Mona's vehicle crept onto the Alligator River ferry.

"I have seen one in my years here. An enormous creature straddled the road, sunning itself. It seemed misplaced among the fox, deer, and bear I see along the way," Mona said.

The three companions stood, leaning against the ferry's whitewashed, splintered rail, shielding their eyes from the afternoon sun. The ferry's engine churned water, turning gasoline power into momentum as it began the long crossing. A freshwater bass broke the flat, slightly brackish water, gobbling up the sky as it sucked in hapless insects swarming the shore trimmed in dish-sized lily pads.

"I'm going to stop in Buffalo City once we cross. You, fine young men, will help me search for a church load of spirits. I'm sure you may have a better sense of direction than I do in this matter," Mona said, glancing into Finch's eyes as he stared out into the periwinkle blue and pink horizon.

"What do you mean, Ms. Mona?" Finch replied.

"I know Ben has scoured Buffalo City looking for that stash of shine, Finch. Don't play ignorant with me. It doesn't suit you."

"I can't talk about it, Ms. Mona. It is law business, and the sheriff has concerns," Finch said, hiding the truth the sheriff had sent him along as protection, knowing Mona would search for the moonshine alone if he didn't intervene.

"What we just did was law business too, and you had no problem going along. You have a sense of loyalty, Finch. But you know I was the one who pointed the sheriff in the right direction. Ben isn't a man who stops until he has what he is looking for. Since the newspaper hasn't been running pictures of you fellows breaking jars, I think the whiskey is undisturbed for a reason. I can't imagine why."

"What about him?" Finch asked, motioning his head toward Mil, who had moved to the end of the ferry, feeding gulls the last of their uneaten fried chicken lunch, which had grown cold and soggy with grease.

"He knows. And by the way, you two need a better rapport. You don't have to like each other, but your common interest should make you a bit more civil toward one another."

"Got nothin' against, Milton. He seems a little odd. All writers do, I reckon."

"He probably overthinks things. No reason not to make peace with him. Both of you have your sister's interests at heart."

"Things been hard for Sparrow. I gotta protect her."

"Your aunt seems to do a good job. I believe you can trust Milton."

"Time'll tell, Ms. Mona."

"There is a couple of hours before sunset. There will be no pictures of the church house moonshine in our next edition. Keep this between the three of us. What you tell Ben is up to you, but I'm guessing he knows what I'm up to. That is why he made sure you came along." Mona said, changing the subject.

"Why's this important to ya, Ms. Mona?"

"I'm not sure I know myself; however, it is."

"All right. I'll show ya," Finch said as the ferry docked. Buffalo City lay a few miles down the unpaved road. Mona turned right onto another dirt road dotted with muddy potholes, jarring her passengers and apples as they inched forward though what was becoming a ghost town. The rows of red and white houses that once celebrated Dare County's boomtown were in decay, being reclaimed by the swampy environment. The town's glory days were over. A few families clung on, squeezing moonshine out of Milltail Creek's tannic waters.

Mona slowed her truck to a crawl. Buffalo City streets were rotting, resting on sawdust and poles keeping the town afloat. Moonshiners had cannibalized old sawmill parts into the pots and columns of stills. The town's centerpiece, the train trestle once spanning the creek, had been towed to Manteo, becoming part of Rawlee's bridge, linking Roanoke Island with Nags Head. Railroad tracks laced through the crumbling town, a steel skeleton laid bare by salvage.

Finch pointed to a shadowy silhouette of a building sitting near a new growth of small trees. The church's clapboard siding was gray with deep cracks and grooves wrinkling its exterior. Mona saw the building as sinister, eerie, and on the edge of nothingness. Mil perceived a vacant house of God, reminiscent of a faith abandoned. To Finch, the building was an empty shell that held a secret best left in the care of his boss; he didn't want to go inside; booze and religion didn't go together. His thoughts flashed back to his father striking his mother, her nose bleeding on her church dress as she heated pork in a pot of field peas after a Sunday morning service.

"We need to go in and leave quick. It isn't safe here," Finch told his companions.

"Everything seems abandoned. But I think you're right. It isn't safe here. Someone has to be on guard," Mil added.

"The fact Ben left no one to spy on the comings and goings means something… I'm not sure what. Let's go inside. I want to see this glass menagerie of bottled moonshine," Mona said, walking with her typical rapid gait toward the steepled husk of a church.

Finch quietly sighed, pushing the unlocked front door open. The church's interior seemed well preserved, ready for the next service that would never come. Sitting in one of two chairs in front of the church, an ancient man stooped over, casting gloom inside the chapel.

"Why is y'all in God's house? What's y'ur business? The Lord put me in charge to keep the sinners out," the man said, snapping closed the breech of a double-barreled shotgun resting on his lap. Finch knew the senescent face; it was the aged face of his father.

The young deputy considered pulling his service revolver to erase decades of grief and anger. But Finch didn't have it in himself to murder. Instead, he looked at the man and said, "Hello, father." Dumbfounded, Mil was face to face with the man who had changed Sparrow's and Finch's lives. He understood why Finch looked away, no longer wanting eye contact with this man who destroyed his family. Mil stood in the church's doorway, questioning whether what he saw was real or another of his dreams.

"Mr. Ambrose? We mean no harm. We'll leave," Mona said, opening her arms to shield the two young men.

"No need to go yet, Ms. Mona. He's guarding what you came to see, I suppose. Let's take a look and go," Finch said, regaining composure, his eyes returning to the man who had brought heartache to his mother and sister.

"The sheriff told me ya were released a month ago. Why come back here?"

"Comin' back? I'm the Lord's servant lookin' over his flock. I'm his shepherd, protectin' his sheep. Shhh," Ambrose whispered, putting his index finger against his lips, his eyes wild.

"Y'ur a crazy man sittin' in an rundown church. Ya serve y'urself and the Devil," Finch said, lifting one of the thick pews to reveal dozens of five-gallon jugs packed under the seats. "There must be thousands of them under these rows. I suppose he's the lookout. He wasn't here when the sheriff found the jars. I wish he weren't here now."

"We've seen enough. We need to go, Finch," Mona said, fearful Finch's emotions might overwhelm him.

"Y'all ain't goin' nowhere until we pray. These are the vessels of God's people. They hold the communion. Soon they will flow out into the mouths of the unholy, filling 'em with the blood of Jesus," Ambrose said.

"I'ld kill the bastard. He has done more harm in this world than any man should be allowed," Finch said, Mona blocking him from moving toward his father.

"Mr. Ambrose… we're going to leave now," Mil said.

"No, son. Y'all must stay as we celebrate God's glory," Ambrose replied.

"We can't stay, sir. We must go set up the tent revival at Manns Harbor," Mil lied, seeing the shell of the man was no longer burdened by the mind of Henry Ambrose. Mil's urge was to protect Sparrow's brother and remove him from the hollow specter of his insane father.

"And he led them in a cloud by day… and all the night by a fiery light. Yes, y'all must go. It'll be dark soon. The demons will come, lookin' for the spirits trapped inside the jugs. I'll stand guard; y'all must go," Ambrose said, his face animated by the demons of his past.

The three moved toward the church's front door, not turning their backs on Ambrose, his fractured mind recalling biblical scripts. Mona shifted her truck in reverse and backed away, her eyes glued on the building, hoping Ambrose would not leave the sanctuary of his madness and follow them.

"Both of ya gotta promise me somethin'," Finch said, his face flush with emotions. "You gotta promise me ya'll say nothin' about this to Sparrow. That man is dead to us and needs to stay dead."

Mona and Mil nodded, neither finding words to offer Finch until Mona stopped her truck at the foot of the Manns Harbor ferry. The ferry didn't normally run at night because crossings were more dangerous after dark. It was difficult to say no to an insistent Mona. Across the sound, lights of Roanoke Island were in the distance, aligned with the dim electric glow of a more distant Kitty Hawk, Colington, and Nags Head.

"There's more to this mystery than I can wrap my mind around. Why is the sheriff letting that liquor stay there, Finch? This makes no sense. Parker doesn't need to know about this, Mil," Mona said. "I'm sorry about your father, Finch. I wouldn't have asked you to go if I had known."

"Knew about the moonshine. I didn't know my… that man was there. Why would a crazy man sit in an empty church, guarding the jars? I don't know the sheriff's plan. Deputies check on the church once a week, and the sheriff has orders not to call attention to Buffalo City."

"There appears to be a gentleman's understanding to do nothing. Well, I'm no gentleman, and I want answers. Tell your boss I want to see him," Mona said, flustered by the day's events.

"I'll pass it along, Ms. Mona. If Sparrow finds out, she'll want to see him. And I rather kill him before lettin' that happen," Finch said.

"What about your aunt?" Mil asked.

"She knows he is out of prison. The sheriff told her when he told me. She doesn't know he is back here. I reckon she would flay him like a fish if she knew," Finch replied.

"Part of me feels it's wrong to keep quiet. Some things are best hidden. You got my word not to say anything unless Sparrow directly asks me," Mil said.

"The Banks has a way of keeping secrets. Those secrets keep piling up," Mona said as she pulled in front of the newspaper office.

"I wonder if keeping secrets protects or does more harm," Mil replied, noticing rust was already starting to form on Mona' new vehicle as he closed the door.

35

⌘

Cut In Stone

Winslow wondered how Milton navigated between the whims of Dick and Parker. There must be a degree of diplomacy budding in the young man. He was certain Milton had a strong will that didn't bend to them, but it must have a sway. Milton was the sort of man he was searching to recruit.

"Where's Boggs?" Dick asked Parker as the two drank coffee over plates of bacon and scrambled eggs. Usually, a pot of coffee was enough to get them to lunch. Today was different. Winslow had asked to meet them at the restaurant, and they couldn't put him off any longer. The aristocratic stranger, who wore his seersucker suits like a uniform, had become a tense fascination for the two men. Both were sure he was from DC, someone sent south on a mission neither could fathom. Winslow was a wildcard in a game they thought they understood despite their gut uncertainties. Two weeks remained before the president of the United States was to cruise to the Banks on a Coast Guard cutter. Dick and Parker had a hunch Winslow's stay on their island home was tied to Roosevelt's pending visit.

"Maybe I can answer. I believe your minister has taken a vacation from Roanoke Island. He was at the Elizabeth City depot a couple of days ago. He purchased a ticket to Baltimore, and he vanished," Winslow said, melting a cut of butter into his bowl of white grits.

"How would you know that?" Dick asked.

"It is my job to keep up with people's comings and goings," Winslow said, probing his grits inquisitively with his fork.

"Humm. My job too. Yet I didn't know Boggs was missing until yesterday when he didn't show up for chorus practice," Parker said.

"I think our roles are quite different, Mr. Woods. You collect current events and sell them. I package facts. Sometimes those facts are ignored, and other times move the nation forward depending on the politics of the hour," Winslow said.

"This fellow sounds like you, Parker… cryptic to the point of being meaningless," Dick said.

"Why are we here, Mr. Winslow?" Parker replied, mildly annoyed by Dick's calling him out.

"Right to the point. Makes my job easier," Winslow said. "I'm a consultant, Mr. Woods. My work is historical investigation. I don't dig up history with a shovel; I collect information in other ways. It can be a slow process. For example, the people I report to almost nicked funding Fort Raleigh. They were convinced locals were wrong about the fort's location. They were certain the fort was on the island but not where people believed it to be. If I had to guess, I would say the colony site is out in the sound, eroded by centuries of storms," Winslow said.

"We're aware, Mr. Winslow. And we know the fort's buildings aren't accurate, and no one wants to talk about the thousands of freed slaves who poured onto the island during the North's war of aggression," Parker replied.

"You are a Southern sympathizer, Mr. Woods. In war, the victor gets to title the conflict. Being from the north side of Chicago doesn't grant you southern roots," Winslow said.

"All right. You hold more cards than we do. There must be a reason to play this game," Dick said.

"It is no game, Dick. It is a question. Simple. Are you in possession of the Dare stone?" Winslow asked.

"And what stone is that, Mr. Winslow?" Dick answered.

"Thought we were not playing any games," Winslow said, eating his grits.

"There are no stones on this island, just shells. Some of them are beautiful," Dick said, trying to keep his emotions in check.

"I agree. The whelk shell is the most interesting. However, the surf breaks them up. Hard to find a good one. My personal favorites are the coquina and calico. They make good ashtrays. Some folks confuse them with conch shells."

"You been to Florida, Mr. Winslow? Lots of conch shells there," Parker asked, feeding off Dick's irritation.

"I prefer the sand dollar. People once thought sand dollars were coins lost by mermaids. There is inescapable beauty in folk tales, don't you agree?" Winslow continued to foil with his replies.

Their waitress poured coffee refills as the impasse lingered between the men. Winslow nor the two Manteo businessmen could steer a course clear of misgivings. Had Boggs been there, he might have been a more successful mediator, but he was on a northbound train, leaving no word of his plans or whereabouts. Boggs often vanished for days. Still, it was unlike him to travel without leaving someone to fill the pulpit on Sunday morning in his absence.

"I'm not sure you are here to help or harm. The Banks' new deal could last far longer than Roosevelt's term in office," Dick said.

"I'm not here to harm, but you can harm yourselves. As for the president, I believe he will be in office for a while. Gentlemen, my question remains. Did Eleanor Dare leave a calling card from the past?" Winslow replied.

"The only calling card we have are Paul Green's words. You saw the play Mr. Winslow. Eleanor, her child, and the colony are adrift in time, waiting for the nation to rediscover them through a symphonic outdoor drama," Parker said.

"So, you think making the stone public would be Roanoke Island's final obituary? Those aren't the headlines you are looking for, are you, Mr. Woods?" Winslow said.

"History speaks for itself. New artifacts from the past would benefit our communities and bring more people across the bridges to enjoy the colony's legacy of sand and surf. That would be good news, don't you think?" Dick asked.

"There is a stone. It is likely a fake planted to boost sales or promote a film producer's plans. How public knowledge of it will affect the Banks is not my concern. History loves a mystery," Winslow said.

"We've heard about a stone. We don't know what it means or where it is. Guess we can't help you," Dick said.

"Is that your story as well, Mr. Woods?" Winslow asked.

"I'm in the business of selling news. What could I gain by keeping such a stone away from the public? Care to share what you know about the rock?' Parker replied.

"Seems we are getting nowhere, gentlemen. I will share this with you. One day soon, the National Park Service will control a sizable chunk of the Banks, including Fort Raleigh. The Banks are about to become civilized. You can delay when these changes come, but you won't be able to stop them. Your Lost Colony has been found. It won't disappear again until the last tourist drives back to the mainland," Winslow said, placing two half-dollar coins beside his coffee cup, one revealing the profile of Sir Walter Raleigh and the other bearing the face of Eleanor Dare cradling a tiny infant in her arms.

"I have plenty of them back at the store. Might I offer you a few more?" Dick said.

"I have enough for my purpose," Winslow replied.

36

When Tomorrow Comes

Sparrow's excitement showed, breaking from her normally tranquil exterior. Her hands were a little more animated than usual, and her eyes danced over the landscape, taking in everything she saw.

"Tomorrow, he will be here," Sparrow said, pointing to a pelican breaking from its squadron of companions to scoop up an elfin fish.

Mil's eyes followed her extended arm back to the profile of her face, the unrelenting sea breeze blowing her hair into the wind. The summer sun had lightened her long brown hair, turning it auburn. He pictured how she looked a few years earlier as a young teenage girl riding in the back of a delivery truck on her way to her new home, her long, thick hair pulled back from her frail, pale features wrapped in wide-eyed innocence. Her childhood face had matured into one of a beautiful woman. The long scar on her arm was still there, faded by the sun, a dim reminder of the bear attack. The innocence was there as well. She had gained an air of self-confidence blending with her curious nature, making her love of life even more apparent to those around her.

The Croatan Inn came into view as Mil and Sparrow drove north above Whalebone Junction. The hotel, its cedar shake exterior graying from sun and salt, was developing a reputation for its cocktail parties and an upscale assortment of guests, including congressmen, the Washington Press, and Joseph Knapp, publisher of the *New York Herald Tribune*, who was launching a Sunday supplement syndicated in dozens of daily newspapers across the country.

These people were merchants of promotion, opening the door wider to tourism. However, the hotel's calling card wasn't the names on its registry; it was the shipwrecked Irma, a three-masted schooner gone aground a dozen years before. The ill-fated vessel had become a tourist attraction with its stern high on the beach as the breakers stripped away its hull, exposing its wooden bones and dissolving it into the sea.

Visitors awaiting Roosevelt's arrival filled the inn. Parker had sent Mil to the hotel with instructions to leave behind a complimentary stack of the newspaper's recent edition, talk to the guests, and report on the pending flood of people expected to attend the *Lost Colony* play the next day.

"There will be plenty to write about. Find something and have it on my desk by 8 am," Parker had said. Mil seized a brief window of opportunity to take Sparrow with him on the assignment, and she hadn't hesitated in accepting his invitation.

"Do you think it is a good thing Roosevelt is coming?" Mil asked.

"Yes, but Aunt Deborah seems fidgety when his name is mentioned, and Finch wants the visit to be over. He is not a fan of things he can't control."

"What about you?"

"Me? Oh. If I get a chance, I'll ask him about Amelia."

"I hope she is safe wherever she is," Mil said, not offering his thoughts that the famous aviator may not have survived her around-the-world attempt. Sparrow's strength was in her sense of hope, and he would not intentionally weaken her belief in positive outcomes. Though he wanted to tell her about her father, he didn't break his promise to Finch. He was certain Sparrow could handle the truth, yet he was unsure how meeting the shattered spectra of her father would affect her. She would likely ask the broken man why he had abandoned his family and listen earnestly to what he might say. Mil didn't believe Ambrose was in any mental condition to offer answers. If Sparrow discovered he was aware of her father's existence, she might hold it against him for not telling her. Mil could live with the secret if it kept another scar from forming.

"Will you ever leave the island? At times you seem restless as if you are waiting for your destiny," Sparrow asked. Her question was general enough that Mil could avoid a direct answer; one secret kept from her was a sufficient burden. Mil let people believe their assumptions. He was a loner who was not lonely on Roanoke Island. His thoughts were too liberal and intangible for a community beholding to a no-nonsense God of practicality, so he kept most of them to himself. He was a dreamer, haunted by a nightmare, who had drifted into the Banks' safe harbor.

"I don't think I will grow old here. I'm not much of a fisherman and maybe not much of a reporter either. Sometimes my words seem out of context."

"I read everything you write. I love the way you talk about the ocean and fishermen. That story you wrote about the boy packing down eel grass with his feet to sell to a furniture company made me laugh," Sparrow said.

"Thanks. There's never a shortage of things to write about here," Mil replied, brushing back her wind-swept hair from her eyes, needing a reason to touch her face.

"My aunt says I can leave the island next year if I want. A sports fisherman who stays at the hotel in the fall and spring says he will give me a job if I can type thirty-five words a minute. The best I can do is thirty words," Sparrow said, looking for a reaction on Mil's face.

"I'm surprised your aunt would agree to that," Mil said, his face refusing to give her one.

"Aunt Deborah isn't as hard as she seems. She trusts Mr. Lyon. He's always kind to us when he stays on the island. Aunt Deborah says if I stay on the island, I will end up serving food to strangers for the rest of my life and picking up their cigarette butts."

They both laughed. Sparrow had added the bit about cigarette butts. What her aunt had really said was that Sparrow would end up pregnant by some local ne'er-do-well. That wasn't an image she wanted Milton to entertain.

"Yes. I've met the man. Jack was from Westborough, which is near where Lyon lives. He told me about the mental hospital where Jack grew up."

"You still miss Jack, don't you?"

"It is hard not to think of someone who keeps coming into your dreams."

"Maybe Jack isn't ready to let go of you yet," Sparrow said, placing her hand on the back of his hand. "I'm here for you."

"I'm here for you, too," Mil replied, taking Sparrow's hand. "Let's walk along the beach."

"Let's look for shells. Mr. Jake, who eats at the hotel, has told me a lot about shells."

"You mean Jake Winslow?" Mil replied, feeling a chill pass through him on the sultry August morning.

"I call him Mr. Jake. He is a nice man who is sad. He lost his wife in May when the Hindenburg exploded. I never knew anyone with so many facts except maybe you." Sparrow smiled, not wanting to dwell on Winslow's sadness.

Mil hadn't seen Winslow as human until then. He was a walking encyclopedia, constantly updating himself, probing for information with the caution of a house cat hunting for its next meal. Mil had refused to let his guard down around this visitor. He saw Winslow as a calculating bureaucrat on a quest for information. Winslow might be trustworthy but Mil didn't want to trust him, unwilling to see deeper inside the man as Sparrow had done.

"Has he asked about Mr. Hammond's stone?" Mil asked.

"Yes. I told him what I remembered. I told him about the turtle shell too."

"What did he say?"

"He said the turtle was probably a diamondback terrapin. He said it was strange that the shell was so far from the salt marsh. Mr. Jake thought about it for a minute and said only a turtle knows a turtle's mind," Sparrow replied.

Mil was not inclined to ask Sparrow questions about her conversations with Winslow. Whatever she shared with the man would be an honest recollection. Sparrow was not someone to guard secrets. Life was an open book to her, and everyone was welcome to read each page.

37

⌘

Everything a Mystery

Mil's fingers toyed with the reeded edges of the Sir Walter Raleigh half-dollar Winslow had given him. The pressed silver image of Raleigh looked to the left toward the words, "E. pluribus unum," the nation's de facto national motto. He flipped the coin over and rubbed his thumb over an impression of Eleanor Dare holding her infant daughter, Virginia. He wondered why Eleanor's depiction was on the back of a coin celebrating the island's colonization. After all, Raleigh had never come to North America, let alone Roanoke Island. Eleanor endured the final trimester of her pregnancy on a wooden boat, destined to die in a strange land on the unfilled promises of a never-established colony. Part of Mil hoped the Hammond stone was a fake. He wanted Eleanor's fate to be different than the tragic ending outlined on a stained rock.

"Fine job. I like how you imagined the Irma anchored outside the hotel, greeting visitors. Excellent use of local color, poetic," Parker said, crushing out his cigarette butt in the yellow calico scallop shell serving as his office ashtray.

"Good quotes are scarce from folks well lubricated. What they have to say sober can be dry," Mil replied, returning the coin to his pocket.

"With East Lake liquor, I hope," Parker said, lighting another cigarette.

220

Mil didn't reply. He found Parker's comment ironic. Parker wasn't aware of the massive moonshine run planned across the Albemarle Sound as the country's president cruised across that body of water on his way to Manteo. Mona, who typically maintained a candid relationship with her husband, had decided not to share what could have become their most significant newspaper headline. Mil didn't question her reasoning, believing in Mona's logic more than he did Parker's ability to navigate how best to handle the stone's future. He knew his decision wasn't objective journalism. The grayness of white lies and omissions blurred moral high ground.

Dick entered Parker's office with none of the civic courtesies customary of islanders. He was on a mission, wearing many figurative hats for his sunburnt forehead to handle. The pressure of running his store in a town overflowing with visitors was taxing. He was a leader under siege from the expected twenty thousand people crossing bridges and ferries to hear Roosevelt speak. His professionalism was there as he answered questions and pumped the hands of strangers in a recognizable imitation of himself.

"He's playing with us. Before he spoke with us, Winslow knew about our involvement with Hammond and the stone," Dick said.

"Seems so," Parker replied, more low-key than Mil had seen him, preoccupied with a folder of paperwork before shoving it into a bottom drawer.

"What can we do about it?" Dick asked.

"Nothing. We told the man the truth up to a point. We have broken no laws. What we have done is not stand behind what likely is a hoax," Parker said.

"Tell yourself that. Neither of us believes the chiseled rock is fake. The words, the message, and the location all suggest it is the real deal. We may have doubts about Hammond, but the stone seems authentic," Dick replied.

"Dick, it all boils down to Hammond. His travels and his actions seem manufactured, not real. Why should we think the stone is real if the man is not legit?" Parker stated.

"What do you think, Milton?" Dick asked, focusing on the young reporter whose studied discretion had earned the town leader's respect over the years. Mil sighed, not wanting to be included in the conversation.

"The stone is convincing; Mr. Hammond's story is not. I can only say we found a turtle shell in the woods, and your daughter took it home," Mil said.

"No need to bring Jeanette into this. She is a handful all on her own."

"Sorry," Mil replied, realizing saying anything was saying too much, even though Dick had asked for his opinion.

"The fact is Hammond and the stone have disappeared. If Winslow wants answers, let him find Hammond and ask him," Parker said.

"The fact is the stone exists. If it is authentic, we should celebrate it, make it public, and let the experts decide what place it has in history," Dick said.

"All opinion and little evidence. You spent time and money trying to find a tombstone in an Edenton swamp. What do you have for your efforts? Nothing. We need to let this go," Parker said.

"It'll not let us go, Parker," he said gravely. "That stone will haunt us for the rest of our lives. We know Hammond was headed south with it, and if it is a forgery, it is too good for him not to cash in on it."

"Every lie has layers. The further he travels, the more distorted the facts become. It's no longer our problem, Dick. We need to focus on the future of Roanoke Island. Not its past," Parker said, staring blankly at another cigarette before lighting it.

"Repeating the past changes the future into something it shouldn't be," Dick answered.

"Everything about the Banks is a mystery, a struggle against what the ocean does extremely well, burying the past under blowing sand. If we replace the mystery with a clear-cut tragedy, how can we build the future we want to take root here? Legends and tall tales are more solid than dunes, fishing, duck hunting, or frying your ass on a sunny beach. If you take away the mystery, there's no Banks, no Lost Colony, no future, just storms poking holes in a worthless strand of sand," Parker said.

"I disagree. We'll have to deal with that stone again someday. Right now, I must ensure Mrs. Sawyer's homemade potato salad doesn't turn the island into a hospital. If you free him up, I could use Mil's help for a few hours. He can assist Jeanette and Sparrow set up a tent to sell those commemorative coins Winslow loves to flash about."

"Not a problem as long as he is in place when the president gives his speech at 3:30. It is going to be quite an afternoon," Parker said, nodding to Mil as he followed Dick out of the smoky office haze.

38

⌘

Jeanette's Pout

Roosevelt's oak armchair arrived before him. He would sit in it once and then gift it to his hosts, Mattie McMullan Toms Buchanan and her husband, John. The L-shaped Buchanan cottage, an exemplar of Nags Head's Unpainted Aristocracy, was built the year before with its eight bedrooms, wraparound porches, hinged shutters, and gabled roof as a summer escape for the wealthy Piedmont tobacco company heirs and their five daughters. Adding FDR's name to her growing guest book thrilled Mattie. People across the sound on Roanoke Island were less excited, feeling slighted the president would eat lunch and spend part of his afternoon among the inland lizards. FDR's security detail fretted about the best way to transport Roosevelt down the East Coast to what they saw as a sandy wasteland. This backwater posed additional risks for a president crippled by polio, who refused to let his nation see him bound to a wheelchair.

Roosevelt's staff didn't understand how taking a day trip to a forgotten beach town in a state that gave lip service, but no genuine support for his progressive programs, was a good idea. However, the president was determined to make the journey. He viewed the Banks as a perfect coming together of his New Deal's Civilian Conservation Corps and the Federal Actors Project, positive examples of how the government could coax a sickly nation back to health. The area's coastal history intrigued him. The saga of Roanoke Island's Lost Colony was an unsung testament of the Anglo-Saxon spirit that helped form the country twenty-two years before Jamestown and thirty-five years before Plymouth Rock.

The night before, Roosevelt left Washington, DC, at nearly 11 pm, taking a southbound train to Elizabeth City. The town's early morning streets were swollen with people from surrounding smaller communities, hoping to glimpse the leader made famous by his radio fireside chats. Roosevelt's eternal smile and endless waves from a caravan of cars taking him to an awaiting Coast Guard cutter enthralled the crowd.

"I thought that when I came to a town as old as this, I'd see rows of colonial houses," Roosevelt queried his car companion, town mayor Jerome Flora.

"We had 'em, but you Yankees burned 'em all up," Flora replied.

"Plenty is at our doorstep. What we once built can be built again, this time with a seat for every American at the table," Roosevelt retorted, flashing a wider smile and continuing to wave to the crowd.

Roosevelt's driver pulled alongside the Elizabeth City waterfront. Paralyzed from the waist down, the president's aides strapped steel bracing to his legs, moving him out of public view, shielded by an assemblage of guardsmen, police, and Secret Service agents. As Roosevelt slid into a waiting wheelchair. A photographer snapped a picture, not knowing or disregarding the press gentleman's agreement never to photograph the president in his chair. A nearby agent approached the man, removed the now exposed roll of film from the camera, and returned the device to its flustered owner. The cutter pulled away from the dock, plowing the broad Pasquotank River, moving east toward the expanse of the Albemarle Sound as the president took his lunch aboard the cutter.

Mil, Sparrow, and VDee, adrift in a crowd of locals and visiting lizards, stood beside the freshly deepened anchorage, awaiting the president's arrival. The three were taken aback by the spectacle of people glued along Manteo's harbor. There was a quiet reverence along the pier as the cutter appeared from the north. The country's president had come in search of a lost colony. For the moment, Manteo was no longer the quaint place of fishermen and salvagers. Mil knitted his brow and squinted toward the clear horizon where sound and sky blended into one.

"He can stay at my daddy's house today. We'll get some fried shrimp and cornbread from the hotel for dinner. Mother had some fancy sheets we can use on my bed, and I can sleep in the livin' room," VDee said.

"I don't think he can stay with you, VDee," Mil said.

"Why not? Ain't we good enough for him? My daddy runs half of the island," VDee replied.

"Not that. You see those lines of police cars. They'll take him over to Nags Head for his evening meal. The president is not spending the night. He is leaving for Washington right after the play," Mil said.

"Hmm. Don't seem right. He came all this way and not spending the night in town. Why's he eatin' over there with those lizards? The folks over here cook food for them anyway," VDee said.

"Think it is his health. You never see him walking on those newsreels. He has trouble standing up. I think he works too hard," Sparrow added, noting that VDee's thoughts were headed toward a bad outcome.

"The president is in a wheelchair. He has braces on his legs, so he can walk a few steps if he has to," Mil said, seeing the empathy on Sparrow's face and the doubt on VDee's.

"My daddy says the country is gonna fall into another depression if Roosevelt don't stop fightin' with the politicians.

And as far as I see, there's no excuse for him not to spend the night with us," VDee replied with a pronounced pout.

"Jeanette, you gotta promise me you won't make a scene. Play nice today. Think what you want, but don't do what you are thinking," Sparrow replied in a tone borrowed from her cautious aunt.

"All right. I'll try to hold it back. No guarantee if those lizards don't act right," VDee replied, biting her lower lip.

Mil stole a look at Sparrow. He took her in all at once, realizing how quickly she was changing, showing practicality and cautiousness in her growing awareness of the world around her. For a second, Mil saw Deborah with her eternally worried expression superimposed over the young woman. Then the visor changed into the raging madman of her father sitting in a swampy ghost town. Sparrow was a product of extremes; a girl stranded on a sheltered island, repeating her daily routines until she became another version of her aunt. Mil thought she deserved more, thining the sea would not be able to protect her innocence if she left the island.

"I see the ship," Sparrow said, pointing to a dot on the horizon as gulls squawked overhead, scooping up the benefits of bored young children tossing bread crusts into the Manteo sky.

39

⌘

Knot That Binds

On the Alligator peninsula, old mail boats, powered boats, and a few over-the-hill luxury yachts anchored near the mouth of Milltail Creek as the Coast Guard ferried FDR to Manteo. A duck blind, thrown together where the Alligator River flows into the Albemarle Sound, was to serve as a lookout for the moonshine fleet. Should law enforcement officers or the Coast Guard appear, the two men nested in the duck blind were to fire a series of shotgun blasts to warn the assembled fleet of moonshine runners to scatter. Dotting the sound were small fishing boats ordered to fire their goose guns if suspicious vessels appeared on the waterway. The moonshine fleet was hiding in plain sight, able to return to hunting, fishing, or leisure cruising without being detected. The plan was to wait until dark and send the East Lake liquor-loaded boats across the sound above Elizabeth City. There they would offload the glass jugs of whiskey onto trucks and move them overland to waiting vehicles that would transfer the spirits up the Chesapeake Bay and to East Coast cocktail bars.

"Is everything going to plan, Mr. Pagette?" asked the silhouette in a suit standing near the rusting tower of an old water tank. It was the man Rev. Boggs met on the streets of Elizabeth City.

"Guys in place. They blocked the way into Buffalo City with trees we cut. Those who still call this swamp home will tend their own business. We'll start loadin' boats," Sawtooth said.

"Very well… begin," the suited man ordered.

"One thang. That church ain't gonna have a seat to sit in when we's done tearing 'em apart getting liquor out," Sawtooth added.

"Doesn't matter. I believe the days of praying in this quagmire are over. This will be the last big run, and this dreadful place can sink back into nothingness," the man said, slapping a deer fly as it landed on the back of his hand.

"People still live here. Folks are doing their best to get by," Sawtooth said, uncharacteristically sympathetic towards the dying town, concealing how he pardoned his misdeeds.

"Don't care, Mr. Pagette. These people mean nothing. We'll deal with anyone who gets in our way the same as we did that preacher. No room for second doubts or second chances. He was a liability, and we know how to handle liabilities. You going to be a liability, Mr. Pagette?" he asked.

"Nope. That crazy fool been watchin' the church is gonna be one. Ain't got the sense God gave a goose. He got our men spooked. Been telling 'em they will burn in hell all mornin'," Sawtooth said.

"Don't let him drink into our profits, Mr. Pagette. Nothing guards a property more than a good dose of crazy. He has served his purpose. Take care of the problem and keep your mouth shut," the man added.

Ben Owens and Finch Ambrose watched moonshine jugs move from the church to a dock along Milltail Creek. They had been there all night. The sheriff sent his young deputy across the mossy points of cypress knees that had once been Finch's home, coordinating information with two other deputies camping out near East Lake and at the Alligator River ferry.

Weeks earlier, Ben concluded he couldn't stop the whiskey run any more than he could keep Mona from moving Eddie out of reach of the local court system. The sheriff could find Eddie if he felt the need. And he could turn this bootlegging operation into shards of broken glass within an hour. Both actions came with a price. Ben chose what he considered a greater good over the letter of the law. Ben knew Eddie wasn't guilty of anything except being the black half-brother of two malicious white men. The sheriff reasoned he couldn't stop the run without turning it into national news which would be bad for the Banks. As much as Ben loved seeing his picture in the paper, he did not wish to read headlines overshadowing the president's visit, portraying the Banks as a backwoods den of moonshiners instead of a gracious host to the country's leader. As for Eddie, the sheriff decided to let Mona determine his future.

Ben was born into a coastal clan of watchers who scanned the sky for storms, and he depended on the guarded words of unflappable fishermen for what he needed to know about his jurisdiction. He told himself that keeping the runners under surveillance was enough, giving the Jersey crime bosses a wide path. Liquor sales were legal again; soon, moonshining for profit would end. Spotter planes could overwhelm the swamp's natural protection from revenuers peering down into the green montage of colors spying small plumes of gray smoke. East Lake liquor was doomed without Prohibition to keep the profit margins high. Ben knew outsider interest would turn the Banks' sand and sea into a different gold called real estate. He wasn't sure the transition was the lesser of two evils.

"See 'em, Pagette brothers, They got sand in their shoes, but you can't make a silk purse out of a sow's ear," the sheriff told Finch. "Their time will come, and I will put them in state prison if it is the last thing I do."

"What'll we do bout 'em today?" Finch asked.

"Every fish needs a good run. Ya gotta know when to set the hook and reel it in. If they see us here, we'll have to do some shootin'. Not what I want to do. Let's leave 'em in peace. Keep a watch on 'em from over at the ferry. I gotta head back to Manteo."

The sheriff arrived in Manteo as the Secret Service guided the president into his awaiting Pierce-Arrow Touring Limousine parked beside the dock. Ben regretted missing Roosevelt's arrival, indifferent to the fact state and federal law enforcement had sidelined his department weeks ago. They didn't know the actual show was unfolding across the western sound.

Roosevelt's limousine served as his legs, taking him to Manteo to make an afternoon speech before being whisked across the Roanoke Sound bridge to hobnob with the Nags Head elite. Rawlee Turnage made sure he would be on duty as a bridge tender that evening as Roosevelt would return to watch the play from his open-topped car in a special parking space inside the amphitheater. A stone recently scribed was waiting near the theater to mark where the President of the United States would watch the Lost Colony's nightly return from its grave.

The mid-afternoon sun was blistering, and efforts to choreograph the visit to hide the president's disability were apparent. Roanoke Island, bejeweled with its marshes and soft sandy roads, strained to hold thousands of visitors. None of this set well with VDee. The president not taking his supper in Manteo, was souring her festival mood. She had not understood why locals called outsiders lizards and dingbatters until now. Hordes of strangers were trampling through her island world, wearing their Sunday shoes on land meant for bare feet, and she didn't appreciate the intrusion.

"These lizards will be here forever. That first night, they parked cars all over. My daddy boarded a family in our extra bedroom. Room's kinda small, and their kids had to sleep on the floor. Daddy let 'em stay for free. It weren't right. I'ld have charged 'em like all the other folks in town are doin'," VDee said.

"I think this will be the way it is from now on, Jeanette. People will keep coming, just like the sportsmen in the spring and fall," Sparrow answered, reserving her friend's nickname for less solemn occasions.

"Lizards gettin' stuck in the sand and can't find their way around. Don't make sense. There's one way in and one way out. Those folks are so dumb they would pay for a glass of water," VDee said, scowling at the crowd.

"The play will end in a few weeks. Aunt Deborah says she hopes they will use the theater for worship just like people are using Fort Raleigh's chapel for weddings. She says people need all the God they can get," Sparrow added.

"Maybe. It's a shame that man can't walk. See how those other fellows are tryin' to keep folks from seein' 'em move him," VDee said, noticing the president's orchestrated progress to speak to the assembled crowd.

"People have their hardships, Jeanette. How they live with them is what matters," Sparrow replied as a tired Roosevelt hid his physical failing behind his Cheshire smile, acknowledging Congressman Lindsay Warren and Governor Clyde Hoey as he started his address. The president admired Warren's passion for guiding the nation toward a rediscovery of the state's hidden coastal jewel. Roosevelt needed Hoey's support as his New Deal programs showed signs of collapse.

"Until recent years, history was taught as a series of facts and dates. Today we are beginning to look more closely...." Roosevelt began his speech. VDee was bored as Sparrow hung on his words. Mil wrote in his notebook that gulls chanted above the quiet crowd as the president began to talk.

"....it is not too much to hope that documents in the old country and excavations in the new may throw some further light, however dim, on the fate of the "Lost Colony" and Roanoke and Virginia Dare," Roosevelt continued as Mil suppressed a grin, scanning the assembly for Dick, Parker, or even, Winslow.

Everyone he knew was displaced in a sea of humanity enamored by a president many saw as a savior.

Roosevelt's oration continued, proclaiming the rights of the middle class, rejoicing the pioneer spirit, how American democracy was unique in the world, and that majority rule is the vanguard of liberty. When the speech ended, the crowd gathered around the smell of fried chicken and fish. The president flashed his unflappable smile, saluting the audience with his ivory cigarette holder seized tight between his teeth as the caravan of cars made its way to Millionaire's Row across the sound to Nags Head.

"You ain't stayin', Mr. President?" Rawlee yelled from his tender station at the Roanoke Sound bridge, showing his anxiety as the string of vehicles in Roosevelt's motorcade crept over his bridge. Outwardly he was not the same old Rawlee; his mouth screwed up within the weathered lines of his face as if he was tasting something sour and unpleasant for the first time. His stomach in knots, he had the disembodied feeling of a man seeing a world he knew like the back of his hand vanish.

"When you come to the end of your rope, tie a knot and hang on, sir. I will be back tonight." The president nodded, sensing Rawlee's uneasiness, as his limousine approached Whalebone Junction.

40

⌘

Beyond Buchanan's Porch

The sun was painting its palette with evening colors as Roosevelt sat on Buchanan's porch, looking out over the Atlantic Ocean. Beyond the horizon, conflicts were brewing in Europe and Japan. He had pledged to keep America out of it. It was a promise he doubted he could keep. Fifty miles behind him on the mainland, a different brew crossed over the Albemarle Sound on a clandestine journey north. Sawtooth was uncomfortable with the run. There were too many people involved, too many boats, and too many moving parts to the operation to suit his liking. The plan was to hide in plain sight, running shine across the sound under the guise of quintessential watermen's life. Two boats had already ramped together at the mouth of Milltail Creek, one of them sinking, taking hundreds of gallons of East Lake Rum to the bottom of the Alligator River. A boat loader on another vessel had his leg crushed between an old mailboat and a makeshift dock at Buffalo City.

"Where the hell is the ol' crazy man who was at the church?" Sawtooth screamed his frustration, unsettling a dragonfly resting on a nearby lily pad.

"He wandered off. One guy saw him in front of an abandoned house near the rail track," Nick replied.

"Go get his sorry ass. And bring him here," Sawtooth said to Nick as the younger brother headed toward the red and white houses lining Buffalo City's fading wooden skeleton.

Nick found Sparrow's and Finch's father squatting in front of a decaying house, his snarled fingers digging into what was once a round flower bed, a half-empty jug of liquor resting near his feet. An image from his toddler years came to Nick as he remembered how his almost-forgotten mother had nursed yellow daffodils from a similar bed. Though he had been too small to see inside the plain box holding his lifeless mother, he slipped three wilted jonquils inside her coffin, confused by the coldness of her folded hands.

"What ya doin', old man?" Nick asked, a certain mellowness creeping into his tone.

"Memberin'," Ambrose said, forsaking the dirt in his hands to reach for the glass jug.

"Rememberin' what?" Nick asked.

"My wife, my young'uns. They ain't here. Don't know where to find 'em."

"Ya reckon that jug is gonna improve memory?"

"This where I buried it," Ambrose said, opening a rusting snuff tin box dissolved by the acidic soil. Inside was a small sand dollar, its perfection spoiled by a chipped edge, discolored touching its container.

"Yeah?"

"I gotta chain for it… made of pure gold," Ambrose said, showing Nick a thin necklace chain, "No one knows where she is. Asked everybody. No one knows, or they won't tell me, so I asked God, and he sent me down to the church."

"You get answers there?"

"Nope. God talked to me, though. I found the blood of Christ there, and the Lord told me to stay and tend to it."

"Seems ya have been drinkin' a lot of Jesus's blood, ol' man."

"God told me to. He said visions would come to me, and they did."

"What visions?"

"Don't know if God needs me to share. He wants me to wait for my wife and my younguns."

"Suppose they don't show up?"

"They will. Gotta trust in God."

"Ya keep swizzling hooch. There won't be no Lord's blood left."

"I don't know ya, brother. Mind y'ur business."

"Well, ol' man, what's in 'em jugs is my business. And I guess the Lord has sent me to bring ya home," Nick said, dragging Ambrose to his feet. "God, or maybe the Devil, is waitin' for ya down at the dock."

Ambrose grabbed his half-empty jug, unable to latch onto it as Nick herded him toward the waiting Sawtooth, leaving the glass jug sparkling in the afternoon sun beside the neglected flower bed.

Sawtooth held his brother in low regard. He thought Nick was weak, taking too long to do the right thing. And the right thing was what benefited Sawtooth. Nick carried emotional baggage, creating an indecisiveness that irked his callous brother. Nick sensed he shouldn't have brought the drunken shell of Ambrose back with him. Now Sawtooth had another situation to deal with. He wasn't in a generous state of mind, as he planned to turn an inconvenient shell of a man into a solution.

"Put him in the little Carolina boat with the rotten bottom. Take him out to the channel marker and chain the boat there," Sawtooth said.

"Why would ya want to do that?"

"Don't ask questions. Y'ur dumber than a box of hammers. Do what y'ur told and get this day behind us."

Nick towed Ambrose over the choppy water and tied the dilapidated craft to the marker. He had misgivings about leaving the old man stranded nearly a mile offshore. Though the water was shallow most of the way, Nick didn't think the wizened drunk could survive a walk or swim across the sound should the leaky boat sink. Nick handed him a battered fishing pole, a dozen spoiled shrimp, and a can of bloodworms to keep him company.

"Ya takin' me here to fish? The Lord needs men who can fish. Used to be pretty good at catchin' stripers. Caught a hundred once in an afternoon. That were a fine day," Ambrose mused.

"Have another fine day then," Nick said, leaving Ambrose alone, the leaky boat chained to the mooring. Nick didn't look back as he made his way back to Buffalo City.

"Ya get him there?" Sawtooth asked as Nick climbed on the dock.

"Yeah."

"Have plans for him if the need arises."

Sawtooth's demands were becoming less important to Nick. He was indifferent to his older sibling's brutal temperament. He missed Eddie. Though he would not acknowledge the black man as his younger brother, he felt the void of Eddie's absence. Eddie had a noble quality, balancing the wickedness of his older brother. Sawtooth turned other people's grief into money, and Nick followed his lead with a dimly aware conscious. Still, the cash wasn't enough to offset the misery of the constant conflicts enveloping them. Sawtooth had encouraged Nick to loathe and mistrust their fishermen's world. Nick's hate was turning inward toward himself and his bully brother. Nick had lived twenty-nine years and had little to show for it except a ragged scar on his left hand from a boating accident and a battered reputation among the locals.

"Three more boats ready to cross. I'll help 'em boys load," Nick said, wanting distance between himself and his brother.

Sawtooth dismissed his brother from his thoughts, walking to the dock where the Jersey man in the three-piece suit was studying a freshwater eel dangling from a set line of hooks strung along the makeshift pier. The long, grayish-green, snake-like creature twisted on the line, wrapping itself into a hopeless tangle.

"This place is filled with odd creatures," the man said.

"It's an eel. Ya either eat 'em or use 'em as bait."

"Yes. I am aware. They are quite popular in bars. I don't eat them myself," the man said, checking a dog-eared manifest.

"No problems so far. The last boats should deliver before midnight, and then it's done. No body the wiser," Sawtooth said.

"Make sure they avoid the Coast Guard as they transport Roosevelt back to Elizabeth City. Stay away from these cutters. We don't want to call attention to ourselves," the man said.

"Those pig-headed federals and police won't know nothin'… just some party boaters watching the president return home. When do I get paid?"

"Your men get paid when the last jugs are offloaded. As for you, I will handle your payment before I leave his horrid place. These insects are atrocious," the man said, hammering a mosquito into a bloody pulp with the manifest.

Further offshore, Ambrose watched water seep into his boat, his bare feet splashing a tune as he sang a mumbled chord of "Jesus Loves Me." Fish weren't biting. Henry Ambrose entertained himself by watching a tub of dead bloodworms floating in an inch of tea-colored water covering the bottom of his boat. Four five-gallon jugs clinked together, buried in a half bale of hay stored on the raised ribs in the bow. Ambrose thought the jugs were filled with moonshine until he saw no seals in the glass. He pulled a corn cob stopper from one. It puzzled him why anyone would store gasoline on a boat without a motor.

41

⌘

Raising Kane

Roosevelt's entourage of vehicles took the long way back to Manteo, cruising the nine miles to the Wright Brothers Memorial before circling back to Roanoke Island for the night's *Lost Colony* performance. The procession moved north on the narrow band of asphalt draped like a misplaced black ribbon running along the sandy expanse. The Atlantic Ocean peeked in through breaks in the dunes pushed high by the WPA and CCC to guard against storm-tossed over wash. Fifteen hundred workers, Milton and Jack among them, dressed in New Deal uniforms, planted beach grass, sea oats, cordgrass, and wire grass, to fortify the one hundred seventy-five-mile-long ridge of dunes along Carolina's coast, towering twenty feet above the surf in places.

The president learned Mil worked for the CCC, which landed him a seat in Roosevelt's limo. The reporter was uncomfortable with his elevated ad hoc presidential tour guide status. Parker and Mona thought it was a grand idea, overruling Mil's vocal resistance. He suspected Winslow had played a part in bringing him on this presidential ride. Mil had done his homework, but he wished he could be the walking encyclopedia Winslow appeared to be.

"We did it by hand, sir, shoveling in six hundred men teams to build up the dunes. When we got to the top, we smoothed it off and hoped it would rain before the wind blew it away," Mil said.

"Fine work, young man. I see the hard work served you well," Roosevelt replied.

"Locals like it, Mr. President. Flooding is not as bad as before. The storms still come across sometimes, though," Mil said.

"Where are you from, son?" Roosevelt asked.

"I grew up in Norfolk, but I'm from a small town near here called Hertford."

"How long did you work for the corps?"

"It was only the one summer, sir. I was going to move back here with a friend, but things didn't work out."

"Sorry, son. What happened?"

"His name was Jack Straw. He was a pianist and a good friend. He died in an accident before we could get back together," Mil added, surprising himself by bringing Jack's name into the conversation. There was no reason for him to do so. Perhaps it was some attempt to make Jack immortal by mentioning his name to the most powerful man alive. Roosevelt lit a cigarette as he passed the freshly painted white and gold two-story block building, trying to make a second go at becoming a nightspot. The word **CASINO** was labeled vertically down one rounded side.

"It's a dance hall, Mr. President. Upstairs dancing and family games downstairs. It used to be a dormitory for WPA workers when the Wright memorial was built," Mil said, happy to return to his role as a junior tour guide.

"Good to see the country come alive again," Roosevelt said, smiling through a puff of smoke as Mil nodded.

The president was sizing Mil up as he sat across from the reporter. Roosevelt didn't care for "yes" men and disapproved of people who sugar-coated information. Mil seemed to be a straight shooter. While the president had a terse relationship with newspaper publishers, he found reporters to be a different breed, partially because they elected not to print photographs of him sitting in his wheelchair.

"That is grand, the way it sweeps into the sky. The Wrights deserve their place in history, though Orville can be a tad difficult," the president said, chuckling to himself.

"Mr. President. May I ask you a question?" Mil said.

"Why, certainly."

"I have a friend who is a big fan of Amelia Earhart. She is worried about Mrs. Earhart's disappearance," Mil said.

"Eleanor and Amelia are good friends. I share your friend's concern for her safety," Roosevelt replied. "I have faith we will find her and her navigator Mr. Noonan. You tell your friend we will keep looking for her."

Mil could feel his face flush for the second time. Earlier, he had tried to plant the ghostly Jack's name in Roosevelt's head. It was out of character for him to ask people for anything, much less to urge the President of the United States to look for a vanished aviator.

The president's motorcade flowed past the towering dune called Jockey's Ridge, skirting the edge of the Unpainted Aristocracy as it passed the newly opened Sambo's restaurant, a pre-fishing breakfast stop for the sports fishermen increasingly descending on the Banks. The caravan turned right, passing the bare bones of a resurrected whale skeleton reassembled near the Roanoke Island causeway to capture motorists' attention to remind them to stop for gas.

42

⌘

Gold in the Creek

Roosevelt's limo stopped at the top of Waterside Theater, parking inside a specially constructed space so the paralyzed president could watch the play without leaving his car. Below him, thousands of people cranked their necks to glimpse the man, swatting bugs with their programs, many paying enterprising children a nickel to mist their feet with homemade skeeter spray. There was tension in the air. The play celebrated a nation rediscovering its first colony. Roosevelt presented himself as a national hero, the leader whose radio voice brought solace into the country's homes. The audience was unsure what to expect as the celebrated events of the past and the hopeful voice of the present came together on a peaceful August night.

"I wanna talk to him," Melvin Twitford from Colington said. "Somethin' I got to get off my chest."

"This is as close as you get," said a Secret Service agent, barring Twitford's approach.

It ain't right what he done. I had one bar, and there won't no need for him to want it," Melvin continued as two agents steered him away from the president.

"You need to leave," the agent said, grabbing Melvin by his arm.

"My gold is to do with as I please. Roo-see-belt has no right to take it. Came to tell him he can have it if he don't mind jumpin' into Colington Creek. That's where I chunked it. He can come get it if he wants to," Melvin said, disappearing in the backward embrace of the two agents. His voice faded on a velvety night as human conversations overcame the cadence of frogs croaking in the marsh.

"I knew it would happen. Someone just had to add their two cents on tonight of all nights," Dick said, thankful the agents had intervened. If Roosevelt heard the commotion, he didn't acknowledge it.

"I think it was more than two cents, Dick. Melvin had a pretty good chunk of gold, passed down through the Twitford family until the president made it illegal to own the stuff," Parker said, walking to his seat along with Dick and Mona, his usual drifting haze of cigarette smoke trailing behind him.

"All Twitford had to do was keep it to himself. He didn't have to throw it in the creek," Dick said.

"He said he threw the gold in the creek? Frankly, I doubt it. Seems he wanted to put on his own show tonight," Parker replied.

"Rocks are more trouble than they're worth," Dick said, watching Parker grin.

"Is that Milton sitting with the Winslow fellow over there?" Parker asked.

"I think it's more of Winslow sitting with him," Mona replied.

"Do you think your boy is telling him anything about the stone?" Dick asked.

"No, Milton would have told me if he had felt so inclined. I don't understand why Winslow has developed such an interest in him," Mona said, genuinely perplexed by the time the two spent together.

"Could be, our boy, as you call him, is destined for bigger things. Maybe Winslow is his ticket. He got him a seat in the president's limo today," Parker said.

The audience became quiet as the waters behind the theater curled on shore. A few random coughs from the playgoers peppered the purple sky. As the theater became hushed, a death cry rang out from the tree near the president's seat. It was a primordial noise causing people to jump. The sound had no less effect on the President of the United States. Unaccustomed to being surprised, Roosevelt rolled his eyes toward the scream and braced himself for the unexpected as a Secret Service agent whispered something in his ear.

"My God, they're going to shoot her," Dick said, losing his customary composure, standing up, facing the direction of the bellow. The beams of two flashlights held by Secret Service agents focused on Jeanette, who was wearing buckskin with her body turned brown and accented with lines of white paint.

"Hoola, Mr. Roosevelt! You made it back for the pageant," VDee shouted from her perch, one leg dangled from a tree branch. She giggled, taking her revenge on the leader of the free world for not eating his supper on her island.

"That was blood-curdling, don't you think?" Winslow said to a startled Mil sitting beside him. "Don't worry. They knew she was there. The country needs no more native blood on its hands."

"Humm," Milton replied, uneasy for Jeanette's safety.

"Adventures happen when we don't expect the unexpected. Don't need any adventures during this visit, Milton. His staff is well versed in handling city crowds, not so much the sandy back roads belonging to a fierce teenage girl," Winslow said. "I trust you had an interesting time with the president today."

"He smokes a lot of cigarettes. I suppose you had something to do with me being there?"

"Yes. You have firsthand insights the president wants to hear."

"I still don't know where you are coming from, Mr. Winslow."

"'*And I fell among some kind of committee from Elizabeth City, each and every one loaded with a gun,*'" Winslow replied, appearing to stray from the conversation. "Robert Frost wrote those words. It is an unfinished poem from his visit to the Banks."

"Yeah?"

"Frost came here as a young man running away from what he thought was a failed romance. He ended up on the Banks with a group of duck hunters. Bob came south to drown himself. Obviously, he didn't kill himself. He returned home and married the girl he thought he had lost."

"Don't know where you're going with that, Mr. Winslow."

"Perhaps nowhere, Mr. Kane. I suspect you are familiar with his poem, *The Road Not Taken*."

"Yes. I read it in one of the old magazines Sparrow likes to keep."

"*Two roads diverged in a yellow woods, And sorry I could not travel both. And be one traveler, long I stood and looked down one as far as I could,*" Winslow recalled a line from the poem.

"I know the poem. I still don't get your point."

"We make most points after the fact when they do little good, Mil. I need an assistant. Would you be open to the idea?"

"I don't understand. We agree on little, and I don't trust you. How is that supposed to work out for either of us?"

"Time earns trust, Mr. Kane. And I, like our sitting president, find it more appealing to be surrounded by people who don't readily agree with me. It keeps me aware."

The play started with light flooding the stage from the right. Two dozen men and women dressed in Elizabethan costumes sang. For a second, Mil felt disjointed, stranded out of place among the make-believe colonists, wondering what to make of Winslow's offer.

43

⌘

Fire Water

A flotilla of Sawtooth's boats gathered to transport the last East Lake whiskey twenty miles across the sound. Still several hours before midnight, Sawtooth drank from an open jug to take the edge off. He knew better than to drink too much. The money he expected to make would be enough for him to leave the Banks and start a new life for himself in the Florida Keys, eight hundred coral islands draped along a hundred and eighty miles of coral sea. The Banks were changing too quickly for his tastes. He needed a fresh start away from the meddling reach of Sheriff Ben Owens. He was done with Nick as well. His brother was another piece of baggage best left behind at the siblings' shagging Wanchese shack. Where he was going, Sawtooth did not need someone to do his heavy lifting, and he had grown weary of listening to Nick's sporadic moral qualms.

"There's boats out there that shouldn't be," Nick told Sawtooth as he climbed from his empty skiff along the Buffalo City dock.

"What ya mean?"

"It's a mail boat and a few smaller ones comin' down the Chowan. They have been sittin' there for an hour now. I pect we got revenooer company."

"I was reckonin' it might go this way. We got options."

"What options? We ain't towing the jugs behind boats where we can cut them loose and pick 'em up later. Our boats are low in the water, filled with moonshine," Nick said, pointing to the seven vessels scattered along the mouth of the Alligator River.

"Grab that 22 and a box of long rifle bullets. Got some target practice to do."

"Ya goin' to take on the law with a little popgun of a rifle?"

"Do what I tell ya and get in the boat."

Sawtooth looped the small craft around the river's main channel, shifting the motor into idle as he delivered instructions to his runners. The message was always the same. "Wait until ya hear a noise and see a fire. Space apart and make a beeline for the other side."

Nick was confused. The others seemed indifferent. Their payday was on the other side of the sound, and that was all they needed to know.

"Ya and me gonna hold off boatloads of feds with a 22 rifle? Don't seem to be a good plan," Nick said as the Pagette skiff sputtered at low speed along the nighttime shadows of tall cypress trees.

"Hand me the gun. It'll take a few shots for this to work."

"What the hell?" Nick said, staring in the direction of Sawtooth's shot. The small caliber gun made a faint echo, absorbed by the darkness of the night. Nick realized Sawtooth was shooting at the small, leaky boat where he had left Ambrose.

"You're tryin' to blow him up, ain't you?" Nick said, the night concealing the shock on his face. "Ya put him there on a boat of gasoline and straw. Don't make no sense. Gas won't blow up that way."

"Add some special potash, a little sugar, and a touch of sulfur, and it'll work fine. Got to find the sweet spot to light the purple fire," Sawtooth said, carefully lining the rifle's sights under the light of a gibbous moon.

"Ya could a blown it up without putting him there."

"Could have… more convincin' this way. No more crazy man to fret about. The law'll take an interest and stop. That's if there's a body left to see," Sawtooth chuckled.

Ambrose was dozing when the first bullet struck the gunnel of his decrepit boat above the water line. The bullet piercing the hull brought him back to near reality. Liquor had left his body, replaced by a dull headache. His lips were dry from the day's sun and wind, and he had a hunger for fried catfish. He loved his wife's cooking. He thought if he left now, she might have supper waiting for him as another one of Sawtooth's bullets freed the sulfur to mix with the potassium and sugar, sending a violet flame into the sky. The boat became an orange, blazing dot on the river as the mixture turned the marker into an inferno. The blast tossed Ambrose's frail form from the skiff ending his thoughts of his wife's biscuits smothered in black molasses.

"That'll keep them busy," Sawtooth smirked as the distant boats powered toward the burning hull. "Skedaddle to the other side."

44

⌘

The Walk

Rawlee sat alone at his bridge tender station overlooking the Roanoke Sound, Manteo ablaze with distant lights glowing from Green's drama. It was after 9 p.m. Roosevelt's security discreetly guarded the passage over his bridge. He frowned, reaching into a paper bag of scuppernong grapes picked from his backyard trellis. He crunched the burnished bronze orbs, releasing their unique flavor on his tongue as his teeth ground the bitter seeds into tiny pieces. Mil had told him the island's first English explorers said the muscadines were so plentiful they overflowed into the sea. Rawlee doubted it, even though Mil had become an expert on Banker history. Rawlee had gotten a cutting from the twisted ancient Mother Vineyard when he moved to Manteo decades before. The first three cuttings died. The fourth took root, becoming his gift from the island. He didn't know much about the Mother Vineyard's beginnings. It was another island mystery. Rawlee left those thoughts to people like Milton and Dick. He was content savoring the grapes' late summer sweetness.

"Just look at 'em. Flutterin' like a sparkle of lightning bugs. The island is on fire with lizards," Rawlee thought as he eyeballed the Manteo skyline, mumbled to himself as he finished the last of his grapes, and tossed the empty paper bag into his dinner box.

That summer had been heartbreaking to Rawlee. Though the money from his charters helped pay the bills, he found no comfort in the visitors invading his island. Living by the sea was challenging, but it wasn't complicated for a man like Rawlee. The bridges had stolen the Banks' simplicity. Mainlanders building cottages reclaimed from shipwrecks was a source of entertainment for him. But even that novelty had grown thin over the seasons, giving him reason to call outsiders dingbatters who poorly understood their summer getaways. Sportsmen making their way to the island were a different breed. They were men he couldn't understand and feared because of what their money might do to the Banks. These men had conquered human enterprise and sought to shellac nature by shooting geese and hauling in trophy fish while throwing back a glass or two of whiskey in the evening.

"That Mr. Roosevelt's car?" Rawlee asked, slapping on the tender station to get the attention of a Secret Service agent standing nearby.

"That's his car," the agent replied as the limo passed over the bridge with no passengers inside.

"What the hell? Where's the president?" Rawlee yelled through the window.

"Two of our guys are taking the limo back to DC. No way were we going to let the president cross that death trap of a bridge north of Kitty Hawk. The Coast Guard took the president back to the train depot in Elizabeth City," the agent said, appalled in hindsight he had shared so many details about the route. "Forget what I said. Let people think he is in the limo if they want."

"Got ya, cap'n," Rawlee replied, grateful the day was almost over, clinging to a small hope island life might return to a slower, less populated existence. As the limo passed, people stood and waved to a president who wasn't there.

Rawlee nodded a somber greeting to the new tender as his shift ended. Manteo was laden with vehicles, so he had left his truck parked in his front yard, not wanting to yield another foot of his property as an impromptu parking space for these outsiders. His walk to the bridge was pleasant enough that morning; however, now that he faced more than an hour's stroll home, he regretted his decision. As he left, he noticed a tall, thin woman walking across the bridge with a burlap bag cradled in her arms. The woman's steps were labored, yet, her purposeful stride suggested she knew where she was going. Rawlee recognized Eddie's grandmother, Delores, bent by age, hard labor and the cancer sucking her life away, white hair poking out from her bonnet.

"How's ya doin', Delores?" Rawlee asked, glad to see a familiar face.

"I'm doin' right good, Mr. Rawlee," Delores said, equally pleased to see a recognizable face. She smiled brightly at a man she had known for over forty years. Their two families had shared a loosely bound history of working for the lifesaving surfmen before the Coast Guard took over the service. The white man and the black woman came from a divided society. They were aware of the separation.

"I reckon y'ur headed home to California. Mind if I keep ya company til we part ways?" Rawlee asked, referring to the Black section of Roanoke Island.

"Be glad to have company, Mr. Rawlee," Delores said, adjusting her bag as she walked. Rawlee considered offering to take her load before abandoning the idea.

"Ya be workin' for those lizards over in Nags Head?" Rawlee asked.

"Busy night over there. White folks sure know how to party. I spent the day baking pies and fryin' up some flounder. They's havin' a fine time."

"Bet they is. Be glad when they take their fine time back where they came from."

"Sure 'nough, Mr. Rawlee. No harm is what they meant. They's takin' in the sea air and havin' 'emselves some spirits. They's nice enough to give me all this food to take home," Delores said. Over the years, she had learned how to deal with whites by flashing a ready smile and remaining agreeable no matter how disagreeable the other race might become.

"They's a-gonna get 'emselves killed with their mommucked ways. They stick their houses on the water's edge, askin' the ocean to gobble 'em up."

"Keeps food on the table, Mr. Rawlee. The Lord has a plan for all of us."

Rawlee knew he would not find a sympathetic ear for life's negatives from Delores. She had lost her husband Matthew years before, and four of her five children died in the times that followed from a fever. Her remaining daughter fell into the servitude of the Pagette brothers' father. Delores clung to being positive the way barnacles cling to the piling of a dock. It was the only way she could survived hardship. Rawlee envied her ability to accept heartache with a smile, not fully understanding her genuine reasons for doing so.

"What the hell ya doin' walkin' with a Negro, you ol' buzzard?" an unfamiliar head shouted from a passing car.

"Mind y'ur damn business, and go back to wherever ya come from," Rawlee retorted, the scowl on his face concealed by night.

"Don't pay 'em boys no mind, Mr. Rawlee. They're funnin' and don't mean nothin' by it."

"Mind if I carry your bag, Delores? It seems heavy."

"No, sir. I got's it. Ain't all that heavy."

"Delores, ya heard from Eddie? I knows he ain't dead cuz Mrs. Mona told me."

"Mrs. Mona's a righteous woman. She helped us after Eddie got in his trouble."

"Is he still in Norfolk?"

"I don't rightly know for sure, Mr. Rawlee," Delores replied, growing quiet as they walked. The balance between saying too much and saying too little was difficult to strike with whites. She knew she could confide in Rawlee, but candor didn't exist between the races. Saying nothing was her grandson's best protection. Eddie had risked returning to the island the month before to see her and his sister. Thanks to Mona, he landed well-suited for the docks of Norfolk, acclimatized to a new identity that was transforming Eddie from a quiet surfman into a hardened version of his former self. Sheriff Owens had seen him the evening of the play's first performance. Eddie feared arrest until the sheriff looked through him, granting pardon to an invisible man.

"Been a fair night cept for all 'em lights they strung over town knocked out the stars," Rawlee said, feeling regret for asking what wasn't any of his business.

"I pect things will quiet down once Mr. Roosevelt goes home. My momma told me the island was a mess when my folks filled it up durin' the Freedom War. She said there were so much commotion that people couldn't figure things out, so life went back to the old way."

"Your mamma was a good 'em, sure knowed how to crack a crab and shuck an oyster."

"Yes, lord. Mamma could cook. She fixed food for rich white folks up the river before the war started. When the men started fightin', she took her sisters and me a-floatin' down the Chowan to live on this here island. I'as just a little tadpole then."

"Must have been hard fur sure," Rawlee said, recalling stories Mil had shared of how Union troops had welcomed runaways during the Civil War, starting a Freedman Colony for former slaves seeking escape to an island protected by federal troops. After the war, the black settlement dissolved into another lost colony as the land reverted to its former owners. A few black families, such as Delores's, remained, buying marshy lots from whites willing to sell.

"Matthew was a hard worker. He hauled in more shrimp than any man I ever seen," Rawlee said, recalling how Delores's Matthew fell ill and died from an infection. Rawlee sat with Matthew as the disease coursed through him, sending his body into seizure-like spasms. Rawlee hoped there wasn't a separate heaven for people like Matthew. Rev. Boggs wasn't clear on the subject. Rawlee missed his old friend.

"Reckon this is where we part ways… Ya have a good 'em, Mr. Rawlee," Delores said, turning left on Bay Street as the weary bridge tender continued toward the bright lights of Manteo.

45

⌘

End of a Line

Nick was dumbfounded as he watched Ambrose's body blown from the skiff, splashing into the sound. He knew the boats waiting in the shadows upriver would come to investigate, giving the last moonshine runners an open route to their destination. Sawtooth was cruel, often for no reason, but this savagery was beyond Nick's imagination. He had helped his brother murder a man, leaving Ambrose to die on a rotten boat hull to make a diversion more convincing. A lingering vision of Ambrose's body ascending into the heavens remained with Nick as he uttered the words, "No redemption," under his breath.

"I'm goin' across… Gonna settle up with them Yankees. Take the truck and go on home. I'll be back by mornin'," Sawtooth told his younger brother as he eased his boat around East Lake and down the shoreline to their truck parked at Manns Harbor. Sawtooth had no intention of returning to Roanoke Island. He would take the moonshine money and head south until he ran out of land. Sawtooth had hoarded enough cash to buy a charter boat in the Florida Keys. He would hire a simple-minded mate who didn't ask questions and wasn't squeamish about fish guts and mop work. Sawtooth would be a free man, free to do anything he pleased in a place where he had no history.

"All right," Nick replied, wanting space between himself and his brother. Something had snapped inside him. It wasn't a good time to think. He needed to be alone.

"Be best if ya wait for the mornin' ferry. Slip back over and work on 'em ol' snagged nets til I get there," Sawtooth said, scoping the harbor for snooping eyes as he navigated the small boat into the broad sound.

"Right," Nick replied, walking unsteadily toward their truck. Emptiness grew inside him as he drove to Manns Harbor. His body didn't seem to belong to him. His stomach knotted with a sick feeling as he replayed his conversation with Ambrose. Nick looked at a distant Manteo too paralyzed by his own loathing to be startled as Finch shined his electric torch through the breath-frosted truck window.

"Why ya here, boy? Shouldn't ya be packin' fish?" Nick asked, trying to regain composure as his muffled voice passed through the closed window.

"I got a new job. What about ya steppin' out of that truck?" Finch replied, noticing but not caring that something was terribly wrong about the man. Nick had rolled down the truck's window an inch, his red eyes seemed to Finch to glow.

"No crime sittin' in this here truck. I ain't bothering nobody."

"Sheriff said to check anyone actin' suspicious. Ya bein' here this late fits the bill."

"Ain't ya heard? Tonight was special. The president came to town."

Finch had observed the moonshiners move their booze across the Alligator River most of the day. The sheriff told him to monitor the operation, not to interfere, and keep him posted. The forced inertia left Finch restless. Though he didn't pass judgment on people, the Pagettes were the exception, and he wanted to poke the bear; he had a score to settle for Eddie.

"Step out."

"Ok. I'm gettin'," Nick said, setting one foot on the ground to face Finch, who was a foot taller than himself. The deputy's light scanned a sheet of canvas draped securely over the truck's bed, haphazardly concealing a dozen jugs of moonshine. Nick could see he was being framed, another victim of his brother's greed. He realized Sawtooth was gifting him to the sheriff, turning another inconvenience into a diversion, another situation that Sawtooth's conniving brain simplified.

"Well, it don't matter," Nick thought as he reached behind his back, feeling for the revolver wedged in his belt, the thought of committing another murder weaving through his fractured mind.

"Ya need to go bout y'ur business. No time to be parkin" here," Finch said, his eyes meeting the other man's stare of disbelief. Nick didn't see how the deputy could ignore what was right in front of him. There were many things he didn't understand about this day. Finch reluctantly followed the sheriff's script. Owens had told his men that, for this one day, any liquid in a bottle was apple cider and to pay it no mind. Whatever the sheriff's motivation, Finch had learned to trust him. The outcomes of the sheriff's strategies appeared more reasonable after the fact than before, so he held his temper and looked the other way. To force Nick's hand would create the attention the sheriff had tried so hard to avoid the past few weeks.

Nick wasn't sure what game his brother or this deputy were playing. He was trapped like Eddie and the crazy Ambrose by his brother's schemes. Whatever the outcome, it wouldn't be in Nick's favor. The words "no redemption" formed inside his mind again as he watched the sheriff's car drive away toward an unscheduled Manteo-bound ferry.

It was Nick who now had a plan. He returned to Buffalo City and awaited his brother's return to the dock. Finch followed Nick unnoticed, his headlights turned off. Nick unloaded the twelve jugs of moonshine stowed in his truck, dropping them into the creek and watching each glass vessel disappear beneath the black water. He linked the jugs together by looping and tying a long cord of hemp rope through their handles, towing the bottles away from the dock, and anchoring the line of jugs to a net pole bobbing near the channel. Nick could hear a boat coming up the creek. He knew it was Sawtooth.

"Hello, brother," Nick said in a lifeless monotone as Sawtooth cut the engine's power, his boat bumping gently against the dock.

"What the hell are ya doin' here? Ya supposed to head home."

"I forgot somethin'."

"Find it and get on."

"There is somethin' out there in the channel. I need ya to check it out."

"Ya check it. I ain't got time."

"You'll want to see this."

"Let's get it done then. I need to put this money in a safe place," Sawtooth said, waving an envelope thick with paper currency. "For the time bein', I'm going to drop it in the fish box."

"I'll tell ya where to go from the front. I need to get up high to see the spot."

Sawtooth, confused and tired, followed Nick's directions, motoring to the pole that anchored the moonshine jugs. His fingers dipped into the chilly water, finding the rope and pulling a crystal flagon above the surface and handing it to his brother.

"What the...?" Sawtooth said as Nick crashed a boat paddle against his skull.

"Were ya there when they crucified my Lord? Were ya there when they nailed him to the cross?" Nick's off-key singing flooded into Sawtooth's thoughts as he regained consciousness. He watched his brother tie constrictor knots around his right foot with the rope, connecting it to the jugs Nick had placed back in the boat while Sawtooth had been unconscious.

"Ya lost y'ur mind?" Sawtooth asked, letting fear show, realizing these were the jugs he had loaded in the back of their truck to set up his younger brother.

"Nope. I need to purge ya from the earth, brother. Gotta be done," Nick said, pushing Sawtooth into the water over the skiff's stern. One by one, Nick returned the jugs to the creek as well, each one pulling a struggling Sawtooth closer to his watery death. His last word was a scream, garbled by a rush of air bubbles leaving his lungs for the last time as the sun bled into the morning sky.

"Oh, sometimes it causes me to tremble, tremble. Were ya there when they crucified my Lord?" Nick's voice had found poor harmony within the rhythmic sound of water lapping on the shore.

Finch rested his back against the grainy siding of a deserted house, trying to understand what he had witnessed. From a distance, he could see Nick and Sawtooth launch their boat down the creek, returning a short time later with only Nick in the skiff. He was ambivalent as to whether it was a calculated crime or an act of long-postponed justice. Finch felt indifferent toward these brothers, his book of secrets growing longer.

46

⌘

Tempest's Song

Hard-boiled eggs sliced on a China plate and tomato juice in a crystal glass waited on a wicker table by an open window. A stiff breeze fluttered chiffon drapes yielding to moist sea air and snapped the linen cloths on a dozen small tables. Mil, wearing a white suit paired with an azure tie, sat across from Sparrow, who was wearing a white lace crocheted dress. Sparrow touched his arm and cast a glance toward an open door. A slender woman seated at a nearby table studied the gray horizon's edge beyond the surging swells. Attired in her pilot's clothing, Amelia Earhart eyed the vista with a worried look.

"Your father. He is not coming home," she said to Sparrow before looking at Mil. "And your friend, Jack, He is over there, waiting for you."

"Mrs. Earhart! You are safe," Sparrow cried as Mil glimpsed Jack wearing Indian buckskins and dressed like an actor from Green's play. The specter disappeared through the dining room's ocean-fronting French doors.

Mil rose and followed him, seeing laundry blowing on a clothesline and a woman hanging up white lace dresses to freshen in the sun. It was Mil's mother, holding a clothespin between her lips, waving to him, motioning for him to join her. He walked toward his mother, looking down at his tiny, bare feet, realizing he was a toddler.

"Momma," Mil heard his child's voice call out as he tugged at her dress. He saw something white moving to his right where the smooth surf line stopped, and stubby foliage grew on the dunes. The creature was a deer as white as his mother's dress. The toddler Mil was awestruck, continuing to tug at his mother, wanting her attention so he could show her the doe. When he looked up at his mother's face, she vanished, and he transformed into the adult Milton. Jack was standing in her place, his hair shaved to one side, braided into a ponytail, white paint running horizontal lines around his face and body.

"You can't solve every mystery, and you can't undo the past, Milton. There is no future spending time staring into yesterday. Bury your sadness here," Jack said, pointing to the dunes.

"You're not real, Jack. Why do you keep coming to me?"

"I don't come to you; you come to me. Remember when the sand pit caved in, and I dug you out and brushed the grit out of your eyes? You cannot see with sand in your eyes and sadness in your soul. It is blindness that steals tomorrow — time for you to see clearly and not be a prisoner. Stop calling me back to you," Jack said, kneeling to scoop up sand so it could run through his fingers.

"*We are such stuff as dreams are made on, and our little life is rounded with a sleep,*" Mil said, remembering lines from Shakespeare's *Tempest*, kneeling beside his dead friend. "We read the play that summer."

"Yes. '*Let us not burthen our remembrance with a heaviness that's gone.*' Those were lines you read."

"Jack, I think I will leave the island. The island gives me peace, but things are changing too quickly."

"Changing? Sands come ashore and leave. In a thousand years, this half land will become a memory."

"Mil, are you here?" Sparrow's voice drifted to find him.

"I'm here," Mil said, seeing her standing in the open door, the scar on her arm red and angry.

"This is a dream, Milton. Don't worry yourself," Sparrow said, waving to Amelia Earhart as she left the room, walking across an empty beach.

"Yes," Mil said. He touched Sparrow's chin, bringing her face close to his. She welcomed his kiss.

"Oh, Mil, she's gone. I don't think anyone can find her," Sparrow said, the couple clinging to an embrace that wasn't real, their eyes fixed on the wing of a Lockheed Electra jutting from the sand like a shipwreck. The wing bore the letters CRO carved vertically down the twisted frame. Mil could see the letters glowing like sea sparkles on the beach as he opened his eyes from his dream.

47

⌘

Where Seagulls Fly

Deborah needed to speak her mind. She surprised herself by turning to Dick, realizing how a lifetime of shared memories had bonded them. It was a union of differing points of view glued into an elemental understanding of each other.

"We need a new spiritual leader, Richard. Mr. Boggs is gone," Deborah said as she ordered flour and coffee beans.

In Dick's mind, Thomas Boggs had served his purpose. His righteous voice made deals with the Devil in the name of a long-gone Virginia Dare. Dick wasn't proud of hiding behind Thomas's actions. He felt there was little goodness in the man. That knowledge made him question himself. He had turned a blind eye to the reverend's methods of bringing outsider interest to the Banks, avoiding consequences and guilt. He nudged Boggs to use his skills and flexible devotion to God to benefit his grand vision for the Banks. After all, Boggs was a hypocrite, a cartoonish figure, and a tool useful to bring growth to the coast. Dick, whose spiritual convictions hovered between belief and dismissal, pondered if his complacency might demand a price for his standing in the shadow of this vanished minister.

"We simply don't know where he went. Some folks say he ended up in New Jersey with the wife of a sawmill owner. That is not true, but...."

"The church don't want him back. I'm not judging the man; that's not the Lord's will. With these outsiders comin' in, Sunday service is growing. We need a shepherd who won't lose his way under a woman's sheets. I'm sorry. I shouldn't have said anythin'."

"Your opinion about Mr. Boggs is well known, Deborah," Dick laughed. "Can't say I disagree with you."

Deborah considered her judgment of Boggs sinful. It was an unrighteous contempt for a man she saw hiding behind a pulpit and making a mockery of her faith. His voice was sweet, and his Sunday words lifted her spirit while reinforcing her shame. Early on, she admired Boggs as a God-sent man to shepherd her church. As the years passed, Deborah saw cracks in his veneer, revealing his hollowness. She hoped the Spirit would reclaim him like Bankers harvesting timbers flowing to shore on the tide until she realized he was a shipwreck eroding into nothingness.

"What is goin' to happen to the island, Dick? So many changes. This is your fault, you and those Woods."

"I don't know why you are assigning blame, Deborah. Manteo is always going to be Manteo. Hunters come and go, fishermen fill their iceboxes, and families pick up a little sunburn and a few shells."

"Ya know what I mean."

"What will happen to our way of life when tourism takes root? More hotels, restaurants, shops, and visitors eager to spend. We've extended the welcome mat. Rolling it back up wouldn't make sense."

"Dick, we're of two minds. The day will come when these tourists do what storms have never done. Manteo will disappear under these paved roads, bingo parlors, and these dance halls."

"Deborah, this is where America began. People with big dreams have ignored Roanoke Island for too long. It's time for our island to dream big."

"Add a sack of cornmeal to the order. Out-of-towners have a hunger for corn cakes and grits."

"So tell me, is it true Sparrow has a job offer off the island?"

"Yes… from George Lyon, Ya know him, that gentleman from New Jersey who stays some during the year to hunt and fish. He has a hunting lodge on Hatteras."

"I know him. He used to hire Dave Driskill to fly his buddies to Hatteras from the Skyco airfield. Is she going to take the offer? Jeanette says Sparrow is thinking it over."

"I don't believe the Lord has put it on her heart what she should do. Dave says the fellow is a businessman who sells car bumpers. Mr. Lyon has been kind to Sparrow and me. He says Sparrow can stay with his family. He has four daughters at home."

"I don't think it is the Lord pulling at her heartstrings. It's that young reporter, Milton Kane."

"Ridiculous. Milton is almost like another brother to her. I see nothin' comin' of it. They are just friends."

"Perhaps you're right. But they do appear to have an eye for each other."

Rawlee stuck his head in the store's front door ringing an attached bell, letting Dick know he had customers. Dick was thinking of taking the bell down. Those quiet Manteo days belonged to yesterday.

"Yo, Rawlee. What Miss Mona got you up to today," Dick said, noticing an glow of excitement about the man, which usually signaled the *Independent's* next major headline.

"The Pagettes done disappeared. Nobody seen 'em in weeks. Their shack is empty, and their boat gone. The sheriff got called their truck is parked over in Manns Harbor. Owens and y'ur nephew are over there figurin' it out," Rawlee said.

48

Tangles

Sheriff Owens smashed the driver's side window on the Pagette's locked and empty truck. Its keys and a box were sealed with duct tape resting on the seat and labeled, "Give to Ambrose gal." The handwriting was crude scribble, but the sheriff recognized Nick's hand made the markings, having seen Nick's signature on the legal papers before.

"What's it mean? Your sister's name is on the box," Owens said, searching for an answer Finch couldn't give him. He reached into his trousers for a pocketknife to open the package.

"Makes no sense. I watched them at the dock in Buffalo City. They went out on their boat. Nick came back and sat there in his truck. There was no one around," Finch said.

"Odd," Owens said, pulling a note from the opened box. It read: "Give this to Ambrose kin. The man who kilted him is in hell. God gave him no mercy."

"Finch, I was waiting for the right time to tell you. I reckon that time is now. Two deputies from Chowan County found your father's body near a burnin' boat the night of the run. I got dental records from state prison this mornin'. Looks like he was drunk and set himself on fire."

"It don't matter. He can't harm my sister; she never has to see his face."

"There's $10,000 here."

"What you goin' to do with that much money, sheriff? There's gonna be questions."

"Questions are what I tried to avoid this entire time. No need to add 'em now. As I see it, you and y'ur sister came into some cash."

"I don't need money, sheriff. Let it go to Sparrow and some to Aunt Deborah and Eddie's family."

"Your decision, son. Stick the money in y'ur pocket. What becomes of it is up to you. Drive their truck to the ferry and take it over to Manteo."

Ben Owens knew Nick wasn't cut from the same cloth as his brother, but he couldn't escape his brother's influence. The sheriff had seen men lose their way through the seven deadly sins, and Sawtooth had been master of all of them. If Sawtooth was dead and Nick had been the killer, Ben saw it as the universe trying to restore balance.

It did not surprise the sheriff when Sawtooth's body surfaced on Milltail Creek two weeks later, tangled in jugs of moonshine lifted from the bottom of the creek by his bloated body. Death set Sawtooth's swollen face with a dumbfounded expression, or perhaps the sheriff imagined it since the marsh terrapins and perch had hollowed out the orbs where his eyes once were.

The Sheriff noted the knotted line tied to Sawtooth's ankle. The binding was not a random tangle. Each knot looped with a precision that couldn't have been an accident. Ben dipped his hand into the cold water, cutting the knots and letting the evidence sink to the tenebrous deep. As far as Manteo would know, Sawtooth got tangled in a string of moonshine jugs, pulling him under to a poetic justice.

Nick's fate was unsolved, leading the locals to speculate the creek also claimed him. Ben kept quiet. He thought he knew how the piece of the puzzle came together but didn't see the point in opening the box. The sheriff decided not to look for Nick just as he had not looked for Eddie. Owens declared the brothers' deaths accidental. In a few weeks, rumors so intertwined with the facts that it didn't matter.

Parker told Milton to dig out as much of the story from Finch as he could. The two men met on the Roanoke Island side of Manns Harbor. Milton had no questions and Finch offered no answers. They spent the morning skipping stones across a glassy sound, letting ripples tell the story neither one had the desire to turn into words. Milton remembered Frank's advice and handed three obituaries to Parker, stating facts without adding anything more. Parker was confused as he read the minimal copy, accepted it and dropped in it his incoming basket without comment.

49

⌘

Mother Vineyard

Jeanette Nancey was furious. She felt betrayed that Sparrow would leave her on an island she no longer ruled as she once did. She would lose the only friend who accepted her as a free spirit and who didn't judge her for being different. VDee couldn't fathom why anyone would willing to leave the island, which was a barefoot haven for her bold spirit.

"Why ya gotta leave?" VDee asked, sifting beach sand between two cups as the wind blew the crystal grains off their mark.

"I want to see the world up close," Sparrow said, determined not to second guess her decision.

"Ya can see what's important right here from Shallowbag Bay. Is it because they found your daddy dead in the river, and ya want to run away?" VDee asked, not meaning to sound as callus as her words seemed.

"Jeanette, I didn't really know the man who was my father. I feel no part of him. I can't grieve for someone who was never more than a bad memory. Aunt Deborah has saved enough money to open a house to tourists, and Finch likes his job. They will be ok without me. Aunt Deborah says I have no opportunities on the island except to clean rooms and cook meals," Sparrow said, leaving thoughts of her father's death in a private place sealed inside herself.

"And what about me? How am I gonna find a new best friend?"

"I'm not going away forever. Maybe I won't even like it away from here."

"You'd be crazy to like it anywhere else. This's your home. We're y'ur family."

"Me leaving will not change how I feel about the island or you, Jeanette."

"Then don't go. Stay where ya belong."

"That's it. I don't know where I belong. I need to find out," Sparrow said, realizing the past few weeks had stripped away some uncertainty and replaced it with the confidence she needed to find herself.

"Hmm," Jeanette pouted.

"Don't be that way, VDee."

"Don't tell me how to be. And what about Milton? Ya gonna leave him, too?"

"Mil has accepted a job with Mr. Jake. He is going to be a researcher and live in Washington for a while."

"Ya leavin' because your boyfriend is leavin'?"

"Milton is my friend. And…"

"And what? Ya two are chickens, cluck, cluck. Y'all won't admit ya have feelin's for each other."

"We have feelings, and we will not stop being friends."

"Do you love him? I see how he looks at you. He can't take his eyes off you. Both of you are stupid."

"I can't be what he needs me to be until I know who I am. I'ld hold him back, and he needs to explore without worrying about me."

"Answer my question. Do you love him?"

"I remember when I thought my parents loved each other. It wasn't enough. The man who was my father kept giving my mother less until he gave nothing. My father learned to hate himself. Everything around him became meaningless until he lost his way. My mother loved him but she couldn't heal him."

"You sayin' Mil is broken?"

"No. He isn't broken. He is not the same man my father was. I know he is strong. He is hurting inside. He has to find answers, and I don't know how to help him find them."

"If ya love him, find the answers."

"I can't. Mil has to find those for himself. What he wants isn't on the island. He has to find those things within himself."

"That's stupid, Sparrow. The island has all the answers anybody could want. If this ain't enough for you, for him, then good riddance. Go live in lizard land," Jeanette said as she bounced to her feet, throwing a handful of sand high into the air.

"Jeanette. VDee!" Sparrow called to her friend as the younger girl stepped inside a thicket and disappeared.

Sparrow felt a sadness to which she was unaccustomed as she took a long way home, walking north by the trellised rows of Mother Vineyard, wanting solitude to sort out her thoughts. Sparrow ambled beside the gnarled trunks twisted into a mat of interlacing branches, suggesting a timeless permanency. Beyond the vineyard's sinister first impression, it had quiet beauty where the sun rose and set over the sounds of Roanoke Island.

This scuppernong vineyard was another Roanoke Island mystery. Mil had told Sparrow the well-ordered plants were there before the first Europeans came to the island. The vines were unique, not the wild variety that populated the coastal plain. The plants existed before written words could explain the symmetry of their planting or the names of the planters who rooted them in Roanoke soil. The vineyard had yielded its bounty for centuries, leaving behind a scattering of dying brown and yellow leaves stubbornly clinging overhead until new buds returned in the spring.

"It's grand here, isn't it?" Mona said, startling Sparrow. "I didn't mean to scare you. Sometimes I take a moment for myself and come here."

"I do the same, Mrs. Mona." Sparrow smiled. "I like this place too."

"These vines are my calendar. Bare in the winter, budding in the spring, shady in the summer, and tasty in the fall."

"Mr. Garrett gives his Virginia Dare wine for the sacrament in church. I asked Aunt Deborah why Jesus's blood came in a bottle labeled by Confederate battle flags. She never answers, only shakes her head."

"That is funny, Sparrow."

"Milton thinks so too."

"Common knowledge you and Milton are leaving the island. Can't say I like it. You two are among my favorite young people. However, I understand life here has its limitations. I'm going to miss you."

"Going to miss you, Mrs. Mona."

"George Lyon is a proper gentleman. Still, I don't see you becoming part of his secretarial pool. I think you have something else in mind."

"Oh, I'm not. That secretarial position is what Aunt Deborah wants me to do. That's not for me. Mr. Lyon says I can live with his family and work as a secretary until I learn to fly. Flying is my dream. It has been since I first read about Mrs. Earhart."

"Good for you, young woman. You got to live your life on your terms. But what about…" Mona stopped short of asking about her relationship with Mil. Mona had had her share of "might have been" romances. She had found a man who let her be herself. Parker was there for her, yet their relationship came at a price. He had never been her soulmate; instead, becoming her life's companion, letting her keep her individuality and gender equality without smothering her. She loved Parker, but she loved the loyalty and freedom of their relationship more.

"Milton? I can't see that far yet. He has been my teacher, my friend, and the person who understands me. If I stay on the island, I will forever be a little girl, not the woman he deserves."

"You are more of a woman than you give yourself credit. Go fly, Sparrow, and see where the sky takes you," Mona said, giving her a firm hug, feeling Sparrow's tears against her cheek.

50

⌘

Salt in the Blood

A slight trickle of blood oozed from the crease of Mil's forefinger as he helped Rawlee pry mullets from a gill net trailing behind his boat. The brackish water turned the red flow into a faint pink stream, disappearing into a pile of fish flapping against the bottom of the skiff. His fingers would be sore the next day as he typed his last article for the Manteo newspaper, which would be his parting thoughts to a land and people he had grown to cherish.

Rawlee pulled tight on the sweep net, scores of fish splashing inside, trying to free themselves from the two hundred feet of webbing drawn in smaller and smaller circles on the choppy waters. The mullet fell from the net into a pile, thrashing on the boat's floor. Many jumped over the net or swam below the four feet deep mesh. The small boat settled deeper into the water as fish rose around their feet.

"Good haul of fish," Rawlee said, not expecting to find a large school of mullet late in the season. "You needs to toughen up those hands." He paused for a second before saying, "Maybe not. You ain't a-gonna to be around much longer."

"Rawlee, I want to try something different. I need to see more of the world. I'll be back."

"Ain't that what you said that John White told the colony in 1587… he'll be back, and three years later, there weren't nothin' to come back to."

"Seems you have been brushing up on your history." Mil grinned.

"Hard not to with all those smarty-pants lizards sunning themselves all over the Banks last summer."

"I thought you weren't paying attention."

"Heard 'em… I was listenin' when you were a-talkin' to the Winslow fellow. I didn't think you cared for the man's company, and now you gonna go to work for him?"

"I surprised myself a little. Winslow is a tough man to figure out."

"All those mainland people are beyond figurin'. Best keep your distance."

"He offered me a job, and I get to travel all over the country. The government seems serious about saving public land, and Winslow knows much about the country. I guess I want to soak up some of that."

"Ya can soak up enough right here. And that sweet little gal. Why would ya leave her behind?"

"I'm not. Sparrow and I are still friends. Besides, she is leaving too."

"So, I heard… Going to be a secretary for one of them bigshot sportsmen a-comin' to the Banks a few times a year."

"I think she has something else in mind, Rawlee."

"Drime. Ya two got eyes for each other, and y'all could have a decent life right here."

"We're standing on a pile of fish soon to bake in the sun unless we get them to Wanchese," Mil replied, wanting to end the questioning.

"I don't understand young folks. They run away from what they want and make it out as if they didn't want it to begin with."

"Not complicated, Rawlee. Not that simple either."

"It ain't none too hard to figure out if ya stop thinkin' with that artsy fartsy brain of y'urn and don't mommuck feelin's. And ya ain't a-gettin' back what ya leave behind."

"I can't erase the Banks from my mind, Rawlee. I wouldn't want that to happen."

"Nobody does. Still, I'm a-thinkin' you are goin' in the wrong direction. Don't throw away what ya got for what ya might get."

"It's a risk I have to take, Rawlee," Mil said, eyeing the sky filled with hundreds of black cormorants speckling the steel blue horizon, blanketing the air with low guttural grunts as they hunted for the next rest stop.

"Those damn birds suck up too many fish," Rawlee replied, beelining his skiff south toward Wanchese.

51

⌘

Footprints and Jellyfish

A bloom of beached jellyfish covered a stretch of shore south of Oregon Inlet. The creatures lined the surf, scattered in a layer reaching high on the tideline like jewels tossed up by the sea.

"They won't harm you," Mil said to Sparrow as they walked barefoot among the transparent sacks of glistening gelatin-like disks of marine life. The swarm had washed ashore on the cooling currents of the Atlantic Ocean, helped along by the winds.

"Mil. They will sting. You remember what happened last summer." Sparrow hesitated.

"Nope. Not these. They had the misfortune of drifting in. The tide may help some return, but most will become bird and turtle food."

"Then maybe we can throw some back in," Sparrow said, placing one on her palm and tossing it back into the ocean.

"Nature will stay its course. In a day or so, they will be gone."

"Sometimes we have to help nature along. Let's sit on the dunes, Milton," Sparrow said, unhappy with his answer. The couple scaled a rippled dune graced with sea oats rising a hundred yards behind the high tide line. A fleeting waterspout swirled through the artificial wall of sand, blowing over the land while the white crested tops of waves marched in from the sea.

The Gulf Stream mixed its warm waters with the incoming zephyr but failed to warm the oceanfront. Sparrow and Mil pulled their coat collars around their faces, protecting themselves from the chilly gale.

"Nature can be unkind. Why does God allow misery? Aunt Deborah says God doesn't take more than he will give back. She says people are too impatient to wait for his rewards. I want to believe her, but life seems more complicated than that."

"What do you think?" Mil asked, stirred by Sparrow's willingness to question what she had been told not to question.

"She says people are a disappointment to God's mercy. He leaves the door to Heaven open, and they're too stubborn in their earthly ways to appreciate his grace."

"You didn't answer my question."

"Milton Kane. I don't have the answers you do. It's more comfortable living in the moment."

"You have more answers than me, Sparrow. When life falls apart, you don't question it. You accept it with that beautiful smile and move on."

"Ahh…. What will I do when you're not there? You're my guiding star, you know."

"And you're mine. But it's the darkness in between the stars we have to make sense of."

The breeze made the sea oats' pointed seed heads rustle as Sparrow picked one of the scaly spikelets.

"You are not supposed to pick those seeds, VDee. They are the fruits of my early island labor."

"Oh, Milton. Don't tease me. I don't think I'm up for it today. My heart is full of missing this…. of missing you," Sparrow smiled, tracing the seed over his cheek,

"I'm leaving with Mr. Winslow next week. You'll be in Detroit by then."

"Yes." Sparrow released a sigh and continued to stare at the spikelet.

"I'll be in Washington for a month, and then we're going west to Wyoming. Jake says there is a place where colored pools of water boil up through the earth."

"So far away. I don't think any place can be more beautiful than here," she said, dropping the dried grass on the dune. "I will write to you every day."

"And I'll write to you too. I'll worry about you. I won't be there to save you like I did when you fell into the sound that first day."

"Don't worry. I don't need saving anymore, I think. My arm is strong, and I know how to swim. Once I learn to fly, I'll barnstorm to see you in Wyoming."

"Barnstorming is dangerous, but I know your mind's made up. Be safe. That's all I ask. Winslow says he has a special project for me once I have the experience to handle it. I don't know what he has in mind. He enjoys surprising people."

"He told me with his very lips that he would keep you safe."

"I see. You have talked to him about me."

"Mr. Winslow believes in you, Mil. He says minds like yours are rare, and you can do great things if you understand each side of the coin. I'm not sure what he meant."

"I think he was saying he is smarter than I am… and I guess he is right about that."

"You are the smartest person I know, except for God and Amelia Earhart."

Mil studied her face, searching for the 14-year-old girl he had met in the back of a delivery truck. She was gone. Her bearing and maturity had blossomed over the summer. Sparrow was ready to leave her little island; she had to explore the world without him. He understood why, yet he was savvy with her decision.

They walked along the beach back to Mona's panel truck. There was a gloominess between them, a melancholy they hoped time would soften into feelings easier to control. Her eyes followed him as he opened the vehicle's door for her after they stopped across the street from the hotel. She wondered how spreading her wings could equally break her heart. Mil slipped the silver 50-cent piece Winslow had given him into her hand.

"Will you keep this for me until we see each other again?" he asked, pressing his lips against hers, connecting a gentle kiss that brought tears to their eyes.

"Milton… I love you," Sparrow said, her words tumbling out.

"It's going to be alright. I'll see you before you leave," he said, adding, "I love you too," after he closed the truck's door and drove a couple of blocks to the newspaper office.

"Nothing I can do to get you to stay?" Parker said, pushing an empty coffee cup toward Mil. "There's hot water and some homemade bags of dry sassafras in the drawer."

"You don't normally offer me hot drinks in the afternoon. Policy change for employees?" Mil uncharacteristically joked.

"I don't normally try to keep my employees on the job. They stay out of habit. It seems your habits are in flux." Parker laughed.

"Part of me wants to stay."

"Then stay."

"I need a… to change."

"Yeah. You're a young man who wants adventure. I've been there. Be careful what you wish for."

"I keep my wishes at a minimum. That way, I'm not disappointed."

"And I thought you were upset with me for cutting out that bit about the Colington fellow cussing out Roosevelt for making him sell his gold."

"I'm sure he didn't sell it. I guess he tossed it into a creek because he didn't want anyone telling him what to do. People make a habit of hurting themselves to prove a point. And no, I wasn't upset. I expected you to cut that out of the story."

"Government for the people appears not to make everyone happy. You sure you want to be a government employee?'

"Quite a few Bankers are government employees of one sort or another. People enjoy the cash flow, but not the rules that follow."

"You aren't a rules guy, Milton. That surprised me when you took mystery man Winslow up on his offer."

"He's not exactly a federal employee. He's more like a contractor, which would make me one too."

"He is a sly character. He knew about Hammond's rock before he approached any of us for information?"

"I figured as much over the months."

"He's tricky. I suspect you can be as well. It's not too late to think about what you are getting into."

"I appreciate the concern. As you said, a young man's adventure. I'll be alright."

"No doubt. I wasn't concerned about you. More concerned with what you and Winslow may do to the country once you join forces. I'm kidding. You are a man of puzzling integrity who understands the value of a secret." Parker laughed, grinding the butt of his cigarette into his shell astray.

"I can say the same about you, Mr. Publisher." Mil grinned over his cup of sassafras tea.

"Sir Walter Raleigh didn't return to search for his Lost Colony? Are you going to be another Raleigh, leaving your treasures behind buried in the sand?"

"I think I'm more of a John White kinda guy. He returned, looking for his daughter and grandchild, according to Mr. Green's play."

"Raleigh left the exploring and colony building to the hopeful or maybe desperate middle class. I see you as a young fellow developing broad shoulders. We build civilizations on broad shoulders, not on the dreams of the self-possessed. When Raleigh got around to looking for the lost hundred and fifteen, all his rescue party returned to England with was a load of sassafras."

"I'm not that obsessive or committed. You've said not much of an employee either at times."

"A frustrated publisher is apt to say anything in moments of stress. Your concern should be with what Winslow has in store for you."

"Then I am glad Winslow isn't a frustrated newspaperman. I'll be alright. He has private agendas he keeps to himself, and the man is not above playing God with the facts when he deems it necessary, not unlike some people I already know. For whatever reason, he kept the stone a secret."

"We haven't heard the last of that damn stone. Even a bar of gold can be fished out of a creek if one knows where to look."

"Yes. This is true," Mil said, placing his empty cup on the table. "Maybe you can get the association to print slogans on coffee mugs, 'Outer Banks: The Nation's Best Kept Secret.'"

"Interesting, but no. People don't want to read the side of a cup."

"Maybe so. I guess I need to go. Winslow is waiting. Thanks for everything. You and Mrs. Mona have been more family than employers. I'm going to miss this."

"Good luck, Milton. Home is where the heart is," Parker said as the two men stood and shook hands. Mil opened the squeaky outside door. He wondered if this would be the last time he left his heart behind.

More than a thousand miles away, Sparrow sat beside George as he explained his love of slingshots and his plan to turn the Bahamas' island of Bimini into his personal paradise. She enjoyed his company. He was unpredictable and fun-loving. Sparrow had known the Lyons were moving to Detroit before she had accepted George's offer. She assumed her stay in New Jersey would be short, and short it was, as Lyon had brief business to conduct in his old home state before rejoining his wife and daughters at their new Detroit residence. To Deborah, any location further than Richmond would have felt like relocating to a foreign nation. Knowing her aunt wouldn't have approved, Sparrow didn't see the harm in delaying telling her about the 1,000-mile detour to America's city of cars, trains, and, more importantly, airplanes. Letters and the occasional phone call back to Manteo would give her aunt peace of mind, still unaware of her intention to become a pilot. Sparrow thought mastering the sky couldn't be so difficult; after all, Mr. Dave had taught himself to fly one afternoon when barnstormer Jimmy Crane left his Curtiss JN-4 Jenny unattended on the Skyco airfield. He had told her the Curtiss naturally found her way into the sky once he mastered taxiing.

From the train station, Sparrow could see the giant arrow sign atop the Penobscot Building pointing to Ford Field in Dearborn. Her excitement fueled her imagination, seeing herself dressed as an aviator and people cheering as she brought Amelia Earhart home. The grandiose vision made her blush, reminding her she had much to learn about flying and about herself before she earned her wings. At times, the fear of what she was doing was nearly unnerved her until she heard Mil's voice inside her head, encouraging her to accept any challenge.

"Is everything ok, dear?" Lyon said, concerned for the young woman who was out of her element.

"I'm fine. Thinking about Mrs. Earhart's disappearance. The world looks so small from the air. Maybe there is still hope she'll be found."

"It was a shock to us all. They may find her yet."

"I pray so," Sparrow said, returning to the world around her, noting a landscape of metal buildings topped by chimneys bellowing plunges of gray smoke. Sparrow missed home. Her anxiety gave way to excitement as the plane taxied to a stop, and she thought back to the Saturday matinee she and Jeanette had seen what seemed so long ago about people who ruled the skies. She wondered if VDee's gum was still under the seat.

52

⌘

Crossing the Sound

The air still smelled of morning rain. Moisture from the wetness lifted into the air leaving behind a crispness that would soon become humidity.

"Ben. What happened to the Pagettes?" Mona asked the sheriff as they ate a lunch of Vienna sausage and crackers on the Manteo waterfront.

"They disappeared, Mona."

"I know that, sheriff. I want to get the why and where."

"Ya writing an article for y'ur newspaper?" Owens replied, peeling the casing from the canned link of pork and beef.

"No, unless you have more to share."

"Ya in possession of facts I don't have, Mona?"

"I don't. I need to close that chapter in my mind."

"Don't think about it then."

"Ben. What happened?"

"I can tell ya what you've run in y'ur paper. Sawtooth Pagette's body popped up from the bottom of Milltail Creek with a line of moonshine bottles wrapped around his legs. It must have been an accident stemming from his illegal activities. As for his brother, he disappeared. Maybe an alligator ate his remains."

"There are whispers of more than that."

"What ya have, is enough information. The president's visit put the island on the map. Moonshining built a few hotels and kept food on the table for a few years, but those days are over. What's comin' is locals setting tables for lizards willin' to lay their money down, nothin' illegal 'bout that."

"Can Eddie come home then?"

"No. If he comes back, he won't be a surfman again. Too many lies have to be told and believed for that to happen. Eddie should remain where he is."

"It is not fair, Ben."

"We each got enough lines on our faces to realize few things are. If people are lucky, they can start over, reinvent 'emselves, and live respectable lives."

"It can't beat eating canned meat beside a dock littered with bird scat. I can see you're not going to tell me more."

"Nope. And yeah, hard to beat this high on the hog life," Owens smiled. "I hear your reporter is leaving today. He and that Winslow guy have passage to Elizabeth City on the Hattie Creef."

"Yelp. Not a regular run for the Hattie C. The perplexing Mr. Winslow pulled his invisible strings."

"I'll be glad when we see the last of him. Anyone askin' that many questions is meddlin' in business that is none of their concern."

Mona greeted Winslow and Mil with a hand wave as they approached the fuel tanks lining Manteo's waterfront cluster of wooden buildings. Mil struggled with his worn travel bag. Winslow walked beside him with the same spectral air that had haunted the town since spring. His style fascinated Mona, almost as if he could see into the future. She enjoyed the suspense but didn't care for Winslow's swagger.

"You gentlemen are taking your leave of us," Mona said, tucking Owens's and her empty sausage cans in a crumpled paper bag.

"Mrs. Woods, Sheriff Owens… good to see you," Winslow said, nodding.

"I got to go do the county's business. Good luck to ya, Mr. Kane. It has been a pleasure, Mr. Winslow. Maybe our paths will cross again," Owens said, moving toward his squad car. "Thanks for lunch, Mrs. Mona. Next time, my treat. I'll bring some potted meat."

"Milton, I need to speak with the captain for a moment. I will give you and Mrs. Woods time for your goodbyes," Winslow said, shaking Mona's hand before climbing aboard the black and white vessel.

"My, my… The years fly. I guess the hermit crab is alive and on the move."

"That sounds more like Parker than you."

"We have been married for so long; some of him had to rub off."

"Thanks for everything. You gave me a job and a home. I will always appreciate that."

"You turned into the best reporter and errand runner in our employ. We'll miss you, but not your spelling," Mona said, rising from her seat to hug Milton. It was the first time she had touched him in all the years he had worked for the newspaper. The hug felt motherly, and each was reluctant to let go.

"I'm working on it, Mrs. Mona. I am working on it."

"Have you talked to Sparrow since she left?"

"No. Her aunt said she got there without problems."

"It puzzles me that Deborah didn't put up a fight to keep her on the island."

"She might have if she had known Sparrow was going there to learn to fly airplanes."

"I think Deborah will be too busy to notice. That place she and Finch purchased is a real fixer-upper. They'll have it turned into a boarding house in no time, especially with Deborah's culinary skills."

"She can bake bread and fry chicken. That should be enough for tourist to beat a path to their door as long as she keeps the seafood hot and steamy."

"Milton. You left much unresolved between you and Sparrow, but I don't think either of you leaving the island is a mistake."

"Hope you're right," Mil paused, taking in the weathered townscape casting afternoon shadows. "Did Dick add purple martin houses to the top of his store?"

"I believe he did. He thinks those birds will keep the mosquitoes away from tourists. Rumor is the Lost Colony will play for another season."

"Winslow was telling me."

"You are a smart fellow, Milton," Mona said, placing a scotch bonnet shell in his hand, "…an empty shell for a hermit crab. No matter where Winslow takes you, this island is your home."

"That was the story Mr. Woods told me when I first came to work for you."

"Who did you think told him that story?" Mona replied, opening the truck's door and sliding behind the wheel, hiding her moist eyes. She watched Milton board the Hattie C., filled with fish and ice and carrying two explorers toward their Elizabeth City train depot destination. Mona hoped Milton and Sparrow would become like Dick's purple martins finding their way back to the roost when the time was right.

53

⌘

Queen of the Shoals

The Hattie Creef pulled away from Shallowbag Bay, plowing across the Albemarle Sound at ten knots. A familiar numb detachment crept over Mil. He wasn't thinking of the island; he yearned to see Sparrow's face and her empathic eyes.

"The Hattie Creef is the most famous vessel to cruise these waters. She is the one who brought the Wright Brothers and their equipment to Nags Head. That was over thirty years ago. The Hattie was in her prime then," Winslow said, watching the boat's wake trailing away from Manteo.

"Is this going to be another history lesson?"

"Depends on you. I share facts, remember. What people do with information is beyond my purview. I suppose you might see it as a lesson."

"And I gather being on the Hattie Creef is such a lesson? There are easier ways to get to Elizabeth City than cruising there on this old girl."

"You are perceptive as usual. That was one reason I offered you employment."

"What are you going to tell me about the Hattie C. that will connect the dots and make sense out of it?"

"Milton, you pick up information well on your own. You tell me about Hattie."

"Not much to tell. She has been around for years, hauling fish and bringing supplies to the Banks. The Wright Brothers made her semi-famous. Hattie doesn't know she is famous, so she humbly keeps doing her job until new owners come along and reinvent her again."

"That is true. The Hattie is a repurposed vessel. She was a sailboat gathering oysters from the sounds. Then the sail came down, replaced by engines, hauling passengers, mail, and freight, linking Elizabeth City with almost every Banks community until the Wrights bought passage. Sources then become conflicted, let's say. Did the Hattie or its bigger cousin, the Trenton, deliver the parts that took the brothers into the sky? Diaries, journals, newspapers, public records, and people's memories seldom perfectly align. That is how folklore begins with hazy recollections. People redact the words until the story becomes an event different from what happened."

"Does it matter which boat they were standing on? They came here to fly, not sail."

"Not unless the vessel becomes a symbol. There is no going back once symbols take meaning and become more important than the fact. Say, one day, the Hattie Creef becomes a museum piece, or she might end her days rotting on the side of the road."

"It would be nice to see her as a museum piece and a tribute to the watermen. Good fit for tourists, giving them a peek into the past."

"We are all tourists when it comes to understanding the past. We visit what might have been and pretend to know what was."

"I didn't expect you to be so relaxed about bagging the facts. You seem as comfortable with fuzzy details as others I know."

"You would be incorrect. Facts must be preserved. Every generation decides what is relevant."

"Are we talking about that stone?"

"That stone is clouded in its own mystery. I was referring to the Hattie Creef and how the vessel struggles every day to adapt."

"She seems hardy enough today except for the smell of seafood coming out of her."

"She is on course to become a symbol, and symbols aren't the property of wood, paint, and rusty nails. George Washington Creef wanted a new type of boat on this shallow inland sea, and he built it. He didn't count on internal combustion engines changing designs, leaving his little Hattie C. to adapt as best as she could. He didn't build it to survive the passing of time. It is up to people like us to transform her from a wooden work boat into something more. There are many of these projects across the country, tangibles waiting to be impressed on our nation's conscience."

"You want me playing with the country's mind, huh?"

"Again, you would be mistaken. The Hattie Creef is a symbol of the Banks, crafted from reclaimed shipwrecks and white cedar timbers, mixed with fish blood, dusted with sugar to feed stills near Buffalo City and to support the wobbly legs of day trippers. The Hattie C. has many chapters and is cruising toward the end of her story. How the vessel's journey concludes is unknown. She plays a role in her own demise."

Mil listened to Winslow; his eyes fixed on the school of fish paralleling the boat as the skiff neared the dock. He looked back; no Banks or Roanoke Island was on the horizon. There was a feeling of deja vu. He felt the same disconnection that haunted him when he arrived on the island.

"Hey, mister. Would ya like to buy some crabs? They're real cheap. My daddy says I can sell 'em and keep the money," a boy, who looked no older than eight, said as he poked at the creatures with a stick, clawing back at him from a tin bucket.

"Need some candy money, I'm thinking? Tell you what, take this nickel and buy yourself some when we get to the dock. Call it a tip for services rendered," Mil said, handing the grinning kid the coin.

"What's a tip, mister?"

"A new way of doing business on the Banks," Mil replied, registering the boy's joy as the child slipped the coin into his blue jeans pocket.

54

⌘

Look Deeper

Winter turned to spring as Mil settled in as Winslow's assistant. Jake's seemingly self-absorbed reserve and cryptic nature labeled his eccentricities. It was his way and not a way everyone viewed as charming or disarming. In private, Mil had peeled back much of Winslow's public veneer and, to his relief, discovered a man humbled by what he didn't know, admitting his gaps of knowledge were vast and disheartening at times. Winslow was mistrustful of anyone too eager to offer their opinions. He was an agent of FDR's New Deal, a hunter of the country's national treasures stored in old attic trunks, dusty bookshelves, conversations, and dirt roads leading to nowhere. Winslow's specialty was cultural geography; he studied how humans interact with natural landscapes to create cultural landscapes. It wasn't hard science. Fearful America might fall to communism or be smothered under the dust bowl that blanketed the county's heartland, the government considered it worth investigating. Winslow believed these hidden treasures of geography and culture could energize national pride by celebrating "...*Spacious skies... purple mountain majesties above the fruited plain.*" He reasoned the country's spirit might benefit from developing national parks and polishing the past by erecting monuments where American dramas outlined the boundaries of 48 states. His plan, or perhaps the plan of those he reported to, was to keep the country from becoming a land of roaming homeless by steering middle-class families into station wagons guided by service station road maps and enough money to spare to recharge the country's economy.

Mil wasn't a fan of the political agenda attached to his new job, but Winslow had the independence that acknowledged no master. His decisions and directions came from a power beyond the red tape and regulations of institutions he worked for and didn't always obey. The dapper gentleman was a man on an almost clandestine journey, adding to a national book of curious unknowns and unresolved. Winslow opened his trove of discoveries if he found others worthy. He welcomed Mil into his fold and was fond of mentoring the like-minded younger man. Winslow had somehow gotten Mil on the National Park Service's payroll as an interdisciplinary archeologist, having himself assigned as Mil's private contract liaison. Winslow's involvement with the service dated back ten years before the organization had a formal name. Whom Winslow reported to was a mystery.

As much as Mil wanted to unearth Winslow's connections with the government, he had learned from Rawlee there was no reason to stand up in a two-person boat unless the intention was to fall overboard. Exploring the country's heritage was challenging enough. Mil's regular nocturnal visits from Jack were becoming less frequent. Mental images of Sparrow's understanding face had replaced the ghostly apparition with a pining serenity. One hole in his psychic was closing while the vacancy left by his separation from Sparrow grew.

Sparrow adjusted quickly to her new life, spending some days watching the Michigan Air National Guard soar in formation over the Wayne County Airport. The benefit of having four "adopted" sisters to introduce her to city life was a welcomed advantage. Her duties in the secretarial pool were less demanding than cleaning the rooms of overindulgent fishermen on holiday, and her typing speed passed sixty-five words a minute. The faded scar down the length of her arm fascinated her new sisters. The old wound reminded Sparrow of a fractured childhood, a roadmap of her past that she had somehow turned into a source of strength. The remembrance no longer brought her anguish. She was free to roam the sky. Her instructor said she was a natural. Yet she missed the Banks and Milton no matter how effortless it became for her to taxi an airplane on a runway and climb into the Michigan firmament. Some days she looked down at Lake Erie, seeing herself flying over the Atlantic Ocean, make-believing Lake St. Clair's vessels were shad boats returning to Wanchese with the day's catch, squinting to transform Erie's islands into the sandy banks of home.

In the beginning, there was a regular flow of letters between Sparrow and Mil, much like the ebb and flow of ocean tides. As often as twice weekly, the post office delivered letters reading like diary entries recapping their days apart. And then there would be nothing for weeks as the postal service had difficulty with Mil's travels across the country. Neither Sparrow nor Mil penned the depth of their feelings to each other in the three-page testaments. Sparrow had included a black-and-white photo of her receiving her pilot wings. Mil had sent a newspaper clipping of him talking to a Tukudika child as he and Winslow interviewed a band of Shoshone living in Yellowstone National Park. He wrote in the clipping margin, "No stone unturned," which made her laugh before she suppressed the sound to keep her "sisters" from hearing. Ever mindful of his surroundings, Winslow gave Mil sheets of photographic acetate to protect what was becoming a dog-eared photograph of his favorite aviator.

"Protect what is important to you. Don't let life wear it into nothingness," Winslow said one morning as the two shared a cup of coffee along the shores of Yellowstone Lake.

"Where did that come from?" Mil replied, reaching for the cup of hot liquid Winslow had somehow favored with a sassafras root.

"It comes from a place I can never visit again. The heart wants what the heart wants."

Mil knew Jake must have been talking about his wife and sipped his drink in silence, leaving Winslow to the privacy of his memories.

55

⌘

Town on Fire

Storms could tug at roofs and fill streets with the rising waters of a flooding sound, but townspeople were not fearful of them. What the town was afraid of was fire. Gasoline, not sails, pushed most vessels out to the spray of waves and rolling water. Manteo was a village of weathering wood; its waterfront anchored by Texaco and Standard Oil gasoline storage tanks.

The fire started with a flickering glow inside Standard Oil's warehouse at 5:40 a.m. Rawlee had been up early to greet the September morning. He wasn't bridge tending, and there were no newspaper errands for him to run on this Monday. He had checked crab pots in Scarboro Creek and shared his catch with Deborah in exchange for a pot of her homemade crab bisque. Her boarding house had become popular in the years since Sparrow had been away from the island, partly because of her cooking and the word-of-mouth advertising offered by her well-traveled deputy nephew. Rawlee was on his way to the siren box when the first blast sent orange fireballs skyward, bringing Manteo residents to their feet.

"This is gonna be a mommucked drime," Rawlee yelled as Dick ran out of his store, covered in a white dusting of flour accidentally spilled from a broken sack.

"We got to get folks out of harm's way. Knew those damn tanks were a hell waiting to happen," Dick said to Rawlee. "If they're not already awake, knock on doors before these flames spread."

The inferno engulfed three-quarters of the waterfront as local firemen battled the blaze, many in their pajamas. Dave from Skyco field flew over the black smoke, taking pictures of the scene before landing his craft, enlisting the aid of the National Park Service and the Coast Guard to fight the fire. A call had gone out to the Elizabeth City and Norfolk Fire Departments, each station too far away to offer quick aid to an impatient conflagration. It wasn't until fifty boys arrived from the nearby CCC camp on the island's north end that the destruction showed promise of ending.

Townspeople dumped the contents of their buildings in the streets as red-hot metal fragments and wooden embers rained down onto the town's rooftops. Men with rifles shot holes into storage tanks to drain them, hoping to keep them from exploding as CCC boys climbed overhead, ripping away burning shingles to hold the fire in check. By the time Norfolk firefighters arrived, twenty-one buildings were in ashes. Manteo's waterfront looked like a bombed-out village as the inferno faded into tiny flickers by noon. People stood along the streets of a vanished harbor, shocked by events that had not taken a single life. As one newspaper reported the next day, "It was Manteo's morning to burn and nobody's day to die."

The town was swift to recover from the destruction. CCC boys stood guard against looters, hauling the street-littered contents of homes and stores back inside, clearing away the charcoal remains of Roanoke Island's third lost community. Rebuilding began within weeks; this time, bricks replaced much of the wood, and a new downtown rose, speeding up Manteo's transition from a quaint fishing village to a town adapted for tourists curious to get a first-hand look at how the village survived the fire. Manteo was reborn, a blending of the old and new.

The play was in its fourth season, and tourism had replaced the smell of fish along the town's waterfront. Locals perfected the art of hospitality, selling goods and services to outsiders entertained by the raw novelty of crashing waves and foot-burning sand.

In a broad sense, life on the Banks was unchanged. Bankers harvested seafood, braved the elements, survived the Atlantic's storms, and found communion through worship and Sunday picnics as they had always done. The footfalls of excited, sometimes temperamental tourists tamed the waterfront, replacing fish blood with dropped cones of ice cream. Winter months remained a quiet time for the Bankers as they prepared for the annual summer crush of visitors from across the bridges.

The growing throng of visitors became too much for people like Rawlee. He decided to live out his days near where he was born a hundred miles down the barrier islands. He knew it would be a matter of time before bridges and tourists discovered his hideaway. Still, he figured that time wouldn't come until he joined his ancestors under the coastal sands. Jeanette and Parker were other casualties of change. Dick decided as long as Jeanette roamed the island, no one would be safe from her impulsive nature. He sent her two hours inland to Greenville to study at East Carolina Teachers College. Once she graduated, he told her she could return to her island home, expecting life among the mainlanders might tame her.

There was no bargain of compromise for Parker. His love of cigarettes had destroyed his lungs on the eve of his bi-weekly newspaper going daily. He took his last breath, inhaling a smoke Mona had secreted into his Norfolk hospital room. The couple smiled at one another as Mona rested the unsmoked tobacco on his familiar seashell ashtray. She held his hand as its warmth drained away. Mona wasn't sure how she would keep the *Independent* afloat. It was her hard work that had built the newspaper and given it spirit. But Parker was its voice, and now that voice was silent.

56

⌘

Overwash

Mil's eyes strayed off the highway as he and Winslow drove south. There was something magical about mountains. They climbed upward almost looking like waves on a stormy, misty day.

"I believe we made a mistake," Winslow said, rifling through a stack of papers in his briefcase before selecting one and reading it.

"What mistake?" Mil asked, absorbed by the road as he drove south, away from the White Mountains. He realized they were going toward Worcester, less than thirty minutes from where Jack grew up in Westborough.

"I think we have shortened its lifespan. Yet, I don't see any other way," Winslow replied as if talking to himself.

"You going to tell me? I can't guess."

"I have been thinking about the Outer Banks a great deal recently. Stabilization of the surf line may hasten its demise."

"I don't see it. Those dunes block overwash and save the paved roads and real estate, right?"

"The Banks retreat toward the mainland as they have for eons. During storms, water and wind migrate sand to the sound side. Those artificial dunes reduce the number of breaches, so the sand doesn't move across as it once did. Instead of retreating, the Banks wash away."

"That won't happen anytime soon."

"Probably not. Nor'easters dragging buildings into the ocean or tossing them about on the shore like chess pieces. The more development, the more likely tragedies will occur."

"The ones that seem to endure are the Unpainted Aristocracy. I think they have a pact with the ocean. Islanders said the tide of mainlanders don't understand or respect the Banks. It hasn't stopped them from building."

"We have to buy it all. That's the solution. Buy every grain of sand available and make the Banks part of a national seashore park."

"The government will have to purchase a good deal of barrier island land first. And the government rarely spends money on park land. Who will donate the land? Local people don't trust the Service."

"…which brings up another topic. Would you be willing to go home and save the Outer Banks from its new notoriety?"

"What?"

"The Park Service wants a man who understands the issues there. I have told them you are such an individual, and they agree. It seems you have people in high places who remember you."

"I left the Banks to travel, learn more about how things work."

"And you have been successful. It has been over three years since we began working together. You know how things work. Your assignment would be to build a rapport with locals and newcomers and make them partners to expand a national seashore."

"That is not a doable job. And why would I want to go back?"

"My young friend, most of you never left. Your thoughts are still in Manteo."

"I don't think so. It was never about Manteo. It was…"

"I know Miss Ambrose is on your mind, and she is in Detroit. I have heard she is quite an excellent pilot. I'm afraid that women cannot afford to be less than excellent to survive in a man's world."

"Yes, she's on my mind. I want the best for her. She's doing what she loves, finding herself," Mil said, fingering the golden-brown seed Sparrow picked during their last walk on the beach together.

"Perhaps it is time for her to stop dwelling on Mrs. Earhart. The rest of the country has."

"I don't think Sparrow would ever stop looking for what she believes in. And she has always believed in hope."

"I expect you are correct. Miss Ambrose is too smart to be a victim of impracticalities. She is tougher than you are, you know. There is a line between being a romantic and a shortsighted dreamer. I think she knows the difference."

"My friend, Jack Straw, the one I told you about, grew up in Westborough. Can we take a detour?"

"Certainly. The afternoon is yours if you don't mind me tagging along."

"I don't mind," Mil said as he saw the turnoff to Westborough State Hospital, realizing the word "Insane" was no longer part of its name. Whatever ghosts and memories Mil thought might exist at the hospital had vanished. The Colonial Revival campus, scrubbed of its earlier stigma, was no longer the chamber of horrors it was to Jack, no longer a prison with secrets locked behind thick concrete walls. How deep was the hospital's makeover? Mil was clueless, his opinion of the facility tainted by stories Jack had shared.

"Your friend Jack came from a well-connected family. Old money has a cruel way of dealing with members who stepped outside the lines."

"Jack's grandfather was a monster. He abandoned his daughter and grandson to rot here."

"True. But there is more to the story."

"Of course, you would know that. Does everything hold your curiosity to the point of irritating your listeners?"

"I want you to see something. Turn here," Winslow said with Mil following his instructions to stop the car.

"Jackstraw Road. I don't understand."

"Oh, there are other places nearby too… Jackstraw Brook, Jack Straw's Hill. Jack Straw Pasture, all here in Westborough."

"You're telling me my friend Jack has history here."

"Well, not your Jack directly."

"What do you mean? What is the point of this?"

"I can't answer that question. Jack's mother was the child of a Boston socialite who spent her falls and springs on the Banks, reading and walking on the sound side beaches while her parents' shot ducks in the winter and partied in the shoulder seasons. Jack's mom didn't care for the beach up close, but she loved the idea of it. She collected folklore and seashells during her visits. The shells went in an attic box, and journals preserved the stories she collected. I discovered them in an old Nags Head cottage. I will share them with you once we are on the train."

"I'm confused. You ran across journals written by Jack's dead mother, and you somehow held on to that information until you could link it with me?"

"No. That makes you sound way too self-important." Winslow grinned as the two men walked along Jackstraw Brook. "It was the name she used for her journals, *Legacy of Jack Straw*.

"Why would Jack's name have any special meaning for you?"

"That is why we are here. Jack Straw is an old, rather unique name. According to Governor John Winthrop, one founder of the Massachusetts Bay Colony, Jack Straw was an Indian who had lived in England and served Sir Walter Raleigh. He served as Winthrop's interpreter and was regarded as a Christian convert. According to records, Jack survived a shipwreck off the Massachusetts coast."

"You're telling me Jack Straw was the Indian Manteo? How can that be?"

"I'm not saying he was Manteo. I am saying there is a possible connection. John White's colony had a pinnacle that could have transported half of the colony up the coast to the European fishing grounds or across the ocean for England if they were under duress."

"Seems like a stretch."

"Stretch is the nature of all folktales… a seed of truth mixed in with speculative storytelling. One legend had it that the pinnacle sailed up the Chowan River, running aground in a shallow creek on its way to the Chesapeake Bay. There is another thought part of the colony headed up the coast and were shipwrecked near Massachusetts. There is no mention of Manteo outside of Winthrop's journal once the Lost Colony disappeared."

"This could be big if we uncover other sources," Mil said, not listening to the conversation, his mind rambling through his own personal history.

"No bigger than a stone you and your friends tried to deny. No more challenging than the Lumbee Indians, who are certain they are the mixed descendants of White's colony, no more bizarre than a dozen other explanations. Sometimes the mystery is simply too good to spoil with a definite answer. I think the Lost Colony is one of those cases."

"Jack's mother picked up on the Jack Straw legend, wrote about him in her journals, and named her illegitimate son after him?"

"Seems to be so. Occam's Razor, the simplest solution, is almost always the best."

"You're suggesting I have spent my adult life trying to find Manteo?"

"I think you found Manteo the first day you crossed the bridge. It just took you a while to make sense of it."

"Maybe I did… maybe it's time I go home." Mil swallowed hard, but the lump in his throat wouldn't disappear. He had never thought he would return to the Banks and now he realized that perhaps there is where he belonged.

57

⌘

Going Home

Mil and Winslow said their goodbyes at the Washington Union Station, with the understanding Mil would lead the National Park Service's quest to expand the country's first national seashore. The barrier of sand wedged between sound and sea was inching toward becoming public lands protected from developers intent on carving the beach into smaller and smaller parcels of vacation getaways. Mil accepted his new job as a mission to help save the Banks from the human expansion creeping over the barrier islands.

It was a chilly day outside of Fort Eustis, the largest WPA camp in the country, charged with delivering material to the Banks. Dave Driskill's Roanoke Island Flying Service had cut the two-and-a-half-hour drive to the Banks to less than an hour's flight. Mil expected to see him pop out of a hangar to fly him to Skyco Field at Manteo. He looked forward to seeing the Outer Banks from the sky.

"Mr. Kane. I see you have a flight to Manteo today. Mr. Driskill is making a supply run to Hatteras. He should return in a few hours. There is a place to get a bite to eat on the other side of those hangers. You can wait here or there if you wish," said a young man working the reception counter.

Mil tried to remember when he had last eaten. He was sure it was on the train yesterday. His stomach was uncertain.

Scrambled eggs, toast, and a cup of coffee might quiet the rumbles, so he headed toward the cafe. Though he had flown across the country a dozen times with Winslow, this trip would take him home with the fresh eyes of experiences he had gained traveling with the enigmatic scholar. Winslow's purpose was sometimes unclear, but Mil had grown comfortable with the man's intentions. Winslow's manner could unsettle people with secrets to hide and be disarmingly polite for those who wished to share them. He had stood in the man's shadow, learning to tease riddled meaning out of obscurity. Now he was on his own, flying to his adopted home with new purpose.

Winslow had convinced him the Banks needed protection, and he had volunteered for the job. A fight would likely come that he might not win. Mil could no longer sit back as a passive listener. What he might have to do could strain old friendships. He couldn't see that far ahead. Mil had chosen this direction, and the challenge was to keep the untamed sands from the human grip that might subvert it into a crowded tourist trap. He had wholeheartedly bought into the Park Service's motto to "preserve unimpaired the natural and cultural resources and values of the National Park System for the enjoyment, education, and inspiration of this and future generations." Mil thought the wording sounded grandiose, a pretension that needed to be changed if the Outer Banks were to endure the ravages of human development.

Mil sat by a large multi-paned window overlooking the bustling airfield. Unlike the scene outside, the cafe was quiet except for a pilot sitting at the counter, dressed in a flying suit with loose trousers, a zipper top, and oversized pockets. A brown faux suede helmet adorned their head, suggesting the pilot was preparing to leave. Mil noticed a large thermos resting on the counter to the pilot's right, enough coffee to keep the aviator company on a long journey.

"I'll have two eggs and some toast," Mil said. The waitress had assumed he wanted coffee and placed a steaming cup in front of him. He was puzzled that the brew lacked the hardy jet black of a bold roast.

"Compliments of that pilot," the waitress said, nodding toward the counter as Mil's nose sorted out the distinctive smell rising from the cup.

"Hope you still have a taste for sassafras," the pilot said, sliding off the counter stool to face Mil.

Mil's heart hammered. His tunnel vision fixed on Sparrow. She was an incarnation of a lost heroine.

"You need a lift to Manteo," she smiled, not moving from where she stood.

"I do. And I see you found her," Mil said, moving toward Sparrow.

"Found who, my precious Milton?" Sparrow asked. "Oh, I understand."

"I love you, Sparrow," Mil said this time so she could hear it. The couple kissed without reservation. Unlike their past hugs, years of separation removed any awkwardness from the embrace. There was an intensity leaving no room for doubt about their feelings for each other.

"I love you more," Sparrow replied. No trace of the uncertain girl remained, her emotional scars replaced by a woman self-assured and eager to show her feelings.

They kissed again, sitting by the window, holding hands, and reliving the past few years with a warmth their letters couldn't deliver. Winslow had added another talent to his long list, becoming their matchmaker in his unique fashion. He had reunited the pair by securing a Park Service job for Sparrow as a Manteo pilot charged with flying supplies and people to and for the Cape Hatteras National Seashore.

Winslow had told the young pilot she would work alongside an old friend tasked with a heavy responsibility. She guessed who the old friend was and readily accepted the position. Winslow suggested Sparrow keep the new arrangement a secret. She agreed, unsure if Mil would see her as a close friend or something more. But there was no uncertainty. Sparrow and Mil were going home without the hesitations that had haunted Milton in the past.

Sparrow's plane lifted from the Virginia airfield into a blue ether. The aircraft flew south toward Elizabeth City, with no clouds blocking their view as boats navigated the Albemarle Sound. Buffalo City hid in the swampy understory of trees along the Alligator River. A narrow band of peninsulas and barrier islands separated the ocean and the sounds by a thin thread of yellow sand on the southern horizon. Below, the Wright Memorial bridge drew a faint straight line uniting the mainland with the beach before changing into a tiny black ribbon of asphalt crossing onto Roanoke Island.

Sparrow placed her hand on Mil's as they viewed the Banks from the air. He felt a warm, round piece of metal touch his palm. It was the coin he had given her years earlier with the engraved reimaged profile of Sir Walter Raleigh, the dapper Englishman from the past, working through the proxy of adventurers as he sought wealth and glory on an unknown shore. On the reverse side, a young mother cradling her infant child, Virginia Dare, ready to brave a new world in quest of a better future. They had been at the wrong place to begin a nation on an isolated bar of sand known for keeping its secrets. There was no mystery between these two adopted Bankers. The future was still unclear, and it didn't frighten them. They were certain they wanted to face the unknown together.

"It's your turn, Milton. The Banks need saving, and I believe in you. Jack called you to the Banks in your dreams. I understand why now," Sparrow said.

"Maybe Jack was Manteo, at least in spirit. I don't know if I'm up to the job Winslow wants me to do, but I'll try as long as I have wings to guide me," Milton said, grinning at his corniness as he kissed the back of Sparrow's hand.

The End

Author's Notes

These Yellow Sands is a work of fiction woven into a tapestry of history that transformed the Outer Banks of North Carolina from a string of small fishing villages into a national tourist destination. This story takes place during the 1930s as the nation begins its recovery from the Great Depression. On a larger scale, the novel's foundation unfolded in 1584, with England's quest to plant a colony in what had been called The New World. The first attempt organized by Queen Elizabeth I favorite, Sir Walter Raleigh, was to study the land and its native people. Early exploration by Spain made many believe only a narrow band of sand separated the Atlantic Ocean from the Pacific Ocean, where riches were waiting for the taking in the spice trade. In reality, what explorers saw was the broad Pamlico Sound beckoning travelers to enter one of many shallow, constantly shoaling barrier island inlets.

A second attempt expedition was in part to establish an English outpost so England could monitor the Spanish treasure fleets headed home to Europe on the Gulf Stream. This oceanic super highway brushing the barrier islands, promised a relatively quick return sail across the sea. The third attempt was a stopover to check on the fifteen soldiers left behind from the second voyage to garrison Roanoke Island. The actual destination for Raleigh's colony of men, women, and children was the deep, sheltered waters and fertile land of the Chesapeake Bay. However, the expedition's navigator, Simon Fernando, refused for some still unknown reason to continue the voyage north, stranding the colony and creating an enduring mystery of the Lost Colony's fate.

The characters in this novel are primarily fictional, drawn from the generations of people who called the Outer Banks home. However, several real-life people populate these pages. Accounts of FDR's visit to the August 1937 performance of Paul Green's *Lost Colony* play are mostly accurate. Roosevelt's interaction with characters in the novel is a product of the author's imagination, except for his car ride with the mayor of Elizabeth City. This blend of fiction and fact is also true for Louis Hammond, Dave Driskill, references to Amelia Earhart, Robert Frost, Ernal Foster, and George Lyon. These people had a role to play on the yellow sands of North Carolina's Outer Banks and were welcomed to this story.

The heart of this work is in the settings, places changed or destroyed by the years, with remnants occasionally visible to the curious today. Buchanon Cottage is still a part of the local landscape. The Hattie Creef was not so fortunate. Manteo's fire changed the town's waterfront. The bridge crossings, highways, and sandy roads have been rebuilt sundry times, and the barrier banks have grown thinner thanks to countless storms over the decades. Purple martins return to Roanoke Island, though not in the sky-darkening multitudes of years that followed this story. Nothing remains of the bones at Whalebone Junction, through shops and restaurants continue to thrive along the causeway. The ferries that crossed the northern and central Outer Banks faded from memories as bridges replaced them. Vehicle ferries still exist on the lower Banks; however, that is a story for another day.

The novel's timeline is in chronological order, drawn from 1930s history, and the plot centers on those events. The Civilian Conservation Corps changed the beach's landscape with a workforce of Miltons and Jacks. An all-black Pea Island Life-Saving Service saved hundreds of lives along the Graveyard of the Atlantic through the bravery of men like Eddie. Buffalo City, now nearly invisible below the Beechland swamp, produced some of the best rye moonshine along the East Coast. The moonshine run described here on the day of FDR's visit remains part of the unrecorded legends about the ghost town. The Dare Stone, a historical artifact housed at Brenau College in Gainesville, Georgia, once viewed as a fake, has found renewed interest in its possible authenticity over the past decade.

While newspapers were many along the outer and Greater Albemarle region of North Carolina in the 1930s, the *Dare Independent* was not one of them. The author created that publication to serve as a hub for the novel. There was no intention to use local newspapers as a business or character model for any of the episodes presented here. The novel suggests there were few publications at the time; in fact, many small newspapers were in print. The age of television was years away, and radio was just coming onto the scene. (In fact, the first known intentional wireless radio transmission in the world occurred in 1902 between Roanoke Island and Buxton as experimenter Reginald Fessenden broadcast himself playing the violin and reading from the Bible across the Pamlico Sound. Again, a story for another day.)

The story of Jack Straw, Milton's spiritual guide to understanding personal loss, is built on a theory that Manteo and some of the Lost Colony fled the Outer Banks in a small pinnacle left behind when John White returned to England for resupplies. Reference to him comes from the journal of the first governor of the Massachusetts Bay Colony.

Gov. WiNTHROP's JOURNAL, p. 25.
April 4, 1631.
" Wahginaeut a Sagamore upon the river Quonehtaeut
which lies W. of Naraganset came to the Governor at
Boston, with John Sagamore and Jack Strawe (an Indian
which had lived in England and had served Sir Walter
Raleigh and was now turned Indian again....

If the Jack Straw of Winthrop's journal was Manteo, it is unlikely any of his descendants survived, based on the historical record. The Jack Straw of this story exists in a spirit world offering an enigmatic hope for the Outer Banks' past and future. Manteo, the man, could be a visionary or a traitor depending on the observer's point of view. When worlds collide, people must seek compromise or be left in a netherworld of lost causes and broken dreams. Manteo remains a gatekeeper between the Old World and the New, seeking an equilibrium between the land of his birth and the hopeful promise of tomorrow.

Though human characters play a significant role, the central figure in this story is not human. **These Yellow Sands** is a novel about the Outer Banks, its way of life, its history, and how the Atlantic Ocean continues to shape its marshy and sandy beaches. It is a place where human enterprise lives in reluctant harmony with the forces of nature, aware that one day this too will become another colony lost, but not forgotten by the sands of time.